Free to Be

Mary Grand

First published in the United Kingdom and worldwide 2015

ISBN 978-1511669436

Printed by CreateSpace

To my husband

for his constant and unqualified support

Welsh colloquialisms
Occasionally, the author has used Welsh colloquialisms spoken by characters in the book. "Oh Duw" means "Oh God". "Cwtch" means cuddle.

Chapter One

'You have chosen the path of darkness.'

Tegan stood on the wooden stage in front of the Community, determinedly staring at the digital clock at the back of the room. 0730. She waited for the dull click. The numbers flipped. 0731.

In the cold, bare meeting room, a shaft of light from the London spring morning crept in through one of the high windows.

'You have been weighed in the balance and found wanting' continued Daniel. He stood to her right, at the other end of the stage, his hard voice echoing off the peeling cream emulsion walls. She didn't dare look at him. The room was silent. Tegan, unblinking, waited. 0732.

'You have chosen the sinful pleasures of the Domain of the Beast. You have grievously sinned against The High One and this Community. You refuse to repent, to curse and reject all that is of the world.' She heard him pause. Even now he was waiting, seeing if she would break. Tegan stood expressionless, very still, apart from the slight rise and fall of her shallow breaths and the secret grinding of her right thumb into the palm of her left hand. Her shapeless clothes hung off her: a calf length dark brown skirt; plain beige blouse; bulky blue acrylic cardigan and large black headscarf, tied at the nape of her neck. The community uniform. Silence. Her eyes crept down from the clock to the tops of the bowed heads of the women at the back of the room. Along the row she saw her mother, Sarah, her hands clasped tight on her lap. She glanced forward and accidentally met her father's gaze, a look that said that this failure was inevitable. She slowly turned her head to her right. Daniel stood, neat white hair and beard, and long loose white shirt intricately embroidered with gold thread, the earthly personification of the High One. She heard his voice, louder, more passionate.

'Tegan Williams, you are commanded to leave this Community. From this time forth you are dead to us, to your earthly parents and the elect. You will be judged with all those in the Domain of the Beast. On the day of judgment the High One will show you no mercy and you, Tegan Williams, will be thrown into the lake of fire, there to suffer for all eternity.'

Her breathing quickened, the grinding into the palm of her hand grew harder. She felt him willing her to look at him. She could not resist. Slowly, she turned her head and met the gaze of the man whose teachings she had followed, the man she had revered and worshipped. His eyes were narrow, eyebrows down and his mouth was tight. His anger was like a volcano waiting to erupt, waiting to burn and consume her.

Then, clenching his fists, he turned, descended the steps and stood with his back to her. The elders in the front row stood and turned their backs to her also, and then the rest of the Community silently stood up and started to turn away. Tegan's eyes darted to her mother, who was turning slowly, stiffly, around. A sharp lightning pain shot through her. This was really happening. This was their final judgment, the end.

Tegan staggered down the steps and left the room alone. The dark hallway was deathly quiet. She climbed the hard wooden steps, brushing past the cold, white, sterile walls. She had been five years old when the Community had moved into this derelict Victorian hospital. She remembered how enormous, empty and dark it had seemed and how she had excitedly run through the huge echoing rooms. It remained sparsely furnished throughout her early years, but the severity of their lives had taken a new turn with the arrival of Daniel. So much had changed then.

She entered her bedroom, the room she had slept in for twenty two years. The room now had white, bare walls apart from a lurid picture called "The four beasts". She knew every detail: the lion with eagle wings; the bear with ribs between its teeth; the four-headed leopard with wings, and the beast with iron teeth and ten horns. They were set in a blood red sky above a stormy sea: all seemed to snarl out of the picture at her. Above it a digital clock showed the time, a constant reminder of the approach of the end of the world.

There were two beds in the room. For years she had shared the room with Esther, who had been her only close friend. Four years ago Daniel had declared Esther was to marry and now Esther's role was to support her husband and their two children. Martha, a critical, pious girl had been given Esther's bed. Tegan had little in common with her but at least someone was there if she woke at night: anything was better than waking up alone. She wondered idly who her bed would be given to next. Tegan turned around quickly, stood on tiptoes, and pulled down a battered suitcase from on top of the wardrobe. It should have been empty, but when she undid the catches she found a large brown envelope inside. She recognised her mother's handwriting, and frowned. Her mother had obviously put this in here secretly. They had not been allowed to communicate for weeks. Maybe these were her final words of dismissal. She couldn't bear to read them, not now. She quickly stuffed the envelope into her plastic shoulder bag. Then she started to take her clothes off the wire coat hangers and fold them carefully: more plain skirts, blouses, acrylic cardigans and black headscarves were placed in the suitcase. Next, her spare pair of brown lace up shoes, grey underwear, light tan tights and two cotton nightdresses. From her bedside table she took her alarm clock. It was a yellow, old-fashioned wind-up clock with a loud tick. Next to this lay a well thumbed copy of "The Revelations of Daniel, The Omniscient." She stroked it, kissed it, and placed it gently in her case. With it she placed the framed verse "He Shall Come like a Thief in the Night". She opened the drawer. She carefully took out a small piece of embroidered material, touched it lightly and packed it. Finally, she reached to the back of the drawer and found a small rectangular silver box with engraving in the top. She took it out, checked the contents, clutched it, and then wrapped it carefully in one of the skirts in her case. She took a deep breath, left her room and walked down the hall to the bathroom. It was a large white tiled room, a row of basins one side, cubicles the other, no mirrors. She found her toothbrush and returned to her room.

Tegan was just doing up the catches of her case when the door burst open. She saw Daniel and, behind him, her parents. 'Tegan, you have filled your parents with shame. They have the right to have the final word.'

Tegan was breathing fast. She dug her fingers deep into the palm of her hand. Daniel gestured to Philip. He shuffled forward with hunched shoulders. He pushed back the round metal glasses with his forefinger and then pointed at her.

'Tegan, you have always been a proud, rebellious child.' His voice was flat, but underlying was the tone of perpetual disappointment he used when speaking to her. 'Your mother and I have spent many hours in vigil for your soul but to no avail. To think we have come to this, for you to blaspheme against our leader Daniel, to doubt and question him in that most proud and sinful way. From this moment we, your parents, with the whole community, disown you.'

Tegan turned to her mother for some drop of mercy. But the look of cold dismissal she saw was even harder to bear than any words.

Philip continued, 'On the Day of Judgment you will be judged more harshly than the world for you were shown the light and have rejected it.' Philip spat out the cruel words. He could have gone on like this for hours but somehow the words from him seemed hollow. She heard an ambulance screaming outside: any minute now she would be cast out into the world to join the damned.

Philip sneered, his finger jabbing in her face. 'You have chosen a wicked, dark place. The animals of the world will tear you apart and feed you to the dogs and in that we rejoice.' He stopped.

Daniel stepped forward and, as if comforting a grieving relative, put his hand on Philip's shoulder. He bent his head, mumbled a prayer in a different language, and they all turned and left the room.

The room was silent. Tegan looked down at the palm of her left hand, dry, cracked, red raw, bleeding, but she felt nothing. She found an old piece of tissue in her bag and with a shaking hand tried to wipe it clean.

Finally, from out of the wardrobe she took a shapeless beige rain coat, put it on and buttoned it up. She picked up her shabby plastic shoulder bag and suitcase, opened the door, and, without glancing back, left the room.

She walked down the stairs and glanced at the clock that hung over the front door. 0750. Next to this was a huge white board. Every day Daniel wrote the date and a verse for them to meditate on, and the date. Today it read March 1st 2006 and underneath that the verse for the day:

"Depart from me, you cursed, into the eternal fire prepared for the Beast and all those in his domain." She guessed Daniel had chosen that for her. She could hear familiar quiet droning prayers of vigil being said in the meeting room. 'Come Quickly Oh High One'. The whole Community including the children would repeat it over and over again for an hour. Every day had started like that for her for twenty two years, but not today. For the first time in her life she was an outsider.

Tegan opened the front door out into the cold drizzly rain and descended the flight of concrete steps. She was hit by a wall of noise: the early morning rush hour. Alone she walked across the concrete forecourt and opened the iron gates. She saw a taxi driver swearing at another driver, a parent shouting to their children to hurry up. The rain added to the sense of urgency as the world rushed about its business. She glanced down at the bins on the pavement and, blinking hard, realised she had been put out with the rubbish.

5

Chapter Two

Despite the rain Tegan staggered across the road to the park and through the familiar wrought iron gates. This was her secret sanctuary, a place she would occasionally visit for a few, precious moments of privacy. She found a wet metal bench, put down her bags and perched on the edge. In an effort to calm her mind she made herself focus on her surroundings. The blossom on the trees above her was still in tight bud, but the daffodils strutted proudly, defying the dreary morning. Commuters clasping umbrellas and briefcases, parents with pushchairs, dog walkers being pulled by their dogs: all hurried past. A group of teenagers proudly underdressed in dripping wet navy school sweatshirts were shouting over their plugged-in iPods. Then she noticed in a quiet corner a woman standing with a toddler, holding the child's upright arms. The little girl, wearing bright pink wellingtons, was splashing in the puddle and giggling. They were in their own blissful world.

Tegan looked over at the Community house and realised for the first time that no one would be missing her. She had ceased to exist to them. She swallowed hard, looked away. Defiantly she picked up her bags and stiffly stood up, aware that the rain had soaked through the back and shoulders of her thin coat. It was time to go.

Tegan left the park, walked quickly down the High Street, past chain stores and cafes, down side streets, past boarded-up shops, small grocers', and sari and charity shops. Her eyes scanned the shop fronts: he had said he lived above a shop, a Spar. There it was. Yes, there was his name on the metal intercom, "Steve Crocker". She hesitated, feeling sick with anticipation. He had no idea she was coming, but he had told her to do this, hadn't he? He had said that she needed to "find herself", be more independent. The last time they had talked, he had touched her arm, kissed her on the cheek. She shivered at the memory. Of course he would be able to help her, tell her what to do.

She took a deep breath, and pressed the intercom. 'OK' a disembodied voice answered. She clenched her teeth with anticipation at the sound of his voice, and heard the door release. Tentatively, she pushed it and went inside. The hallway was grey concrete. She started to climb the stone steps. She could see a front door open on the landing, hear the radio blaring "Soldiers' wives have asked for a meeting with Tony Blair."

As she neared the top she heard Steve shout 'One day you'll remember your bloody keys.'

Puzzled, she approached the open door, and stood in the doorway. She could see Steve sitting at an old wooden table, a mug in his right hand, the other holding open a book lying flat on the table. There were books and old newspapers strewn everywhere, a tatty sofa; on the walls framed maps and a poster for a production of Hamlet. Steve glanced over casually but, on seeing her, clumsily put his drink down, spilling it over his book.

'Tegan. My God.'

'I'm sorry.' Tegan stammered and looked away, deeply embarrassed.

She watched him register her embarrassment, then realised he was only in his boxers.

'God, sorry,' he said, and rushed into the bedroom.

She heard him stumbling around as he shouted 'Come in.'

Her stomach twisted with embarrassment. She stayed in the doorway.

Steve came back into the room wearing a crumpled checked shirt and doing up his jeans. Still she blushed, aware of the intimacy of the situation. She hadn't imagined it like this.

'Come in,' he repeated impatiently.

Tegan took one step forward. He took off his red-framed glasses and, with the other hand, rubbed his forehead, ran his hand over his close shaved head.

'So what - I mean, how? God, Tegan, why are you here?'

'I've been cast out. I've left the Community.'

'What?'

'It's complicated, but I've been told to leave. It was awful - but you said it would be good to get away, didn't you?'

'In theory,' he said evasively, 'but you said it would be very difficult.'

'I know it's a big thing, but I thought you'd be pleased.' Tegan searched his face but there was no reassuring smile.

'But what will you do?'

'I don't know. I thought you would tell me.'

'Why did you think that?' he asked. Then he looked perplexed. 'How did you know where I live?'

'You mentioned the Spar.'

'Right-'

'I thought you'd be pleased,' she repeated. He didn't reply. She put down her bags.

'I know I haven't any money but I can get a job. Of course, I wouldn't want to move in-' Her voice was getting more desperate. 'You said it was the right thing to do. We can be together now.'

She heard the downstairs door open, and saw Steve's eyes dart to the front door, which was still ajar. The look of consternation on his face was turning to panic. A female voice called breathlessly.

'Sorry it took so long. I had to wait for the croissants. Still they are really hot.' Steve stepped forward just as a woman appeared in the doorway. In an abandoned gesture she kicked the door fully open and flung open her brown fake fur coat proclaiming 'Just like me!'

Tegan stared in horror as the woman revealed skimpy scarlet underwear. What kind of world had she come into? The woman, however, seemed unabashed.

'Shit! Didn't know we had company,' she said, glancing at Tegan and laughing.

Steve turned to Tegan and spoke in harsh tones she had never heard before. 'This is Alice. She is my fiancée.' It was brutal.

Tegan blushed and looked down. She dug her nails in to her hands.

'Alice and I are getting married.' Steve enunciated the words as if he was speaking to a child.

'I'm sorry,' she stammered, still not daring to look up. 'I didn't realise-'

The room was spinning. Steve's words were echoing far away. Tegan grabbed hold of the back of the chair. She swallowed hard, and then forced herself to look at Steve. Their eyes met.

'You are getting married?'

He nodded.

'But what about us?' she asked quietly.

'There is no us Tegan, there never was.'

Tegan glanced at Alice, who had pulled her coat together, and was walking towards Steve.

'Who is this?' There was no anger, just total bewilderment in Alice's voice.

'This is Tegan. I met her a few times at the library.' He smiled at Alice. 'There's nothing going on.'

'Well, obviously,' Alice grinned, 'but why is she here?'

As Steve and Alice both turned and looked at her, Tegan remembered the time she had found an enormous toad in the garden. Captivated by the beautifully ugly creature she had looked at it in the same way they were looking at her.

'She's in a bit of bother, says she has left this religious group she's been living with, you know, the group who live in that big old building by the park.'

'Oh God, well, would you like a coffee or something?' asked Alice, obviously not sure what to do with Tegan. She reached forward and touched Tegan's arm. 'Shit, you're drenched. Hang on. I'll get you some dry things. Have some croissant or something.'

Tegan shot a look at Steve, but she saw an infinitesimal shake of his head: his eyes were pleading with her. She couldn't ignore the fact that he was desperate for her to go.

'No, no thank you,' Tegan said, as she started to pick up her bags and walk to the door.

'You will go back to them won't you?' said Steve.

She couldn't answer. Steve came and stood between her and the door. 'Go back. You must, you know that.'

She pushed past him, stumbled down the stone steps and out into the street.

Steve went to the window and watched Tegan walking away. From up here she looked even more fragile and vulnerable. Swamped by that long shapeless brown coat and enormous headscarf, she walked in flat brown shoes like a clumsy school child.

'Poor girl,' remarked Alice. 'Has she got learning problems or something?'

'Actually, she's bright. She's just led this very strange life.'

'She obviously had feelings for you.'

'Rubbish.' Steve looked away, hiding a spasm of guilt.

'Steve, she wouldn't come here for nothing. You said she came to the library. There must have been more to it than that?'

'We did go for coffee. I was interested. Her life in the community is fascinating, and I'd never met anyone like her.'

'And how did she know where you lived?'

'Apparently I mentioned the shop. I don't remember that. Mostly she told me about her life in the community.'

'So you found her interesting, a novelty?'

'No, not just that. I felt sorry for her,' insisted Steve.

'Did you say you'd help her?'

Steve squirmed. 'No, of course not. I may have suggested that she should leave the community-'

'And that she could come to you?'

'No, No. For God's sake, Alice. I never said that, it was nothing. I never thought she'd leave. Look, enough of the interrogation, she'll be alright. Come on, let's have some breakfast.'

10

Down below, Tegan was staggering blindly down the High Street. What had she done? People impatiently pushed past her. She stepped off the pavement.

'Move, you stupid cow -' shouted a driver over his horn. Tegan got back on the pavement and went and sat on a seat in the nearest bus stop. Pigeons pecked close to her feet, looking for crumbs among the cigarette butts. She pulled her feet back. She hated birds. They were always waiting to peck and scratch you. She wanted to curl up and die. Tears poured down her cheeks. She felt so ashamed at how she had behaved, what she had seen. To have loved someone like that. She had trusted a heathen man. She had ignored all the warnings.

"No pure thing can exist in the Domain of the Beast." Steve had deceived her. She had thought he was a good man and that he would tell her what to do.

The rain grew heavier. What was she going to do? She sat chewing hard on the quick of her thumb. She was hunched up, rocking slightly. Dreams of proving to the Community, to her mother, that she could come out here in the world and live a pure, good life were crumbling. She was alone: no money, no food, no friends, nor anywhere to stay. *"A valley means a wrong turn."* That's what they said. This was all her fault.

What was she going to do? Daniel knew her heart; he would never let her back in the Community. She stared at the traffic. Then she remembered the envelope from her mother. She pulled it out of her bag, and opened it, numbly. It contained a letter and two envelopes. She took out the letter. It was written on a scruffy piece of lined paper.

'Tegan, I am writing this without permission. For this I shall pay penance. You have chosen the world over your own family, rejected those who have loved and cared for you all your life. I fear for your soul. This is the last thing I shall do for you as your earthly mother. You must resist the temptation to live in sin with this heathen man. On the back I have written the address of my sister, Aunt Hannah, and her husband, Uncle Ellis, and their phone number. Contact them. I believe they will give you shelter. Be warned. These relations are not of the elect. Trust no one. You will need what is in the larger envelope. I am ashamed of it. I am glad to get rid of it. Despite the terrible hurt and suffering you have wilfully inflicted on us I will do vigil for your soul. Yours in Him, Your Mother.'

Tegan stopped reading. Despite the harshness of the words, this letter must have been very difficult for her mother to write. Her mother must still care. She turned over the page, glanced at the address and grimaced. That was ridiculous, how on earth did her mother expect her to get there? She replaced the letter. Full of curiosity, she pulled out the thicker envelope. It had the name "Sarah" written on it in fountain pen. It was held together by an elastic band. She took this off and put her hand inside. Frowning, she started to extract the contents. As they were revealed, her eyes widened, her hands started to shake. Alert, she glanced around at the people around her. Had anyone else seen? She quickly shoved the contents back in, re-tied it with the elastic band, and returned it to the envelope. Quickly, she replaced the whole lot back in her shoulder bag, zipped it up, and squashed it tightly under her arm protectively. What on earth was she going to do?

Chapter Three

'Bloody Daffodil' muttered Ellis Davies, trying to pin the drooping flower on his jumper: St David's Day again and a hectic day ahead. But he was excited: so much work had gone into this concert. Of course, it was a far cry from the professional concerts of his life before retirement, but the thrill was still there. He stood in the music room of the Georgian Manor he had moved into with his wife Hannah on his retirement five years before. He looked out of the long patio windows, and mentally shut out the sounds of the builders above with their radio. Out there were his Cambrian Mountains. Over thousands of years they had remained miraculously unchanged. Today the distant hills were blue green, traces of the remnants of ice and snow on the highest peaks. He saw a red kite, enormous flashed wings, soaring high in the sky. His face relaxed. Further down the valley was a small cottage, "Hafan", his childhood home. That was his reference point. He still went down to the cottage to work sometimes, and revelled in its remoteness. Of course, the manor was a beautiful old building. He could understand why Hannah had wanted to live here. Also, the farmhouse on the land was perfect for his daughter Cerys. He had been pleased she had her own place. Tucked away in the garden, it was perfect for her. But, for all that, his heart was down there in that tiny cottage.

'You struggling with that daff?'

He turned to Ruth. Petite with short brown hair, Ruth was the wife of the village publican. She idolised Ellis, choosing to imagine a far greater level of fame and prestige than he had ever actually attained. He knew she found his appreciation of her work organising the choir and concerts deeply flattering. The bulk of his fortune had actually been made, not from solos in great opera houses, but in the royalties received from his chance involvement in music for some major films. However, he did nothing to dispel the myth, and Ellis, for his part, thoroughly enjoyed this more glamorous version of himself.

Ruth put down the programmes she was carrying. 'God, Ellis, the poor thing is completely mangled.'

Ruth plucked a fresh daffodil from a vase and broke the stem. Even though he was broad rather than tall, she had to stand on tip toes to pin it on his jumper. Her hands were shaking but she pinned it perfectly.

'What would I do without you?' he asked.

Her dark brown eyes shone with pleasure. 'You know Martin has dropped out? Well, I was thinking, why don't you do it, you know, sing "Maffanwy"? People would love to hear you: it would be the highlight of the concert.'

He smiled, but shook his head. 'No, I won't sing, not in this concert. You know that I never do it on principle. It's about discovering new talent. Actually, I have given the solo to James.' He spoke the words with an air of martyrdom. It seemed a long time now since he'd enjoyed the applause of an audience and he missed it more than he cared to admit.

He picked up the programmes for the concert. The layout was not particularly inspired but the contents were accurate. He saw Ruth watching him anxiously, waiting.

'Marvellous.' She beamed in response.

'I hope we fill this concert hall, it's so much bigger than any other place we've used.'

'Oh we will, thanks to you. When I think how amateurish we used to be before you came. You know, already three quarters of the tickets have been sold.'

'Fantastic. Let's hope the rest go as well.' He heard the house phone ring and grumbled, 'Not more last minute changes.' He picked it up.

'Yes?'

'It's Sarah.'

'Sarah?' He was trying frantically to remember who she was and what was she doing in the concert.

'Yes. Sarah, Philip's wife.'

14

He gripped the phone, his mind erasing any connection with the concert. 'Duw' he said, sitting down, his hand shaking. He started to scratch at his greying beard, coughed, and cleared his throat. 'I didn't recognise your voice. It must be more than twenty years. How are you all?'

'It's Tegan,' Sarah said.

'What's happened?'

'She rebelled, Ellis. She's been cast out.'

Ellis was aware of Ruth standing close by, looking at him curiously. 'Coffee?' he mouthed in a bid to get rid of her. She nodded obligingly and left the room.

'Sorry Sarah, what do you mean?' he asked, trying to speak more slowly, more reasonably. However the answer did nothing to assist him.

'She's been shunned by the Community, put out into the Domain of the Beast,' came Sarah's reply.

'Sarah, what the hell are you talking about?'

He heard Sarah tut irritably. 'She has been made to leave here.'

'Let me get this straight. She has been living with you and Philip in the Community but now she has been thrown out?' He spoke as one translating a foreign language.

'That's right. She refuses to repent, to curse the world and the works of the evil one.'

Ellis couldn't believe this was the Sarah he used to know. She had always been serious, but now she sounded so intolerant.

'It all sounds very traumatic,' he said, 'but she must be twenty seven or so now. I guess she'll go and live with friends, get a flat or something?'

'The only person she knows in the world is this man who worked in the library. I pray she will resist the temptation to live in sin with him.'

'But what do you expect her to do? Has she friends from work who can help?'

'We have kept her pure from the world. She has never been to school or worked in the world.'

'I didn't realise.' He felt overwhelmed. 'So I assume you and Philip will be leaving as well. Do you want to come here?'

'Philip and I will not be leaving. We will have no more to do with Tegan.'

'Duw, you can't mean you are not going to look after her?' He was stunned. How could Sarah act in such a callous way?

'We have taken care of her all her life, but now she has shown she neither respects nor appreciates anything that has been done for her.'

'I'm sure that's not true, but in any case you can't abandon her to the streets of London. You can't just disown your own daughter. How do you expect her to cope? How much money does she have?'

'She has some cash, no bank account of course.'

Ellis took a deep breath. Exasperated and shocked, he said 'It sounds to me that her only realistic option is to go to this man then.'

'I have urged her to resist a life of sin. Actually, there is another option. I have suggested that she contacts you.'

'Contacts me?'

'You do see that you and Hannah must provide her with shelter, don't you?'

'You can't possibly expect Hannah to help after the way you've behaved.'

'That was different. I have told Tegan to come to her aunt and uncle. I have provided her with enough money to travel to you.'

'But it would be so difficult and, in any case, she doesn't know us from Adam.'

'Ellis, it is your duty to help.'

'Oh Duw.' He could see there was to be no reasoning with Sarah. 'You say she has money. Does she know how to get here?'

'She has your number. She must contact you and sort that out.'

'I think you'd better give me her mobile number,' said Ellis reluctantly.

'She is not allowed to own a mobile phone.'

'Bloody Hell, Sarah. She's so vulnerable. Anything could happen to her.'

'She has chosen to rebel. She must bear the consequences. She is very fortunate I am helping her at all. I really shouldn't be doing this,' said Sarah, her voice tight.

'So she will have to find a phone box then. Hope she can find one that works. Otherwise, what will she do?'

'She must find her own way now.'

'Aren't you at all worried about her safety?' he asked desperately.

'From this time forth she is dead to us.'

'Sarah, that is a terrible thing to say,' he said quietly. She didn't reply. He sighed and said, 'So I just have to wait and hope she gets in touch.'

'I have done what I can. Listen Ellis, Philip must never know I have phoned. Don't contact us. I shouldn't have used his phone. I'd get into terrible trouble if he found out.' The voice that had been so stern sounded like it was verging on hysterics.

'You don't even want me to tell you she's safe?'

'No, I want nothing more to do with her. And there is one more thing Ellis-'

'What?'

'If she does come to you, you must keep your promise, you must say nothing. Tegan knows nothing. You mustn't tell her.'

'Of course, you know you can trust me Sarah.'

'I don't trust anyone in the world. I will go now. I can do no more.'

With that she had gone. He sat shell-shocked. How could the Sarah he had known speak, behave, like this? She'd had a wonderful singing voice but there had been no hint of beauty or music in her voice today. He guessed life married to Philip would be pretty tough. A hard, fanatically religious man, Philip had the gift of crushing any hint of joy out of life. What

17

had life been like for Tegan? He guessed she would go to this boyfriend. Sounded like she'd finally had enough of the community place, wanted to make her own life. How prepared was she though? He couldn't help being worried about her. What if she didn't phone? It was terrible to feel so helpless.

Ruth came back into the room carrying coffee.

'Hope you put something in that' he said.

'What's happened?'

'That was Hannah's sister, Sarah. Hasn't spoken to us for years. Apparently her daughter is in some kind of bother. She was asking me to help if the girl contacts me.'

Just then he received a text. He took a deep breath.

'What now?' asked Ruth.

He sighed with relief. 'It's only Hannah wishing me luck.'

'I'm surprised she remembered. I mean, she's busy enjoying New York isn't she?'

'I guess so. Actually, maybe it's as well she's away at the moment. Anyway, come on. Let's get on with the concert, eh?'

In London Tegan thought about the money. *"Mammon will burn your soul."* Five hundred pounds! It was sinful to even handle this amount of money. Her mother would never steal, but how on earth would she have got hold of this amount of money? It was extraordinary that she should have such a sum. Tegan started to walk aimlessly down the street. She saw a young girl lying in an old sleeping bag in a doorway.

"A valley means a wrong turn" she heard again. What had that girl done? What sin was in her life to lead to this? Tegan looked at the girl: cold, alone. People skirted round her, looked the other way, and treated her like some unpleasant mess on the pavement to be avoided. She would not end up like that girl. She was stronger than that. But what would she do? Could she live out here, away from the Community, stay pure? People pushed past her. The rain got heavier. She had to find shelter. She started to walk down the street, and saw a large, rather squalid,

Bed and Breakfast with vacancies. She swallowed hard. Could she really go in there on her own? Would she be safe? She thought about these people in Wales. Maybe it would be safer with them at least for a few days, but how would she get there? Why on earth did her mother suggest people so far away? She was getting very wet and tired. What was she going to do?

Chapter Four

As people pushed past her Tegan made a decision. She would try and ring these people: if nothing else they may be able to suggest people in London she could stay with for a day or two.

She started to search for a public phone. There were some open kiosks, but then she spotted an old fashioned red phone box. It looked safer, more private. She went over and pulled open the heavy door. She was immediately struck by the overpowering stench of urine, and realised there was broken glass on the floor from one of the smashed panes. She took out the letter from her mother, looked up the phone number, and then she took out one of the twenty pound notes, picked up the receiver and read the instructions. Frustrated, she realised she needed coins or a phone card, thrust the letter back into her bag and went back out of the phone box into the rain.

She went into the first newsagent's she could find. It was full of wet school children buying crisps and ice creams for their breakfast. It felt very strange to be in here on her own, no Community purse, and no list. She froze, wondering what to buy. So many sorts of chocolate bars, crisps, snacks. How to choose? She recognised Kit Kats. She'd get one of those, but which sort, size? She picked the smallest, plainest one and went to pay at the counter. Children kept pushing in front of her. They were so badly behaved. In the Community the children would never have dared push in front of an adult. In the end the shop keeper took pity. 'What?' he shouted impatiently over the children's heads.

She showed him the bar. 'How much does this cost please?'

He grabbed and scanned it. 'Forty two pence,' he said impatiently. He didn't look at her; he was too busy trying to police the children in his shop.

Tegan put a twenty pound note in his hand. The man held it up. 'Anything smaller?'

'Sorry, no. I'm sorry' said Tegan. The children were impatient, a man pushed past her, put down the money for his newspaper and left. She didn't know what to do.

The shopkeeper muttered, 'Bloody Hell' and opened the till. He roughly pushed a pile of coins and notes in her hand. Tegan smiled, embarrassed. The coins fell on the counter and the floor. She grovelled on the floor picking them up.

She was glad to get out of the shop. She looked at the Kit Kat. She couldn't remember when she had last eaten. She put it in her pocket. Tegan returned to the phone box and pulled open the heavy door. The smell was awful but the noise of the traffic was muffled in there. She felt cocooned. She read the instructions again, picked up the receiver, put in a pile of coins, took a deep breath and punched in the numbers. The phone was answered.

'Ellis -' The voice spoke sharply.

'Um, hello, this is Tegan, Tegan Williams-'

'Oh, thank God you've phoned.' The voice softened into gentle Welsh. 'Sorry, busy day. Your mam said you might ring.'

'My mam?'

'Your mother, she rang earlier on your dad's phone. She told me you might need help, but I guess you're going to live with your boyfriend?'

'No, of course not.' Tegan was shocked that he thought she would do such a thing.

'Why not?'

'It's not the right thing. Anyway, I got it wrong.'

'But what will you do then?'

'I'm not too sure. I wonder, do you know if I have any relations up here in London?'

'I don't think so, and in any case your parents haven't spoken to anyone for years.'

'No, sorry, no, of course they haven't.' She felt embarrassed, wishing she hadn't rung.

21

'Why don't you try to go back to the community? I'm sure whatever you did can't be that bad.'

'No, that's not possible. I can never go back there.'

She heard Ellis pause, and then he said, 'Your mother's idea was for you to come here.'

She could hear the reluctance in his voice.

'Oh no. No, I'll be fine,' she said quickly.

'But what will you do?'

'I don't know. I'll think of something.'

'Look, I really think you had best come here, at least while you find your feet,' said Ellis more decisively.

'Don't worry, I'm twenty seven. I can look after myself.'

'But you've never been on your own before, have you?'

Tegan was suddenly aware of the rain being blown in through the broken window. Her feet were getting wet and cold.

'I think I'd better go' she said.

'Don't go, wait,' he urged. 'Your mother wanted you to come here.'

'No thank you, it's OK.' Tegan looked out at the wet streets, wondering what real alternative she had.

'Please, we should look after you. Come just for a few nights. We have loads of room. Also, just think, you could meet your cousin Cerys. You're about the same age.'

Tegan was watching the money eaten away by the machine. She pushed in more coins.

'I'm sorry, I can't. I mean, I don't even know how to get there. I mean, you're in Wales, aren't you?'

'Now we're not a million miles away, you know. It's quite straightforward. You get a train from Euston, change at Birmingham and come to Aberystwyth.'

Suddenly a woman holding a broken umbrella started banging on the window, shouting to Tegan to hurry up. She panicked. The woman looked very cross. She was wondering what to do when she became aware of Ellis speaking to her.

'Tegan, are you still there?' asked Ellis.

'Sorry? Yes.'

'I was saying you can get a train to Aberystwyth.'
She sighed. She was going to have to go along with this.
'Oh, right. So, where do I start?'
She heard him sigh. 'You get a train from Euston, change at Birmingham -'
'So I buy a ticket a ticket at Euston?'
She heard him sigh again.
'I'm sorry,' she said.
'It's OK. Now, let's take this slowly.'
Tegan cringed. She felt about ten years old. The woman knocked again on the window. She turned her back to her, tried to concentrate on Ellis' directions. When he had been through the journey in minute detail he said,
'So, you've got that?'
It sounded an enormous undertaking. She panicked.
'Actually, sorry, I don't think I'll come after all.'
'Bloody Hell, Tegan. Don't be stupid. Of course you should come.'
She gasped, shocked at his language, but didn't dare defy such a man.
'I'm sorry. Of course I will come, thank you.'
'Good. Now, find something to write with?'
Tegan rummaged in her bag, found the envelope from her mother and a pencil.
'OK.'
'This is my mobile number. Write it down.'
Tegan did as he instructed.
'You can get me on that at anytime. I'm very busy today but you must ring me. Let me know when you expect to arrive in Aberystwyth. Either me or Cerys will be there to meet you. You should be in time for the concert, chance to meet everyone.'
'Oh I don't know-' said Tegan faintly. 'How will you find me at the station? Know who I am?'
'We'll find you, don't worry, you take care now.'

Ellis put the phone down and scowled. This girl sounded odd, so much younger than twenty seven. He thought of Cerys.

She lived with them most of the time but she was very independent. Maybe Tegan just wasn't very bright. She certainly sounded very vulnerable, needy. Ruth came over to him.

'We're short of music stands. We need to pick some more up from the hall.'

'Mmm.'

'Ellis, are you alright?'

'My niece, she's coming here.'

'When's that then?'

'Today,' he said, still in shock.

'Good grief.'

'Yes, she'll need picking up. I'll have a word with Cerys. I'm sure she'll help out. This girl she sounds very uncertain, young-like, you know, and the house is in chaos-'

'Oh Ellis, I'm sorry. You have so much to put up with. Listen, would you like this girl to stay in the pub? We've got spare rooms.'

'Thanks, but no.' He looked out of the window. 'Hang on, I've just had an idea. I think I'll put her in the cottage. Yes, that's just the right place.'

Ellis sighed with relief.

In London, Tegan had gathered up her things, and staggered out of the phone box. The woman waiting scowled at her but she pushed past her. Cold hard rain hit her face; her headscarf clung to her head. She tried to pull up the collar of her coat but it did little to stop the rain creeping down her neck. In the distance she saw the steps leading down to the underground. She had to go. She had no choice. She walked quickly towards them and carefully descended the slippery steps. On the wall she could see a map of the underground. She needed to figure out her journey. The writing seemed very small. It was a mass of coloured lines. She was close to tears. She had never been on the underground. She couldn't do it. She was starting to panic when a voice behind her asked 'Need a hand?'

Chapter Five

Tegan turned to see that the person speaking to her was a girl with a backpack. She must have been in her teens.

'Where are you trying to go?' she repeated.

'Euston. Don't worry, I'll ask at the desk,' Tegan said, thinking it would be too difficult for the girl. However she replied 'Oh, that's easy. I'm going that way, just one change at Oxford Circus.'

'Oh,' said Tegan. 'Um, so do I need to get tickets over there?'

The girl laughed. 'You new to the underground? On holiday? Come on, I'll help you.'

Feeling very foolish Tegan followed the young girl to the ticket office, and then through the tunnels to the platform. The noises echoed off the white tiled walls, the music of buskers mixed with the sounds of wheeled cases and people shouting. Tegan went to speak to the girl who was helping her but she was listening to music. She seemed to be in her own world.

Tegan, shocked at the enormous garish picture of a woman in skimpy underwear on the wall opposite, thought briefly of Alice back at Steve's flat. The world was such an immoral place. She glanced around but no one else seemed to be bothered by it. It was claustrophobic and a cold, dusty wind seemed to be whistling down the platform. The track seemed very close. She was frightened of being pushed onto it. She stared at the black tunnel, waiting. Eventually two bright lights like huge eyes appeared and the train came screeching in.

'This is us,' shouted the girl and they boarded the train on a wave of people. Tegan had to stand and hated all the people pushing up against her. Being short, she had rucksacks and people's armpits jammed in her face. Squinting past them through the window, she eventually saw they had arrived at

Oxford Circus. They piled off, trudged though more tunnels and eventually boarded another train. Finally, they arrived at Euston. The girl showed her the way to the over ground station, smiled, and walked away.

Tegan was surprised at how easily the girl had helped her. In a wicked world she had been very generous and unfussy in that she had just helped. She hadn't even expected payment.

Tegan saw the girl disappearing into the crowd and suddenly felt very alone. What was she to do now?

In Wales Ellis left Ruth in the music room and went out into the garden in search of his daughter Cerys. He had a deep affection for her; she shared his love of this place. When she had been a young child growing up at home with them in Swansea, Cerys would come and stay for the summer holidays in the cottage with his mother. She would return to him, full of her Nanna's folk stories about fairies, the Tylwyth Teg, and the trips to the Holy Well in the woods. However, Cerys was at heart very practical and down to earth and he found this very reassuring.

Despite the icy wind, he knew he would find her in the garden. Whatever the weather she would be out here working. As he approached, her black and white cocker spaniel, Dylan, came running over, jumping up at him. He bent down to pat him and pushed away the muddy paws.

'Hiya,' shouted Cerys, slowly unbending. This was her natural habitat. She was planning to restore the grounds to their former glory.

'Hi, lovely. How's it going then?'

Her round face was red with exertion. Despite her mother, Hannah's, best efforts Cerys paid no attention to her appearance and lived in old jeans, a shapeless fleece and Wellington boots.

'The ground is rock hard. I'll move on into the greenhouse in a minute, loads of work in there.'

Ellis understood that the passion he had for music, she had for gardening.

'Something has cropped up' he said, close to her now.

26

'What's that then?'

'I had a phone call from your Aunt Sarah. You know, Mam's sister.'

'Wow, what's she doing ringing here then?'

'It's about her daughter, Tegan.'

'What's happened to her?'

'You know they live in that community place? Well, Tegan has been thrown out for some reason.'

'That's awful. But then she must be in her twenties, isn't she?' asked Cerys.

'Yes, she's about your age but she's never lived away from her parents, from the community.'

'Poor thing. I suppose she'll have to go and live with friends.'

'That's the problem. I don't think she has any. She has not been allowed out much, never went to school or to work.'

'Are you sure?'

'That's what Aunt Sarah said. And the thing is, she's asked if Tegan can come here.'

'Here? God, Mum won't want that, will she? Anyway, Tegan wouldn't want to come here, would she?'

'Well, I've spoken to Tegan as well. She really sounded lost, very vulnerable. I have said she must come here.'

Cerys blinked at her father. 'Dad, have you said anything to Mum?'

He shook his head.

'Oh Dad!'

Ellis was suddenly aware of the cold wind eating its way into his jumper and of a concert waiting to be organised.

'Look I'll deal with your Mam later. Tegan is on her way now. I was wondering if you could pick her up for me?'

'Well, yes, suppose so. Shall I get a room ready? Shame my roof is being done. Still, you've plenty of room in the manor.'

'Actually I thought she could stay in Hafan. What do you think?'

27

Cerys raised her eyebrows and then nodded. 'Actually, not a bad idea. When was Hafan last used?'

'It must have been when those friends of Bethany's used it for a few weeks around Christmas.'

'Well, it'll need going over and airing. I'll pop down when I've finished here. You say Tegan's on her way?'

Ellis sighed with relief. Cerys was so practical.

'She should get in about teatime. She'll let me know when she has an arrival time.'

'OK then Dad. I'll finish off here and get down to the cottage.'

Ellis went over and put his arm around his daughter. She was short like him but broader, stronger.

'Thanks so much, love. I'm sure she'll be here in plenty of time for the concert, wouldn't want you to miss it.'

Cerys grinned and bent down. She had had enough chatting.

'I'll see you later,' he said and went inside out of the wind.

Tegan walked around the busy concourse. People pushed her, voices echoed from the tannoy. She found the ticket office and waited in a queue. Finally a woman smiled at her, asked her where she was going, and what kind of ticket she wanted. The information was very confusing but Tegan could feel people behind her getting impatient and the fixed smile on the face of the woman was slipping. She bought a one-month return and, clutching her tickets, went to find her train.

This was not simple, but after asking a guard for help she found out that the train she wanted was in. She pushed her ticket through a machine and boarded her train.

Inside, it seemed very cramped. She realised she had to find somewhere to put her case, and copied others, putting it on a rack. Finally, she found a seat with a table next to the window and sat down.

Tegan took a deep breath, and then looked around the carriage. Everyone seemed focussed, working on laptops, giving instructions on mobiles, and reading. A voice asked 'Is this seat free?'

She nodded as a man in jeans and a black jacket sat next to her. He put his laptop on the table and opened it. Tegan felt his arm brush against hers and moved closer to the window. It was so physical, too intimate. The train jolted and set off. She watched through the window as, slowly, London ebbed away. The flats were replaced by houses; the gardens got bigger. She was fascinated by the stuff people filled their gardens with: trampolines, furniture, sheds and summerhouses. The Community garden was completely given over to vegetables and fruit. Flowers were considered an indulgence, frivolous. She had enjoyed some of the gardening. It had been propagating the seeds that she found the most intriguing. She would have liked to study it more but the books in the Community were very limited.

She looked over at a student sitting with her text book propped up on the table, typing notes onto her laptop. Tegan thought of her old fashioned exercise books. She had loved them, the hours of writing and drawing diagrams. She clenched her fists as she remembered Philip taking the books from her. It was the day she was told she was not allowed to have any more lessons, and she had protested. She had watched Philip take the books outside and put them in the bin as the dustcart arrived. She had stood crying, but it was too late. That anger, she had swallowed it, stored it, and it had never gone away however much she had outwardly conformed.

Tegan sat back in her seat. She had to relax, calm down. She closed her eyes, tried to imagine her safe place, the cottage, and was just starting mentally to open the front door when strange noises in the train startled her back to reality. She opened her eyes to see an enormous trolley being pushed along the aisle. The woman pushing it mumbled 'Hot drinks and sandwiches,' daring anyone to place an order. Tegan watched as the woman opposite her courageously asked for coffee and a chocolate biscuit. She realised she was hungry and she looked at the array of sandwiches, crisps, and sausage rolls but didn't dare order anything. She caught the eye of the man sitting next to her.

'Would you like a coffee?' he asked.

Tegan caught her breath in panic. 'Sorry, I don't know. I mean, sorry, thank you.'

He ordered them both coffees.

'Are you going far?' the man asked as he placed the coffee in front of her.

Tegan just nodded, and looked back out of the window. He went back to his laptop. Tegan breathed a sigh of relief. Thank goodness the man was leaving her alone. She had thought it would be rude to turn down the coffee but now hoped he hadn't been propositioning her. Then she wondered if she should have offered to pay for the coffee but decided not to. She remembered the third envelope in her bag and looked for it.

She nervously opened the envelope and poured on to her hand a round silver locket. It was very unusual, quite heavy, in the shape of a wheel, decorated with continuous Celtic knots that wrapped all around its circumference. She had never seen it before.

It had a fiddly clasp, and was difficult for Tegan, with short bitten fingernails, to open. Inside were faded photographs, one of a young fair haired woman, shyly smiling; the other of a young man. She wondered who they were. The woman was pretty and looked so happy. The photograph of the man had been scratched. It was impossible to see who it was. Maybe it was her grandparents. Tegan decided the safest thing was to wear the necklace. With some difficulty, she put it on. It felt strange. It was the first time she had worn a necklace.

She went back to staring out of the window. Finally, she saw that they had arrived at Birmingham New Street. She awkwardly pushed past the man sitting next to her, found her case, and left the train.

She had been unaware just how closely he had been observing her. He was an art teacher on his way to a residential course. As soon as she left he turned over the page of his sketch pad. He closed his eyes, pictured her and started to draw. She had been sitting bent forward, still, apart from the shadow of a rocking motion, hardly breathing, sore, red hands. One was clutching a horrible fake leather handbag as if it was stuffed with priceless jewels, the other occasionally lifted to her mouth where she methodically gnawed at her thumb. Her body tightly bound; legs squeezed together, arms jammed against her body. Her face was make-up-less, tiny, lost behind old fashioned tortoiseshell glasses. Her hair was almost completely covered by an ugly headscarf; only a fringe of black hair dared peek out underneath. He had glanced over her body. The bits he had seen were very thin. A fragile neck supported her head. Stick-thin legs protruded from her coat. God, that coat: where the hell had that come from? It rivalled the handbag for ugliness: a beige thin tent with buttons. Not like the chic vintage his students wore, but rather the bri-nylon of fashion. It was however very clean, like the rest of her, scrubbed and sterile. He had felt sorry for her but fascinated by her. He sat back and looked at his drawing. Part of him felt uneasy. It was a good representation of the girl but he knew instinctively she would have been deeply upset by the fact he had studied her, drawn her. It felt voyeuristic. When he got back he knew he should destroy the picture.

Tegan left the relative safety of her carriage, and tried to find her way around. It was difficult. She had to use escalators to change platforms. It was chaos all around her. She was hungry but the tight knot in her stomach meant she couldn't face food. Eventually she found the platform for her next train but then remembered she hadn't told Ellis the time of it. She had to go back up the escalator to find a phone booth, went through the same rigmarole as before and waited. He answered quickly.

'Hello. Is that you Tegan? How's it going?'

'I've got to Birmingham.'

'Well done.'

'I have a while to wait. I think I'll get to Aber - Aberystwyth is it? - about half past five.'

'Great. Cerys will pick you up and don't you worry, it's paradise here after London. I promise you, it's a different world.'

Chapter Six

Tegan watched her train arrive and boarded it. This time she found a seat that didn't have a table. It was in a pair facing the back of the seats in front of it. She tucked herself next to the window and put her bag on the next seat, hoping no one would sit next to her. Slowly they left the city behind. The scenery became more rural. She saw fields, mountains. Her focus went from the mountains to the dirty window sill inside the carriage and she closed her eyes. She woke with a jolt, aware of a man standing over her speaking in a loud, over-bright Welsh voice. 'Ein bod ni'n ar Aberystwyth.' She looked at him and blinked.

'We're at Aberystwyth,' the guard explained, smiling.

Tegan glanced out of the window. The train had stopped, and the carriage was empty. She glanced at her watch. It was only half past five but she felt she had been away from the Community for days. She got off the train feeling very disorientated. In the distance she saw mountains and stopped, looked over at them: incredible. Who would have thought you would see mountains from a platform in a railway station? Above her seagulls screeched, the air smelt damp. She realised she had come somewhere not far from the sea and panicked. She had never seen the sea, only heard tales of the beasts that come from it. Somehow she must try to keep away from it. She looked for the way out, and panicked when she thought all the signs were in Welsh. Then, with relief, she realised there was an English translation underneath. The first people she heard speaking were speaking in Welsh. What would she do if everyone spoke like that? How would she understand anyone?

''Scuse me lovely' a voice said. Tegan turned to see a sprightly grey haired woman smiling at her.

'Sorry' she mumbled, then took a deep breath and started to walk along the platform. After the anonymity of

London, the familiarity with which people smiled at strangers was disconcerting. Eyes met, they gave each other space and time to walk. She realised no one was bumping into her and liked it: the feeling of space, room to breathe.

Outside the station, Cerys was standing in the car park, holding onto Dylan's lead. He was excitedly pulling and sniffing. She was trying to keep an eye on the people coming off the train. She saw a group of students in tight jeans and fashionable jumpers and sweatshirts, chatting noisily. There were older short Welsh women, with neat hair-dos, and sensible rain coats; middle aged business people: weary, mentally still at work. Then she saw a girl in a strange headscarf, with anxious eyes, looking around. Was that Tegan? Everyone was walking past her purposefully to their cars. It must be her.

'Tegan?' she shouted.

The girl walked slowly towards her. Dylan lunged forward on the lead, trying to greet her.

Tegan stepped back horrified as the dog tried to jump up at her clean coat. The girl didn't seem bothered and laughed. 'Hiya, I'm Cerys. Dad asked me to come. The car's over by there. Let me take your case. How was your journey?'

'It went alright, thank you' she replied, and followed Cerys to a small, mud-splattered red estate car.

'Throw your bags on the back seat and jump in' said Cerys. Tegan reached into the back of the car. The seat was covered in rubbish, old towels, empty plastic bags, and old Wellington boots. Dylan was put in the back, behind a dog guard and he flopped down exhausted. Cerys sat in front of the wheel and started to back out of the car park. Tegan glanced at Cerys. They both had black hair and blue eyes and were about the same height, but Cerys was plump and her hair was in a short scruffy bob. Tegan glanced disapprovingly at the mud on Cerys' trousers and wrinkled her nose at the smell of wet dog emanating from Dylan at the back.

'Sorry about the stink' said Cerys. 'I took Dylan down the beach before coming here and he rolled in some seaweed, but that's dogs for you. Can't stop them, can you?'

'So, do you live by the sea?' asked Tegan anxiously.

'Oh no, we're out in the hills. Anyhow, sorry to hear all that's been going on with you' said Cerys. 'It sounds dreadful.'

'It was my fault' said Tegan.

'What did you do?'

Tegan didn't reply. Cerys changed the subject. 'Have you visited anywhere around here before?'

'Oh no' said Tegan.

'I ought to bring you back into town soon, do the touristy things like the electric railway, and take a bracing walk along the seafront. To be honest, though, I'm always glad to get away from here, out to the mountains.'

'Do you live in a very isolated place then?' asked Tegan.

'You could say that. It's just outside a small village, Ty Ffynnon. It's in the heart of the Cambrian Mountains.'

'Sorry, the Cambrian Mountains?'

'Don't worry. Lots of people haven't heard of them. It a glorious wilderness between Snowdonia and Brecon.'

Tegan stared out of the windows. Soon they were leaving the town and the landscape became increasingly wild.

'Look over there: miles of fields and hills,' said Cerys. She took in a deep satisfied breath. 'It's lush here, isn't it?'

'Mmm' said Tegan. She wasn't really listening, just staring out of the window. She had never been in such a vast empty space: no buildings, no cars, nothing.

The roads became increasingly narrow and undulating. She started to feel very sick.

'Sorry. Please, can you stop?' Tegan asked.

Cerys pulled over to the side of the road. They both got out. Tegan was shocked at the ferocity of the wind and held her coat tightly round her. She felt sympathy for the sheep and lambs in the fields: such an inhospitable place. The air battered her face, demanding attention. She would have described London air by smell: the fumes, cooking smells from the pubs, even the perfume from strangers. But here she was only aware of the feel of the wild uncontrolled wind. She took deep breaths. Slowly the nausea was subsiding. She looked towards the horizon but then saw two enormous menacing birds, gradually getting closer and closer. Her heart started to race. What were these wild beasts?

'Red kites,' said Cerys. 'See, they have forked tails and those wings span nearly two metres.'

Suddenly Tegan could feel the talons, grabbing her hair, sinking deep into her head. Tegan screamed, closed her eyes, put her hands on her head. She felt Cerys touch her arm. She opened her eyes, the birds still far away.

'Hey, it's OK. They won't come near you, I promise,' said Cerys.

Tegan was shaking. She could see Cerys was bewildered,

'Come on, let's go' said Cerys. Tegan was relieved to get back into the safety of the car, though she was still shaking. What must Cerys think of her? But this place felt reckless, unpredictable.

They travelled further into the hills, the fields a patchwork of heather, bracken and purple moor-grass. On the horizon Tegan spotted a line of tall white towers. She peered at them. She could see they had large white blades rotating.

'Wind turbines,' said Cerys, 'sprouting up everywhere, they are.'

'What are they?' asked Tegan.

'You've heard about wind farms haven't you?'

Tegan daren't reply.

'The trouble is they are getting bigger and more intrusive,' said Cerys. 'It's very difficult, isn't it? You know, balancing the needs of people and wanting to preserve all this.'

Tegan couldn't understand the dilemma. Daniel said this would all end soon whatever we did. In fact, the sooner the earth was destroyed, the sooner the end times would come.

Eventually they entered a long driveway that led to the manor. There were a few workmen's lorries parked outside, and scaffolding covered some of the building, but still it looked impressive.

'I just need to pop in and pick up the keys,' said Cerys.

Tegan stared out through the windscreen. It was enormous, a palace. Were these people millionaires? Where on earth had she come? Cerys saw her face. 'Don't worry. It's not as posh as it looks. Obviously, at one time it was wonderful, and then it got hacked about and was a hotel for about fifty years. Mum dreams of restoring it, fancies herself as lady of the manor. Still, the garden is very exciting and I have a lovely house the other end of it. Come on, I think you might catch Dad.'

Cerys turned off the engine and let Dylan out of the back. Tegan followed them into the house. The hallway had a dark, oak floor and graceful curved staircase. It was very light with enormous windows streaming light which reflected off the white and Wedgwood-blue walls. A middle aged woman with a ponytail, wearing a tabard was energetically vacuuming in a side room, losing the battle against the constant dust and dirt from the builders.

Cerys tried shouting over the noise, 'Donna!'

The woman turned around, but left the vacuum on.

'Donna, is Dad around?' Cerys shouted.

'No, your Mam's just come back, though.'

'But she's not due back yet! Does Dad know?' said Cerys. Tegan was surprised by the horror in Cerys' voice.

'Don't think so. She only just came, said it was a surprise.'

'Thanks Donna,' said Cerys. She turned decisively to Tegan. 'Dad can sort this one out. You go on out to the car. I'll just find the keys.' Tegan turned and left the house, mystified. Cerys caught her up and stood outside the car talking on her mobile. Tegan sat in the car wondering what was happening, why she couldn't meet Cerys' mother, her aunt. Where was she going? It seemed so rude to be rushing out like this.

At the concert hall on the outskirts of Aberystwyth Ellis and Ruth were busy with the final preparations for the concert. Ruth had just finished a call.

'Great,' she grumbled. 'That was Fiona Matthews to say they are incorporating a flipping clog dance into their act. That's the third call like that since lunch time. At this rate we might as well throw the programmes away.'

'Never mind' Ellis replied soothingly. Then his phone rang.

'Hiya Dad' said Cerys.

'How's it going?'

'I've got Tegan. Did you know Mam's home?'

'Oh Duw, no.'

''Fraid so. Anyway, I've got the keys and we're going straight to the cottage, alright?'

'Um, yes, OK. So why's your Mam home early?'

'No idea. I didn't speak to her. You can do the explaining.'

'Fair enough. Damn, I'll have to get home and speak to her before the concert. So is Tegan OK?'

'To be honest Dad, she's a bit weird, like.' Cerys spoke in a low voice.

'What do you mean?'

'I don't know. Her clothes and things. Anyway I'll bring her along later.'

'OK. Thanks, lovely. I'll try to catch you in the interval.'

He sighed as he finished the call. Ruth was coming towards him. She saw the look on his face.

'What now?' she asked.

'It's Hannah. She's come home early.'

'Has she now? I wonder why?' said Ruth sulkily. 'I mean, she was so excited about going to stay with Megan and Wynn in that flat in New York, didn't think she'd want to leave there early to slum it at our concert. Still, I suppose she's heard it's a posh do now, wants to swan round in some designer dress.'

Ellis didn't reply. He pushed away the picture of Hannah, crying, pleading with him to go with her, insisting she

37

was desperate for a break after years of caring for her parents. No, he'd rather Ruth saw him as the downtrodden husband of a spendthrift, discontented wife. After all, it hadn't been an easy time for him either and he wasn't waltzing off on expensive holidays. He noticed the disappointment on Ruth's face, took his coffee and smiled gently.

'Well, some people don't need designer dresses to look beautiful.'

She smiled back, gave a brave sniff and returned to the preparations.

Cerys got back into the car and drove them back down the driveway.

'You'll be staying in Hafan, the cottage' she explained. 'You'll like it down there. It's real quiet, like. We'll just pop to the village and pick up some bits.'

Tegan felt increasingly anxious. What on earth was going on? Why was she being put in a cottage on her own? Was there something the matter with her? Was it because she'd sinned? Were they scared she would contaminate them? But no, they were worldly, they couldn't be thinking like that. Why then wasn't she invited to the manor? There must be loads of spare rooms. She didn't want to go to some cottage away from everyone.

'This is the village, Ty Ffynnon,' said Cerys, pulling up in front of a shop. 'We'll pop in the Co-op. There's nothing in the cottage at the moment.'

Tegan got out of the car and looked around. In London, people, buildings, cars dominated. Here they were secondary to the mountains. The houses seemed smaller, more insignificant, because of them. Opposite the Co-op was a gift shop. Next to that was a large pub called The Red Dragon. At the end of the high street she saw a church steeple. A lot of the houses were terraced, some painted in pastels, white, pink or blue. They entered the shop. It was quiet apart from a small dark-haired woman behind the counter chatting excitedly to a customer in Welsh.

Cerys shouted 'Hapus Sant David Dydd Helen.'

'Oh Hapus Sant David Dydd, Cerys.'

Tegan stood still, her eyes darting between the two women. Then she heard

'Mae hyn yn Tegan, mae hi'n aros yn Hafan.' Cerys grinned at Tegan. 'Just telling Helen you're staying at the cottage. She likes to know what's going on.'

'Prynhawn Da Tegan' Helen said to Tegan.

'I'm sorry, I don't speak Welsh' she replied, embarrassed.

'Never mind' Helen said. 'Lovely to meet you. Cerys, you should have got our Donna to give the cottage a good going over for you.'

Cerys ignored this and said to Tegan, 'Helen is Donna's sister,' and then, turning back to Helen, said 'I just saw Donna up at the manor. She tells me Mam is back early.'

'Oh, come for the concert I expect' said Helen. 'So, Tegan. You here on your own?'

Cerys interrupted. 'Don't tell her, Tegan. Let her work it out.'

'I hear you were out with that Robert again last night,' Helen said to Cerys. 'We're all so pleased, about time he got a new girl, we all think.'

Cerys grinned but said to Tegan 'Grab a basket from over there. I'll pop out and give Dylan a quick walk if that's alright. Be back in a minute.'

Tegan looked at her in panic. 'Is there a list?'

'No, but just get basics, you know.'

Tegan looked around the shop with a glazed expression.

'Would you like me to stay and help?' asked Cerys.

Tegan nodded but felt humiliated. Cerys picked up a basket.

'Right, what kind of milk?'

Tegan stared.

'Ok let's get semi-skimmed,' said Cerys. 'Fancy lasagne? And some chocolate, cereals, muesli?'

Tegan followed Cerys round the shop and then saw the toothpaste and soap.

'Sorry, I need to get them,' she said.

They went to the till.

'I can pay.' Tegan pulled out her envelope.

Helen accepted the notes, and gave her change.

'There you are now,' said Helen. 'You can always phone through for anything. Do you want a newspaper?'

Tegan wondered why she would want that. 'No thank you.'

'OK then. Let's go. Bye Helen' said Cerys.

'Do most people around here speak Welsh?' Tegan asked as they left.

'A lot, yes. I had Welsh lessons at school in Swansea but I'm not fluent like some people round here. Mam and Dad don't speak it. In any case, everyone here speaks English as well. Don't worry: they'll understand you!'

They returned to the car. Tegan looked out of the window as they pulled away and drove up a narrow steep road leading off the high street. Initially they were hemmed in by high bushes but after about half a mile they were in open countryside and on a rough track which ran through a field and circumvented a small wood. Ahead Tegan could see that the track led to a wooden gate, propped open, and the track continued into the front garden of a small stone cottage. It looked rather abandoned among the wilderness of fields and was dwarfed by the hill behind. Cerys drove in and parked.

'Come on then, out we get. This is where you will stay. This is Hafan' said Cerys proudly.

Chapter Seven

Cerys let Dylan out of the back of the car and he tore off running around the garden, nose glued to the ground, tail wagging furiously. Tegan had to battle the wind to open the car door, but managed to stagger out.

'The manor's a ten minute walk down there,' shouted Cerys, pointing to a path to the left of the cottage. Tegan turned and looked into the distance at the mountains painted with white gloss snow. She stepped off the track on to the grass, which felt soft and springy under her feet, and stood spellbound. Out here nature ran riot: no fences, and no boundaries. Nature adapted to survive: the daffodils were short, the trees all bent in the same direction, sculpted by the wind. In the London parks people were in control, with organised paths and borders, each tree and flower planted and preserved for a purpose.

As Tegan looked she felt an inexplicable deep feeling of sadness. It was too much freedom, too much beauty. She didn't know what to do with it. She stood very still and closed her eyes. She realised that the absence of traffic did not mean silence. She could hear crows screeching in the woods nearby, the gentler trill of smaller birds. In the distance sheep brashly bleated. The wind buffeted her face. Calmer now, she opened her eyes turned and walked slowly towards the cottage.

However, her new found sense of calm was soon shattered. She stopped and stared at it in horror. Cerys misinterpreted Tegan's expression. 'Sorry, the garden's a bit of a mess. I should have come down and tidied up.'

Tegan didn't answer. Slowly, panic seeped into every part of her body. She started to shake. This was impossible. This couldn't be happening.

'What's wrong? Don't you like it?' asked Cerys.

'It's my safe place, my cottage.' She whispered, and, then turning to Cerys, she said in desperation 'It's impossible, but it is.'

Tegan could see Cerys looking at her, baffled.

'Don't you see? My Mum made it up' she said. 'It's not real. So how is it here? My mother made up an imaginary place, but this is exactly like it. I mean, it's identical.'

Tegan touched the red wooden door, then bent down and stroked the stone owl.

'Well, lots of cottages look a bit like this. Don't worry about it,' said Cerys. 'Come on in.'

Tegan dreaded entering, but knew she must. She followed Cerys, and then swallowed hard. The layout was exactly as she would have predicted. One large room with a hearth, inglenook, and beams. A kitchen led off it. However, the interior of the cottage disturbed her more than the exterior. It was more than just a picture painted by her mother. There were sounds, smells, objects, that her mother had never described but which were somehow familiar. This place felt part of her own experience. But that was impossible. She heard ticking, and swung round. There it was: the large grandfather clock with unusual painted flowers on the face. She went into the kitchen and there was the wooden dresser with the carved birds on the top.

'It's ever so small' Cerys was saying. Tegan looked down at the flagstones. She knew how cold they would be on tiny bare feet.

'Do you want to look upstairs? You can bring your bags. I'll show you your room.' Then Cerys laughed. 'That sounds very grand. There are only two. I thought you'd like the one at the front. It looks over to the woods.'

Tegan followed her up the wooden stairs and went into the room she was directed to. She gasped. It was just the same. She sat on the bed looking up at the beams. On the wall she recognised an intricate framed embroidered picture. She went and looked and she remembered the detailed picture of the cottage and hills. 'I think I'm going mad' she thought.

'My Nanna did that,' said Cerys. 'She did beautiful embroidery work. You'll find it all over the cottage on cushions and cloths.' She opened the window. The wind blew the curtains. 'Come and see the wonderful view of the woods.'

Tegan joined her and stood breathing in the fresh air.

Cerys' mobile phone rang and she left the room. Tegan started to calm down: she was being foolish. Then she turned and looked at the bed, the duvet. She didn't recognise that, thank goodness. She felt drawn to the bedpost, and went to look at it. Nothing- but she pulled out the pillow and then she saw it. A small fist clenched in her stomach as, with shaking hand, she reached out and her fingers followed the simple outline of an owl. She could picture a hand scratching it into the wood, using an old ball point pen. She tried to imagine the person's face but couldn't see it. She took her hand away quickly, pushed back the pillow, and returned to the window.

The woods were starting to become a silhouette against the orange-red sunset. Soon the sun would disappear; the night would come. She shut the window. In the Community the nightly vigil would have started. She felt the knot in her stomach getting tighter.

'That was just a friend calling' Cerys explained, coming back into the room. 'What are you looking for?'

Tegan didn't answer. The light switch, where was it?

'Tegan, what's the matter? Are you still worried about the cottage?' asked Cerys gently.

'It's not just that.'

'Tell me,' insisted Cerys.

'I'm sorry, it sounds so stupid. It's when I feel the night coming on, I get nervous.'

'You don't like the dark?'

Tegan didn't know how to explain. 'In the Community as soon as it gets dusk we put on all the lights, you know, getting ready. It could be that night; the High One could come... ' Her voice trailed off as she saw Cerys' raised eyebrows.

Tegan was embarrassed. Cerys clearly thought she was talking nonsense, maybe even thought she was crazy. She looked again out of the window. The fear was creeping, sliming its way into her body.

'I can stay down here with you if you like,' said Cerys.

'I couldn't ask you to do that.'

'It's OK. I'm staying with Mam and Dad while I have a new roof put on my own place. It's fine. I'm happy to come here if you like. It will get very dark later. It can throw anyone from the town. Not many people are used to pitch blackness.'

'I'm sorry to be a nuisance, but thank you. So does this cottage belong to your Dad?'

'That's right. The cottage, the field in front, and the woodland. It was where he was bought up. Mum would like to sell it but I can't see Dad ever doing that. She even thought of renting it out but Dad doesn't want strangers here. Still, it's a shame it lying empty so much' explained Cerys.

'It's very kind of them to let me stay,' said Tegan.

'No problem. I'll take Dylan to Mum and Dad's for tonight but he'll have to come back here to stay tomorrow. Mum can't take much of him.'

Tegan cringed but replied 'That's fine.'

'I'll leave you to unpack and go up to the house and sort out some things, wash this smelly dog. I'll be back in a minute now. See you later.'

As Cerys was leaving the cottage Ellis' car was screeching to a halt in front of the manor. He leapt out and ran inside, up the staircase and arrived at the bedroom door. He took a deep breath, gripped the handle and pushed open the door.

Hannah was carefully hanging up a long sequinned dress. A neat pile of cream silk underwear was piled up next to a new designer handbag on the bed. She had obviously spent a fortune in New York, but now wasn't the time to argue about that.

'Hiya, sorry. Only just heard you'd come home. You know, it's the concert. Everything is chaotic.'

Hannah finished carefully arranging a dress on its hanger, then turned around.

'This place is filthy. The workmen haven't used anything like enough dust sheets,' she responded. There was no hint of the Welsh accent she'd worked so hard to eradicate.

'You came home early?'

'I thought I would come to your concert, even though naturally I have not been invited.' Her mouth moved into a tight smile that had been painted on with the perfectly applied make up.

'You've not wanted to come to anything since we moved here-' Ellis muttered. 'Anyway, how was New York?'

'It was good to get away. I was right. I needed a change. Do you know, it's the first time for years that I've been away without worrying about how my parents were, dreading phone calls. I wish you had come with me, though. I went to so many galleries. It was wonderful. It would have been fun to have gone to them with you.'

Ellis shrugged. 'You knew I had the concert. I'm glad you had a good break anyway. How were Megan and Wynn?'

Hannah went back to hanging up clothes. 'Things aren't so good there, very tense. You know they've always seemed an odd pair, him so good looking and her, well, let's face it, very frumpy. All she thinks about is her damn horses and the stables, but they've managed to stay together for nearly thirty years.'

'Well, he likes money and she has plenty of it,' said Ellis.

'True, and she fusses over him all the time. It seems to suit them both. I hadn't realised before I went away with them how obsessed he is with what he eats, what he looks like, and Megan just rushes around trying to make sure everything is exactly as he likes it.'

'But you say things seemed tense?'

Hannah turned to look at him. 'Yes, they were arguing a lot about the flat. Megan wants to sell it, and to be honest I can see her point. They hardly ever go there. However, Wynn is adamant he wants to keep it. While we were there, he arranged for someone to come and completely re-do one of the en suites.

It'll cost a fortune. I've never seen Megan get so angry with him.'

'I think the flat is in her name, so really it's up to her, isn't it?'

'In theory, but really she usually does what he says.'

'Ruth was hinting at something about Wynn. Made me wonder-' said Ellis.

'What?' asked Hannah curiously.

Ellis took a deep breath. 'I'll tell you another time. Listen, something important has cropped up.'

'Is it Cerys?' asked Hannah, suddenly anxious.

'No, she's fine.'

'Good.' Hannah started to arrange her cosmetics on the dressing table. 'So I assume it's something musical.'

'No, it's not that either.'

'For God's sake, Ellis spit it out.'

'The thing is, Sarah, your sister, she phoned.'

Hannah turned around quickly, and stood very still clutching a large bottle of perfume.

'Sarah phoned you? Why?' she demanded.

'It's their daughter, Tegan. She's been thrown out of the community where they all live.'

'That's nothing to do with us,' Hannah said dismissively, and turned away. However, her hands were shaking. She knocked over an open box of earrings, sent them flying all over the floor. She didn't appear to notice.

'The thing is, Tegan is here. She's going to stay in the cottage.' Ellis held his breath, waited for the explosion.

'You are joking?' said Hannah.

'No, it's true. Sarah's daughter has come here.'

'When did all this happen?'

'Today. I'm sorry, it was all so sudden. Sarah rang and then Tegan. She sounded so desperate. I couldn't say no. They have disowned her and thrown her on the streets. I had to do something.'

'Hang on, I don't believe this. My sister, who called me a whore of Babylon, has thrown out her own daughter, and you've said we will look after her?'

'Um, well -'

'No way Ellis. You get down there now and tell the girl to get the hell out of here. I will not have her here.'

'For God's sake, have a heart. It's not her fault. She's got nowhere to go.'

'Surely she can go to friends or something,'

'The trouble is, I don't think she has any friends outside of the Community. She's had a very isolated sort of life. She knows no one, has nothing.'

Hannah picked up the pile of underwear, put it in a drawer and slammed it shut.

'First thing tomorrow, you phone my sister and tell her to take her back, OK?'

'They won't. Honestly, Hannah, they've disowned Tegan. They don't want any more to do with her.'

'I don't believe that. Not even my sister would disown her own daughter.'

'Honestly, she sounded more fanatical than ever. She said the girl was dead to them.'

'Oh God' gasped Hannah. 'That's what she said about Mum and Dad. But surely she can't say it about her own daughter? I can't believe it. No, you see, she'll be missing her soon enough. You know how kids can wind you up. Just send the girl back.'

'I can't, I told you. Listen, she is our niece. Let's at least keep her off the streets for a few days.'

Hannah sighed, and then asked, 'So have you met her? What's she like?'

'I haven't seen her yet. Cerys picked her up. She'll be at the concert tonight though.'

Hannah looked at him curiously. 'Why have you put her in that cottage anyway?'

'Because, as you said, it's chaos here.'

'But down there?'

'Why ever not?'

'It's damp, awful. Why you won't sell the place, I'll never know.'

'You know I can't. It's tied up in all sorts of ways. Anyhow, I wouldn't want to. It's my family home,' he said quietly. 'I think it's a good place for Tegan. She can tuck herself in there as long as she likes.'

'Are you tucking her away from me?' Hannah asked quietly.

'No, no, of course not, but it will be easier this way.'

Hannah bit her lip, tweaked her hair, and then changed the subject. 'Most people have replied by email about the party,' she said.

'Party?'

'Our anniversary-'

'Oh, of course. Sorry, I forgot. Well, I didn't forget. My mind is full of the concert. So is everyone able to come?'

'Looks like it. Also, I have had another email from the trust about the manor. We need to give them a reply soon. This offer won't be there for ever.'

'For God's sake, Hannah. Not now, I'm up to my eyes!'

'You're always too busy-'

Ellis heard footsteps coming up the stairs and along the corridor. The door opened and Cerys and Dylan entered the room. 'Hi Mum. How was New York?'

'My God. Cerys, what do you look like? What will people think of you? And don't bring Dylan upstairs. My God, he smells worse than ever today.' Hannah pushed the dog away.

'That's the seaweed. Dad told you about Tegan then?'

'He certainly did.'

'Good. Dad, I'm going to stay in Hafan for a few days. Tegan's very nervous. I think she's scared of the dark.'

Ellis cringed. Hannah groaned. 'Oh my God, Ellis.'

'I'm sure she's fine,' he said.

'I hope you're right.' Hannah looked at her watch. 'OK, you two, out of here. Someone needs to make an effort for this evening. I shall be wearing this season's Ralph Lauren.

Impressive, eh?' She looked at their blank faces. 'No, you don't get it, do you? Might as well be Primark.'

Ellis and Cerys left the room but before she left him Ellis grabbed Cerys' arm. 'Do you think Tegan has real problems? Is she safe down there?'

'She's very strange Dad. You know, I'm not into clothes and things, but hers are so old fashioned and she wears a weird headscarf. And then she gets freaked out by little things, like she thought the red kites were going to attack her. You know, she got spooked by the cottage, thought her mother had told her about it or something.'

'Did she really think that?' asked Ellis.

'She's so on edge. Talks weird, religious like.'

Ellis sighed. 'Oh dear. I'm sorry to land this on you. Do you mind staying with her?'

'Not really. Listen, I'll go and pack a few things. Can I leave Dylan here tonight? I'll give him a quick hose down. I can pick him up tomorrow.'

'Of course. Is Tegan alright with the dog?'

'Not sure, but she'll get used to him. Right, see you later and good luck this evening.'

Ellis gave her a quick hug. 'Thanks. I'll get them to reserve two tickets for you at the desk.' Cerys smiled and went along the landing to her bedroom.

Meanwhile, down in the cottage, Tegan was waiting. She walked around upstairs. It was very quiet. She didn't know when she'd ever been in a house on her own. It was very luxurious compared to the Community house. The bathroom shone with white tiles, and a pretty border co-ordinated with the shower curtain, and the accessories. She returned to the bedroom. The duvet was thick and soft and the cover was a design of beautiful red roses which matched the curtains. On the wooden floor were thick rugs.

She wondered whether she should unpack. Cerys wasn't there to ask what to do. Maybe she'd better. She hung up her clothes carefully, although they looked lost in the huge wardrobe and the underwear looked scruffier in the smart lined drawer. She put Daniel's book, her clock and framed verse on the bedside table. She started to put her silver box in the drawer and then realised she didn't have to hide it here. She put it proudly next to the other things. She touched its smooth surface, looked again at the writing. She was pretty sure it was Welsh. Her mother had never told her what it meant, and she must ask someone here. She opened it, checked the contents were not broken. Next to it she put the piece of Elizabeth's embroidery.

She went downstairs and wearily sank into the thick cushions on the sofa. She leant back, thought of the hard plastic chairs in the Community and went to look out of the window. She gazed up at the sky. It was a mixture of a deep blue ink sky and gathering grey clouds. She wondered when Cerys would be back. What to do while she waited? She looked at the TV: obviously not that. She sat down on the sofa again: she must just wait. The room was getting cold, darker. Suddenly the phone rang; the sharp trill startled her. She panicked. What was she meant to do? It seemed to get louder; more urgent. She looked at it on the window ledge. Was she allowed to answer the phone? The ring seemed to get shriller. Slowly, she stood up, reached out towards the phone, her hand shaking.

Chapter Eight

Tegan stood at the window holding the telephone, staring out. She watched as Cerys got out of the car, grabbed her bags and pushed open the front door with her elbow.

'Hiya, are you OK?'

'The phone-' stammered Tegan, looking at the handset.

'Oh, right, is Dad on the phone?'

'He's gone now.'

'Right, well you can put it back then' said Cerys, looking at her strangely. 'I see all the lights are on?'

Tegan looked down. Cerys walked into the kitchen.

'I've got the booze for later,' she said, lifting up the bag she was clutching. 'Fancy a cup of coffee before we go? Do you need something to eat?'

'Uh, no thanks. Coffee would be nice though.'

Tegan sat on the edge of the sofa watching Cerys busily making a drink. It was odd to feel so helpless. In the Community she was always busy, and out here she felt useless. She started to think about the concert. Would the theatre be like the ones she had seen from the outside in London? She had never been in. Daniel called them Houses of the Devil. She had imagined all sorts of lurid, shameful things that might happen in them. This was very difficult.

'I should of course obey your father,' she said to Cerys as she was handed a drink, 'but could you tell me what will happen at this concert?'

'Usual thing, although it will mostly be in Welsh I'm afraid, but then it is a St David's Day concert. There will be singing, dance, poetry, harps of course.'

'Will there be a lot of well, swearing and things?'

Cerys laughed. 'God no, all very tame and worthy I'm afraid.'

'-and we just sit and watch?'

'That's right.' Tegan could see Cerys looking at her strangely, and decided to stop asking questions.

'Your Dad seemed very insistent-' Tegan said.

'Yes, but if you're too tired-' said Cerys.

Tegan thought of Ellis swearing crossly on the phone earlier that day. 'I ought to come' she said. She looked down at her clothes. Looking at Cerys she guessed it was quite informal. In any case, she didn't possess anything any smarter.

As Tegan closed the front door behind her she stared in horror at the sheer blackness in front of her. No cars, streets light, people: nothing. Cerys called her and she felt she was stepping off the end of a precipice into a dark, bottomless sea. She was glad to get in the car and drive away but even then the darkness seemed to envelope them. "You have chosen the path of darkness." The words shouted at her. She was in the Domain of the Beast, fraternising with the world. She shouldn't be going to the theatre.

'You alright?' asked Cerys.

'Is it always so dark?'

'Well, often the sky is full of stars, but it's overcast tonight. When I first came here I found it quite scary, you know, all this blackness.'

'Really, you were scared too?'

'Oh yes. I mean, no street lights, buildings. Still I've got used to it now, even like it. You know people come here because of it. It's meant to be good for star gazing and things.'

Eventually, as they drove into Aberystwyth, the street lights started to appear and spread a comforting glow.

'There you are, civilisation. That feels better doesn't it?' said Cerys.

Tegan nodded, pleased that Cerys seemed to understand. Finally, Tegan spotted the concert hall. Cerys parked the car. The streets were full of people, all of whom seemed to be heading purposefully in the same direction. There was a buzz of excitement.

'Wow, Dad will be pleased. He was dead worried about filling this place,' said Cerys.

Tegan looked up at the large modern building. Lights shone from the enormous windows. Tegan could see inside, hoards of people streaming up the stairs. They looked very smart. It was a sophisticated world she had never been part of. Daniel would disapprove, despise this opulence. She felt a surge of panic. It had been a long day. She was very tired. All she wanted to do was go home.

Cerys took her arm. 'Come on then, in we go.'

Tegan stood self-consciously in the foyer. Smart confident people greeted each other in English and Welsh. She frowned disapprovingly at such opulence. "Vanity, vanity, all is vanity". Her thin coat rubbed shoulders with pashminas and expensive suits. Cerys in jeans at least fitted in with the younger and more rebellious types who wore their jeans as a sign of non-conformity. No one was dressed like Tegan. She glanced at Cerys, who was just grinning.

'You know, a few years ago this concert was held in a church hall. People turned up in jeans and bought a ticket at the door. We had a glass of wine served by ladies from the church. Now look at it. My Dad's done this.'

She laughed, but there was pride in her voice. 'Come on, let's find our seats.'

There was a buzz of expectation around the room. An orchestra was tuning up.

'It's very grand' whispered Tegan.

'Well, it is for round here. I expect you go to professional concerts all the time in London, but, still, this should be pretty good. People fight to take part now. Here, look at the programme.' Tegan took it from her and glanced uncomprehendingly at the pages of Welsh writing, but was relieved to find an English version at the back.

The small orchestra at the front struck a chord. The hum of chattering subsided in expectation. The lights started to dim. Tegan's heart began to race. She clutched the arms of her seat.

53

She stared at the curtain on the stage, a spotlight trained on it. The curtains opened. A woman stood alone. Tegan stared at this woman standing brazenly waiting to perform. Nobody joined her. The music started and Tegan realised that she was going to sing on her own in front of all these people. She glanced around. From what she could see in the darkness everyone seemed to think it was normal. She sat back and started to listen to the singing. The woman sang well but seemed happy to flaunt herself. She would have done better to sing more quietly and with others. Still, the audience applauded enthusiastically.

Next, another woman came on who played a harp. The instrument was enormous, but the woman seemed to embrace it and produce the most incredible sound. Tegan was soon lost in the unusual sounds. It gave her a feeling of floating and she was sorry when it finished. The concert continued with more singing and then dancing. She was more uncomfortable about this. It seemed rather immodest: the outfits rather tight and revealing. She glanced at Cerys but she didn't seem bothered by it so Tegan decided it would be best just to look down until it had finished.

The final performance of the first half was by two children. The boy announced in a clear, rehearsed voice "Ar Hyd Ar Nos" and they sang a duet that was sweet and tuneful. It was a lullaby her mother had sung to her, years ago. She had used English words "All through the night." Tegan closed her eyes and could feel the closeness of her mother, the comfort of knowing she was safe. Her mother was with her. The singing ended and, reluctantly, Tegan opened her eyes. She felt an overwhelming sense of loss. She wanted to go home. The applause seemed far away. Tears slowly trickled down her face. The lights went up, people started to stand.

Cerys grabbed her arm. 'Come on, let's get to the bar, see if we can find Dad.' Tegan took a deep breath, and quickly wiped the tears away. She hadn't realised they would be going to a bar. She couldn't go there. However, Cerys wasn't looking at her and she had to follow her through the crowd of people. They quickly reached the bar. The noise was deafening. People were greeting each other, hugging and kissing, shouting excitedly in Welsh and English. She hated the feel of people pushing against her. She found the smoke stung her eyes. The unfamiliar smell of alcohol forced its way up her nose.

'There's Dad,' shouted Cerys.

Tegan was very apprehensive about meeting the rough man. He seemed so loud, hugging, kissing, greeting people enthusiastically. He had a mass of jet black hair flecked with grey that matched his beard, and a presence far greater than his physical body. When he noticed them he came over, arms open.

'Hiya lovely,' he said warmly to Cerys, and then turned to Tegan. 'Now, you must be Tegan.'

He stepped back, put a hand on her shoulder and stood very still. His head on one side, he stroked his beard thoughtfully. He was blinking fast. 'Duw' he said quietly. She wondered what was wrong. He spoke softly, his voice breaking slightly. 'Lovely, really lovely.' She tried to pull back; uncomfortable at the intimacy. How could he talk such nonsense anyway? Here she was in her headscarf, skirt and blouse. Did he think she was stupid? She knew she looked anything but lovely.

'Thank you for letting me stay Uncle Ellis' she said, formally.

He smiled. 'It's a pleasure. Do call me Ellis. Now, how was your journey?'

'Rather long, but thank you for your help.'

'You don't look much like your Mam.' He seemed spellbound. 'She was so fair. Look at you, real Welsh with that black hair and blue eyes, lovely.'

Then, to her horror, he reached forward and touched the locket round her neck. She shuddered.

'My mother's' she explained, stepping back. He nodded. She didn't understand the emotion in his eyes, but it was painful to see.

'Are you enjoying the concert?' He spoke quietly, his mundane words at odds with the look of intensity.

'Yes. The harp, I've never heard one before. I liked it very much. And the song "All through the night", my mother used to sing that to me.'

'Your Mam had an incredible voice.'

A man suddenly clamped his hand on Ellis' shoulder. 'Well done Ellis, marvellous,' he shouted, and walked away.

The gesture seemed to pull Ellis back to the present. 'Tegan, anyway, it's good to have someone who appreciates the music. There are some real gems coming up.'

He turned to Cerys, shaking off his mood. 'I've given James a solo.'

'Oh Dad, no. He'll be unbearable.'

Tegan followed Cerys' glance and saw a good looking young man, gelled spiky black hair, and clean shaven. He stood upright, head tilted back, hands confidently in his pockets. He was immaculately dressed in an evening suit. Attractive girls were standing hanging on his every word, giggling. James, she noticed, was not so engrossed but was glancing around.

'I know, but he has a wonderful voice, and it's nice for Wynn and Megan to see their son's gift recognised' said Ellis.

'Have you seen Mam?' Cerys asked anxiously.

'I talked to her before the concert. I think she's outside at the moment.'

'Should I take Tegan to say hello?'

'Look, try and avoid her tonight. She's really upset, you know, about things.'

Tegan watched a knowing look but didn't understand their silent communication.

Then she noticed a tall, very fair haired younger man, scruffy despite his evening suit, standing by them. He seemed lost in thought.

Ellis turned and saw him, reached and grabbed the man's arm. 'Sam, this is my niece Tegan.'

Tegan had to strain her head back to meet the gaze of the man who looked down, but she had a feeling he wasn't really seeing her. He didn't speak.

'Sam is our accompanist' explained Ellis. He glanced at Sam, but he missed his cue.

'So, all organised for later?' he asked Sam.

Sam blinked and then gently smiled at Ellis. 'Oh, the concert, yes, of course.' His voice was quiet, gentle, but not Welsh.

'You look distracted' said Ellis.

'I was thinking about a stray Amy had in earlier today. I've just thought of something I want to try on his leg.'

'Well, don't go before the end of the concert' laughed Ellis.

Cerys turned to Tegan. 'You think he's joking, but Sam's quite capable of disappearing off.'

She saw Tegan's puzzled look and explained.

'Sam is a vet in his Dad's practice in the village. We all think a lot of him.' She grinned, and turned to Sam. 'The trouble is, word about you has spread. People are coming from all over the place to see you. Dylan had to have someone else give him his inoculation last week. We were not happy.'

Sam smiled absently and then asked intently 'How's Dylan's ear?'

'Much better, thanks. It made such a difference when you found out exactly what caused the infection. He's looking really good now.'

'Excellent. Bring him in early one morning, before surgery. I'd like to have a look at it, make sure it's completely cleared up.'

'Tegan is staying up at the cottage,' interrupted Ellis.

Sam's face lit up. Tegan felt she had become interesting, although when he looked at her he didn't quite meet her gaze. 'I think there are Kites nesting at the edge of the woods there; I must get up there again soon.'

Cerys smiled. 'So when's Angharad due back?' she asked.

Sam blushed, looked down, scratched the back of his neck, spoke to the floor. 'Soon I think. She has a lot of work to do for her finals.'

Then Sam took a long swig of his beer.

'Right, I'd better circulate,' said Ellis. 'See you later in the pub Tegan.'

Tegan was about to object, but he had gone. She stood panicking: she couldn't go to a pub, no way, but actually she was surrounded by people drinking. The High One was looking down. He could see her in this place of sin. The High One could be telling Daniel what she was doing. The panic rose like a storm crashing inside her and she started to dig her fingers deep into the palm of her hand.

Chapter Nine

'Tegan,' a voice shouted.

Tegan blinked. She looked at Cerys blankly.

Cerys smiled. 'It's Sam. He was talking to you.' Tegan slowly reoriented herself, and glanced up at Sam. 'Oh, sorry. What did you say?'

'I was asking if you want a drink,' Sam said.

'Oh no, of course not, nothing,' she said abruptly, stepping back. She was in some kind of nightmare, the devil tempting her into sin.

Sam blinked and looked down. 'Oh fine.'

'Tegan-' said Cerys, shocked.

Sam shrugged. 'Don't worry. Cerys, can I get you something?'

'That's kind' said Cerys, pointedly glancing at Tegan. 'Half a lager shandy would be great, thanks.'

Sam left them and Cerys turned to Tegan. 'He was only being friendly.'

'I don't drink alcohol. He shouldn't try to make me get drunk,' she said firmly.

'Sam wouldn't try to make you do anything. In any case, there are soft drinks as well there. You could have had orange juice or something.'

'Oh, I'm sorry. I didn't know-' Tegan stammered.

But Cerys was now distracted. Tegan noticed that she was nervously playing with her necklace, a silver pendant of a letter "T".

'Oh God, Mam' said Cerys.

Tegan followed her gaze. She saw a sophisticated older woman, who looked a lot younger than Ellis. Tegan found it hard to believe that this woman was her mother's sister. Granted, her mother was tall, but painfully thin rather than slim, and her grey hair was restrained in a tight bun. Even for the Community she dressed very plainly and severely. In stark contrast Aunt Hannah had shoulder length bobbed hair, ash blonde with highlights, and she wore a stunning strapless silk lilac evening dress which seemed to search for places on her slim body to cling to. It made all the dresses around it look prosaic.

Cerys turned to Tegan and groaned. 'That is my mother.'

Tegan stared at the extraordinary woman and then she saw Hannah grab the arm of an older man who was passing. She took his glass of champagne and drank from it and he smiled a dazzling smile in return. He was very good looking, tall with dark hair, greying at the sides. He looked immaculate in his evening suit. Tegan watched horrified at this woman, her aunt, throwing herself at the man.

'That's Wynn, James' Dad, our very own George Clooney' explained Cerys.

Tegan looked at her blankly, and then asked 'Should I go and introduce myself?'

'Not now. As Dad said, best leave her be for now.'

Sam returned with Cerys' drink. He held it out, spilling some of it on her arm. 'Oops' he said, smiling shyly. He seemed to move like a large marionette puppet being worked by a very distracted puppeteer.

Cerys laughed. 'You're so clumsy Sam.'

'Yea, drives Angharad mad. Right, better go and check my music. Don't tell your Dad, but I think I've forgotten the music for Calon Lan.' His face lit up in a mischievous grin. It surprised Tegan.

'Oh Sam, really' said Cerys.

'Don't worry, I'll busk it,' he said, winking, and left them. Tegan noticed he didn't look at her: no doubt he had written her off, but then that was the price of living in the world. Just as they were about to return to their seats she glanced over at Hannah and Wynn. A woman in a stiff tweed suit approached them; firmly put her hand on Wynn's arm and, unsmiling, escorted him away.

Cerys laughed. 'Megan keeping her husband in check! She'll be wanting to get him back to their seats. Wouldn't want to miss any of James' performance. Honestly, she worships him.'

Tegan noticed Hannah looking around and then felt Cerys' hand on her arm. 'Come on, let's get back.'

They returned to their seats. It took longer for people to get seated for the second half as people reluctantly left their socialising, but eventually the audience settled back. There was some Welsh poetry reading which Tegan sat through, totally mystified. And then a man about her own age strode on to the stage, smiling easily at the audience.

Cerys nudged her. 'The wonderful James! Look down there: you can see his Mam, Megan, sat on the edge of her seat.'

James stood, upright, confident, enjoying being centre stage. It would be easy to write him off as cocky, but then he started to sing. He sang an old Welsh ballad, "Maffanwy". At the end the room fell silent before breaking into applause. He bowed, smiled at the audience, and bowed again.

'Honestly!' exclaimed Cerys.

'He sings very well.'

'I know, but he's so full of himself. Still, it's made his mother's evening.' Cerys pointed down to Megan, who was standing, clapping enthusiastically. Tegan watched as she reached down to her husband, forced him to stand and then managed to make the audience around her follow suit simply by a meaningful glance. All the time she clapped, but never once did Tegan see her smile.

It took a while for the next and final act to arrange themselves. It was a large choir. Tegan saw Ellis busily rearranging the music stands and then he left the stage. When the choir were arranged, Sam walked on quickly, took a brief bow and gratefully sat behind the piano. Ellis made much more of his entrance, and absorbed the applause. He stood proudly smiling out at the audience, bowed, and then turned to his choir.

As the audience hushed Cerys whispered, 'I'm a member of that choir.'

Tegan's eyebrows shot up.

Cerys laughed. 'I go to rehearsals but, to be honest, I hate performing.'

'Doesn't your father mind?'

'Oh no, he knows I'm not singing. I hate being out the front like that.'

The choir sang a selection of Welsh hymns and songs, and the audience joined in. Tegan listened, impressed with the enthusiasm of the singing. At the end the conductor and pianist received a standing ovation.

Ellis opened his arms and spoke. People hushed to listen.

'Dioch a fawr' he said; more applause. He spoke some more in Welsh. Tegan had no idea what he was saying but she closed her eyes, relishing the sound, hearing the rise and fall of the mountains reflected in the gentle tones. Ellis started to speak in English.

'And so, thank you so much for coming and for all your kindness. Now, before we finish I must thank all who have performed and in particular I want Ruth to come out and take a bow. We all know that without her this concert would never have happened.' Self-consciously a pretty young woman came on to the stage. One of the choir members came forward and gave her a huge bouquet of flowers and a bottle of wine. Ellis embraced her enthusiastically and kissed her on both cheeks.

'Who's that?' asked Tegan, very confused. Who was this strange woman Ellis was kissing? Is this how the world carried on?

'That's Ruth. She helps Dad with the concerts, hero worships him. It's sad really, but Dad laps it up.'

Everyone got up and Tegan was glad to leave.

'Come on.'

Tegan would be glad to get back to the cottage. However, Cerys drove back to the village and into the pub car park.

'We don't need to stay long' she said, and started to open the car door.

'I'm sorry, but I can't' shouted Tegan in panic.

'What?'

'I can't go in the pub.'

'Why ever not?'

'It's not allowed. It's wrong.'

Cerys sighed. 'It's the drink thing is it?'

Tegan nodded.

'It's alright, you know. All sorts go there. There's a restaurant and everything. You don't have to drink-'

'I'm sorry. I just can't.'

Cerys sighed and closed her car door. 'Right, back to Hafan then?'

Tegan cringed. 'I'm sorry. I can wait in here if you want to go in.'

'Don't be twp,' said Cerys.

Tegan felt close to tears. It had been a long day.

Cerys seemed to sense her upset. 'Hey, come-on. It's OK. Actually, that lot after a concert are unbearable. All that 'Weren't you wonderful?' –'Oh thank you but not as fantastic as you.' It's horrendous. Come on. Let's get going.'

Back at the cottage Cerys immediately went into the kitchen and took the bottles of wine out of the bag.

'I'm going to open a bottle. You don't mind do you?'

Tegan sighed. It was all so difficult. 'I think I'll go on up to bed if that's alright.'

'But aren't you hungry? I'm starving. Fancy a lasagne?'

'No. Thank you-'

'Sure?'

'I'm OK.'

'Don't you want to watch something before you go up?' asked Cerys.

Tegan blinked in horror. 'I'm sorry. I'm very tired.'

'OK, if you're sure' said Cerys. 'I'll watch down here for a bit, hope you sleep well.'

Tegan climbed the stairs. It felt very strange. The cottage was very quiet and dark. In the Community there was always a group on vigil all night and the lights would be left on. She put her bedroom light on and closed the curtains. It was nearly eleven. She knelt by her bed.

'Come quickly Oh High One' she repeated over and over. Then she confessed her sins for the day, so many; she pinched her arm very hard. The High One must know she was truly sorry. She must try harder tomorrow. At half past twelve she got into bed. She had never slept in a room on her own. She wondered how Esther was. Was she missing her? Maybe Esther despised her like the rest of the Community. It was what Daniel had instructed. It hurt terribly to think of Esther feeling like that towards her. She left her light on and lay listening to the strange sounds. No traffic or sirens, no groups of lads shouting to each other. Instead she heard owls calling, and a strange howling sound. She would like to have looked out of the window but decided to stay safe in her bed. It was comforting to know Cerys was downstairs. She thought about her mother and prayed 'High One, look after my mother. I know I have no right to ask you anything, but please look after my mother. Also, help Elizabeth sleep tonight. Help me stay pure.' She opened her eyes, and thought about Steve. How did she get it so wrong? She thought of that girl, the girl in the scarlet underwear. The world was so wicked. And Steve, he had said there was 'no us'. How could he? She was a stupid, sinful, person to have got it so wrong. She cried, hard hot tears into her pillow until, finally exhausted, she stopped and lay on her back looking up at the beams. She was tired. She must rest. She tried all her usual ways of getting to sleep: making lists, trying to relax. Nothing seemed to work tonight. Eventually she dozed off but she had vivid, hectic dreams. Enormous beasts with wings flew down, pecked at her face. It was bleeding, sore. Then she was in hell. The fires burnt her flesh. She could hear screams of fear and torment. She was screaming for her mother to save her but all she could see was Daniel's face, despising, rejecting her.

Chapter Ten

Tegan awoke in a panic. Where was she? Everything was so quiet. Where was everyone? Had the end come? She felt the softness of the duvet, and then heard unfamiliar bird song, the sound of someone downstairs. Slowly, she reoriented herself. She was in the cottage, in Wales. She started to calm down, saw a crack of light through the curtains. She had made it through the night out here in the world. She heard the familiar loud ticking and was shocked to see it was seven o'clock. In the Community she would have been at vigil for an hour by now, would have looked at her rota for the day. She got out of bed and went to look out of the window. The ground was covered in a thick frost. She could see a large man wrapped up in a thick anorak; his dog, oblivious to the cold, running ahead over the frozen grass. She turned off her light, then put on her skirt, blouse, cardigan, headscarf, and went downstairs. Cerys was up and offered her toast and coffee.

'Hiya, sleep well?'

'Yes thank you.'

'I heard you shouting out in the night. Are you alright?'

Tegan was embarrassed. 'Sorry. I hope I didn't disturb you.'

'It's OK, but you sounded very upset. Maybe you should see Doctor Khan, Nadia. She could give you something to help you sleep.'

'No, I don't need medicines,' Tegan said quickly. 'I will pray for a better night tonight.'

'Well, have some coffee. There's some toast there,' said Cerys. Tegan made herself a drink and sat down at the small pine table. The ticking of the clock seemed to emphasise the silence.

Eventually Cerys asked, 'So what sort of house did you live in in London?'

'It was a huge building, used to be a nursing home. The rooms were quite bare and cold but it was good not to waste money on luxuries.'

'You must be finding this place tiny then?'

'It is very small, and of course so quiet. It is odd, though, you know, it being so familiar, but I'm getting used to that now. It's cosy.'

'I wouldn't exactly call this the Ritz' said Cerys. 'I used to come here when I was little, stay with Nanna. Loved it then. Dad loves it, of course, but then I suppose he grew up here.'

'I think it would be a wonderful place to grow up.'

'Were there lots of you living in this house in London? You call it a community, don't you?'

'I suppose about fifty; some families, some new disciples. Daniel has started a new house somewhere recently. He's had a real vision in the past year or two for outreach.'

'So was it a kind of commune, everyone equal, go self-sufficient and all that?'

'Well, we did try to grow a lot of our own food, but I wouldn't say we were equal. The men, particularly the elders, were always in charge.'

'Is there a leader?'

'A man called Daniel. He came with his wife Deborah when I was about ten. Then we did vigil a lot more, and a lot longer. He showed us how to make money to support the community with sewing and knitting.'

'So did you go out to work?'

'No.' Tegan looked down. 'I couldn't. I didn't have any qualifications.'

Cerys frowned. 'You never did exams?'

'No. I was taught by Deborah, Daniel's wife, but never took exams.'

'You've had a very different sort of upbringing haven't you?'

66

'I suppose so. It's the only life I've known, though.'
Tegan suddenly felt very home sick, a deep longing to return to her own kind, to be somewhere she fitted in.

The clock ticked loudly. Cerys coughed. 'I'm going up to the manor this morning. I need to get on with the garden.'

'It's a busy time of year, isn't it?' said Tegan quietly.

'Would you like to come up with me now?'

Tegan sighed. 'I ought to help, yes. I should do something useful.'

'Great. I have so much to do.' Cerys stood up.

'You work for your parents then?'

'Yes. I had a really boring job down in Swansea. Mum and Dad had bought me a house on the Gower. I lived there with my partner Gareth.'

'Oh, you are married,' said Tegan, surprised. Cerys hadn't mentioned a husband.

'No, thank God. We lived together for about a year. I think really he liked the house more than me, and anyway he found someone else with an even bigger house and left me. I was miserable, and then Mum and Dad moved here.'

Tegan was trying to get over the shock of Cerys having lived in sin, but Cerys didn't seem at all ashamed.

'Dad gave me the farmhouse on the land,' continued Cerys. 'You see, I have been very spoilt. And now I'm doing the garden. It's my dream. I love it here so much.'

'It must be a huge garden.'

'Gosh, yes. I couldn't possibly manage it on my own. David, a lecturer from the local college, is involved, and some of his students. I have to compromise but, still, it's worth it. There's a lot of woodland and we are creating the most wonderful wild meadow.'

'So do people come in and visit it?'

'Not yet. A trust has offered to take on the manor and gardens. It's very exciting, but Dad is driving Mum mad. He won't decide what to do.'

'But where would he and your Mum live?'

'They could still live there. It's a very good set up. They'd live in the manor, still own it, but they have to commit to most of it being open to the public, including the gardens. In return the trust will pay for a lot of the renovation work.'

'Oh, right' said Tegan, though she was rather confused.

'Mam is keen. She would like to be involved in the work. She's done lots of research into the house.'

'But your Dad?'

'Oh, he typically won't make a decision. My Dad has this crazy philosophy that life somehow sorts it out. It's very frustrating for Mam.'

'I'm looking forward to seeing it all' said Tegan.

'Great. Well, you'd better get changed after breakfast. We need to get on.'

'Changed?'

'You can't garden like that. You need to put on jeans, sweatshirt, that kind of thing.'

Tegan was embarrassed. 'Sorry, I don't have any of them. When we wanted to garden we used the community boots and coat.'

'Good gracious. Well, let's get up to the house and I'll see what I can find you.'

Tegan was horrified. 'You can't give me your clothes. Please don't do that.'

'Well, I know my clothes aren't fashionable,' said Cerys, looking offended.

'No, I didn't mean that, but I couldn't make you short of clothes.'

Cerys laughed. 'I have been jumping up sizes in the past few years. I'm not intending to give you any of my current clothes: they'd drown you. No, I have things I wore a few years ago. They may be OK.'

Tegan tried to smile, but it was awkward to be given clothes like this.

'Oh by the way,' said Cerys, 'we ought to swap mobile numbers, just in case I need to get hold of you.'

'I don't have a phone,' said Tegan, cringing

68

'Really, wow. How do you manage?'

Tegan shrugged. She couldn't think why she should need one.

⊕

After breakfast they shut up the cottage. It was a dry morning. The wind was cold and hurt Tegan's cheeks. She noticed Cerys looking at her.

'What's wrong?' Tegan asked.

'Oh, nothing. It's just, well, do you always wear a headscarf?'

Tegan nodded. 'Of course. Daniel said it was about us women knowing our place.'

She saw Cerys' look of disapproval, and stopped trying to explain.

They left the cottage behind. Tegan felt lost in so much open space.

'This will be full of wild flowers' said Cerys. 'There will be a mass of bluebells in the woods soon, and then wild flowers, orchids, yellow rattle. It's fantastic.'

Tegan suddenly grabbed Cerys' arm. 'There's one of those red kites. Sam said he thought there may be a pair nesting in the woods?'

'Yes that's right. Magnificent isn't it?'

Tegan watched the bird wheeling, carried on the wind: a silent predator searching for prey.

⊕

Ellis was tired and fractious. It had been a late night. He had chosen a bad time to check the credit card bill. He found Hannah sitting in the dining room nursing a cup of coffee, looking through a book about Georgian interiors. Her smart linen trousers and blouse contrasted with her tired, grey face.

'It's your own fault you feel so rough. I saw you packing away the champagne last night with Wynn.'

'At least he talked to me. I make all that effort for you and you disown me.'

'When I came to find you, you were outside smoking. I thought I'd leave you to it.'

69

'Was Tegan there? '

'Oh yes. She came with Cerys. I saw her in the interval.'

'You or Cerys should have brought her to meet me.'

'You were far too involved with Wynn. You'll meet her soon enough. Anyhow, I've been going through the bank statement.'

'Oh God, not money at this time in the morning.'

'You've been spending money like water in New York, and before that the bills for this place were astronomical. I mean, over two thousand pounds for bloody wallpaper.'

'Well I can't just go and pick something off the bargain shelf at B and Q. The place needs sorting out, Ellis. If only you'd get on and sign this thing with the trust-'

'I don't know. I told you. I don't want to live in a tourist attraction.'

'We would have part of the place private. It's the sensible thing to do. We could travel.'

'I suppose so. Oh, I didn't mention. I've been offered work at the university in September.'

Hannah threw down her book in exasperation. 'Ellis, we bought this manor together. You promised we would do it together, and look what you do. Throw yourself into a load more bloody music stuff.'

Ellis groaned. 'Not this again, it gets so tedious, Hannah. Anyway, you could help with the choir, the concerts-'

'No, Ellis. I've done that all our married life. We were going to make a new start. I was to do some art courses,'

'Nothing is stopping you. For God's sake, you just like to complain. All you want to do is spend money.'

They stood in silence, both discontented, both too weary to carry on arguing. Hannah reached out first.

'So what has Cerys been up to while I've been away? She certainly hasn't been out buying clothes, but she looks happier. Has she seen any more of Robert?'

'I don't know. Wouldn't harm, though, nice bloke. And it would suit Cerys to be married to a farmer. Mind you, I wouldn't want to lose her.'

70

'Hardly flying the nest, the next bit of land along, is it? You ought to encourage her to be more independent. Now James, he's good looking, and with a bit of encouragement from the right woman he could make something of himself.'

'Fortunately Cerys has more sense.'

At that moment they heard the front door open. Tegan and Cerys had arrived.

Cerys gestured for Tegan to follow her into the dining room.

'Mam, this is Tegan.'

Tegan peered at the glamorous woman of the night before who now looked harder, older. Suddenly she could see the similarity with her mother.

'Hello Aunt Hannah. Thank you so much for having me.'

She was aware of Hannah just staring at her, slightly open mouthed. Then she saw Hannah shoot a glance at Ellis.

Cerys coughed. 'I'm going to show Tegan the garden.'

Hannah blinked. Then she spoke quietly, still staring at Tegan.

'Please call us Hannah and Ellis. I mean to say, aunt and uncle makes us sound ancient.' She seemed to shake herself. She stepped back away from Tegan. 'You don't look like my sister. I see you dress like her though.' Then Hannah glanced down at Tegan's hands, and in a softer voice said, 'They look sore. Anyway, how are you getting on in the cottage?'

'It's very comfortable, thank you.'

'You think so?' Hannah said, carefully. 'I can't imagine that. I don't know what possessed Ellis to put you down there. So, I hear you were asked to leave the community. Why was that?'

Tegan looked down. 'It's a bit complicated.'

'Well I guess it wouldn't be difficult to gain disapproval from my sister; but I expect it will all blow over. You can't have done anything that awful. I know my sister can be strict but I'm sure she'll sort things out for you to return soon.'

'No, I have sinned badly. It's not my mother's fault. I don't think I will ever be allowed back.' Tegan sensed the animosity towards her mother, wanted to defend her.

'Well there's no rush for any of that,' interrupted Ellis, 'and there's the party coming up, good chance to meet people.'

Cerys groaned. 'Oh God, that's still happening, is it?'

'Cerys, you're as bad as your father,' said Hannah sharply. 'But, still, what the hell is there to celebrate any more?'

Without explanation she turned and left the room. Tegan was horrified. No woman in the community would have argued with her husband like that. She saw Ellis cringe.

'Oh, Dad. I'm sorry,' said Cerys.

'Don't worry. She'll calm down.'

Cerys sighed and turned to Tegan 'Come on, let's sort out some clothes.'

As they were leaving the room, Dylan came bounding to greet them. It was Cerys he wanted to see. She patted him. He rolled over and she tickled his tummy. 'It's OK, I've come back' she said, laughing. 'Cocker spaniels are not called velcro dogs for nothing. I only have to go to the toilet and he greets me like I've been away for a year.'

Tegan followed Cerys up the expansive flight of stairs. This led to a crescent gallery with heavy wooden doors. On the wall were some charcoal drawings of female nudes. Tegan blushed. She wanted to walk away but then she saw the faces: they had a look of deep despair, loneliness. They made her want to cry.

'Good, aren't they?' said Cerys. 'Mam did them.'

'Your mother?'

'Yes, years ago now, when I was little and she was still nursing.'

'She was nursing when my Mum was doing her medical training wasn't she?'

'That's right, same hospital in Cardiff. She had always wanted to go to Art College but her Mum and Dad, our Gran and Grandad, didn't approve, so she did it in evening classes instead.'

72

'I never met any of my grandparents. Mum never visited hers, neither did Philip.'

'I never liked Mam's parents very much. They were so strict, very religious. I don't think Mam got on with them, but she looked after them when they were ill, I suppose from a sense of duty. She said they never thanked her. To be honest I think your Mum was the favourite but she never went and visited, never even went to the funerals.'

'I didn't know they were ill' said Tegan. 'Mum never talked about them once we went to the Community.'

Cerys sighed. 'They were both really poorly. First Grandad, and then Grandma. She died last year. Mam was nursing them both for years. It changed Mam, you know. She became very tired and uptight. It's a shame your mother never helped. Maybe that's why Mam's being a bit funny to you'

'My mother would have thought she was doing the right thing, you know, keeping out of the world, but I suppose to your mother it can't have seemed fair. I've never thought about it but it's sad I never met my grandparents. What ever were they like?'

Cerys smiled. 'Well Dad's parents were lovely, so I'm glad I knew them. It's sad that our families never got on, isn't it? I mean me and you are both only children. It would have been fun to have been friends growing up.'

'You're right, yes; it would have been nice to see you.'

Tegan followed Cerys into a large bedroom. The backcloth of the room was expensive reproduction furniture, but it was overlaid with a chaos of clothes, gardening books, and sketches. Tegan noticed some delicate water colours of flowers.

'They're lovely. I think there are pictures like this in the cottage.'

'I took them down there to brighten the place up.'

'So you painted them?'

'Yes, it's just a hobby.'

'But they're so good. That's interesting, an orange poppy.'

'The Welsh poppy, sometimes yellow. They'll be everywhere round here soon.'

There were also posters and statues of strange things Tegan knew nothing about. She looked at the pictures but found them vaguely disturbing.

'I put all these up in my teens. My Nanna, Dad's Mum, taught me about them. That's Arianhod, the Welsh moon goddess' explained Cerys. 'I really loved Nanna. She was lovely, always made a fuss of me. She was interested in this stuff because she said it was part of our heritage. She always said, though, that it was stories. I must never be frightened of it. Some day I must take you to the well.' Then she pointed to a very intricate crystal on the window sill. 'And this is a special crystal my Nanna gave me to attract the Twyleth Teg, the fairies.'

'It's very pretty.'

'Yes, but actually it led me into some quite major problems. I keep it more as a warning than anything else.'

'What do you mean?'

Cerys bit her lip, looked away. 'Maybe I'll tell you about it one day.'

Cerys opened a wardrobe. 'Right, now then, let's get down to business. This is full of unworn clothes. They are for my mother's daughter.' From beautiful padded hangers hung silk dresses, designer jeans and tops.

Tegan was confused. 'You haven't got a sister though.'

'No, I meant the girl I was meant to be.' She sounded sad and bitter. She shut the wardrobe, and then opened one of the chests of drawers.

'Right. In here I have some clothes from my distant past when I was a size ten. Here we are.'

She pulled out jumpers, jeans. There were rows of Hunter wellies in different colours and sizes with socks to match.

'Try the clothes and choose some wellies. Oh, socks to go in them as well.' Tegan was embarrassed. She had never undressed in front of anyone before, not even Esther. They would leave the room and let each other change.

Cerys saw her face. 'I'll go on down, see you in a minute.'

Tegan took off her skirt and put on the jeans. It felt very strange. Her Mum would be horrified. Wearing "men's clothing" was strictly forbidden. The trousers were very loose. She found a belt and did it up on the tightest notch: better. The jumpers were soft wool. She put on a navy blue one with a round neck. It swamped her but she liked the feeling of being encased in it. She was amazed at the selection of wellies, all pristine. In the community there were a few old black pairs with worn inner soles that rubbed her feet. First she put on the warm, soft socks and then chose some boots. They were a bit big but so comfortable. Tegan stood in her new clothes feeling very self conscious. She looked at the stranger in the mirror: who was she? What was happening to her?

Chapter Eleven

Tegan heard a knock at the bedroom door, and turned around self-consciously as Cerys entered.

'That's better' said Cerys. 'You just need a decent coat now. Hang on, I know just the thing.'

She went to the wardrobe and produced a navy padded coat, with a hood. It still had labels on it from the shop. 'Here you are.'

'But it's never been worn. I can't wear this in the garden.'

'It was my mother's idea of a gardening coat. Hang on, let's take the label off. The thing is, it was much too small for me. She must have known.'

'Are you sure you don't mind me wearing it?'

'Of course not. I'll be glad to see the back of the thing.'

Tegan tried on the coat. It was big but very comfortable. She had never worn such a luxurious coat. She put the hood up. It was huge, but she could adjust the poppers so that it wrapped around her head.

'Your Dad won't mind me, you know, dressing like this?' she said, looking down at her clothes.

'Of course not. Come on, let's go down.'

As they left the bedroom Tegan could hear that Hannah was in the hallway arguing again with Ellis.

'Honestly Ellis, she looks very odd. She needs to go back where she belongs. She'll never fit in here.' Hannah's voice echoed around the hall.

'Keep your voice down' urged Ellis.

'But she can't stay here.'

'I can't see why not. Why do you have to make a fuss about every little thing? Your outburst about the party, really, it's so embarrassing-'

'Everything I do is embarrassing to you, isn't it? If you could just once stick up for me, put me before your damn music and other people's opinion.'

'Oh God, not this again-'

Tegan went red with embarrassment. Cerys coughed loudly. Hannah glanced up and walked away again but Ellis came over to them as they descended the stairs.

'You're all togged out then Tegan' he said. 'Listen, take no notice of Hannah. You must stay as long as you want.'

Tegan couldn't reply. "She looks so odd, she'll never fit in." That is what Hannah had said. That is what people must think about her.

Ellis was still talking. 'You know, it's good for Cerys to have some company. By the way, Bethany, our vicar, asked me last night to invite you there for coffee any time. She said she was free later this morning.'

'A vicar? But why does she want to see me?' Tegan asked, alarmed.

'Oh, it's just part of her thing to welcome visitors. She's OK, is Bethany.'

'I have to go to the village later' said Cerys. 'You could come with me. I'll show you where she lives. She's got a gorgeous retriever called Rex.'

Tegan nodded. She felt she had no option but to go along. She followed Cerys into the garden. Dylan came racing out with them.

Tegan breathed in the crisp air. The wind was cold, but it was the beauty of the garden that took her breath away. 'Cerys, it's wonderful.'

'Do you think so? All I see is all the work that needs doing. I'm so glad you like it. Come on, I'll show you round.'

Cerys had come alive. She walked briskly, her face glowing with passion. There was a long brick patio running the length of the manor, and then a large rectangular lawn. Individual gardens led off from this. 'I like it because it makes each one its own private space. The students have areas, means they can experiment a bit. We have a really odd mixture of old and modern planting and design. Practically, it works for us as well.'

They walked up some old stone steps. 'This is my rose garden. I won't let them touch this.' Cerys was talking, walking fast. 'This is the cottage garden.'

As they moved away from the house and through the gardens there was a wilder feel.

'This area is a wild flower meadow. It leads to the orchard over there and then the woodland surround, and tucked away in here is my home' she said proudly.

They came to a small farmhouse surrounded by scaffolding. It was very neat, probably twice the size of the cottage. Cerys took Tegan inside. The rooms were generously sized, white-washed walls, warm, rather untidy, but comfortable.

'It's a lovely home' said Tegan.

'Thanks. I love it.'

They went back outside. Despite it being a cold day, Tegan was starting to feel very warm in her coat. They walked down one side of the garden, when she noticed a large wooden door set into a beautiful old brick wall.

'What's in there?' asked Tegan.

Cerys laughed. 'Ah, that door hides a terrible mess.'

'Can we see inside?'

'OK, come on. David would love to do something with it.'

They went into a large rectangular overgrown piece of ground surrounded by brick walls on each side.

'Apparently this was a walled garden. David wants to work on this.'

'I've read about them. They would have provided the manor with all the vegetables, fruit, even flowers if needed.'

'You know your stuff don't you?'

'Only a bit about vegetables' said Tegan earnestly. 'Anyway, what would you like me to do today?'

Cerys rubbed her hands. 'Come into the greenhouse. There's lots to do in there.'

They went in. The smell was earthy, comfortable. Cerys glanced down at Tegan's hands and gave her some gloves. 'Mam's right. They're very sore. Would you like to wear these?'

Tegan and Cerys worked happily. Tegan loved the smell of the plants in the greenhouse. The soft brown compost crumbled between her fingers. In the community she had asked for a greenhouse but it had never been allowed. This was so organised and efficient; she loved it. All too soon, though, Cerys said 'Sorry, if you're to get to Bethany's for coffee, we have to go. Alright to walk? I'd rather leave the car here, and then we can walk back to the cottage after you've seen Bethany.' They went in to the house. Tegan took off the boots and was about to remove the socks when Cerys said 'I'd keep those on, and the clothes if I were you. You can pack up your skirt and blouse. We're in for a really cold spell.'

'Won't Bethany mind me wearing trousers?' asked Tegan.

'Of course not.'

Tegan went upstairs and put her clothes and shoes into a carrier bag. They looked very flimsy and old. She went downstairs and they were about to leave when Cerys said 'Hang on. I've something for you.' Cerys ran back up the stairs.

Tegan could hear piano playing coming from one of the rooms. She followed the sound and found Ellis playing. It was the tune from the night before "All through the night".

She stood listening.

'Ar Hyd ar Nos' whispered Ellis.

She nodded. 'When I was little Mum sang it to me, when I was frightened at night. When I was older she said enough of these stories and songs, I must do vigil. She didn't come to me at night any more then.' She stopped and was aware of a deep unspoken but always existing sadness.

'Your Mum had an exceptional voice, you know.'

'I loved it when she sang, but then she said it was vain and boastful.'

'So do you sing?'

'My mother and Philip always discouraged it.'

'Really? That's awful' said Ellis. Then he frowned. 'Why do you call your father Philip?'

Tegan blinked. 'You know, I haven't thought about it. When I was young he asked me to and I just thought it was normal.'

Then he looked at Tegan gently. 'You've had a strange upbringing, haven't you? I'm sorry.' He coughed. 'Anyway I wouldn't mind betting you can sing. Do you read music at all?'

'Not really. I play a bit by ear, that's all. To be honest, I always found the manuscript very tiny, hard to read.'

'Really?'

Ellis held up a piece of music. 'Can you read this?'

Tegan peered at the music. 'No, see, it's all blurred.'

'Lots of my students have refused to wear glasses because of vanity but you have a pair. I think they must be the wrong prescription. When did you last go to the optician?'

'Oh I never go there.'

'What do you mean? You have glasses.'

'Of course, I just get them out of the box.'

'The box?'

'When I was about eight I told my mum I couldn't read things far away very well. She said they had a box of glasses. I was told to get a pair out of there. I just tried a few on and found a pair that suited. Every time one pair stops working I just choose another one.'

'You've never had an eye test?' asked Ellis, his voice betraying his concern.

'Oh no. We never go to things like that.'

'What about the dentist, the doctor?'

'I've not been to them for a long time now. I went when I was little, but it's discouraged, better to pray.'

'Pray?'

'Yes, fast, do vigil. '

'For God's sake. Sarah was training to be a doctor before, well, before she gave up. That's really bad Tegan.' He looked angry.

'My mother didn't really have much say' said Tegan defensively. 'Daniel and the elders decided on a lot of stuff when I was growing up.'

'OK. Well, I want you to see my optician, Grace'.

'Oh no. I won't go' she said firmly.

'We'll see. I'll make an appointment. You say you play the piano by ear. Come and show me.'

'Oh no.'

'I insist.'

She nervously went to the piano, and played the tune he'd just been playing.

'But you never had lessons, did exams?'

'Oh no. Philip said it was a waste of money.'

Ellis scowled. 'That was a dreadful waste of talent. We have a choir, meets on a Wednesday. Cerys comes sometimes. You should come.'

Tegan didn't reply, but she had no intention of singing in public like that.

He sat on the piano stool next to her and played the tune "All Through The Night". 'I'm going to sing. See if you can join in.'

Ellis sang. His voice was rich, deep like liquid, dark chocolate. His gaze was far away, looking at the mountains. She started quietly, hummed. Then she realised he'd stopped: she was singing on her own. Immediately her throat tightened. She couldn't swallow or breathe.

Ellis stopped. 'What's the matter?'

'I can't, I'm sorry' she said tearfully. 'It hurts. Philip told me it was God's way of punishing my vanity.'

'Philip is a fool. I think you could have a good voice and you should be proud of it. I think the reason you can't sing is because of stress. We can work at that. Come to choir sometime. Also, I can teach you some exercises that will help sometimes. Singing with others is easier, less pressure.'

Tegan tried to smile, but no way would she be going.

Hannah met Cerys as she was running back down the stairs.

'Oh, Cerys, will you give this to Tegan?'

'Hand cream?'

'Yes. I mean, her hands look terrible.'

She saw Cerys' look of surprise. 'I'm not a monster Cerys. Just because I think Tegan should go back to her family doesn't mean I am heartless. Actually, I feel rather sorry for her. I'm glad you've at least given her some warm clothes, however scruffy she looks.'

'I'll give it to her Mum. I've got her a mobile' said Cerys, and went into the music room. Hannah followed her, stood in the door way.

'Your cousin can sing, Cerys' Ellis shouted. 'You must bring her to choir on Wednesday.'

Cerys laughed. 'I'll try. I've got this phone for you, Tegan.'

Hannah watched as Tegan looked at the handset in horror. She looked really frightened of it.

'Please, I can't' she stammered.

'Go ahead' said Ellis. 'It's our old spare. Cerys tells me most people wouldn't be seen dead with it.'

'I have no idea how to use one,' Tegan said desperately.

Ellis put the phone in her hand. 'It's simple, don't worry. Cerys can easily show you how it works and it means you can get in touch with people. It has mine and Cerys' numbers on it.'

Hannah watched as Tegan tentatively took hold of the phone. Cerys started to explain to her how it worked as if it was the most normal thing in the world. Hannah noticed how Tegan's hands were shaking, as she typed in a number, making a practice call to Cerys. She held the phone to her ear.

Cerys answered her phone. 'Hiya. Congratulations, you are through to my phone.'

Tegan put the phone into her pocket. Hannah saw the fear in her face that was going unnoticed by Ellis and Cerys. She thought, that girl is really frightened. I bet she's been told she'll go to hell or something if she uses a phone. Ellis and Cerys have no idea. God knows my Mum and Dad were bad enough, but I reckon she's been through worse.

Then Hannah saw Cerys give Tegan the hand cream. She watched as Tegan took the pot, unscrewed the lid. The cream was white, rich. She touched it delicately, lifted it to her nose, smelt it and smiled. 'It's lovely.' She glanced over at the doorway and they looked at each other.

'Thank you very much.'

Hannah nodded, moved by Tegan's reaction to the cream. Cerys would have hated it, but this girl seemed to appreciate beautiful things. It would have been wonderful to have someone to spoil for once, someone on whom she could lavish all the things she never had when she was a child. Of course, she'd tried with Cerys but that had never worked.

Hannah watched as Ellis smiled indulgently at Cerys and Tegan. Still childlike, he chose to ignore anything complex, difficult: hide away in his music. Well, that was not possible this time. She knew far more than he realised, and as much as it would have been fun to buy lovely things for Tegan the truth was that the girl had to go back to that community, and go back soon.

Chapter Twelve

Tegan left for the village with Cerys and Dylan. The wind felt like ice hitting her face. Tegan put the hood of her coat up, over her headscarf.

'Wow, this is so warm' she said to Cerys. 'Only my nose is cold now.'

'I don't think I've ever appreciated clothes like you do.'

The sky was grey and heavy.

'Looks like snow' said Cerys. 'We'd better stock up in the shop later.'

Once in the village Cerys put Dylan on the lead and then pointed down the road. 'You turn right at the gift shop. The vicarage is down on your right. When you've finished ring me, OK?'

Tegan nodded and left her. As she turned the corner she stopped and looked in the shop window. There was an assortment of gifts, but the main items on sale were expensive hand-made clothes. She appreciated the craftsmanship, the hours of work involved. The soft silks and wool were luxurious. Tegan watched as a woman appeared from the back room and stood in front of a mirror. She was trying on a blouse. She looked very sophisticated, beautiful. Tegan thought of her own ill-fitting nylon blouses and cardigans, the baggy skirts. For the first time she was aware of a grumbling deep resentment of the way she had been forced to dress. Then she became aware of a tall dark-haired woman smiling at her from inside the shop. Embarrassed, she backed away and walked quickly on.

She arrived at the vicarage and stopped. She really didn't want to go in. Daniel had warned of false prophets who led people astray. She must stay firm. Nervously, she rang the bell and heard barking. The woman who came to the door looked extraordinarily ordinary. She was short and plump with tidy red hair. She wore black trousers and a bright smocked top with a white clergy collar. She had a generous smile and for one awful moment Tegan thought she was going to hug her. Instead she spoke breathlessly, 'Hiya, you must be Tegan? Come in. Gosh, it's freezing today.'

A large dog blocked the hallway. Tegan didn't know what to do. Bethany nudged it gently out of the way. 'Come on Tegan, just push past him.'

Tegan had expected a vicarage to be plastered with Bible verses on the walls and crosses. However the house felt very cosy. There were just some innocuous prints of mountains and in plain pottery vases bunches of daffodils radiated warmth. She liked it but thought it was strange that it wasn't very religious. She followed Bethany into the kitchen, where she made coffee.

'Rex is a rescue. He was taken to Amy's rescue centre in a terrible state. Still, Sam worked really hard on him and look at him now,' chatted Bethany. Tegan watched the dog walking beside her, his golden hair shining. Bethany proudly held out a plate of scones.

'You bake well' said Tegan.

'Oh no, I'm dreadful. I got these fresh from the WI stall this morning. You must pop along, although all the decent stuff will have gone by now. There's a small market in the next village on Fridays. It's worth going to, lovely local stuff: lamb, fish, bread and of course cakes!'

Tegan was thinking how extravagant it all seemed. They would never have bought cake in the community.

'One or two?' asked Bethany, busily buttering a pile of the scones.

'Half of one would be fine, thank you.'

Bethany laughed. 'No wonder you are so skinny. I could eat the lot. How come I had breakfast two hours ago and am starving again now? Come on, let's go and sit down.'

They went and sat in the living room. There were shelves full of books, a TV with games and DVDs lying around it. On the table was a half finished model. Bethany sighed. 'I'm not sure who makes more mess, my husband Mark or my grandson Rhys.'

Tegan looked up at the photographs on the wall. She saw a young freckled boy smiling self-consciously in his school uniform. 'This is Rhys' said Bethany proudly. 'I can't believe how much joy he has brought us, and so bright! He'll be five on Sunday. Don't know where the time goes. He already knows all his letters and can count to a hundred. Anyway, come on. Let's sit down and have a scone.'

The room was very quiet, warm. Bethany stretched out her legs. 'Gosh, this is bliss. Rhys was having nightmares last night so I got up to give Rhiannon a break.'

'Rhiannon is your daughter?'

'That's right. She lives here with her son Rhys.'

'Oh, I see. What does her husband do?'

Bethany smiled. 'There is no husband, never was. But of course we stood by her.'

Tegan didn't understand the 'of course' at all. She remembered rumours going around the community of one of the girls being pregnant. The next thing she heard was that the girl was cast out; her parents disowned her. Tegan wondered for the first time what had become of the girl and her baby.

The doorbell rang. Bethany got up quickly to answer the door. Tegan heard Bethany's voice in a rather forced friendly way say 'Oh Megan, come on through. I have Tegan visiting.'

Tegan looked up as Megan entered the room. She recognised the woman from the concert. She looked far better suited to today's outfit of sensible trousers and waterproof.

'How are you? How was New York?' Bethany was asking.

'It's difficult. Wynn talked me into buying the flat, but it costs a fortune, and we don't go there much. We've been made such a good offer but still Wynn says he wants to keep it. I tell him he can choose to go to all sorts of glamorous places for holidays with the money we would save. I've come back and of course the place is a pig sty. James hasn't a clue how to even put a dish in the dishwasher. Anyway, I've came round with this for you.' She held out a cake tin.

Bethany took it and looked inside. 'Oh Megan, you shouldn't have. It's gorgeous.'

'Well, I thought Mark looked like he could do with feeding up.'

'He'll love it. Chocolate is his favourite.'

'I know. Now, I came to pick up the rest of the magazines to be distributed. I've done mine of course, but I guess no one else has bothered to take any.'

'Well no, no one has yet. Come in. They're in the sitting room.'

Bethany put the cake down on the sideboard. 'Oh Megan, meet Tegan. She's staying up at Ellis' cottage.'

Tegan stood up. Megan looked her up and down, and then put on a cold straight smile. 'Good to meet you Tegan. So are you here on holiday?'

'Sort of,' said Tegan, awkwardly.

'Hmm' said Megan, the smile tightening. 'See you've been gardening.'

Tegan immediately felt scruffy, aware of the mud on her trousers. 'I've been helping Cerys up at the manor.'

Megan tutted. 'Waste of her time. She should get a proper job. Why Ellis and Hannah ever bought that monstrosity I will never know.'

Bethany interrupted. 'Here you are,' she said, offering a pile of magazines.

'You want me to do them all?'

'Oh, sorry. I thought that's what you were offering.'

'Well OK. You know what they say, if you want something done, ask a busy person.'

'That's very kind, um, would you like coffee?'

'Goodness, no. I haven't time to sit round drinking coffee. I have all these to do. Alan's coming to the stables to look at one of the stallions, and I am doing shopping for Mr Groves. You know his wife is in hospital don't you?'

'Of course. I'm going to see her later.'

87

'Good, right. I'd better be off.'

Megan left quickly.

Bethany came in and sighed. 'Sorry about the interruption. Poor Megan, so little joy, all her life, kindness measured out in drops, each accounted and paid for.'

Bethany took a bite of her scone and then smiled. 'So, how are things going?'

Tegan sighed. 'The cottage is very comfortable.'

'I'm sure you have been made very welcome.'

'Oh, yes. Cerys has been very kind, and Ellis has said I can stay as long as I want.'

'And Hannah?'

'Well I think she had a few problems with my Mum. I think she would like me to go soon.'

Bethany looked thoughtful. 'I know Hannah can be prickly. She's always winding people up. Spends money like water, puts on all these airs and graces but really, you know, I think she's OK. Ellis of course has all the charm. Everyone loves him, and Cerys worships him. However, Hannah was very good to her parents. I really think she has a good heart.'

Tegan wondered if this was some kind of criticism of her mother but Bethany carried on chatting.

'Anyway, it's lovely up at the cottage isn't it? I should take Rex up there more. Some friends of mine stayed there last Christmas. It has all mod cons, like TV and internet, doesn't it?'

'Oh yes, although of course I don't watch the TV.'

'Why not?'

'We believe it is evil' said Tegan firmly, glancing at the rows of DVDs.

'Really? Tell me, this community you were in, what is it called?'

'The Last Week Community.'

'I haven't heard of it. So, it's a religious community?'

'I'm not sure what you mean by that. We do believe we are in the last week of time. Our leader Daniel is the final great prophet. You know, before him there were Abraham, Moses,

Elijah, Daniel, Belteshazzar, Jesus, and now, of course, Daniel. Well, Daniel, The Omniscient is now his full title.'

'Oh, and what does Daniel teach?'

'That we are to stay pure, do vigil. The end is near.'

'And at the end?'

Tegan was not surprised that Bethany did not know about these things. Daniel had said people outside were ignorant of them. 'Well, at the end of time The High One will judge the world.'

'Sorry, the High One?'

'I suppose you might call him God, but he has revealed to Daniel that this is the name he is to be known by now in these last days. It is how we know we are meeting a fellow member of the elect: they know the name.'

Tegan stopped. Bethany was sitting looking wide eyed. Tegan realised that Daniel was right: the world was blind to his message.

'So your community is based on the teaching of Daniel?'

'The Community had been set up before Daniel came actually. We believed the end could be at any time. If we were not pure we would be left to the time of tribulation. We would suffer for eternity in hell. No religions were leading the pure life we were striving for. Then of course Daniel joined us. Slowly, more and more was revealed to him. We knew then that he was the final prophet to reveal the ways of The High One.' Tegan stopped, worried that she was saying too much about the Community. Was it right to be telling this heathen woman so much?

'I see you're wearing a headscarf. Do all the women wear them?'

'Of course. Yes.'

'Why's that?'

'I know that you probably don't agree, you being a vicar, but in the Community us women know our place, and the headscarf shows that.'

'But you left this Community?'

'I was cast out, but I deserved it. It was the right thing for them to do.'

'But you must miss your family?'

Tegan shrugged. They sat in awkward silence. Tegan was desperate to get away.

Bethany put down her cup, her face very serious. 'Why were you made to leave?'

Tegan's breathing speeded up. She put down her coffee and went to stand up. 'I think I ought to go and meet Cerys now.'

Bethany seemed flustered. 'Oh, right. Hang on, before you go.'

Tegan watched her get up, find a card and hand it to her. 'You might contact these people. They may be able to help you.'

Tegan took the card. She read what was on it and stared at Bethany. She was furious, mortified. How dare this woman give her this?

'Well, do come again' Bethany was saying quickly. Tegan was too upset to speak. They walked to the front door. 'I'll see you again soon?'

Tegan nodded. She tried to smile.

Bethany closed the door, went back into the kitchen and made another cup of coffee. She heard the front door open.

'Hiya. Just popped back for some tools.' Mark was a plumber, but could fix most things. He was kind, practical: her rock. He only came to church for Christmas and Easter and to fix things. She understood, but sometimes felt lonely. Her work seemed very divorced from her family. Mark came into the kitchen.

'Want a coffee?'

'Just a quick one.'

Bethany was aware of him spilling out of his overalls. They really ought to eat better, she thought, buttering more scones.

'Did I see that new girl leaving?'

'Yes, she's called Tegan.'

'She's staying at Ellis' cottage isn't she?'

'Yes, she seems much stressed. I'm worried about her.'

'You worry about everyone.'

'This is different. She has real problems.'

'I thought she dressed a bit dowdy.'

'It's more than that. I think she's been brought up in a cult, or I think you're meant to call them a High Demand Group, something like that. Anyway, she's had a rough time. The trouble is I don't think I handled it very well.'

'She'll be alright.' He took a scone. 'I've just been up the manor.'

'Oh. Why's that?'

'Hannah wants work done on the bathroom. They've got workmen everywhere up there, must be costing them a bomb.'

'I wonder if I should have a word with Hannah about Tegan.'

'Don't go there Bethany. Hannah looks really stressed. I wouldn't want to be Ellis, having to cope with her full time.'

'Maybe he's not as easy as he appears.'

'Rubbish. Good man, Ellis. Everyone likes him. I wouldn't want to live with her though. Anyway, I need to get back to work.'

Bethany went into her study and sat in front of the computer. She googled "Last Week Community" but found nothing. What was the name of the man who was leading the group? That's it, Daniel. She tried googling it, but there were pages of references, mainly to the Biblical character. She clicked on some of the more obscure ones. Finally, on a blog she found a reference to a Daniel and his community. As she read it she felt sure this was referring to Tegan's community. She read it again and her face became more serious. Her instincts had been right, but what on earth was she going to do?

Chapter Thirteen

Tegan walked into the village quickly, very upset from her visit with Bethany. Daniel was so right: the world had no idea of the truth. How dare that woman judge her, call herself religious, when she had no idea of how to stay pure? Tegan tried to send a text to Cerys. She punched in letters angrily but half the words didn't make sense. When she tried to send the message it disappeared. Exasperated, she put the phone away. That would teach her for messing with worldly things. Then she received a text from Cerys. 'Meet me at The Red Dragon.' She stormed to the pub and saw Cerys coming down the road with Dylan.

'Have a good time?' asked Cerys, smiling.

'No. No, I did not.'

'I'm surprised. Normally you at least get a nice piece of cake with Bethany. Listen, shall we go in and have some lunch? I'm starving.'

Tegan pursed her lips. 'You know I can't.'

'Oh, come on. Honestly, it's a really nice family pub. It'll be a chance to meet some people.'

Tegan shook her head. 'No, I refuse to go in there and really, Cerys, you shouldn't be going in there either.'

'I think that's up to me, don't you?'

'I can't stop you.'

'No you can't. I'm going in for lunch. What will you do?'

'I'll go back to the cottage. I have a key.'

'Good. OK then, see you later.'

She watched as Cerys walked away. Tegan knew she had offended her, but she was only trying to protect her. Cerys joined a group of people, all shouting and laughing. Tegan dug her nails into the palms of her hands: if she dug hard enough she knew the pain would drown out all the anger and upset. She walked away, alone, making her way up the long path and then through the fields to the cottage. The hedges seemed frozen, still and quiet, but she felt better away from everyone. She was on her own, nothing to prove, no one watching her.

Inside, the cottage felt very empty. She knew what she would do. She poured herself a glass of water and went up to her room. She knelt rigidly next to her bed, clasped her hands tight and began her vigil. 'Come Quickly Oh High One' she repeated over and over. Slowly, she started to fell calmer: her mind clouded over; she didn't have to think any more.

At about four o'clock she heard Cerys and Dylan come in. She took a deep breath and went downstairs, thinking she must try and be friendly, but Cerys was frowning. 'It's freezing in here. You should have lit the fire.'

Dylan went rushing up to her. She gingerly patted him on the head, and then he started sniffing around the unfamiliar room.

Tegan realised her hands were icy cold: she should have done something. 'Sorry, I didn't notice.'

'It's OK' said Cerys. 'Have you ever lit a real fire?'

Tegan shook her head. The idea was very frightening: flames, heat, and hell. Oblivious, Cerys took her coat off, and started making up the fire. Slowly, the fire came to life, the flames crackled. The tongues of fire darted upwards. Tegan could feel the heat on her face. She had a picture of a devil laughing at her standing among flames. She could feel the heat burning her flesh. She continued to stare at the fire, transfixed with terror.

'Tegan, are you alright?' Tegan turned slowly and looked at Cerys. Her heart was pounding. It hurt.

'What's the matter?' asked Cerys.

Tegan shook her head.

'Is it the fire?'

Tegan stayed still, frightened to move.

Cerys frowned. 'Look, hang on a minute.'

She rummaged in a small cupboard and pulled out a fire guard. 'I knew Nanna had one somewhere.' She put it in front of the fire. 'There, that's better now, isn't it?'

Tegan nodded. She felt so stupid, but still her heart was racing. Dylan flopped down on the rug in front of the fire.

Cerys carried on chatting. 'Coffee? James was in the pub, still showing off from the concert. Apparently, he has been asked to audition for something.'

Tegan sat on the end of the sofa furthest away from the fire.

'He does sing well-' she replied. Her mind was still racing but she had to act normally.

Cerys gave her coffee and then picked up her laptop and opened it. 'God, the internet is so slow here. Oh, it's hopeless today.' Cerys shut the laptop and went to the kitchen.

Tegan noticed that the skies were darkening and got up, put the lights on, and closed the curtains.

Cerys opened a bottle of wine. She held it up. 'Sure?'

'No thank you.'

Cerys poured herself a glass and then went upstairs. She returned with a thick cotton craft bag. 'I brought this knitting just in case, but I don't know why. Still, I spent a fortune on the yarn. I ought to try again.'

'What are you making?'

'It's meant to be a shawl. I saw one in Rachel's window in the village. It was lush but cost about £200. I bought the stuff online from a specialist supplier. Mad really, I never could even do plain knitting.'

Cerys took an unruly tangle of knitting with needles poking out from the bag. She took a long swig of wine. 'God it's hopeless. I think I might have to just start again.'

'Would you like me to have a look at it?'

'You knit?'

'It's what I did in the Community.'

'OK.'

Cerys handed over the knitting. The yarn was a combination of silk and cashmere, fine, like sewing thread. The needles were very thin, and the pattern an intricate design of peacock feathers in light blues, greens and gold.

'It's beautiful' said Tegan. 'This is the kind of thing we made.'

'You're kidding. You mean you really can make this kind of thing?'

'Oh yes.'

Tegan inspected the knotted mess with holes. 'I think really you need to start again.'

'Can you start it off for me then?' Cerys' voice held something akin to awe.

Tegan's nimble fingers carefully cast on the new stitches and began the work.

'You're so fast' said Cerys, clearly impressed.

'It's just practice. I find it very relaxing.'

'I don't suppose you'd like to do some more?'

'Yes, I'd like to.'

'Great, in that case I can look at my gardening magazine.'

Later, Cerys took Dylan out and then they had tea.

'Shall we watch TV?' asked Cerys.

Tegan looked up, cringing.

Misunderstanding her, Cerys said 'Sorry, I know it's very small. It's ancient-'

Tegan shook her head. 'No, it's not that. I don't watch television, and to be honest, Cerys, you shouldn't be either. There are all sorts of terrible things on there, and they will corrupt you.'

'What?'

'All this going to the pub, drinking wine, watching TV, it's not a Godly way to live.'

Cerys took a deep breath. 'Tegan, I don't mean to be funny like, and you are entitled to your opinion, but I think I have a right to choose how I live.'

Tegan blushed. 'I'm sorry, but I'm trying to warn you.'

95

'But I don't need warning. You have your beliefs and I have mine.'

'But there is only one way.'

'What? Yours?' For the first time, Tegan heard anger in Cerys' voice. She looked down. Why, her words sounded so odd out here. 'I think I'll take the knitting up if you don't mind,' she said quietly.

'OK.' Cerys said more gently. 'Look, I'll bring you up a hot chocolate if you like?'

'Thanks' replied Tegan, recognising the olive branch. She picked up the knitting and went upstairs.

Cerys went into the kitchen and made herself a sandwich to go with her glass of wine. Then she made Tegan's chocolate and took it upstairs. She could hear Tegan's quiet repetitive voice 'Come Quickly Oh High One'. She found it creepy, unnerving. She knocked briskly on the door. Tegan came and opened it wearing a thin grey-white nightie.

'Are you warm enough? I have thicker nighties if you'd like to borrow one?' Cerys asked.

'Oh no, I'll be fine. I can put a cardigan on if I'm cold.'

Cerys went over to the bedside table to put the drink down. She flinched when she looked at the framed black picture with the words "He Shall Come Like a thief in the night" written in blood red. Then she touched the silver box.

'That's pretty.'

Tegan smiled. 'It's very special to me. My mother gave it to me when I was little.'

'It's lovely.'

Tegan picked up the box. 'I remember the day so clearly. Mum was making bread and I was reading. The men had gone to a retreat for the day. She suddenly said we were going to the park. I assumed we would be giving out leaflets but she said we would just go and enjoy the sunshine. I was amazed. We had never gone out just for fun. I remember the park was very busy. There was music and people dressed up, dancing. It was so exciting, like a wonderful dream. When we got back to the house Mum gave me this. I couldn't believe it: we never had presents.

96

She told me to hide it, not to tell anyone.' Cerys watched Tegan as she carefully replaced the box. The story had been so moving, so sad. To think that was the one day Tegan remembered doing something for fun, her one present.

Cerys blinked hard. 'Your life, it's been so different to mine.'

'Yes, I'm starting to see that. Anyway, thanks for the chocolate.'

Cerys left the room, baffled by the sad fleeting picture of Tegan's life in the community. She turned on the TV and settled to a film. Her phone rang. It was Robert. He was a local farmer she'd been seeing the past few months. He had been widowed five years ago, and was healing slowly. When they had met it had been a sense of relief that they had each finally found a soul mate who was kind and dependable. To Cerys he seemed to be carved from the same stone as the mountain. Welsh was his first language although he spoke to her in English.

'How are things?' she asked.

'Terrible. The weather is awful for the lambs. It'll snow soon. I'm sure of it.'

'Shall I come up tomorrow to help?'

'That would be great. Unless, of course, you need to stay with your cousin?'

'To be honest, I don't think she'll want to do anything I suggest. She's gone to bed now. She's very strange.'

'What do you mean?'

'She's had such a weird life. I feel sorry for her, but she disapproves of everything I do. You know, drinking, watching TV, everything normal. She wears a headscarf all the time and then at nights I hear her in her room chanting away. It's dead creepy. She shouts out in her sleep, terrible screams, sounds absolutely horrific.'

'Oh dear, she doesn't sound quite right.'

'I don't know. I don't get her at all. You know she did some knitting earlier. It was really good, and she seems bright enough, but just, well, weird.'

'Well, you look after yourself. What time will you be up?'

'About eight?'

'Great, see you then.'

Cerys smiled. It was never a long chat with Robert. She poured herself another large glass of wine.

Upstairs, Tegan quietly closed the bedroom door Cerys had left open. So that is what they all thought: she was some kind of freak. Daniel had said the world would not recognise them. She remembered listening to those words in meetings about being among the elect. She had had a warm smug feeling of being safe among the chosen. But they had been such a small group. She could see that now. Out here there were millions of people who didn't follow Daniel and his teachings. Were they all wrong? Going to the pub, watching television: was that so evil, would that send them to hell? Tegan knelt next to her bed. This doubting was from the devil, and she must do her vigil: she must stay pure. After an hour she got into bed, picked up her knitting, drank the forgotten cold chocolate. As she knitted she thought about Steve. It was surprising that she had thought about him so little since she had come here. Surely she should be missing him more? But she was honest enough to realise that she hadn't known him very well. But then, would any relationship out here work? She was so different to everyone else. She was a stranger in a strange land. Never in her whole life had she felt so abandoned, so alone.

Chapter Fourteen

The next morning Tegan went down early for her breakfast. She dreaded seeing Cerys. However Cerys looked up and smiled. Dylan came over to her, wagging his tail. She leant down and patted his head nervously. He rolled over on his back for her to rub his tummy. She stood up, not sure what to do.

'Any luck with the knitting?' asked Cerys.

'I did get on with some.'

'Go and get it. I'd love to see it.'

Tegan went upstairs, returned, and shyly showed Cerys what she had done.

'Wow. Well done. It's lovely. You know, my Nanna used to knit me things. She made me very pretty cardigans with hand made lace edging.'

'If you need me to do any more-'

'Please do as much as you can face. I'm off to Robert's this morning.'

'Robert?' asked Tegan.

'He's a farmer I'm seeing.'

'Oh, a boyfriend?'

'I suppose you'd call him that. I said I'd go up and help him this morning.'

Tegan made toast and sat down with Cerys.

'So, is Robert's farm near here?'

'Well it's not his farm, it's his parents', but it'll be his one day. He still lives with them. The farmhouse is massive, and Robert even lived there when he was married. I have stayed there a few times but to be honest I find it awkward, you know all sharing the kitchen and things and then they all speak Welsh. It's so fast I've no idea what they're talking about.' Cerys stood up. 'Right, I ought to get on. You'll be alright?'

'Fine. I'll do some more knitting.'

'Look, would you mind if I left Dylan with you? Say if it's awkward.'

Tegan looked down at Dylan. How on earth did you look after a dog? Maybe though for once she could say yes? 'OK, um, what do I do?'

'He'll be glad to stay in the warm but let him out when he needs it. Actually, you could take him down to the woods if you like.'

'Oh, right. OK then.'

When Cerys had gone Tegan looked down at Dylan. He plodded philosophically over to the hearth and lay down. Quietly she picked up her knitting, realising it was nice to have his company. She had never spent so much time on her own. In the Community her day was so busy, starting with early vigil, and they never stopped. Here she sat quietly knitting. It was so calm. After a while her eyes started to tire, so she got up and looked out of the window. The sun was shining; trying to break through the cold day. She looked at the fields: crisp, the light bouncing off a layer of frozen dew. It would be lovely to go out there. She realised that Dylan was standing next to her, wagging his tail expectantly. Then with a shock she realised that they could just go out, no-one to ask permission from. No-one was going to stop them. She looked at Dylan. 'Fancy a walk?'

Dylan seemed to recognise the word, stood up and wagged his tail even more. She smiled. Feeling very daring, she put on her coat and her wellingtons, and opened the front door. Dylan rushed out ahead of her.

She walked around the garden. The daffodils were starting to unfurl. The birds were darting around and singing. Cambrian Spring was nervously starting. The wind was still there, cold but refreshing rather than buffeting her.

Where to go? There were no concrete paths to guide her. Cerys had suggested the well but she had no idea where in the woods to find it. Dylan raced in front of her and headed to the hill. Then he stopped and looked back at her.

'OK, we'll go that way' she said, and started to climb. Soon Tegan was out of breath. She stopped and looked down.

She could see the roof of the cottage now. She continued walking but stopped frequently. She heard, and then saw, a pair of red kites wheeling above her. She cringed but kept walking. The air was so fresh, cold. Her cheeks burned. The higher hills in the distance were very white. The cottage below became smaller, the trees like sticks of broccoli. She could still hear the sheep, which were tiny white specks on the hillsides. It was surprising how well sound travelled. She could hear a dog barking far away and the lambs shouting at their mothers. She surveyed the endless vista jewelled by small lakes in the valleys.

Then her attention was caught by the sound of a bird hovering high above: that must be the sky lark she had been reading about. The song was extraordinary. It trilled high then low. The bird seemed to manage to hang suspended overhead. It was extraordinary. She looked around for Dylan, called him

'Quiet' a voice demanded in an urgent whisper.

Alarmed, she turned and recognised Sam, the accompanist from the concert. He was standing looking through binoculars. She didn't know what to do. This was the man she had offended, and she was up here alone, miles from anywhere. Dylan came racing over to her.

'Alauda Arvensis' Sam whispered. She looked at him mystified.

'Sky lark,' he explained. 'A male, he's trying to dominate that patch of sky, incredible.'

He put down his binoculars. 'So, what do you make of this place?'

Tegan gazed down at the fields below, the hills that seemed to stretch on endlessly. She felt a sense of peace seeping in through her pores. It was majestic, awe inspiring. She turned and realised that Sam was looking at her. 'I think it's beautiful. It just goes on and on.'

'It's great you like it. You know, I've had people come here to stay who actually get scared out here, say it's too wild. Others, well they say it's plain boring. One friend, I took him up the hill, we looked down and I said 'Well, what you think?' and

101

do you know what he said? He said 'Is that it? What are we meant to do now?''

Tegan laughed. 'I can imagine some people in the Community saying that. They would think it was a waste of time walking out like that.'

'Well I'm glad you don't think that.'

'Oh no, it's like somewhere to escape to, you know, away from it all. Or is that silly?'

'It's alright. You're not the only one to come up here to hide from their past you know.' She noticed his serious expression, and wondered what he was thinking.

'You know they used to call this place the Green Desert' said Sam.

'Why was that?'

'Because they thought there was nothing here, just empty wilderness. Of course they were wrong. What was it I read? One hundred species of breeding bird recorded, thirty-five species of mammal, and thirty types of butterfly.'

'You know so much about this place.'

'Oh, sorry. Angharad says I go on too much.'

'No, it's interesting. It's a whole world I didn't know existed. Wonderful, it's so quiet. I would sit in the park in London but it was never like this.'

'That's because we're miles from cars and roads. You know I can walk up here all day and not meet anybody.'

'Don't you worry, you know, being all on your own?'

'Not at all. I feel more at home up here than down there.'

'So is all this Cambrian Mountains?'

'That's right. You know the gold for the royal wedding rings comes from here. Has Cerys taken you to the well in the woods?'

'She mentioned it but I haven't seen it yet.'

'It's a lovely spot, means a lot to Cerys. You must go there. It's quite something to have our own Holy Well here. You must ask Cerys all about it.'

Tegan looked at him puzzled. 'You don't have a Welsh accent.'

'No, we came from the Isle of Wight, nippert,' he said in an exaggerated accent.

Tegan looked puzzled.

"Nippert' is just used in a friendly greeting. I got teased a lot about that when I first came here, like when I talk about 'the island' not the Isle of Wight. Mind you, the Welsh are ones to talk with all their 'Duw' and 'twp' and all the rest of it.'

Tegan smiled. 'Yes, and what's this 'I'll do it now' thing?'

Sam interrupted. 'Don't get me started on that. In work they say they'll do something now and I know it'll take ages. Still, it's good to try and fit in. I was lucky I had played rugby at school, as you can see.' He pointed self-consciously to his nose. Tegan looked at his nose closely. She realised that at the bridge it bent to the left and then seemed to come straight again. Sam grinned. 'Been broken a few times, a badge of honour around here.

'Anyway, we were talking about this language thing. You know Amy calls me brawd now.'

'Brawd?'

'Welsh for brother. Amy is my sister. I share a flat with her.'

Suddenly, out of nowhere a pair of red kites swept overhead. Tegan, petrified, covered her head, and stood very still.

'What's the matter?' asked Sam.

Tegan couldn't speak. Her heart was racing, and she couldn't breathe.

'It's only birds' said Sam. The birds flew away. Slowly, Tegan removed her hands, and tried to breathe more slowly. They stood for a few minutes, and then Tegan was suddenly aware that she had been up here alone with a man for a long time.

'I think I'd better go now' she said suddenly.

103

'I'll walk down with you. I promised Amy I'd pop into the rescue centre.'

'Rescue centre?'

'Amy works there. It's a place for abandoned animals.'

'Is she a vet like you?'

'No. She dropped out because of, well, all sorts of reasons. You haven't met her. You ought to go down the pub, meet a few people.'

Tegan twisted her hands together. 'I don't really go to pubs.'

Sam grinned. 'I know you don't drink-'

'I'm sorry.'

'It's alright. You're entitled to not drink, although maybe you need to find a better way of refusing.'

She was relieved to see him smile.

'You always wear that headscarf?' asked Sam.

'Mmm-'

'Shame, you have pretty hair. You don't dye it like Amy.'

'So does Amy have a boyfriend?'

'Oh, of course, you don't know. Amy is a lesbian. She's in a relationship with Rhiannon, Bethany, the vicar's daughter.'

Tegan stopped walking, and stared at Sam. She didn't know which bit of information shocked her more. 'Lesbian? Rhiannon? But she has a child?'

Sam looked very serious. 'Yes, it's complicated. Amy has been very good to Rhiannon. She's had a hard time.'

Tegan frowned. It really was a different world out here. 'Did your parents mind about Amy? What about Bethany? She's a vicar.'

'My parents had no problems. Bethany, well, as I said, it was complicated, but her and Mark have been great. I mean, parents are always there for you, aren't they?'

Tegan suddenly felt angry. 'My parents have every right to disown me. I rebelled. I sinned. I deserved to be judged.'

Sam's eyebrows shot up. 'Hey, hang on, where's this coming from? All this talk of judgment. What right have you to

104

judge Amy and Rhiannon? Why does everybody think they can dictate how other people live?'

Tegan stared at him. His mild-mannered face was red, his eyes wide with anger. Suddenly she was frightened. He lifted his hand. She started to scream 'Don't hit me,' and then saw his hand reach to the back of his neck and scratch.

He looked confused as well as angry now. 'Of course I'm not going to hit you. What sort of person do you think I am?'

Tegan burst into tears. 'I don't know, just leave me alone.' She turned and started to run down the hill.

'Stop. Tegan, come back.' She heard, but she kept running. Dylan ran by her, excited at this new game. She ran to the cottage, went inside, and slammed the door. Breathing hard, she felt sick, closed her eyes.

When she opened them Dylan had flopped in front of the fire. With hands shaking she found a pencil and paper, wrote in large letters 'Doing vigil, do not disturb' and ran upstairs.

While Tegan was attempting to do her vigil in Wales, in London her mother, Sarah, was on her knees in the garden trying to weed the vegetable garden. The ground was frozen, the trowel old and rusty. It was hard work but she didn't mind that. It was good to be busy, waste of time thinking. She continued trying to force the tool into the earth. She slowly became aware of a voice calling her name and she looked up from the ground. She frowned as she saw Philip walking towards her waving his mobile phone. She panicked. Was there some way he could have found out she used his phone? She didn't understand the thing. She swallowed hard.

'Is something the matter Philip?'

'My phone. I've been checking it. There's a phone call to Ellis, made on Wednesday.'

Philip was close to her now. He wore no coat. Obviously he had rushed out, and his words were carried on vapour visible in the cold air.

'Sarah, did you make a call?'

She nodded. She daren't speak.

'But why? You know you are not allowed to use a phone without permission. And why phone him?'

He looked very angry. His hand was shaking.

'It was Tegan,' she said quickly, and went back to her digging.

'What do you mean?' he demanded.

She squirmed, and sat back on her heels. 'I don't know. I thought she may contact him, thought I'd warn him.'

'What? How could she do that?' Sarah bent over again, dug harder, and tried to ignore him.

Philip bent over and gripped her shoulder. 'What is going on?'

Sarah bit her lip, wiped her hands and stood up. 'When Tegan left I gave her their address, their phone number, wrote them down. That was all.'

Philip turned pale. 'You did that? How could you?'

Sarah was breathing hard. 'I panicked. I'm sorry. I just thought it was someone she could ask for help.'

'But how could they help? I mean, she didn't even have the money to make a phone call.'

Again Sarah shrugged. 'Anyway, when I spoke to Ellis he hadn't heard from Tegan.'

Philip seemed to relax. 'Good, I still don't know why you rang Ellis not Hannah.'

'I didn't know you had numbers for both' she answered quickly.

'You know you should never have used the phone.'

'I know, and I did extra vigil. I'm sorry. It won't happen again.'

'Tegan has been cast out. We have a duty to forget her. She has made her own choice now, and you know that.'

'I do. I was weak but I promise it won't happen again.'

Sarah knelt back down, and returned to her digging. Relieved, she heard Philip walk away. Her hands were shaking; she felt dizzy, missed the earth and dug the trowel deep into the back of her hand. A terrible pain shot through her, blood and mud covered her left hand. She didn't speak. The pain was a comfort, and this was her judgment for disobedience. She went into the house and ran her hand under the tap. It was a deep cut; it bled heavily, and it was her fault. In the cupboard there were torn up cotton sheets. She took a piece and wrapped it round her hand. It stung badly. Esther came into the kitchen. She looked exhausted.

'I was sick this morning-' she grumbled. Then she saw Sarah's hands. 'Oh dear, what have you done?'

'Been stupid.'

'Make sure you get all the earth out of it.'

'I have. You know I was training to be a doctor. I know what I'm doing.'

'It's nasty, though. Look, you need to change the bandage.'

Sarah sighed. 'You're right. In the world they'd rush me off to casualty. Probably give me stitches. Still, we don't need all that here. I will do extra vigil. I'm sure the High One will heal me.'

Esther smiled. 'I wish I had your faith Sarah. You must miss Tegan. I know I do. I know I shouldn't but I do worry about her, feel I should have done something to help her. I hope she's safe.'

Sarah stood up stiffly. 'She has chosen the way of the world and she must now live with the consequences.'

Chapter Fifteen

Tegan had stayed kneeling by her bed until dusk. Cerys returned and offered her food but she refused. She had to get back to living a life devoted to staying pure. She had cried, shouted to the High One, asking for forgiveness, for answers. Nothing came. She must try harder. As night fell she closed her curtains and put on the lights. Her head felt light, she was dizzy, and she must not stop, but finally she fell asleep on the floor next to her bed.

She was shattered the next morning and stiffly staggered down stairs to find a note from Cerys to say she had gone up to the manor to do some gardening. She had taken Dylan with her.

It seemed very quiet without Dylan. She missed him: at least he always seemed pleased to see her. She had a bad headache. Looking out of the window the day looked lifeless and dull. She made coffee, and then picked up the knitting. She would sit and do that: it was safe.

However later that morning she heard a car arrive. She peeped out of the window, saw it was Ellis and groaned. Hopefully, if she ignored him he would go away. He knocked on the door. She didn't answer. However, he was persistent and shouted 'Tegan, I have to talk to you.' Reluctantly, she went and opened the door.

'Hiya, how are you?' he asked with forced brightness.

'I'm fine' she replied defensively.

'The thing is, Tegan,' Ellis spoke quickly, nervously. 'I want you to come somewhere with me.'

'What do you mean?' she asked cautiously.

'It's nothing to be worried about. I've made an appointment. I want you to come to the optician.'

'No' she shouted, backing away.

'I knew this would be difficult, but, come on, come and get your eyes tested. Please.'

'I won't.'

'Yes. Come on, it'll really help you.'

Tegan shook her head. 'No, no. I can't.'

Ellis looked very serious. 'I've been talking to Cerys. I know things have not been easy for you.'

'You don't understand-' she stammered.

'No, I don't. I know that community place is strict. To be honest, I don't understand how your mother could have stayed there with you. Anyway, you are here now. You have to try and fit in.'

Tegan shuddered. 'No, I can't. Don't you see?'

Ellis looked at her sternly. 'Tegan, that is enough. You have to come. We have to update those terrible glasses. I mean, you can't see properly, and they look awful.'

Tegan blushed, embarrassed. Did they look that bad?

'Come on' he persisted. 'You have a right to see properly.'

'But I can't.'

'Why not? Tell me.'

'Daniel told me it would hurt me. They would try to blind me.'

'Duw, Tegan. You've been taught some dangerous nonsense. Of course it won't hurt. They're there to help you see, not blind you, for God's sake.'

Tegan was so confused. How could Daniel and Ellis both say such opposite things but sound so sure? She watched as Ellis stood, impatiently scratching his beard. His outburst was frightening: he was the head of the household, and maybe she should do what he said. A wave of weariness came over her. She was too tired to fight. 'I suppose I could come.'

'Good, right, get your coat now. Come on, you'll be able to read, knit for longer.'

Tegan sighed. She reached for her coat, and followed Ellis to the car. It was a shock to feel the fresh wind on her face. She looked around, and remembered that first day she had arrived. It seemed such a long time ago, and yet that feeling of wonder at the vastness and beauty of the place felt as fresh as ever. In the distance she saw Sam and Bracken. She quickly got in the car.

'Nice chap that,' said Ellis, glancing over. 'Workaholic of course. Wonder when Angharad will return?'

'His girlfriend?'

'Yes, she'll have to come back soon. I think she has exams. Shame really. I like Sam and I worry about him.'

'Why?'

'Just something Ruth said. Mind you, she's never liked Angharad.'

They drove straight to Aberystwyth. Ellis parked down by the seafront. Tegan sat in the car staring ahead of her. She had never seen the sea before. Her eyes were drawn to the horizon. Between her and it was a vast, grey-blue mass. Ellis knocked on her window and opened the car door.

'Out you get then.'

She saw him look down at her.

'What's the matter?' he asked.

Tegan held on to the edges of her seat.

'Tegan, come on.' She could hear he was getting impatient and made herself get out. She tried to keep her back to the sea but Ellis walked towards it.

'Marvellous, isn't it?'

Then he looked at her face. 'You look scared to death. Why's that?'

What was she meant to say? She didn't know the answer. All she knew was that the sight of the sea made her feel sick with terror.

Ellis shrugged, looked at her as if she was very odd, and said 'Well, never mind then, let's get to the optician.'

They walked up steep vertical streets, past small department stores, greengrocers and bakers, and then Ellis pushed open the door of the optician.

A young girl looked up and smiled. 'Ellis. Hiya, how are things? How's Cerys? What's she up to these days?'

110

'Morning, Jenny. Cerys is fine. I left her gardening as usual. This is my niece, Tegan. I rang first thing. You said you had a cancellation?'

'That's right. So, Tegan, you've not been here before?'

'Oh no, I've never been here before.'

'I explained that Tegan has not had an eye test before' said Ellis.

'Oh yes. OK. Fill in this form then.'

She handed the form to Tegan with a pen. Tegan looked at Ellis helplessly.

'Put the cottage as your address for now, and my mobile number.' Ellis dictated the details.

'But I have no idea who my GP is-'

'Just put a line for now. I'll explain.'

When Tegan had filled in all she could she handed the form to Ellis. He scanned it and frowned. 'You've only put your year of birth.'

She shook her head. 'To be honest, I don't know the exact date.'

'What? You are joking?'

'No. Mum and Philip said I didn't need to know. This is the first time it's ever been an issue.'

Ellis scowled. 'You've never, ever, celebrated your birthday?'

'It's alright. We have a Community birthday.'

Ellis sighed and handed the form to Jenny. She was busy typing. Tegan was momentarily distracted, wondering how Jenny could type with such incredibly long, lavishly decorated finger nails. Then a conservatively dressed woman came from the back room. She acknowledged Ellis with a brisk nod.

'This is Tegan. She's taken the cancellation,' explained Jenny. 'She hasn't had an eye test before.'

Grace frowned. 'Come this way, Tegan.'

Tegan stood up and tried to breathe slowly. Her heart was thumping. Her walking felt clumsy and uncoordinated. She followed Grace into a room and was directed to a large leather chair. The room seemed very gloomy, claustrophobic.

111

'Is it correct that you have never had an eye test before?'

Tegan was very embarrassed. 'Yes.'

Grace looked shocked. 'Seriously? But where did you get your glasses? They don't look shop bought.'

'I got them from a box of glasses we kept in the Community. You know, you would try pairs on until one suited.'

Grace gasped. 'What?'

Tegan clung onto the arms of the chair. She couldn't breathe.

Grace looked at her curiously. 'You really haven't had an eye test before?'

Tegan shook her head.

'OK, right. Well, don't worry. Let's get started. Firstly, I need you to take off your glasses.'

Nervously, Tegan raised her hands and removed her glasses. She felt naked. Grace took them from her and inspected them.

'These are very old and scratched. I'm amazed you can see anything through them.'

Tegan's heart was racing. Grace put an uncomfortable pair of frames on her face, and started swapping lenses, asking questions. She found the close proximity to Grace disturbing. But it didn't hurt, and Grace was very efficient. Her detachment made it easier to cope with.

After a while Grace said 'You have significant problems. You are actually short sighted in one eye, long sighted in your right. You need a very specific prescription. How on earth have you been coping with those old glasses?'

'I suppose I didn't know any different.'

'But you must get problems reading, and seeing ahead for that matter. Do you get headaches?'

'Actually, yes.'

'Well, we can make things a lot better for you.' The tests continued. Grace sat back. 'Good, we're getting there now. It's bound to take a long time, but I'm getting a base line. I will need to see you regularly. The reason you have coped at all is that one eye is significantly better than the other. Now, try these.'

With a few adjustments Tegan finally had a pair of lenses that she could see through clearly to read. In fact she had never seen things so well. 'It's incredible.'

'Good.'

'No, really, it's like a miracle. Look, I can read all those letters, even the bottom ones.'

Grace smiled. 'I'm pleased. Now I don't want to, but I'll give you these back for now. I need to prioritise your new glasses though. Go out and choose some decent new frames, and I'll make some phone calls.'

'So is that it?'

'For now.'

'Oh good, right.' Tegan quickly put on her glasses but was shocked at how blurred everything was. Odd, nothing had hurt. No-one had tried to blind her.

They went out to where Ellis was waiting. Grace said to Jenny 'Will you help Tegan choose some frames? I want to rush this through.'

Tegan looked at the prices on the frames. They were very expensive. 'Can't I keep these?'

'No, you must get new frames' said Grace.

'Of course' interrupted Ellis. 'Come on, this is on me.'

Tegan went to the basic frames.

'No, I'll get you some really nice ones for once' insisted Ellis.

Tegan was very self conscious. It seemed to take ages, looking in the mirror trying on frames. Instinctively she had wanted old fashioned chunky tortoiseshell glasses, but Jenny was good at her job and gently persuaded her to try some more suited to her tiny face and features. Finally they found some.

'You look lovely' said Ellis. Tegan looked at herself. It was very odd, like seeing a stranger. She felt very exposed, but she did look a lot younger. The headscarf of course did not quite go with them but all the same she did look better.

She turned to Ellis. 'Thank you very much.' He smiled. She was surprised at the emotion in his face.

Jenny went over to the computer. 'OK, sounds like these should be ready soon. I'll phone you as soon as they're in. Have you got a mobile I can phone?'

'You've got mine' said Ellis. They left the optician, Tegan relieved it was over.

On the way back to the car Ellis said, 'You can come to choir now, you'll be able to read the music.'

'Oh, I don't think I will. There is no way I'll be up to the standard of the people in the choir.'

'You don't need to worry. I know you can hold a tune.'

'But I can't sight sing.'

'That's OK. I'll come round, give you a few lessons, help you get your confidence. How about that?'

Tegan didn't reply. She was looking ahead, down the hill. She could see glimpses of the sea, and started to panic. Averting her eyes, she concentrated on her feet, counting the steps, just raising her sights enough to avoid bumping into people. Finally they were back at the car. She was glad to get back in.

When they arrived back at the cottage, Ellis said 'That wasn't too bad, was it?'

'No, thank you. It was fine. It's difficult when you are told things. Maybe Daniel doesn't know about opticians. Maybe they have changed since he went.'

'You think so?' Ellis sounded sceptical.

Even as she had said the words Tegan knew they sounded wrong. Daniel the Omniscient - he would know surely? How could he be wrong?

Just as she was opening the car door Ellis said, 'One more thing-'

'Mmm'

'You know when you told me you were scared of the optician? It was strange but I didn't mind. It helped me understand. Maybe you should try that, telling people what you are thinking.'

'Maybe, but you know I don't want everyone thinking I'm mad. Sometimes it's better not to.'

'Well, OK, but just think about it.'

She thanked Ellis for the lift and got out of the car, glad to return to the safety of the cottage. She made herself a drink and then pulled off the shelf a book about the Cambrian Mountains. She started to read about the rocks which it said had been laid down 400-500 million years ago, the Bronze Age stone circles, standing stones, Cairns. She frowned. Surely Daniel had said the world was nothing like as old as that? He said talk of evolution was wicked, but this book stated completely the opposite as fact. Who was she to believe?

At the Community, Philip was sitting in the cold, empty meeting room. He had spent the night in vigil and a lot of the morning in vigil, but his mind was distracted. He was deeply shocked at what Sarah had done. He knew that she was clever. He always thought she willingly deferred to him, recognised his position in their marriage. But was it all a charade? Inwardly, did she despise him? And Tegan, where was she? What if she had made it to Hannah and Ellis? He couldn't bear that. He had to know what was happening. He felt in his pocket for his phone, thought carefully: no, he couldn't talk to Ellis, it had to be Hannah.

He found the name and pressed "phone".

Hannah was on the patio smoking. She knew Ellis was out with Tegan. She was wondering if Tegan had agreed to go to the optician when her phone rang. She picked it up and saw it was Philip calling. She shuddered. She was tempted to leave it go to voice mail. Then she thought that maybe he was coming to get Tegan: she should speak to him.

'Hello Philip' she said coldly.

'Hannah, I need to talk to you.'

Hannah took a long drag of her cigarette. Philip continued, his voice flat and hard.

'I understand Sarah gave Tegan your contact details.'

115

'Apparently,' she replied.

'Now, listen Hannah. If Tegan contacts you, on no account are you to receive her.'

'Well you're a bit late. She's here staying in our cottage.'

There was silence. She felt rather smug, like somehow she had outwitted him.

'She's with you?'

'Yes. She rang Ellis, got directions, and came down Wednesday evening.'

'How could she phone or travel? She has no money.'

'Ellis said Sarah gave her some. She came down on the train.'

'You're lying. Sarah has no money to give to Tegan.'

'I am not lying. Why should I lie about this? How dare Sarah do this, after the way she treated me and Mum and Dad. She has no right to be asking anything of us.'

'Well I don't understand any of this. Sarah has no money.'

'Look, Tegan is here, and what are you going to do about it? I want her out of here but Ellis insists she stays as long as she wants.'

'I don't want Ellis to have anything to do with her,' said Philip firmly.

'Actually, he's taken quite a shine to her. He's taken her to the optician this morning' taunted Hannah.

'That's terrible.' He sounded very angry now. 'No. She cannot stay there under your influence. I will not allow it.'

'But you and my sister have thrown her out.'

'It was her choice. She rebelled.'

'I can't believe she did anything that bad: it's madness. Anyway, I don't see why you're angry with me. At least we have kept her safe.'

'She's not safe with you. Her soul is in peril.'

Hannah dropped the cigarette butt. She ground it into the path with the sole of her shoe. She heard Philip take a deep

116

breath. 'I don't know what should happen, but she should not be there.'

'Well, I can see her being here permanently unless you do something pretty quickly.'

'I don't know what to do. I think I must go and do vigil, pray to the High One and then talk to Daniel-'

'I think you should try to get her back there.'

'I don't know. Does she show signs of repentance?'

'I hardly see her. She sounds pretty miserable, hides away in the cottage most of the time. I don't think she fits in at all.'

'Well that is something to be grateful for. I will contact you again. Goodbye.'

The call ended abruptly. Hannah sat shaking. "Your influence." What was that meant to mean? No thanks, nothing. Hannah sat up, the memories churning up deep anger, resentment and hurt.

She heard the front door open, quickly put the cigarette packet into her pocket and went inside. She stormed over to Ellis.

'I've just had my brother in law on the phone' she said crossly.

'Philip?' Ellis sounded worried.

'Yes. He didn't know Tegan was already here, rang to tell us not to take her in. I told him it was a bit late for that.'

'Duw. Well, I suppose at least Sarah will know she's safe now. Can't imagine he's too pleased though.'

'He's furious. He's angry about Sarah phoning, and now he's found out she gave Tegan money.'

'Oh heck, poor Sarah. He's going to have a real go at her now.'

'Poor Sarah can look after herself' said Hannah angrily. 'Of course, the thing he's really angry about is Sarah sending Tegan here. I can see that. I mean, they think we live this life of wild debauchery. In fact, I keep wondering why Sarah sent Tegan here. Think about it Ellis, why here?' Hannah watched him carefully. She could see his eyes darting back and forth. He fiddled with his beard; he looked like cornered prey.

'She didn't have much choice. I expect she just panicked that's all' he mumbled.

'No, Sarah doesn't panic. She'd have definitely had a reason for doing this. You really can't think why?'

They both held their breath. Then Ellis shrugged and turned away.

'Never understand people' he said. 'Anyway, bit of good news. Tegan came to the optician. Now I'd better go and sort out the music for the choir.'

Hannah watched as he quickly walked to his sanctuary in the music room. She turned and went out on to the patio and, with shaking hands, lit another cigarette. Sometimes she wished she could be like Ellis. He parcelled up problems, and put them to one side. He would be in his music room now, immersed in planning for choir, the problems outside the four walls completely forgotten. Like his mother with all her talk of fairies, he hid from the real world. Hannah took a long drag on her cigarette. Anger, resentment seethed inside her. It was people like her that were left to pick up the pieces. She was the one who nursed her parents while her sister hid away in London. She had done her duty then but she refused to let her sister off the hook again. Tegan was Sarah's responsibility and she could damn well have her back.

Chapter Sixteen

'So will you go to church today?' asked Cerys the next morning.

Tegan looked out of the window, shocked. She had forgotten it was Sunday. She realised she had only been there five days but had completely lost track of the days. It felt so much longer. She was slipping into sinful ways without even noticing it.

Tegan put down her glass. 'I should spend the day in prayer and fasting. Are you going?'

'Oh no. I haven't been for years, well, unless you count the odd carol service. Surely you're not going to do more fasting and praying,' said Cerys. 'Don't you get bored, hungry?'

'Of course not' answered Tegan automatically.

'Well, OK. I'm up to the manor gardening this morning, so I can leave you in peace. I'll take Dylan.'

'OK.'

Cerys stood up, then she bit her lip, and looked questioningly at Tegan. 'Actually, this afternoon I'm going to help with Rhys' birthday party. You know, Rhiannon's son. Bethany wondered if you'd like to come. Lots of families will be invited.'

'But I was going to have a quiet day, and in any case I didn't really get on with Bethany last time I met her' replied Tegan.

'Oh come on. You know, Bethany was telling me she is really worried she's upset you.'

Tegan frowned. 'But what will happen at this party?'

'It's just a normal children's party,' said Cerys, sounding so impatient Tegan daren't ask any more questions.

'Come on Tegan,' said Cerys. 'It would be friendly. You can't hide in here for ever and it's very low key.'

Tegan sighed. 'Maybe. What time is it?'

'About three, at the Vicarage. Make sure you come, now.'

Cerys left. Tegan went up and knelt next to her bed. Questions fought each other inside her brain but nothing answered back. She started to repeat the words of the vigil. Slowly they sent her into a dream-like trance. She felt calmer. Then she opened she her eyes, and looked out of the window. She could imagine the wind on her cheeks. She longed to go out there. Tegan remembered her meeting with Sam and cringed, but surely she wouldn't meet anyone today?

Tegan left the cottage. It felt very daring to be out and about like this on a Sunday.

It was very quiet, cold but peaceful. Slowly she climbed the mountain, feeling as she did before that she was leaving the world and its complexities behind. At the top of the hill, out of breath, she sat down and screwed her eyes up, watching a skylark trilling above her. She looked at the rocks: were they really millions of years old?

A voice interrupted her thinking. 'Hiya again.'

She looked up, saw Sam, and panicked.

'Look, I'm glad I've met you' he said awkwardly. 'I don't know what happened Friday. One minute we were having a nice chat and then suddenly-'

She looked down.

Sam sat down. He spoke gently. 'Tell me, Tegan, why did you start crying?'

'You sounded so angry' she said quietly.

'I thought you were having a go at Amy and Rhiannon. You know, when you said about judgment, you being religious and everything.'

'Well, Daniel did not approve. I know, he did have someone cast out, an older man who said he was gay. He was made to leave his wife and children behind in the Community.'

'That seems very cruel' said Sam.

'Well it's what happened to me, isn't it? It's the way the Community works. I was upset because I thought you were criticising my parents. I know people around here find it hard to understand but it's how the Community works.'

'I'm sorry. I'm very protective over my family. We've, well, been through a lot-'

'What happened?' asked Tegan.

'We don't talk about it. We came here for a fresh start' he said firmly. 'The trouble is, the past is always there, isn't it? In your head, I mean? I find up here is one of the few places I can really be at peace.'

He looked up at the sky lark and smiled.

'Alauda Arvensis, male,' said Tegan quickly. 'Out there, one hundred species of birds, thirty-five of mammals, and thirty types of butterfly.'

His eyebrows shot up. 'Blimey, you remember stuff, don't you? Hope I got my facts right.'

'I was reading yesterday, the rocks. Do you believe they are really millions of years old?'

'Yes, it's incredible, isn't it?' Sam sat next to her, looked ahead.

They sat quietly listening to the sky lark. Tegan realised how tired she was: tired of thinking, reasoning, arguing with herself. Up here nature just somehow got on with living. She glanced at Sam. 'Your girlfriend, she'll be back soon won't she?'

'Angharad? Oh yes. Next week, sometime.'

'You must miss her.'

'Mmm-'

She looked down at her wrist, no watch. 'Do you know the time?'

'It's about twelve.'

'I'd better go down, have some lunch. Cerys has asked me to go and help with Rhys' party this afternoon.'

'You're brave.'

'I didn't really want to go.'

'Go on. Chance to met people, and chance to help.'

Tegan nodded. 'I suppose so. I can always leave, can't I?'

121

'You can. Come on, I need to get down as well. I've got work to do.'

'But it's Sunday-'

'I know, but there's always paper work. I want to check on a cat that's been in overnight and also I like to go into the rescue centre everyday, just in case anything has cropped up.'

When they reached the bottom, Sam suddenly grabbed her arm.

'Look, over there.'

She peered towards the woods. She saw high in the sky two red kites, but they seemed to be flying in a strange way.

'What are they doing?' she asked, relieved they were a distance away.

'It's a courtship dance. Maybe two getting back together after the winter. You see, they are flying towards each other very fast and, yes, did you see that. Their talons nearly touched, and now they turn and twist away from each other. It's a wonderful dance. You know they may nest down there. At the edge I expect.'

Tegan found the idea of the enormous birds nesting so close to the cottage worrying but said nothing.

'Right, better get back to work' Sam said. He turned and smiled. 'It's really nice to talk to someone who is interested in this place.'

Tegan's eyebrows shot up. She thought he was joking, but, no, he was serious. He really did seem to have enjoyed talking to her. 'Thank you,' she said quietly. They stood looking at each other, the wind gently blowing. She smiled shyly at Sam.

'You look so different when you smile' said Sam.

She looked down and blushed. He coughed, embarrassed. 'Well, better be off.'

She watched as he walked briskly away and she went back to the cottage.

Tegan had lunch and then left to go to the party. She walked briskly through the fields and down to the village, wondering what would happen, worried about seeing Bethany

122

again. Also, what happened at a children's party? She guessed there wouldn't be alcohol, but what would they do? Maybe they watched a film: she could always look away during that. When she reached the Vicarage she saw balloons tied to the gate post. She swallowed hard and knocked on the door. This was opened quickly by a short plump girl with a mass of red hair. 'Hi, I'm Rhiannon. Welcome. You must be Tegan. Cerys said you may come.'

Tegan followed Rhiannon into the living room where she found Cerys.

'Tegan,' shouted Cerys. 'Great, come and blow up a balloon.' She handed Tegan a balloon. Tegan copied her and started to try to blow it up. Suddenly Cerys fell back in the chair. 'I'm stuffed from lunch.'

'Was it good?'

'Lush. It was the full Sunday roast, fantastic. And the Yorkshire puddings are to die for.'

Bethany came in. Tegan wondered what she would say but she seemed completely absorbed with organising the party. 'Tegan, ah good. Can you help make up the pass the parcel? Really, we've left so much to the last minute.'

Tegan went to the table.

'Right. I put a present in each layer. See, like this. I can't face their poor little faces when there is only one at the end, can you?'

Soon a young red haired boy ran in. 'Nanna, they're coming!'

Bethany smiled. 'Come on then Rhys. Let's go and let them in.'

Tegan noticed that each child was carrying a present. Rhys was running around unable to cope with the excitement. The children were very eager for him to open their presents, usually telling him what was in them before he opened them. Tegan was amazed at the presents. She had never seen most of the toys before. There was an animal game which Cerys told her was based on the film Madagascar that had come out the year before, and then there was Lego and Playmobil. They looked

123

very expensive and exciting. Bethany stood the cards up on the shelf as Rhys handed them to her, although he was showing little interest in them. One was written in Welsh. The words looked vaguely familiar to Tegan but she was distracted by Rhys running up to her with a car with all lights and horns blazing.

Rhiannon was in the garden waiting for the children. Bethany brought them out and they started energetic games of Musical Bumps, statues and Oranges and Lemons.

'Enjoying it?' asked Cerys.

'It's lovely' said Tegan, smiling. 'Look at Rhys. He's having a wonderful time.'

Standing to one side she saw a young fair-haired girl, earnestly watching, not smiling, and not joining in. She saw Rhiannon go to the little girl and ask her if she wanted to join in but she shook her head. Tegan felt sorry for her, wondered what the matter was.

Bethany was close by and saw Tegan watching. 'That's Halina. Her parents came over from Poland over a year ago. They've moved around. Started in Llanelli but came up here for work. It's hard. Halina has very little English. She must feel very lost.'

'Poor thing' said Tegan. 'She looks so unhappy.'

Bethany looked at Tegan. 'Over there I've put a box of children's books. Maybe she'd like to look at some with you?'

Tegan wasn't sure, but went to the box to pick out some books. She was flabbergasted at the beauty and range of the books: to think that these all belonged to Rhys. She picked out a few, mainly picture books, and went over to Halina.

'Would you like to look?' she asked, showing her the books. The little girl looked at the books curiously and gave a little nod.

They sat down and soon Tegan was reading her the stories. The little girl was enthralled. Another child came and joined in. Soon Tegan had a group of four children all listening to the stories.

Bethany called out. Halina held Tegan's hand as they went into the birthday tea.

124

Tegan sat with Cerys watching the children tuck into sausage on sticks and rabbit shaped jelly.

Cerys grinned. 'Brings back memories, eh? Good to see children can still enjoy an old fashioned party. I remember mine, don't you? You can imagine the fuss Mum made, way over the top, but it was exciting.'

'Mm.'

'You alright? You look a bit sad.'

'Oh, I'm sorry. I'm fine.' No way was she going to admit to never having seen such a party: not even before the days of Daniel would such a thing have been allowed. She had never had a birthday party, birthday presents. She blinked. She must stop all this covetousness. It was very wrong and ungrateful.

Bethany brought in a huge cake in the shape of a train with five candles on it. Tegan listened to them all singing "Happy Birthday" and then watched as Rhys blew out his candles. Mark, his grandfather, went round taking photographs, and then it was time for more games.

Tegan sat with Halina and they joined in pass the parcel. Tegan watched the carefully engineered game. Every child had a turn.

The children were starting to get fractious, but just in time Bethany introduced a magician. Finally, parents arrived to collect tired but happy children. Tegan saw a young woman with light brown hair come for Halina. She was quiet and didn't join in the loud chatting of the other parents. Bethany went over and spoke to her but she left quickly.

When all the parents had collected their children, Bethany came over to Tegan.

'Well I'm off to the church, gets me out of the tidying up. Evensong in half an hour.'

'You have another service?'

'Yes, you can come if you like.'

'I'm not sure.'

'It's very quiet. Just me and a few others. You can just sit and rest if you like.'

Tegan realised that out here there would be no other meetings like the Community. She wanted to try and do something as it was Sunday. 'OK, I'll come.'

Rhiannon came over and hugged her mother. 'Thanks so much, Mum. That was wonderful.'

Bethany smiled. 'I'm off to set things up for the service. Sorry to leave all the clearing up. I'll see you later Tegan. We start at half six.'

Tegan looked around the kitchen: the piles of plates, paper from the presents, and games everywhere.

'Would you like a hand?' she asked.

Rhiannon looked out of the window at Rhys running aimlessly around the garden.

'You know, would you mind reading to him, like you did with Halina earlier? All this is easy. Me and Cerys can clear it quickly.'

Tegan went into the garden. Nervously she went over to Rhys, and asked him if he would like to read. She was surprised at how willingly he agreed and soon they were sat on the grass reading endless Thomas the Tank Engine books together.

When all the work was done Cerys left and Rhiannon brought Tegan out a cup of tea.

'There you are, you deserve this. Thanks so much for helping' Rhiannon said.

'Can I watch telly Mum?' asked Rhys.

'Of course,' Rhiannon said.

Rhys ran inside.

'Thanks so much. He just needed to calm down' said Rhiannon. She flopped down on the grass.

'Your Mum did well' said Tegan.

'Yes, she did this last year as well. I think she's worried about Rhys fitting in, you know, being accepted, so she makes a lot of effort.'

Tegan looked at her questioningly.

Rhiannon looked directly at Tegan. 'You must know all the gossip about me.'

'Um, I know you were young when you had Rhys-'

'I was sixteen actually. It was a difficult time. I had just started to tell people I was a lesbian. Just family, close friends-'

'You were very young' said Tegan.

'I'd known for a few years.'

'What did your Mum say?' asked Tegan.

'She was upset actually. Thought I was too young to know. Anyway, then I got pregnant.'

Tegan frowned.

Rhiannon saw her face. 'I know, doesn't make sense, does it? There were people at school who had bullied me when I came out. I started to wonder if it was all worth it. I went to a party, got really drunk and slept with this boy. I think I was trying to prove to myself that I wasn't a lesbian. What a mess, eh?'

Rhiannon started to pick the heads off the daisies on the grass.

Tegan was very shocked, sat forward, and looked at Rhiannon. She was talking calmly, but it must have been so traumatic.

'The boy denied he was the father and moved away with his parents. Mum stuck by me. I went to counselling, and had Rhys. I stayed here. Mum and Dad have been wonderful.'

'It must have been very difficult' said Tegan.

'It was. Some of the people in the church and the village were pretty horrible to Mum, said she should resign. Some people left the church.'

'Oh no.'

'Yes, she got anonymous letters and everything. But Mum is a fighter. We could have moved but she wanted to stay. And really it's not worked out too badly. Rhys is lovely. I can't imagine life without him, and Mum and Dad worship him. You know, life is changing. There are children with all sorts of backgrounds in school, and Rhys fits in fine. And now of course I have Amy.'

Rhiannon smiled warmly. 'We were so lucky to find each other. I mean, it's a small village and yet to meet here, well, after Rhys, it's the best thing to happen to me.'

'I haven't met Amy yet. She runs the rescue centre doesn't she?'

'That's right. She works really hard, like her brother Sam. We keep our relationship quite low key. We have friends who live in the cities who say we should be a lot more assertive about everything but we have to do what is right for us and that includes Mum and Rhys.'

Tegan could hear the toll of a church bell in the distance.

'Ah, time for church' said Rhiannon, standing up. 'Sorry, pouring out my life's story to you.'

'It's OK,' said Tegan.

'Gosh, look at those clouds,' said Rhiannon. 'I think we've been really lucky with the weather.'

They walked to the front door.

'Thanks again. You know, you are really easy to talk to. Thanks for listening.'

'That's OK. Nice to meet you. Thanks, I really enjoyed the party' replied Tegan. She realised she meant it. It had been a good afternoon. Nothing had made her feel odd and she had even helped with that little girl. To hear Rhiannon's story had been very moving; out here in the world she was meeting so many different sorts of people. The Community which had been so all-encompassing was shrinking; the teachings less and less relevant to how most people lived.

Tegan made her way over to the church. Dark clouds had started to gather. Spots of cold rain fell on her head. She started to feel very sick and anxious. She noticed the church was surrounded by graves. Most of the grave stones were old, the engravings worn away over time. It started to pour with rain. The grey sky seemed dark and heavy. The church did not look picturesque, but rather it appeared threatening, looming over her. Tegan walked up the wet steps and pushed open the wooden door of the church.

Chapter Seventeen

Inside the church Megan was standing giving out hymn books. 'Good evening Tegan. Glad someone has made the effort to come out on an evening like this. Well done.'

Tegan tried to smile.

'Wynn and James are down there on the left if you would like to sit with them.'

Tegan glanced down at two stiff suited backs. The church was bitterly cold. She wondered why they didn't have coats on.

Bethany came over. 'Tegan, go on down the front. It's warmer down there.' Tegan walked down the aisle. Her footsteps echoed on the stone floor. Unlike the Community meeting room with its plain walls, there were crosses and a crucifix, and large stained glass windows. She looked at the colourful banners hanging on the walls and a huge wooden cross at the front. She sat on the hard wooden pew, and looked up at the brass pulpit, the eagle with its wings staring at her. She was so cold. She started to shiver. Then her eyes drifted to a painting tucked away. It was of Jesus on the cross in terrible agony. Blood poured down his face, but it was the hands she couldn't stop looking at. They had nails in them. They were covered in blood. She felt her own hands, so sore; but it was good, wasn't it, to have pain, to atone for her sins? She started to scratch her hand: deep, hard scratches. Then she looked up at the clock: the red second hand creeping round, time passing. The end was near and she was out here in the world. Her heart started to pound. She couldn't breathe; her heart beating fast. It hurt. She had to get out. She stood up and started to stagger down the aisle. She saw Bethany, but her voice sounded far away.

'Tegan are you alright?'

She felt a hand guide her to a seat. She felt very sick. Slowly the room stopped spinning. Bethany was very concerned. 'What's the matter?'

'I'm OK. Sorry. I think I need to go back to the cottage.'

'I'll get Mark to run you home.'

Tegan stood up quickly. 'No, it's fine really.' She started to walk quickly out of the church. Bethany ran after her.

'Tegan, you can't walk home. It's pouring with rain.'

Tegan started to feel giddy again, and grabbed Bethany's arm. 'I think you're right.'

'Hang on, I'll phone Mark.'

Mark arrived quickly. Tegan was very grateful but embarrassed. She saw Megan looking at her disapprovingly and guessed that she saw her as attention seeking. But she felt terrible; she couldn't stop shivering.

Mark helped her into the car, and she sat huddled up. She looked out of the window. It was dark. She was drowning in the blackness. Mark chatted about the weather. She found the aimless talk comforting. They drew up by the wooden gate.

'Please drop me here.'

'Shall I walk you to the door?'

'I'll be fine. Thank you.'

She waved Mark off and started to walk towards the cottage. She was concentrating on making her way through the blackness and the rain, when, out of nowhere, a large black monster came charging at her. She saw huge white teeth, a flaming tongue. There were wings on his back. She screamed in terror. The beast: it was the beast come to get her. She fell to the ground.

'Bracken, leave. Come here' shouted a voice.

The dog left Tegan in the darkness. She tried to stand.

'Let me help you. I'm very sorry.'

Tegan recognised Sam, then Bracken. 'I'm sorry' she cried, very embarrassed but still shaking.

'Are you hurt?'

'No, no.' She was sobbing.

130

'Let's get you back to the cottage.'

Sam held her gently by the elbow and led her. He knocked on the door.

Cerys opened it. 'Tegan, are you alright? You're as white as a sheet. Come in quick.'

Tegan couldn't stop shaking.

'I'm sorry. I'm always lecturing people about training their dogs' said Sam.

'It's alright. Look, why don't you come in for a drink?' asked Cerys.

'We're soaking wet. I've got Bracken with me.' Sam glanced at Tegan.

'That's OK. Come on in.'

Bracken obediently gave himself a shake and was allowed in. Sam took off his coat and wellington boots, Tegan her coat. Cerys had built up the fire. Dylan jumped up and ran to Tegan. She leant down and stroked him. Then he went to greet Bracken.

Sam leant down. 'Let's have a look at that ear, Dylan, while I'm here.' Dylan sat patiently as Sam examined him, occasionally diving to lick him.

Sam stroked him and sat back. 'That really is looking good. I can see you've been cleaning his ears like I said. Well done.'

Cerys glanced over at Tegan and noticed her staring at the fire. She moved the guard in front of it. 'Come here Tegan; you look freezing.'

Tegan stared at the flames. She moved her chair back.

'I've never been in here before. It's very cosy' Sam said.

'Wine, Sam?' asked Cerys.

'Thanks.'

He sat on the sofa by the fire. Cerys' phone rang and she went into the kitchen to answer it. Tegan sat, her hands clasped in her lap. She stared at the floor.

'I'm so sorry. Are you alright?' asked Sam quietly.

Tegan nodded. 'It's been a long day: the party, church-'

Bracken walked slowly over and lay down at her feet.

'He knows he's upset you. He won't hurt you.'

'I know. Sorry, it was out there, you know, in the dark-'

'He's very gentle, honestly.'

Sam called Bracken to him. Bracken put his head on Sam's knee and wagged his tail, narrowly missing the vase on the coffee table.

Sam patted his head. 'Have you ever had any pets?'

'No. It was seen as a terrible waste of money.'

Sam's eyebrows shot up. Tegan held her breath, suddenly realising what she'd said. She waited for him to shout at her, and storm out of the cottage. Instead, his face slowly broke into a smile. 'Well, I don't know, people like you could do me out of a job.'

She breathed a sigh of relief and stared back into the fire. She was exhausted, confused and frightened. What was the matter with her? Was she mad? Cerys came back from the kitchen. She gave Sam a glass of wine and Tegan a cup of hot chocolate. Tegan sat back and stared at the wall. Cerys and Sam became a distant noise chatting to each other.

Cerys was saying, 'So, Angharad will have her finals this year?'

Cerys turned to Tegan and explained. 'Sam's girlfriend, Angharad, is in her final year of a biology degree. Sam has been coaching her, and it's how you two got together, isn't it?'

'That's right.' Sam turned to Tegan. 'She loves me for my brains, not my money.'

Cerys laughed and then chatted to Sam about people in the village. Tegan sat staring at her lap, trying to ignore the heat from the fire. That beast, she could still feel the teeth biting into her flesh. And then, a long way off, she was aware of someone calling her name.

'Tegan' Cerys repeated. 'I said Sam is leaving now.'

Tegan blinked. 'Oh sorry. Right, well, goodbye.'

Sam stood up and looked around for Bracken. 'Come on you, out into the cold.'

As Sam was doing up his coat he said. 'I think I'll pop up to see Robert later, check how things are going up there.'

'I really like Sam' said Cerys as she shut the front door.

'Dylan was good for him.'

'He's just amazing with animals, very kind. They love him. You know, he can do it all. Handle them, tell you what's the matter, everything. To be honest I think he's better than his Dad, Alan. Alan is good, mind you, but he's on edge all the time. It can unnerve the animals.'

'Sam was telling me he came from the Isle of Wight.'

'I heard that. Alan and Rachel, his parents, moved here not long before we came.'

'What are his family like?'

'Difficult to say. Alan, his Dad, is quiet, shy like Sam, but a good vet. Rachel looks a bit stressed to be honest, but I like her.'

'And Amy?'

Cerys laughed. 'Amy is something else, a one off. Very different to Sam.'

'So how serious are Sam and Angharad?'

'Don't know really. He was helping her with her work, next thing they were together. He looked completely besotted at first. Really, I don't think he knew what had hit him. And she, I have to say, seemed to reciprocate, which was surprising.'

'Why?'

'She usually goes for the, you know, alpha male types.'

'Pardon?'

'Never mind. Sam's much quieter than her usual men.'

'What's she like then?'

'Extremely pretty. You know. I mean, really, really pretty, and clever, sexy, the lot. She has all the men chasing her.'

'As long as she doesn't encourage them, I suppose it's not her fault'

'Oh, she encourages it all right, loves the attention.'

'She's very fortunate to have found a man like Sam.'

'Suppose so. To be honest, though, I think he's too good for her. Deserves better; someone kinder; someone interested in his work and things. I don't reckon she even likes nature or animals much, but there you are.'

'So where does she live?'

'Oh, either at the pub with her Dad John or in her flat in Aber.'

'Ruth at the concert, she's married to John? So she's Angharad's mother?'

'Ah, nothing so simple. John's first wife, Angharad's mother, left him years ago. Took Angharad off to France with some bloke she'd met. Apparently John was devastated. It's lucky he found Ruth really. She's helped him a lot.'

Cerys went and poured herself another glass of wine. 'Anyway, enough of me bitching. You must be tired; you've had quite a night of it.'

'That's true. I think I'll go on up.'

Tegan changed, knelt beside her bed, and began her vigil. It was hard to concentrate. Every time she closed her eyes, images of the hands in that picture, the blood dripping down, kept flashing into her head. In the end she crawled into bed and tried to sleep. She lay listening to the owls and remembered the owl shape on the bed post. She pulled back the pillow and looked at it. Who had drawn that? She touched it. She could see a hand, an arm, but no, no face. Who was it? It was so frustrating. It didn't make any sense but she knew somewhere in her head she had the memory locked away, but nothing seemed to unlock it.

The next morning Cerys went out. Tegan sat knitting. She received a phone call from Bethany.

'Just checking to see how you are.'

'I'm alright.'

'Well, you did look very upset.'

'I think I was tired, but thank you for asking.'

'Listen, Tegan, the person on the card. Well, he works with people who've been in cults and things.'

Tegan stiffened. 'I wasn't in a cult. Daniel said the world says that, but it was definitely not a cult.'

'I'm so sorry, but where ever you were it seems to have hurt you in some way. The reason I gave you the card is because that man is someone who may understand what you are going though, you see. Most counsellors have no idea really.'

'It's alright. I can cope. Don't worry' Tegan said firmly.

She heard Bethany cough. She sounded nervous. 'Your parents, if anything happened in the Community, if for any reason it was to break up, what would they do?'

Shocked at the idea, Tegan replied 'I've no idea. They gave all their possessions, all their money, to the community, and they have no alternative. But then, they don't need one, do they? Nothing will ever stop the Community's work. Daniel will make sure of that.'

'Maybe. Well, OK. You know where I am, if you need anything.'

'Thank you, but I have Cerys. She's very kind. I'll be fine.'

'Ok well the offer is still there.'

Later, Cerys came in. 'Bloody hell, it's cold out there.' Dylan came running over to Tegan wagging his tail. She patted him. They made lunch: soup, cheese and bread, and sat in front of the fire.

'Bethany phoned' said Tegan.

'Worried about last night?'

'I think so. Listen, she seems to think I was in some kind of cult. You don't think that do you? Is that what people are saying?'

'To be honest, people do get pretty confused about you. Your life has been so different to ours. You know, it's like you've been living on another planet.'

'It sounds like that?'

'Kind of. Take this being thrown out. I mean, it's not normal, is it? You know, last time I heard someone getting chucked out of their home was a lad in the next village that stabbed someone for money to buy drugs. Don't tell me you did anything like that?'

135

Tegan stood up and looked out of the window. 'Of course not. See, it's so frustrating. You'd never understand.'

'Look, try me. Tell me what happened.'

Tegan bit her lip. She was very nervous, but suddenly she wanted to tell someone.

She took a deep breath. 'Last September, I was out distributing leaflets, inviting people to meetings. Anyway, I was stood there and it started to rain. I looked over at the library. I knew I wasn't allowed to go in there but there had been something I wanted to find out about. I couldn't get any answers in the Community.'

'Hang on. You weren't allowed to go in the library?' said Cerys, aghast.

'No. When I was little I was told there were lots of evil books, knowledge in there that wasn't safe for me. Daniel said he was protecting us by not allowing us to have computers, read newspapers, and things.'

'So you weren't allowed to read things for yourself?'

'Daniel said we were to *"gouge out the eyes of reason"*.'

'But that's crazy.' Cerys shook her head in disbelief.

'The idea was that it showed we trusted him. Often, someone would go out the front at meetings and they would have to honestly agree with whatever Daniel told them.'

'I expect they just said it to shut him up' said Cerys sceptically.

Tegan shook her head seriously. 'Oh no. You see, they believe Daniel is omniscient. He could see into their heart, know if they were lying.'

Cerys shuddered. 'Blimey, all sounds creepy. So you believe that?'

'I don't know. I'm very confused. Anyway, there was something I desperately wanted to look up. I told myself I'd just look up the one thing and then leave. I walked straight over the road and pushed open the door.'

'And?' Cerys leant forward.

'I went in. I just opened the door and went straight in. It was so easy, all those years of waiting, wondering what would happen if I went in.'

'And-'

'Well, in some ways, you know, it was a bit of an anticlimax' said Tegan. 'I expected all sorts of terrible things, but it was all so normal. There were obviously lots of books, posters for art classes and things. There were old people, mums and toddlers. No one seemed to take any notice of me.'

'And what did you think?'

'I was surprised. You see, there were all kinds of books. I had been worried it would be full of, you know, immoral books, but there were books on all sorts of things: gardening, cookery, and even children's books. I peeped in the children's library. There was a group of toddlers and their mums, singing and having stories read to them. I had never seen such beautiful books. I had only ever been given tatty old books, mainly Bible stories.'

Cerys frowned. 'That's sad.'

'Yes, I must admit to feeling really envious of those children.'

Cerys shook her head. 'It's incredible. I find it really hard to believe you'd never been to a library. Mum used to take me a lot.'

'I went into the adult section. A librarian asked me if I needed any help. I asked him for medical reference books. He showed me where to look. He said I could use the computers for free if I wanted, but I didn't dare do that.'

'So what happened then?'

'I found a medical book, sat and read. I was shocked. I looked in more and every book I looked in seemed to say the same.'

'What on earth were you looking at?'

Chapter Eighteen

Tegan found it embarrassing to tell Cerys what she had been so keen to read about. She looked down, blushed.

'Tell me,' said Cerys. 'What were you so worried about?'

Tegan took a deep breath. 'I wanted to read about pregnancy, problems that may occur.'

'Really?' said Cerys, surprised.

'I knew very little about such things,' said Tegan shyly, 'but it wasn't just curiosity. Deborah, Daniel's wife, had died a few years before. She had been late on in her pregnancy. It was a terrible time, but nobody would talk to me about it.'

'What happened?' asked Cerys.

'It had been a surprise when she became pregnant. She was in her late forties. She never went to any doctors or things. Daniel wouldn't let her.'

'Why ever not?'

'He said we must do vigil, not rely on the heathen-'

'You're kidding. That's dreadful. What happened to her?'

'She started to feel very unwell. I suppose she was somewhere in the middle of her pregnancy. She went to see a doctor without telling Daniel and he told her she should go into hospital, something about heart problems. Anyway, Daniel refused to let her go in. The baby wasn't due for another couple of months, but one night I heard lots of screaming. Daniel ordered a special vigil, but in the morning Esther's mother persuaded him to call the doctor. I was looking after Elizabeth when the doctor came. The doctor wanted Deborah admitted straight away. Daniel argued. It all got very heated. Eventually Daniel gave in. Deborah was taken to hospital but later that morning we were told Deborah and the baby had died.'

Tegan sat, tears slowly, silently, falling. She had never talked about it to anyone, never dared, but it hurt so much.

Cerys clasped her hand over her mouth. 'Oh no Tegan, that's tragic.'

Tegan wiped the tears. 'It was. I remember going to Mum crying. She told me off, said it was judgment from the High One. They should never have called a doctor. No one talked about it again. But it always worried me.'

'Daniel must have felt very guilty.'

'No. It seemed to make him harder and more fanatical. He said the end was very near, things like that. His daughter Elizabeth was so upset, you know, losing her mother. It was a terrible time.'

Tegan stopped. 'I wanted to find out what it could have been.'

'And do you know?' asked Cerys earnestly.

'Not really, but the more I read the more I became convinced that Deborah and the baby might have survived with the right medical help.'

'Did you say anything back at the Community?'

'I couldn't say too much. In any case, nobody would talk about it. But inside, you know, I felt really angry and frustrated.'

'And did you go back to the library?'

'I told myself I wouldn't. However, the following week I gave in, and went back in. There was a different librarian on this time. He came and asked me if he could help me. It was the first time I'd spoken to him.'

'What was his name?'

'Steve. It was the first time I talked to Steve.'

Cerys grinned. 'So, romance, eh?'

'No, not really, but we talked. He showed me how to use the computer, told me I could join, borrow books, you know, take them home, for free. I don't know what got into me. It was like being someone else, and someone who could do anything she wanted.'

'And what happened?'

'Well, I borrowed books, read them secretly. The hardest bit was reading the news on the computer.'

'Why was that?'

'Daniel said all suffering was judgment for sin. But when I read about the earthquake in Pakistan I kept thinking what had the children done that had been so terrible to deserve this? I remember Steve coming over to me as I sat crying. He seemed surprised that I had known so little of what had been happening. I was very upset.' Tegan blushed. 'I'm sorry, it was all rather emotional.'

Cerys smiled. 'That's alright. Maybe we should all cry about these things a bit more.'

'Steve said something like that. He was very kind, and in fact that was the first time we went for coffee. He asked me to go with him, next door to a café. Of course I knew I shouldn't, and in any case I had no money. But he insisted, and so I went.'

'It sounds like he took a real interest in you.'

'Oh no. I got that wrong, but he asked me about my life. For the first time I started to understand how different my life was to most people. I would sit there looking around at the other people in the café, all chatting.'

'It sounds quite romantic.'

Tegan blushed. 'Well, I suppose I did like him a lot. You know, he was so friendly, listened to me. I did think he liked me but I was wrong about that.' Tegan looked down. Images of walking into his flat, the girl in the fur coat, the deep, excruciating embarrassment, all came flooding back.

'All seems harmless enough to me.'

'No, no. You see, it wasn't. There were so many things wrong with it.' Tegan felt frustrated.

Why didn't Cerys understand the enormity of what she had done?

'Steve said I should leave the Community. He got so excited, talked about starting a new life.'

'Did he want you to go to him?'

'The trouble was, when I was with him, everything seemed simple. I felt I could do anything with him. Maybe there was a part of me that wanted to get away, leave the Community, but I hadn't really thought about it. All I knew was I loved having coffee with Steve. It's what I lived for each week.' She stopped. Whatever would Cerys think of her?

However, Cerys just smiled. 'First love, eh?'

'I don't know. The last time we had coffee we were sitting talking. He put his hand on mine, kissed me on the cheek. I knew it was terrible, but I was so happy.' She stopped, smiled at the memory. For that brief minute it had been wonderful.'

'So what happened then?'

'What I hadn't realised was that Naomi from the Community was walking past. She saw us, went back to the Community and told the elders. When I returned the elders were waiting.'

Cerys looked bewildered. 'But surely you were able to explain? I mean, you really hadn't done anything wrong, had you?'

'I had disobeyed, communed with a heathen man. Oh yes, I'd done plenty of things wrong. I was put into isolation, and then the elders started to quiz me about what had happened. I asked questions. That made it even worse.'

Tegan remembered the faces of Daniel and the elders. Their lips hard pressed together, eyes of stone. 'Daniel was particularly furious about Steve. Prostituting myself with a heathen man, he called it. He said Steve was a heathen man, full of sin, who deserves to burn for ever in hell.'

Cerys drew a breath in shock. 'My God. What happened?'

'It went on for days. They would leave me for hours and then start again. Shouting at me to curse Steve, the world. To vow I would never question Daniel again, promise to never read another book without permission, never leave the building on my own again. They kept asking more and more of me.'

'Didn't your Mum stop them?'

Tegan shook her head. 'No. It wasn't her place to do that.'

Cerys shook her head. 'That's awful.'

'I realised I was in danger of being thrown out, but then I thought maybe it would be better. I thought Steve would help me find somewhere to live and then I would show them that I could come out here, live a pure life. I was angry with them, wanted to prove I could do it without them.'

'And how do you feel now?' asked Cerys quietly.

'I don't know, Cerys. I really don't understand anything any more.'

They sat in silence, and then Cerys spoke.

'Tegan, I never realised what you went through, but maybe you're well out of it. I mean, it's awful about your Mum and Dad, but it does sound a weird, horrible place.'

'But it wasn't all terrible. You know, I had company. Us women would sit, knit and sew together. To be part of an elite, special, was nice.'

'But they used to run you down as well. You had no freedom, you weren't allowed to make decisions, have nice things, see the doctor. It's not right.'

'I suppose so, Cerys. It's very confusing.'

Cerys put her hand on Tegan's shoulder. 'I know it's been hard but people don't hate you. Maybe they're a bit confused by you, but they don't hate you. And look out there: it's a beautiful place you've been brought to.'

Tegan sighed. 'I suppose you're right, but I don't feel I belong here. I'll never fit in. And anyway I miss everyone. My Mum, we've never been apart you know, not even for one night.'

'Surely you could go and visit just for a short time.'

'There is no just popping in to see them. It's all or nothing with them. You are in or out, no in-between. And now I am out.'

'Oh, Tegan, that's cruel. I'm so sorry. Maybe your Mum will persuade your Dad to leave with her, and then you could be together again.'

Tegan laughed coldly. 'Philip will never leave, and my Mum, well, she's changed over the years. When I was little there was softness there but it's gone now. No, she would never leave.'

Cerys sat thinking, and then she spoke more pragmatically.

'What you've been through is awful, but it seems to me that you are out here now and somehow you are going to have to adjust. You know, you may even enjoy it, if you give it a chance. Maybe it's time to compromise a bit, meet people half way, otherwise you are going to be very lonely.'

Tegan scowled. 'Ah, you think I should go down the pub, get drunk, sleep around. Is that it?'

Cerys' face changed. She looked angry. 'No, of course I don't. For goodness sake, Tegan, don't just assume the worst in everyone. It is possible to go to the pub without getting drunk, you know.'

Tegan bit her lip. 'But I've seen people coming out of there drunk.'

Cerys grinned. 'Look, I'm not saying these things don't happen, but you don't have to be part of that. I mean I don't come home rolling drunk, do I?'

'No, I suppose not.'

'Well, think about it next time we're going out.'

'I'll think about it.'

Cerys looked at the time and stood up. 'Right, I'd better get on. See you later.'

Tegan sat alone, thinking. Cerys made it sound so easy: just join in. Maybe that is what she should try to do. She could still do vigil, stay pure, but maybe she should socialise more. She smiled at the thought of Sam. It would be exciting to see him more, maybe go up on the hills. He didn't sound too keen on this girl and she couldn't be as pretty as Cerys made out. No, she would make more of an effort. She could do this, and she could live out here.

Meanwhile, in London, Sarah was about to face a new dilemma. She had finished in the garden and was about to enter the women's room when Philip appeared. She knew he had spent the last two nights in vigil. She had hardly seen him. He looked exhausted but very stern.

'We have to talk. Go upstairs.' His face was white, his lips tight and thin.

She followed him to the bedroom and waited.

'On Saturday I spoke to Hannah. I have been in vigil since.'

She automatically backed away. 'You rang her?'

'I had to warn Hannah and Ellis not to let Tegan go down to them.'

'Oh. And had they heard from her?' asked Sarah.

'Yes they had. Tegan is with them.'

Sarah breathed out, didn't comment.

Philip stood over her, his face turning red. 'Daniel has prayed for me.'

'What have you told Daniel?'

'You know he is omniscient. He knew something was wrong with me. He actually asked me if I was thinking about Tegan.'

'What did you say?'

'I told him Tegan had gone to relations, that you had been instrumental in her getting there.'

Sarah gasped. 'Oh no. What did Daniel say?'

'He was very upset. Sarah, you do know you cannot go unpunished. You have used my phone, and helped Tegan when she has been cast out.'

Sarah started to tremble. The thought of being cast out was terrifying.

'However-' Philip said.

She heard the hint of hope and said 'What? Tell me.'

'I told him how unhappy Tegan is, hiding away all the time.'

'You think she is repentant?' asked Sarah.

'She could be. Daniel and I spent sometime praying together. He said he has been told by the High One to show Tegan exceptional mercy. If she is willing to truly repent, he said she would be allowed to come back.'

Sarah burst into tears of relief.

144

'I can't believe it,' she said breathlessly, 'and does that mean I will be shown mercy as well?'

Slowly, Philip nodded his head. 'Daniel recognises that our family have made an enormous contribution to the Community. Tegan had gifts with Elizabeth, and sewing. And you, until now that is, must be the most pious follower here. We are greatly blessed.'

Sarah sighed with relief.

Philip sat next to her. 'But Sarah, you must tell me everything. The money, did you give Tegan money?'

She took a deep breath. 'Yes. I gave Tegan money.'

He sat shocked. 'But how?'

'I'm so sorry.' Her voice was shaking. 'I had money from Cardiff, cash. I sold my mother's jewellery. I had it hidden in my case. Honestly, I wasn't going to spend it without telling you.' She sat staring at the floor, wringing her hands together.

'You mean that all these years you've been hiding money from me?'

'I have. I'm sorry, but again I have repented, and in any case that money had no place here in the Community. I'm glad it's gone.'

Philip grabbed her arms and squeezed tight.

'Ow' screamed Sarah. Her left arm was so tender, her hand still bandaged from the cut. She tried to struggle free. However, the harder she pulled the deeper he dug his fingers into her arms.

'But you lied to me and the Community and to the Lord your Judge. Remember Ananias and Sapphira? I don't understand why you haven't been struck down.'

Then the grip loosened. Philip stood away. 'You have made a full confession now, but it is up to Daniel to decide your punishment. At least we know you will remain here, whatever that may cost. You will stay with the elect.'

Sarah's eyes filled with tears. 'I will spend my time now in fasting, praying and working.'

Philip left the room. Sarah sat on the bed. She was shaking. This was all Tegan's fault. Why had she rebelled, brought this shame on them all? Since a little one she had questioned, challenged, them. Tegan had always been wilful, difficult. And now, because of her, she had disappointed their leader, she, who strived to be perfect. It was Tegan's fault: she was the stumbling block in her life.

At this time, in a world away Sam's girlfriend was sitting on a sun lounger on the patio of her mother's hotel in the south of France. On the floor next to her lay the abandoned revision books. Angharad sat staring out at the brilliant blue sea. She tried to block out the cold rainy days back in Wales, those endless bloody fields, people always wrapped up in layers of clothes. She sighed. Only a few days left. In the distance she saw her mother leaning over, watering plants. She stepped bare foot on to the stone patio, savouring the warm breeze blowing her long golden hair. A thin long silk skirt gently caressed her long legs.

'Maman' she called. From a distance her Mum looked in her thirties, very slim, tanned, thick blond hair. However, as Angharad approached the illusion gradually disintegrated. Despite face lifts and Botox, or maybe because of them, her mother had a plastic immobility to her face, like she was wearing the mask of a much younger woman.

'You recovered from last night then?' Angharad asked.

'Not yet,' groaned her mother. 'I can't take the drink like I used to. Still, Pascal likes to party.'

Angharad smiled. Her mother's latest partner was fifteen years younger than her and she was struggling to keep up. 'You ought to find someone more your age. You know there are plenty of men looking your way.'

'I know love, but they make me feel so old.' Her mother smiled sadly. She stood up, rifled through her pocket, took out a cigarette and lit it.

'It's time you gave up that up.'

'I can't, I'll end up enormous. Listen to you. What's going on with you? Last night you didn't drink. I saw you slope off at nine. Poor Jacques was abandoned.'

'Poor Jacques quickly picked up a very attractive guest and has yet to emerge from her room. Mum, I told you. I've settled down now'

'Not with this chap Sam? You can't settle down with a vet, and certainly not in that wet dreary village.'

'Look, I'll do my exams, and then work on Sam. I have no intention of staying there. You know that.'

Her mother sighed. 'Good. You are like a rare exotic bloom. You'll fade and wilt back there. You're like me. We need the sun. Anyway, what happened to that other chap you were talking about last time you were here? He seemed something special.'

'I came out here to think. That's finished Mum. Doing this degree with a load of younger students has made me realise my age. I'm nearly thirty. I can't wait around for ever. I want a home and kids.'

'There's years enough for all that. What's the rush?'

'Sam's a good steady man. He adores me, and he'll be loyal, look after me. He's a good man to have a family with.'

Her mother sat up. 'God, it sounds deadly.'

'It'll be fine. I've been looking things up. There are ways to make decent money as a vet, and I just need to get him away from bloody sheep and castrating the local cats. He's a clever chap. He doesn't need to stay buried in that village.'

Her mother stood up, started to walk away.

'Actually, Mum, when you come to my graduation in July, you will stay for a few days won't you?'

'Why?'

'I have a plan, that's all, and I want you there.'

'What do you mean?'

'Just something I've been talking to Dad about. So you will stay around?'

'I could. Maybe I'll bring Pascal, take him to London, and see some shows. Don't get much culture down here.'

'Good.'

'Right, I'm off to lie down. My head is thumping. They'll have to manage lunch without me today. Still going back Wednesday?'

'That's right. Work to do, life to sort out.'

Angharad closed her eyes and lifted her head to the sun, content. No way would she end up like her mother, desperate, chasing men half her age.

She laid back, a gentle smile on her perfect pink lips, stunningly beautiful and her face looking angelic, and calm. This was, however, very deceptive. The thoughts were far from innocent and the plans she had in mind would shatter lives back in the village of Ty Fynnon.

Chapter Nineteen

Tegan was sat at the table knitting. In front of her lay an ornithological book. She had started looking up sky larks, and then owls. It was very interesting and she had been reading most of the day. She was still reading when Cerys returned for her tea, and was only half aware that Cerys was vaguely wandering around. Then Cerys spoke.

'I have a big favour to ask you. The thing is, I wanted to ask you to come out for a meal with me, tonight.'

'Oh.'

'It will have to be the pub.'

Tegan was about to speak.

'Please, don't just say no. It's tonight, just a meal. Honestly, it'll be fine.'

'I don't know. What about Dylan?'

'He can come, as long as we eat in the bar area. Please come.'

Tegan looked at Cerys. She looked so desperate, and she'd been so kind. Daniel had been wrong about the optician. Maybe if she was careful she could go to the pub, stay pure.

'OK, yes. Thank you.'

Cerys beamed. 'Great. Come on. Let's go before you change your mind.' She put Dylan on his lead, and they went out to the car and headed straight for the pub.

Tegan sat in the car, scratching her hand and staring out at the darkness. They arrived at the pub too quickly. Tegan had to force herself to get out of the car. She stood in the pub car park, her hands sweating. Her heart was thumping so hard it hurt. The High One was watching and judging her.

'Come on' said Cerys. Trembling, Tegan followed her in.

'Sorry we have to eat in the bar because of Dylan' shouted Cerys. It was a foreign land. The smoke stung her eyes. The smell of alcohol made her feel sick, and the loud Welsh voices shouting made her cringe.

'Can't wait for the smoking ban' shouted Cerys. 'Come on, let's get a drink.'

Fighting the desire to run, Tegan stayed close to Cerys. It was busy but Cerys stood on her tip toes and elbowed her way to the front of the melee. Tegan noticed a family chatting. She was shocked to see children in there. She recognised James, the good looking singer from the concert, sitting with an attractive girl, their faces nearly touching, the girl engrossed, him looking around over her shoulder.

The landlord, John, came to serve them. 'What can I do for you ladies? Now you must be Tegan. Croeso i Gymru.'

'Oh, um, yes.'

'Can we have a menu?' asked Cerys.

John reached behind. 'There you are. Specials are on the board.'

Tegan read the dishes written on the blackboard. Steak pie made with Welsh Black Beef, grilled sardines, squid with coriander and chilli salsa, and rack of Welsh lamb, with white bean and fennel salad. It all seemed exotic and very expensive.

Cerys spotted Sam next to her. 'Are you eating?'

'No, just popped in for a drink with Rhiannon. She's over there.'

'Can we sit with you? It's really busy.'

'Of course.'

'Right then,' enquired John. 'What are you girls eating?'

'Do you have a plain omelette?' asked Tegan holding out the menu.

'Of course. Cerys?'

'I'll have the steak pie. '

'OK.' He tapped the order into the till. 'Tab?'

'No, we'll pay now' said Cerys.

Tegan felt for her envelope. She must get herself a purse.

'No, this is on me' said Cerys.

'I heard from Angharad again this morning Sam,' said John, with a knowing look.

Sam nodded. 'She needs to get back to work.'

She'll be back soon. I guarantee it, and with a few surprises up her sleeve for you. I've so much to thank you for. You're the reason she's stuck at her studies. Fancy having a kid at university. Can't believe it.' John beamed with pride, and then turned to Cerys. 'Drinks?'

'Orange juice and half a lager shandy please.' Cerys turned to Tegan. 'Can you take Dylan over with you to sit with Rhiannon? I'll bring the drinks over.'

Tegan made her way through the crowd, and found Rhiannon, who tonight had her hair piled high. Rhiannon grinned down at Dylan, who wagged his tail enthusiastically. 'Hiya you' she said, stroking him.

'Sam said we could join you?' asked Tegan nervously.

'Great. Nice to see you again.'

Tegan sat down. Dylan sat at her feet. It was comforting having him there. She sat stroking his velvet ears.

'I left Dad and Rhys playing some of his new games. Chance to escape for an hour,' said Rhiannon. 'It's been really busy at the salon this afternoon.' Without warning, Rhiannon reached out and touched the fringe of hair sticking out from the bottom of Tegan's headscarf.

'You know, I reckon under that headscarf you have really nice hair. Do you have to wear it for religious reasons?'

Tegan nodded.

'That's a shame. Sorry, I'm a hairdresser, professional curiosity. Oh good, here come the drinks.'

Cerys and Sam came over.

'You have a fan' said Sam, looking down at Dylan.

Tegan smiled. 'I never realised what it was like having a dog around.'

'See, not just a waste of money.'

Tegan glanced at him concerned, but was relieved that he was smiling. Dylan looked up, and she stroked under his chin.

151

'Now, how are things going with you and Robert?' Rhiannon asked Cerys.

'OK at the moment' Cerys replied cautiously.

'Good. I reckon he's ready to settle again. I can see you as a farmer's wife.'

'Are you coming on Friday to my parents' do?' asked Cerys.

'Free booze, chance to dress up, - yup, I'll be there' said Rhiannon. 'It'll be a good night, Tegan: champagne, the lot.'

'I don't know anything about it, but I can't imagine-' stammered Tegan.

'Remember. Dad mentioned it' interrupted Cerys. 'He said it would be a chance to meet people. Come on, at least it will be good food.'

'You think I ought to go?' asked Tegan earnestly.

'Of course.'

'But I have nothing to wear to something like that.'

'Don't be daft. Remember all those dresses hanging up in my wardrobe? You can have your pick of them.'

'And I could do your hair for you' interrupted Rhiannon. 'You have to leave your headscarf off for a party.'

'No, I can't.'

'Why not?'

Tegan felt herself blushing. 'I just can't-'

'But what do you mean?' persisted Rhiannon. 'I mean, you must have a very good reason for wearing that all the time.'

Tegan could feel herself getting upset, but there seemed no escape. Cerys, Sam, Rhiannon, were all looking at her waiting for an answer.

'Well, it shows the men are the head of us, and we have to hide our beauty from the angels, from men.' She found herself struggling to explain. She had never thought about it that much.

'What?' asked Rhiannon.

'Um, well, so they don't desire us' said Tegan, cringing. This really sounded odd out here.

Rhiannon burst out laughing. 'Bloody hell, that's so sexist.'

Tegan felt overwhelmed and miserable. Rhiannon stopped laughing. 'Hey, sorry. I shouldn't mock your religion. Take no notice of me.'

Cerys turned to Sam. 'So how's work?'

Tegan sat back, glad the attention was off her. She was finding the atmosphere in the pub claustrophobic. If only she could get out, get some air. She glanced over and saw the door bearing the sign "to the garden".

She whispered to Cerys. 'I'm just going to get some air.'

'You OK?'

'Fine. I won't be long.'

Tegan handed over Dylan's lead and then made her way self-consciously across the room. She pushed open the door. The air was bitingly cold; dusk was approaching, but she felt calmer out there.

'You alright?'

She turned to see Sam. 'Yes, I just needed some air. You know, that's the first time I've been in a pub.'

'Really? How do you find it?'

'Smoky, claustrophobic, but actually not as bad as I thought it would be. Anyway, why are you out here?'

'This is going to sound really daft,' Sam said sheepishly.

'What?'

'I want to go and have a look at a nest. Does that sound really odd?'

Tegan looked nervous. 'Is it a red kite nest?'

'Oh no, something much smaller. Look, come on. I'll show you.'

She followed him to a quiet part of the garden where he pointed to a small pile of twigs in the tree.

'See that?'

She looked up.

'I've been watching a long-tailed tit building that nest. Takes about three weeks to build. The older birds, like the one building this, try to get an early start.'

Tegan felt herself calm down as she looked at the nest. It was so intricate, a work of art.

153

'I've been reading about owls today' she said.

'Really?'

'There is one I hear every night. I think it was a tawny owl, but there were other sounds as well.'

'Could have been the same owl. They have at least twelve main calls.'

'No wonder I was confused. In London the night sounds are usually people, shouting, and, of course, ambulances, traffic, but it's so hard to know what's going on here.'

'Ah, you need to go out at night, get to know the place. There's a whole other world at night, and it's exciting.'

'I wouldn't do that.'

'You shouldn't be so frightened of everything. Tell me, what do you really love, really like doing just for fun?'

Tegan blinked. She tried to think. 'I don't know. I really don't. I suppose since coming here I've discovered the hills.'

Sam grinned and stamped his feet.

'It's really cold.' Tegan smiled. 'Could explain why we're the only ones out here.'

Sam smiled back at her and then said 'Your food should have arrived.'

Tegan realised that, despite the cold, she would much prefer to be outside with Sam, but agreed, and they started to walk back into the pub.

'Reckon there'll be snow tomorrow' said Sam. 'Can you tell Rhiannon I'm off to work?'

Tegan nodded and watched him walk away. She returned to sit with Cerys and Rhiannon. The food had just arrived. Tegan had never seen such an enormous fluffy omelette, accompanied by a bowl of chips and warm granary bread. Cerys' pie was steaming hot. When she cut into it thick brown gravy flowed onto the plate and a heavenly smell filled the table.

'Gosh, this place just gets better. Here, Rhiannon, have a chip, there's too much even for me here.'

They all sat comfortably eating. Tegan started to relax and enjoyed her meal.

At the end of the meal Cerys asked 'Alright?'

'Yes, thank you very much.'

Rhiannon touched Tegan's hand. 'Hey, I'm sorry for having a go at you like earlier, never did know when to stop.'

Tegan shrugged, but Rhiannon continued. 'The thing is, please come anyway. Honest, you can put your headscarf on after but I could give it a good condition, tidy the ends, please.'

Tegan sighed. 'I don't know.'

'Please, my way of saying sorry.'

Tegan could see Cerys egging her to say yes. 'OK I'll come.'

'Great. See you Friday afternoon.'

Tegan and Cerys made their way back to the car.

'Was it OK? Sorry it was a bit chaotic in there, and what with Rhiannon and everything-' asked Cerys.

'It was OK actually. It was bound to be strange but, just think, I went in, came out. I did it and nothing awful happened.'

Cerys laughed. 'Well, quite a low base line but still-'

'Oh, and the food was very good, thank you' said Tegan quickly.

'Good. Come on, let's get home.'

Sam was right. The next day everyone in the Cambrian Mountains woke up to snow. Tegan opened her curtains and blinked at the brightness. Snow fell thickly and silently. It was extraordinary to see miles of untouched white snow. Everything merged into a continuous series of white shapes, even the woods, silently covered overnight in white dust sheets. In London people would already have scraped the snow off their cars, roads would have been cleared, and life would be slowly getting back to normal. With a jolt she realised it was only a week since she was last there, in London, wondering what she was going to do. Ellis had said it was a different world down here and he was right. Each day here seemed a revelation: look at it today, the world transformed once more. Her breath clouded the window. She watched a red kite gliding in the grey sky.

She put on jeans and the jumper Cerys had given her and went downstairs. She noticed the fire crackling in the fire place.

She glanced away but was glad of the warmth. The whole room looked whiter, reflecting the snow outside.

'Freezing isn't it?' Cerys glanced over at the window, adding 'This place could do with central heating.'

'Beautiful though.'

'There's more to come by the look of the sky. Did you sleep any better?'

'I think so. Hope I didn't disturb you?'

'No, I was fine. I'm going up to Robert's for the day, see if I can help. What about you?'

'I'll stay in, read or something.'

Cerys stood up. 'Actually, can I leave Dylan? He doesn't like the snow much.'

'Of course.'

'Thanks, right, better get some layers on, and I'll see you later.'

Later that afternoon, outside the cottage, the sky was growing increasingly grey and heavy. Tegan went to take some stale bread out for the birds and was hit by a freezing cold wind. Quickly, she retreated, put on her boots and grabbed her coat. Dylan watched from the doorway. She went out, threw the bread on the ground and then noticed something small and white resting on the snow, tucked amongst the frozen daffodils. She peered over. Maybe it was a dead rabbit? But no. She knelt down and saw that it was a kitten. What was it doing out here? Its eyes were closed. It was lying very still. Then she saw an eyelid flicker. Tegan looked around in panic. What was she meant to do? Then she thought of something. She pushed back her hood and pulled off her scarf. Nervously, she reached out and touched the kitten. It lay, frozen, still, but then she saw a slight, shallow breath. She leant forward; her knees covered in snow, took hold of the kitten, and awkwardly wrapped it in the scarf. It was difficult to stand up, but she managed, and staggered back over to the cottage. Holding the kitten, she kicked off her boots, grabbed her mobile and knelt by the fire.

'I've found a kitten' she said hysterically to Cerys when she answered.

'Oh my God. Is it dead?'

'Not yet. I've brought it in. What do I do?'

'Hang on. I'll send you Amy's number. Ring her.'

Tegan waited for the number and then, with shaking hands, rang the rescue centre. The voice that answered was brisk. 'You've found a kitten? How old is it?'

'I don't know. It looks very ill. I've no idea what to do.' She was close to tears. 'I think it's dying.'

'Hang on. Where are you? Who is this?'

'It's Tegan at Ellis' cottage, "Hafan".'

'Oh, you could be in luck. I think Sam is up that way. Wait. I'll use the other mobile.' It seemed to take ages. Finally Amy came back. 'Yes, he is up that way. He'll come when he can. Just hold tight. Keep it warm.'

Amy rang off.

Tegan sat on the floor close to the fire trying to keep the kitten warm. Dylan was naturally interested and was persistent in trying to sniff it. She pushed him away. He sat patiently next to her but whimpered with excitement.

'Poor little thing.' Tegan stroked the kitten. It was so cold and painfully thin.

Eventually there was a knock on the door.

'It's open. Come in,' she shouted.

Sam bashed his boots and came over. Dylan jumped up at him. Sam stroked him briefly.

'Off you get now Dylan. I need to see this poorly kitten' he said, pulling off his gloves. Sam's face was bright red from the cold. There was snow on his shoulders but he was totally focused on the kitten. He handled it, gently, expertly.

'Right. It's female, not feral, surprisingly. I expected a farm cat. I guess she's about ten weeks old. Bit of a mystery. No collar, and yet she's a pedigree cat. Look at that.'

'What?'

157

'See, half a tail. Wonder if she's been dumped? I'll need to take her back, check her again, see if she's micro chipped, you know, the chip we use for identification.'

'You think she'll live?' asked Tegan earnestly.

Sam looked at her. 'I think she'll be fine. If we can't trace her owner, I'll take her to Amy. Nice little thing though.' Tears of relief started to flow down Tegan's cheeks. Sam smiled at her. Then he spotted the book about the Cambrian Mountains, lying next to him on the sofa. 'Still reading that?'

'Mmm.'

'You've got beautiful hair.'

Tegan reached up to her head in panic. 'I forgot-'

'It's alright. I won't tell. It's a shame you have to wear it, though. Your black hair, blue eyes, you're very pretty you know.'

Tegan looked down. 'No, not like normal people.'

'You don't want to become like everyone else. You're just right as you are. Don't ever change.'

He lifted a hand and gently touched her hair. She felt a shiver of excitement. Then a gust of wind sent snow crashing against the window.

'It's building up again. I'd better get back with this little one down to the surgery. If you give me your mobile number I'll let you know if there's any news.' Tegan found her phone and gave him the number.

'Are you busy?' she asked, realising she didn't want him to go.

'Chaos. Lambing in the snow, no joke. I saw Cerys up at Robert's. She's working hard. Right. Oh, your headscarf-'

'It's alright. I've more upstairs.'

'OK. Well done then. She wouldn't have survived much longer out there.'

Sam left, holding the kitten under his coat.

Cerys returned early in the evening. 'Gosh I'm exhausted. Tell me. How's this kitten you found?'

'Sam came. He took her back to the surgery, and he thinks she'll be alright. He doesn't think she's a farm cat though.'

'That's odd. How on earth did she end up here?'

'Sam said she might have been dumped.'

'Gosh. People can be such scumbags. By the way, where's your headscarf?'

'Oh, I put it round the kitten. I meant to get another one.'

'It's nice to see your hair. It's very pretty.'

'Sam said he liked it.'

'Did he now?'

'Oh it was nothing. I mean, he has Angharad, hasn't he? Do you think that is serious?'

'Maybe, who knows? Maybe you've provided him with a better alternative.'

Tegan looked down and blushed. Her phone sounded a text

'Oh it's from Sam' she said to Cerys. 'It says 'kitten is fine, with Amy now.''

'That's good, let's hope she finds a home soon' said Cerys and she built up the fire.

They opened tins of mushroom soup, sliced the bread thick and added cheese and butter to the table. They sat down in front of the fire, both eating hungrily. Tegan moved her chair back from the fire and read. Cerys closed her eyes and was soon asleep. Tegan quietly picked up her knitting, thought about Sam, felt the gentle touch of his fingers on her hair and smiled. Then she stopped. She shouldn't be thinking about a heathen man like this. It was sinful, wrong. But still another part of her mind wondered, who knows, maybe he would break up with Angharad and then who knew what might happen?

159

Chapter Twenty

The snow continued to bring the Cambrian Mountains to a standstill. Tegan woke to the familiar white glow behind the curtains and went and looked out on virgin snow. There was a watery sun today and the thin shafts of sunshine made parts of the snow glisten a brilliant white. It was still eerily quiet.

She went down to find the fire lit and a note from Cerys to say she had gone up to help Robert and she hoped Tegan didn't mind but she had left Dylan. Dylan jumped up from in front of the fire and ran over to greet her. Tegan ate breakfast and settled to a day of reading and knitting.

That afternoon, Sam was in his office. The kitten was healthy but not micro-chipped, and so was settled in with Amy at the rescue centre. He hoped it would be claimed or adopted soon. The morning had been hectic, first with surgery. Then his farm visits had all taken longer with the weather. Now he had a pile of paper work to catch up on before the next surgery, and he wrapped his hand around his hot chocolate in an attempt to warm up. Suddenly, he heard a gentle knock at the door.

'Come in,' he shouted, without looking up.

'Bon après-midi Sam' said a quiet, seductive voice.

He looked up, flustered. She was back. Angharad stood in tight jeans, pink cropped jumper, her hair golden, pouting lips and huge baby blue eyes. It took his breath away. He had forgotten just how stunning she was. She went over to the desk, pulled his chair round, sat on his lap and kissed him fully on the mouth.

'Tu me rends fou.' She saw his blank expression. 'You drive me crazy. When are you going to learn French?'

He coughed, blushed. 'You're home early.'

She smiled and kissed him again. 'I was worried about the snow, so I got a very early flight, but then the trains and all were running normally. Miracle isn't it? So, tell me, have you missed me?'

'Of course. I hope you've been doing plenty of revision.'

'I tried, but without you somehow I can't concentrate. You have no idea how much I've missed you.'

Her voice was an irresistible fusion of soft Welsh and southern French. It made him shiver.

'I guess you've been too busy to miss me' she said, fluttering her eyelashes.

'I've been really busy and this weather makes everything harder. I haven't stopped,' he stammered.

'Well, come on over to the pub and have something to eat. I bet you've not eaten since breakfast time.'

'I can't. I have to get this done.'

'You need a break. Come on,' she said, pulling him away. The phone rang. She picked it up and replaced the receiver.

Sam was horrified. 'That could have been an emergency.'

'You need food, and you are not the only vet here. Come on.'

'What do you mean? What's going on?'

'I need you to come somewhere with me. You are in for the most wonderful surprise of your life.'

Reluctantly Sam stood up, grabbed his coat and followed Angharad out. When they got to the pub she grasped his hand and, laughing, said, 'Not the front door. Come on round the back.'

She took him to the garden and she showed him to a covered seat. 'But it's freezing out here' he complained.

'We need privacy. Now, just sit there. I'll only be a minute.'

He pulled his coat around him, got distracted by the long tailed tit's nest, watched and waited.

161

Angharad returned wearing a woollen jacket carrying a plate with a hot pasty on it. He ate hungrily.

'Now, me and you, I think we have something very special, don't you?' Angharad said.

He looked up and put his head to one side. 'We get on well, yes.'

'No, it's more than that. You know it.'

Sam ate the final crust. 'Maybe we need to talk about this some time. I do need to get back.'

'No, you're not going anywhere' she replied crossly. Then she smiled, spoke more softly. 'While I've been away I've been thinking. I think it is time to, you know, start thinking about settling down.'

'With your degree, the world will be yours for the taking.'

'But I don't want the world' she said, leaning towards him. 'You must know what I want.'

He peered at her. She looked very serious as she said 'I think me and you should settle down together.'

He coughed, choked. 'Hang on; you're saying we should live together?'

Angharad looked cross, no childish pouting this time. 'What I mean is that we should get married. Neither of us is getting any younger. Why wait?'

He sat, speechless.

'Come on, what do you say? Me and you work well. You're a workaholic but if you're not careful, one day you'll turn around and find you've missed out on a home and kids. As it is, you have me, like a ready meal if you like. You don't have to go through all that terrible dating lark again, and look what you get.' She opened her arms and smiled. 'You must admit you never thought you'd end up with someone like me.'

Sam shook his head. 'I don't know what to say. I'm shocked. I'm sorry but I don't think I'm ready-'

'Come on Sam, you think about things too much.'

'No, Angharad, I mean it. I don't want to settle down.'

Angharad burst into tears. 'But you told me you loved me, wanted to be with me for ever-'

Sam cringed. 'That night-'

'I don't know what I'd do if you turned me down.'

She seemed so full of despair. He felt terrible.

'Sam, without you I couldn't cope. I don't think I could carry on.'

'But Angharad, we were never that serious. Honestly, look at you. Look at me for that matter. I'm not the sort of person you want to settle down with.'

'You underestimate yourself. You are just the sort of person I should settle with.'

'But-'

She leant forward. 'We've been very close, told each other things, haven't we?'

'What?'

'Family stuff. You know, we trust each other not to tell anyone else things, don't we? We trust each other because we are together, a couple-'

He looked up, stared at her. Surely she couldn't mean-

Then her phone rang. She answered it. 'OK, I'll come now.'

He looked at her puzzled, and then she knelt beside him. 'Sam, je t'aime du plus profond de mon coeur. I love you from the bottom of my heart. Will you marry me?' She took a small box out of her bag and held it up. With trembling hand he took it, and opened it. Inside there were two rings, one was a man's signet ring, the other a huge sapphire and diamond. Before he could speak he heard John's voice.

'Congratulations.'

Sam stared as he saw John and Ruth coming towards them holding a bottle of champagne. Behind them were Alan and Rachel, his parents. His father was tall, fair like him and stood, as always, just behind his mother. She was tall, with long brown hair, and with an 'arty' appearance of long skirt, layers of tops, and large jewellery.

163

In a daze, he stood up. Angharad put his ring on the ring finger of his right hand and her ring on her left. She whispered in his ear, smiling. 'I'll send you the bill.' Everyone came forwards and hugged and kissed them. Strangers from the pub came out, oblivious to the snow. They ran and hugged them. Sam looked at his Dad in panic. His father caught his eye anxiously, but raised his glass of whisky.

John then held out an envelope. Sam opened it. Inside was a reservation for the Brook Country House Hotel, for a wedding reception for two hundred people on the 11th July. He blinked.

'Yes son' said John, laughing. 'It's all booked. Angharad and I have been busy. To get into somewhere like that last minute even on a Tuesday was a miracle, but I pulled a few strings. Yes, only the best for you two. It's all paid for. It's all signed and sealed. All you have to do is turn up.'

Sam glanced at his mother. Her face was in a fixed smile but at least in her eyes he could see she was checking, trying to gauge his reaction.

John grabbed his arm. 'Come on, son. Gosh, I like the sound of that. Let's go in. We have a long day of celebration.'

'But work -'

Alan leant forward and said quietly 'It's OK. You have the rest of the day off. I'm going back in a minute.' Sam realised that it would be no hardship for his father to leave the party and return to work. They went into the pub, Angharad glowing. Sam sat down with his mother.

'You alright, love?' she asked. She held her glass suspended in mid air. Her bangles jangled on her wrist.

'It's all happening so fast,' he said quietly.

'Are you happy? I mean you do want to marry her, don't you?'

He scratched the back of his neck, leant forward and looked into his mother's face. She was sitting forward eagerly.

'Well, she's an amazing girl. I mean, look at her.' He looked again. Angharad had rushed up and changed into a beautiful fitted short white woollen dress. Her golden hair hung down to her waist. She seemed to sense his gaze, looked around, blew him a kiss. Then Sam looked at his dad. John had his arm around him.

'John seems to have taken to Dad.'

'Oh, John's into the whole "We're now a family thing". He came to tell us about the wedding. He's so excited. He's very fond of you, you know. Anyway, you know John's cousin has taken over that huge stables outside Lampeter, well, they're looking to give the work to a new veterinary practice. With John's recommendation, it could be Dad's.'

'Wow. That would be good money.'

'I know. Dad is a bit uneasy actually. As much as he would love the work, he'd rather have got it on his own merit.'

'But he's very good with horses.'

'I know. Don't worry, he won't turn it down.'

'I suppose it would make him feel on an equal footing with the other partners as well.'

'Exactly. You know, he was so crushed when we came here, and so grateful to be given work. It's good for him to feel he's bringing fresh work in. But, Sam, love. That is all by the by. Is this really what you want?'

Sam looked over at his father's glowing face, and then at his mother, saw the ingrained years of worry. 'I'm fine Mum. You know me, not used to rushing things, that's all. Come on. Let's get some of this champagne.'

Cerys returned to the cottage at about four.' I'm shattered. I don't know how Robert keeps going. How's Dylan been?'

'Really lazy. I've made us a casserole.'

'Oh, how wonderful. I'm starving.'

'Well, it needs another hour.'

Cerys had a drink and then slept until it was time to eat. 'This is really good, thank you' she said as she ate. Her phone signalled a text.

'Oh God, she's back.'

'Sorry, who?'

'Angharad. She's back. The text was from John. He wants us to go down the pub this evening.'

Tegan looked out of the window. 'But the weather-'

'I know, it's odd. I expect the pub is empty. Maybe he's trying to drum up business. Choir's cancelled. I suppose we could go down.'

Tegan sighed. 'I don't think he will expect me.'

'Oh, come on. You did really well the other night. Come tonight before you lose your nerve again.'

Tegan sighed. She didn't want to go out in the cold. Even less did she want to see Sam with this girl. He was one of her few friends and she guessed now he would be taken up with his girlfriend. 'So I'll get to meet Angharad?'

'Yup, lucky you.'

'Is she really as pretty as you say?'

'Come to the pub and you'll find out.'

At half past six Tegan rushed upstairs, put on a headscarf and then went down to put on her coat. They trudged through the snow together. It was bitterly cold. They pushed open the door of the pub. It was no easier going in. Tegan could hear the loud voices, smell the alcohol and smoke.

'Wow, it's packed' shouted Cerys. 'What on earth is going on?'

Chapter Twenty One

Tegan and Cerys pushed their way into the crowded pub. Then Cerys grabbed Tegan's arm.

'Look, look at that,' she shouted, pointing to a banner above the bar.

Tegan frowned. 'What does it mean?' she enquired.

'Congratulations Angharad and Sam' read Cerys. 'You know what, I reckon they've got engaged.'

Tegan swallowed hard. Sam was getting married.

'Shock isn't it?' a strange girl said to her.

Tegan was momentarily distracted by the sight of the girl speaking. She was short, with bright red hair, tattoos and piercing. Tegan found her rather alarming. She shouted at Tegan. 'Hi, I'm Amy, Sam's sister.'

Tegan couldn't believe it. She looked so different to her brother.

'How long have you known about the engagement?' asked Cerys.

'Today, the same as Sam.'

'What do you mean?' asked Cerys, wide-eyed.

'She proposed to him today. Honestly, I'm not joking. I don't suppose she wants people to know that, but it's true. The ring is a mystery, though. She wouldn't have bought that herself would she?'

Tegan looked over and then she saw her. She saw Angharad for the first time. Tall, slender, perfect hair, body. She glowed, she radiated beauty and confidence. 'She's incredible. I don't think I've ever seen anyone so beautiful.'

Cerys grinned. 'She's quite something, isn't she?'

Tegan stared. She must have been mad to think Sam would break up with someone like that.

'Well done about the kitten by the way' said Amy.

'Pardon?'

'The kitten. She's very sweet.'

'Oh, yes. Is she alright?'

'Yes. Heaven knows how she got to you. I think Sam is right. He reckons she was dumped by a breeder who couldn't sell her.'

'So can I get you a drink?' asked Cerys.

'Nah, I'm off back to the centre.'

'Shouldn't you stay?'

'No. I don't understand what Sam is playing at. I mean, he can't love her, can he? Anyway, I'm out of here. Can't stand any more of this.'

Cerys and Tegan went to the bar.

'The first one's on the house' shouted John, magnanimous with pride and champagne.

Cerys ordered wine and orange juice. They went to find a table and then saw an older couple.

'Congratulations' said Cerys. Then, turning to Tegan, she explained, 'These are Sam's parents, Alan and Rachel.'

Alan was drinking whisky. 'Good to meet you.' He was smiling confidently, but he blinked fast. His eyes seemed to dart around, and he took frequent sips of his whisky. Rachel was taller, fair. She stood quite still, but her hands were tightly clenched. She exuded an air of weary alertness. Even talking to Tegan seemed a lot of effort. 'I hear you are up at the cottage, Tegan. It's lovely up there.'

'Yes. I'm very lucky. I have been up in the hills sometimes.'

'Sam goes up there a lot. I do as well when I have time.'

'Sam told me you came from the Isle of Wight?'

Rachel looked alarmed. 'What did he tell you?'

Tegan felt she had said the wrong thing but wasn't sure why. 'Just that you came here, that it was a lovely place' she explained.

Rachel sighed. 'Yes, it was beautiful there. I miss the long sandy beaches. The downs were gentler but, still, we could have done a lot worse than come here.'

'Mum and Dad are over there' said Cerys. 'Are you coming over?' she asked Rachel.

'Oh no. We'd better stay at the bar, I think. Anyway, nice to meet you Tegan.'

Tegan followed Cerys over to the table where a large group were sitting. Hannah and Ellis were sitting next to Bethany and her family. Tegan was very surprised to see Bethany, a vicar, in a pub.

'Hi girls' said Ellis. 'Good to see you coming out Tegan.'

'I'm surprised to see you in a pub' said Hannah. 'Your parents wouldn't approve, would they?'

Tegan immediately felt guilty. Hannah was right. Her parents would be horrified.

'Don't be silly Mam' interrupted Cerys. 'It's good that Tegan is coming out and socialising.'

Tegan sat down next to Cerys. On the other side of her she recognised James, who grinned at her.

'Good to meet you at last. How are you settling down?'

Before she could answer, James' father leapt to his feet and leant over, kissing her enthusiastically on both cheeks. 'Great to meet you' he said.

James laughed. 'Sorry about Dad. He always goes over the top.' Tegan felt herself blushing.

'James, you must tell Cerys who you've been asked to audition for' said Megan, proudly. James, however, was suddenly distracted. He sat up and grinned at someone approaching. Tegan looked up and saw that it was Angharad approaching the table. Close up she could see perfect skin and large baby blue eyes peeping out shyly, seductively, from under her fringe.

'James,' she said her, voice drawing out his name in warm French tones.

James sat back and grinned. 'Angharad, you look even more stunning. Love must suit you. Congratulations.'

She smiled. 'Merci, although I think it is Sam you are meant to congratulate on his catch isn't it? By the way, I got the tattoo you said about.'

'What tattoo is that?' asked Wynn sharply.

Angharad didn't have to lift the hem of her dress far to reveal a small Welsh dragon on her thigh. Wynn reached out his hand: a whisper of a touch. Angharad looked down at him and laughed.

Megan coughed. 'So how is your revision going Angharad?'

'OK. Sam has been emailing me work. He's such a slave driver.'

Tegan saw Sam standing awkwardly away from them. Angharad gestured to him to join them. He made his way though the tables, and then stood next to her, scratching the back of his neck, looking down.

'Ah, bless' said Angharad. She tucked her arm under his, wrapped herself around him, whispered loudly in his ear 'Mon amour' and kissed his cheek. He looked up, blushed and smiled awkwardly. Tegan watched. He didn't seem to be the Sam she knew. He sensed her gaze and gave her a half smile. Angharad saw the exchange and, for the first time, seemed to notice Tegan.

'Ah, so you're the new girl in town. Tegan, isn't it?'

Tegan looked down.

'Sam has told me about you. He wasn't exaggerating was he? I love your headscarf. Amazing. I want to hear all about that weird cult you've been brought up in sometime.'

Tegan blushed, deeply embarrassed. What had Sam been saying about her?

Sam said uncomfortably, 'Angharad, don't-'

But she turned to Bethany. 'I think Dad has mentioned the date?'

'He has.'

'Good, we will come soon and sort out the details.' Angharad hugged Sam. 'Can't wait. Now come on, babe. We need to circulate.'

170

Sam let himself be led away.

Cerys sighed irritably. 'I think that's enough for one evening. Shall we make a move?'

Tegan nodded and stood up.

Bethany said 'Nice to see you again Tegan.'

Tegan couldn't speak. She was glad to leave.

As they made their way home through the snow Cerys said 'I'm sorry about what Angharad said. She can be a right cow.'

'Sam obviously sees me as some kind of freak.'

'That's just Angharad. Honestly, don't take any notice. God, what a shock though.'

Tegan didn't reply but assumed Cerys was, as usual, just trying to be kind. She was hurt, though. She had thought Sam liked her. What had he said? 'Don't change'. What did he mean by that when he obviously loved someone so different? He was one of the few people she had felt at least tried to understand her, and if he thought she was weird what hope did she stand with everyone else?

The next morning Hannah sat staring out of the window. The anniversary party was the next day and usually she would have spent the day having her hair done, manicures, the whole works. Somehow, though, there seemed little point. She had expected Ellis to change when he retired, pay her more attention, but somehow he seemed to be clinging on to his past, still using music to validate himself, leaving her in a state of constant discontentment. At that moment the phone rang; she answered it.

'Philip here' the voice hard, cold. 'I've spoken to Daniel. He has been very merciful. He has been told by the High One that Tegan has repented in her heart. Tegan has permission to return.'

Hannah sighed. 'Well, thank God. Are you coming to get her?'

'Of course not' shouted Philip. 'No. She finds her own way back. She must show true repentance and then she can be a member of the Community again.'

'Well do you want her mobile number then?'

Silence, then 'No. You are to speak to Tegan, and tell her that if she repents she can return.'

'You want me to do that?'

'Yes.'

Hannah smiled. She could hear that he hated asking her to do something for him. 'Well, alright, I'll try. I'll talk to her. If I don't get anywhere, though, it's back to you.'

'Good. Yes, that is, good, and well, um, thank you.'

Hannah sat down, thinking. So Tegan could return. Although she was pleased, she would rather not be the one to be telling Tegan. Ellis and Cerys would think she was pushing Tegan away, and she could do without their disapproval. Still, someone had to face the reality, and the truth was that Tegan did not fit here and everyone, including Tegan herself, would be a lot better off if she returned to the Community.

Late afternoon the next day, Tegan was knitting. She had been quiet all day but fortunately Cerys didn't appear to notice and was busy on her laptop. However, Cerys suddenly looked up. 'Fancy coming to see the well?'

'The well?'

'Our Holy Well. Come on, it hasn't snowed for a few hours. In fact there's a bit of a thaw. I love it down there.' She held the pendant on her necklace. 'You know my Nanna gave me this pendant once when we were down there.'

'Sam mentioned the well, said I should go with you to see it.'

'Right, well come on then. It's special. It'll be lovely on a day like this.'

Tegan could see how much it meant to Cerys. 'OK then, but not too long.'

They put coats and wellingtons on. Cerys led Tegan and Dylan across the snow. Cerys made snowballs for Dylan which he played chasing. Tegan enjoyed herself and they kicked the snow and laughed.

'I used to make all sorts of things in the snow. Mum would come out with me and we would make snow dogs and cats, even a dragon once' said Cerys.

'Your Mum did that?'

'Yes. Honestly, sometimes she was really good fun. Dad being away so much meant we did a lot together. When I was young I let her dress me how she wanted. It was only in my teens we fell out over all that. Still, it was good fun when I was little.'

They reached the edge of the woods. Tegan looked up at the towering beech and oak trees. It was like entering an ice cathedral. The long trunks like stone pillars, the only sound the snow occasionally falling in clumps off the branches. They walked through the trees carefully as the snow was deceptively deep in places. Eventually they arrived at a clearing with what appeared to be a small frozen pool of water surrounded by flat stones.

'This is our Holy Well.'

Tegan was surprised. It didn't look anything like a well. Cerys smiled. 'It's more a spring, I suppose.'

'But what are they?' Tegan pointed to a collection of stone statues around the edge.

Cerys carefully brushed the snow off one of the statues. 'This one is of the Madonna. It's the oldest.'

'Did people come to worship her here then?'

'Not exactly. You see, people have always come to wells for healing. They were seen as an entrance to another world and the water could be used to heal or curse. When Christianity came, the leaders tried to stop people coming, but then they gave up and instead adopted them. Maybe someone was healed here and put the statue here in thanks to Mary.'

Tegan was nervous. 'You mean thing like spirits and demons are here?'

'No. Not spooky stuff.'

Cerys wiped the snow off another heavy stone statue. This was of a woman sitting breast-feeding twins. Tegan thought it rather shocking.

173

'Nanna put this one here. It's the star and moon goddess, Arianrhod. You know, the one I showed you in the poster. People believe the dead are carried on her oar wheel to Emania, the Moonland, or land of death. The moon, you see, is the archetypal female symbol, representing the Mother Goddess, connecting womb, death, rebirth, creation.'

Tegan felt very uncomfortable. 'So these statues don't frighten you?'

Cerys frowned. 'No, I said to you before, Tegan. I see it as part of our Celtic heritage.'

'But you said that the crystal, it had caused you problems.'

'Ah, what happened was, I left home and I started to collect crystals, got really superstitious about them, and wouldn't let anyone touch them, carried them to bring me luck, put them in special places. From the same shop then I bought angel cards, then tarot. I was getting very obsessed with it all. Some of it comforted me but a lot of it actually frightened me. I kept thinking bad things would happen if I put things in the wrong place, if I forgot to look at the cards.'

'So what changed?'

'Mum came round. She moved some of the stones. I went ballistic, started shouting, crying, saying she had ruined my life. She was so shocked. I was the sensible down to earth one. I actually went to a therapist and talked. Instead of taking responsibility for my own life I had become dependent on all these external things. It was driving me crazy. I went home and got rid of them all. Apart from, of course, the crystal from Nanna. That was different. It was such a relief, not to be frightened and worried all the time.'

Tegan was shocked that someone as practical and down to earth as Cerys had ever been so caught up in all those things. Cerys pointed to the statues. 'These things are only stone statues. I don't worship them or anything. This place is my link with my Nanna. It's very special to me.'

Tegan spotted the owl. 'Why's that statue there?'

'Oh, it's one of the older ones. My Nanna put it here as well.'

'It looks like a piece of jewellery I have in my box. Is the owl significant?'

'Well, Nanna told me that Arianhod, can shape-shift into an owl.'

'What does that mean?'

'Well she changes form. She is meant to see through the owl eyes into the darkness of the human subconscious and soul.'

'That sounds rather creepy, but for some reason I find it comforting.'

'I don't think it's meant to be creepy. It's said she can fly through the night and her wings of healing spread to give comfort to people who seek her.'

'I suppose that sounds better.' Tegan looked at the bushes near the well, and realised that what she had thought was snow was pieces of frozen wool tied onto twigs. 'What are those?'

Cerys blushed. 'I'll explain it one day. You do like it here don't you?'

'Yes, of course.' She spoke quietly, but the sun had gone in, the white branches seemed to reach out to get her, the sky behind them grey and threatening.

'I'm getting cold now-' said Tegan.

'I'd like to stay for a bit.'

'Why don't I take Dylan to the cottage?'

'OK, thanks.'

Tegan walked quickly through the woods and headed straight back for the cottage, around the woods. As she approached she saw Hannah waiting in her car.

'Hello. Sorry, I think Cerys is still in the woods.'

'No, that's fine. It's you I want to see. I have something important to tell you.'

Chapter Twenty Two

'You've made it very cosy,' said Hannah, as she entered the cottage with Tegan.

'Coffee?' asked Tegan.

'No thanks.' Hannah sat on the sofa. Dylan went over and rested his head on her lap. Hannah pushed the muddy head away. Tegan stood wondering what to do.

'Now sit down, Tegan. There is something I need to talk to you about.'

Tegan sat in a chair, watching Hannah sitting on the edge of the sofa nervously.

'The thing is, Tegan, it's been lovely having you here,' Hannah began.

'Thank you. It's very kind of you.'

'It's been good for Cerys to get to know her cousin.'

'She's been very helpful' Tegan replied, waiting as the unspoken 'but' hung in the air.

'Good,' said Hannah awkwardly. 'The thing is, yesterday I had a phone call from your father.'

'Philip? What's wrong?' Tegan asked, alarmed.

'Nothing's wrong. In fact, it is good news. Apparently your leader Daniel has said you can go back.'

Tegan was stunned. 'Go back? That doesn't make any sense. He's the one who said that was impossible.'

'Well, I think he said he knows you want to repent or something. Does that sound right?'

'It sounds incredible. I thought I would never be allowed back in the Community, never be able to see my family ever again.' Tegan felt tears welling up.

'It's good, isn't it? It's your home,' said Hannah earnestly.

Tegan looked around the cottage, remembered the cold bleak house. 'Yes, of course.'

'You will be pleased to see your mother?'

'Yes, of course.'

Hannah put her head to one side. 'Do you like it out here?'

'In some ways, the cottage is cosy. I can read, go for walks, but then there is so much I don't know about and so much I know to be wrong. I've tried to compromise but it is very difficult to live in the way the Community expects out here.'

Hannah seemed to relax, and then looked at her curiously. 'Were you happy in the Community?'

'Happy?' said Tegan. It was a strange notion. 'It was simpler in some ways. Daniel, our leader, he always told us what to do, how to think. It was easier really.'

Tegan stood up and looked out of the window. 'I'll miss all this, the wildness, the freedom, though. You know, just to be able to go out in this. I'll miss it.'

'I think you appreciate it here more than I do,' said Hannah, 'but then me, maybe I'm the sort doomed never to be content. But you, well at least in the Community you have somewhere you fit in, belong. You'll get such a welcome, won't you? They will all be pleased to see you.'

Tegan grimaced. 'It won't be quite like that. No, I have sinned and there will be a price for that, I'm sure. It might be that I am never treated quite the same again.'

'But it's got to be better than sitting in pubs feeling an outsider?' persisted Hannah.

Tegan swallowed hard. 'I know I look different-'

'But it's not just appearance, is it? Look, Tegan, let's be honest. You have had a very strange life, and, well, you're not what most people consider as normal, are you?'

Tegan swallowed hard. 'Pardon?'

'I'm sorry, but I think you ought to face facts. You don't belong here, do you?'

'I've been trying.'

Hannah gave her a hard smile. 'I know, but it's not working is it? I'm sure your mother is missing you.'

'Do you think so?'

'Of course, it's only natural. I mean, even my sister must have some maternal feelings. And Philip, your father, of course, you must miss him. By the way, why do you always call him Philip?'

'He just always wanted that. I suppose he must love me, mustn't he? I mean, he is my father but, I don't know, he's not too good at showing it, that's all.'

Tegan went and sat back down, her mind rushing. Somehow returning had seemed so impossible that she had been scared to contemplate it. But to think she would see her mother, and her friends, Esther, little Elizabeth, the garden: it would be good to see them all again. And just think, no one would be trying to change her. She would look like everyone else again. There would be a cost, though. Nothing was free in the Community. Hannah could have no idea the depths of humiliation, the long periods of ridicule and isolation that probably awaited her.

Hannah stood up. 'Well, I'm pleased to be able to bring such wonderful news. I've brought you Philip's mobile number. I'm sure he's dying to hear from you.'

Tegan found her own phone and Hannah put Philip's number on for her. Then she watched as Hannah smiled and stood up.

'Oh, can you afford the fare? I mean, did you get a return ticket?' asked Hannah.

Tegan blinked. She was trying to remember. It seemed such a long time ago. 'Hang on, I'll go and find it.' She went upstairs, found the ticket, ran back down, and handed it to Hannah.

'Well that's lucky. It hasn't run out. I guess Saturday will be as good a day as any. Come to the party on Friday, good way to say good bye to everyone.'

Tegan nodded. It seemed so soon, so definite.

Hannah opened her bag. She handed Tegan money. 'Here, use it on the journey. You know, for taxis and things.'

'Oh, thank you.'

As she left, Hannah said brightly, 'Now don't forget, you must come to the party tomorrow. Promise?'

Tegan nodded, and then watched Hannah leave. So she was going back, back to the Community where she belonged. Hannah's words "not normal" echoed in her head. That really was how everyone saw her. Cerys had told Robert she was odd, and look how she'd been in church. Tears fell silently down her cheeks. She had tried, she really had. Gone to the theatre, the pub, but she was fooling no one. People were just being kind, felt sorry for her. That was all.

She looked around at the cottage. It was sad; she liked it in here. Compared to her cold cell at the Community, this was like a warm nest. Her warm bedroom with soft duvet, thick rugs, and the hot shower.

She stopped; how materialistic she had become. These things, her comfort, had become more important than her mother, than following the truth. All her proud boasting that she could keep pure out here, well, it was rubbish. Here she was reading worldly books, going to the pub, talking to heathen men. And she was becoming so vain, all this talk of her singing, compliments on her knitting, even the temptation of having her hair done, so wrong. She must realise she was worthless, proud. She must humble herself and be guided once more by Daniel and the elders. No more doubts. She was becoming like the world. She would be judged dammed for ever with them. She had to go back, be safe, saved with the elect. In the Community she knew where she was, and she had people who talked and dressed like her. Daniel, well, to think he was prepared to forgive her; to be approved by him again would be wonderful. She could learn to live with the teachings again. She just needed to get her mind sorted out and put away the doubts. She took a piece of paper and wrote again "doing vigil, do not disturb" and went upstairs.

While Tegan was still at vigil that evening Sam was taking Angharad to a pub in the next village. Angharad peered out of the car window. 'God, this place. Look, nothing, and it's so cold. Mum's hotel is covered in lights at night. It looks so beautiful at night. All the cafés in the town with fairy lights, it's like magic.'

'I'm glad you bothered to come back then' Sam said crossly.

'That isn't the only reason I've come back; you know that' she said laughing, putting her hand on his knee. 'So, tell me, how is work?'

'Busy. I told you, in this weather everything takes twice as long.'

'You know, there are ways you could earn so much more.'

'What do you mean?'

'I was reading online that in America you can earn a fortune doing plastic surgery on pets. You know, nose jobs and things.'

'You are joking. That's obscene. In any case, why should I want to go to America?'

'It could be a good life out there. You know, Wynn was telling me about living in New York. It sounds wonderful.'

'Wynn?'

'Oh, he sent me pictures of the flat. It looks fantastic.'

Sam shook his head. 'I would never leave here. You do know that, don't you? Do you really hate it around here?'

'Of course not' she laughed. 'As along as I am with you, it's all I ask for.' He drove into the car park.

As they entered the pub, Sam noticed the appreciative looks glancing Anaghard's way. The pub was very busy but the barman came over and found them a table quickly. Sam watched Angharad smile sweetly but seductively at the barman. It was all the reward the man needed. 'What charmed lives beautiful people lead' Sam thought. They ordered food.

'We need to talk,' he started.

'Not yet. Please, not so serious. Come on, I've got all the news of France first.'

She told stories, light, entertaining. Sam found himself laughing, and slowly they started to swap anecdotes. The food was excellent. Moules Marinières followed by Salt Marsh Lamb. A gentle Welsh jazz trio played. It was very relaxing and romantic. Sam had forgotten how much fun he had with Angharad. They chatted about choir and then Angharad started to ask about Tegan.

'She really is odd, isn't she?'

'She has some problems but, you know, you shouldn't have said that about the cult and things.'

'It's only what James told me.'

'James knows nothing about her.'

'Well, you know how word gets round. His mother had told him things. He passed them on to me.'

'You seem to have spent your time in France emailing the village. I hope you did some work.'

'Of course.' She leant forward, and stroked his cheek.

He caught a whiff of expensive perfume.

'It's wonderful to see you: you have no idea how much I've missed you.'

He took a deep breath. 'Look, about the wedding-'

She leant forward, her head to one side. Sam looked at the seductive expression in those beautiful blue eyes. She really was lovely.

'I know it's all a bit sudden. I'm sorry. I swept you off your feet rather, didn't I?'

'It's not just that.'

'But Sam, if I wait for you to decide things it would take for ever. I finish my degree this summer. The timing is perfect. We can start off living in my flat, and then move on to buying our first home. I know Dad will help. It will be so exciting.'

'What about Bracken?'

'You know he can't live with us, but Amy will be fine with him I'm sure.'

He sighed, looked down.

181

Angharad sat back, pouted prettily. 'Really, Sam you make it all sound such an effort. We'll be married in less than six months.'

'I know, your Dad is going to be spending a fortune.'

'Of course, you didn't think he'd scrimp on my wedding did you?'

'No, but this is crazy.'

'For God's sake, Sam. Would you marry me in some town hall registry office with half a dozen guests?'

'Sounds ideal to me.'

Angharad put her hand on his. 'I know how shy you are, but this is the most important day of our lives, a start of a new life together. Who knows what the future may hold for us?'

'Not doing nose jobs on dogs for sure,' he said.

'OK, let's not argue.'

'The thing is, Angharad, I know it's awkward but I don't think I'm ready for all this. I mean, we hardly know each other that well, do we?'

'What's happened to you while I was in France? You seemed keen enough when I went off.'

'Nothing. I just don't want to rush things.'

'Is it this girl Tegan? I saw the way you looked at each other last night. What's been going on there?'

'Nothing.'

'Thought you'd started to fancy freaks or something?'

'She's not a freak. She's bright, interested in nature. She's read up all about the hills. She loves it here.'

Angharad sat back. 'So you do fancy her. Who'd have thought it?' Her face hardened. 'Now, listen to me. There is no way I am calling off this wedding for some ridiculous whim of yours. She's just a novelty but you don't see it. You and I are getting married this summer. We're too far along to change direction now.'

'But we've only been engaged a day, for God's sake.'

She sat forward, looked down, her voice very soft, breaking, 'Sam, I can't live without you, you know that. If you were to break up with me, I think I would kill myself.'

'That's rubbish-'

She looked up intently. 'It's not rubbish. I mean it, Sam. You break up with me and you'll see how serious I am and then how will you live with yourself? Live among your precious hills?'

He sat back and took a deep breath. 'You can't mean that, Angharad. Really, you can't possibly feel that much for me.'

'But I do. I promise you're the man I have been looking for all my life. No one else will ever do.'

He scratched the back of his neck, shook his head. 'It's not right, is it? We need time.'

Angharad sat upright, her expression harder. 'Dad has put down the deposit. It's all arranged.' She sat back. The tone of her voice changed; she sounded firmer, older, almost threatening. 'I will not have his heart broken, and you know the promises he has made to your father. He may have to break those if he knew the things I know.'

'You wouldn't say anything would you?' said Sam, shocked.

'Look, we keep secrets. That's what you do in relationships, but once they have ended, well, there's no reason to do it any more, is there?'

Sam shook his head. 'Angharad, what is going on? You seem desperate. All I'm asking is for more time to get to know each other.'

Angharad shook her head. She looked very serious. He dreaded her hurting herself over him, and what about his family? He looked at the beautiful girl sitting in front of him. What was wrong with him? She was gorgeous, funny, clever, sexy: he must be mad. He put out his hand decisively, squeezed her hand. 'OK, let's get out of here.'

She grinned. 'Good, come on. Let's go home and I'll show you why we got together in the first place.'

Sam shook his head. 'No. No, I'm sorry. I have to go to the centre.'

Angharad smiled softly. 'That's alright. I know how much your work means to you. Another time soon, eh?'

They left the pub. Sam took her back to the Red Dragon and drove to work.

It was late into the evening. Tegan had heard Cerys coming and going and finally going to bed. She needed a drink, so she crept quietly downstairs. To her surprise, she found Cerys sitting reading.

'Hiya' said Cerys. 'I couldn't sleep, thought I'd come down and read for a bit. You alright? I saw the note about the vigil.'

'I just need a drink' replied Tegan. She looked at Cerys and decided she must tell her.

'By the way' she said, trying to sound casual, 'I'm going back to the Community on Saturday.'

'What?' exclaimed Cerys. 'How come? I didn't think you were allowed to go back?'

'Well, your Mum came to see me. She spoke to Philip. Daniel has said that if I repent I can go back.'

'Hang on, they say now you can just go back like nothing's happened?'

'I'll have to show I've repented-'

'And are you sorry? Do you regret going to the library, reading, meeting that chap Steve?'

'I think so. That's why I'm doing vigil. I must prepare my heart to return.'

Cerys sighed. 'But Saturday is so soon.'

Cerys scratched her chin and then started to play with her necklace 'The thing is, Tegan. I don't want you to go. It's really nice having you here.'

Tegan blinked, surprised. 'But I've been such a nuisance.'

'It's been different, I'll admit, but, you know, sitting at the well, I felt very relaxed. I can talk to you. I'll miss you if you go.'

'But you have so many friends,' said Tegan.

'Not really. Most people think I'm a bit odd to be honest.'

Tegan tried to smile. 'That's my role, isn't it?'

Cerys sighed. 'Anyway, it's up to you, and I can understand you must miss your family.'

'I do. It's my home, where I belong.'

'It's the party tomorrow. You'll still come, won't you?'

'Yes. I promised your Mum I'd go.'

Tegan got her drink and then returned to her room. She knelt beside her bed, tried to do her the vigil. It was such hard work. Her mind kept drifting off: the mountains, the wind, the snow, the kitten, Cerys, Sam, and the red kites. Then she thought about the glasses she would never get. She would never be able to see properly. And that feeling when she sang, never again. She blinked back tears, but then spoke to herself harshly. She had drifted a long way from the truth. It would not be long now. She should be back there, with the elect, safe, where she belonged.

It was two in the morning. Her head was nodding forward when she suddenly remembered there was something that had to be done. Stiffly, she stood up went and found it. She would do it. It had to be finished.

Chapter Twenty Three

It was dawn when Tegan staggered downstairs. Dylan ran, excited to have company so early. She let him out of the front door, made strong coffee, let him back in, and went back upstairs. Finally, she went down again and was sitting nibbling toast when Cerys came down. Busying herself making up the fire, Cerys asked 'You OK? You look done in.'

'Fasting and vigil are good for me.'

'Really? You look knackered. Anyway, Dad said the party is on.'

'Your parents' party?'

'That's right. People should be able to get around today. Now, I promised to find you a dress didn't I?'

'Oh, please don't bother. I can wear my skirt. It's not worth it.'

'Nonsense, wait till you get there. I have to go and fetch something for myself, usual cheesecloth thing I should think. I have a dress in mind for you, though. I never did fit into it but it might do.'

Tegan realised there was no point in objecting. As long as the dress was decent she would wear it.

'I'm off to Robert's now. Don't forget about going to Rhiannon's this afternoon.'

Tegan groaned. 'I can't go, Cerys. I really can't.'

'But you said you would. Go on. What are you worried about?'

'Well, it's so vain.'

'Rhiannon will be really hurt. Please go.'

'But there's no point. I'll be back at the Community tomorrow.'

'I know, but Rhiannon is expecting you. You said you would go.'

Tegan sighed. At least all this would be over soon. 'Alright, I'll go, but it's a waste of time.'

'Good. I don't see why I should be the only one making an effort tonight. Right, I'll take Dylan up with me now. He can stay up at the manor then.'

Up at the manor Hannah was clearing tables for the caterers, throwing together piles of sheet music, throwing them in a heap. Ellis' first words in bed that morning, the morning of their wedding anniversary, had been 'Cerys rang me and told me you went to see Tegan.'

'So?'

'Cerys said she seemed upset.'

'Oh, really? I was just checking she was coming to the party.'

'And the rest. I hear she's talking of going back tomorrow' he said angrily.

Hannah had got out of bed and put on her dressing gown.

'Listen, I didn't tell you, but Philip rang me again. Tegan can go back. It's better for her there.'

'But we can help her, look after her.'

'No, Ellis. It's too much. She can't cope.'

'But she's going out more. She's been to the pub a few times now.'

'Ellis, it was agony for her there. She needs to go home.'

'But this could be her home. Cerys was telling me why she was thrown out. She's been taught some pretty awful things, not allowed to sing. I don't want her to go back there.'

'I'm sorry for what's happened to her, but the bottom line is that she can't cope out here. She has to go back. Now, leave it, Ellis. No more arguing today. Fine start to our anniversary this is.'

She saw him sigh, irritated, but he responded, 'OK, no more arguing today. I promise, but I shall talk to Tegan tonight.'

187

With that he had left the room. Not even a 'Happy Anniversary', no card, no flowers, nothing. Hannah sighed as she picked up yet another pile of music. She glanced over at her wedding photograph. Still sometimes they would laugh at the same thing, catch each other's eye, realise the spark was there. But she seldom felt really loved, cherished. It hurt but he didn't care enough to see it.

After lunch Tegan reluctantly made her way to the hairdressers'. She found "SIAN'S" and peeped through the window. It seemed very smart and sophisticated to Tegan. She pushed open the door. Rhiannon tottered over to Tegan in very high stilettos. Tegan wondered how she could stand in them all day. She greeted Tegan with a big smile. 'Welcome, come on in.'

There seemed to be mirrors everywhere. Rhiannon took her coat, put an enormous black cape around her shoulders and took her to a large black leather seat. Tegan felt very uncomfortable.

'Right, can you take your headscarf off?'

Tegan took a deep breath, and with shaking hands she began to untie the knot at the nape of her neck. She put the headscarf on the shelf in front of her next to tall exotic bottles of hair products. It seemed to glare at her accusingly.

Rhiannon smiled. 'Well done. Wow. Just look at this.'

Rhiannon touched her hair. Tegan shivered. It was very intimate. Rhiannon began brushing her hair in a business-like manner. Her hair seemed to expand. It fell in a mass of thick black waves down her back. She glanced in the mirror, then down.

'Right. Let's get you washed and we'll use a really good conditioner.' Tegan had to move to another seat, this time with her back to a basin.

'Would you like to take your glasses off?'

Tegan felt she should, but felt very vulnerable without them. It hurt, straining her neck back and she panicked when she first felt the water on her head.

'Is that OK?' Rhiannon carried on. Tegan was actually very uncomfortable, but she didn't say anything. The pressure of Rhiannon's finger tips massaging her scalp didn't exactly hurt but it felt awkward. She had a feeling it wasn't right. Rhiannon used a lot of conditioner. It smelt of flowers and almonds.

'Right, we'll leave that on for a bit. Here, have some magazines.'

Tegan fumbled for her glasses and looked at a magazine. She looked at endless pictures of people she had never heard of. Apparently they were too fat or too thin, possibly pregnant, possibly getting together or breaking up with someone else she had never heard of. Eventually, Rhiannon returned. Tegan took off her glasses and Rhiannon washed out the conditioner. Tegan went back to her seat. More brushing.

'Now, I'd like to style this around your face a bit and tidy up the ends. Would that be alright?'

Tegan nodded. She felt powerless, sat without her glasses in this strange place. She stared at her lap.

'You should use a good conditioner. This hair could be really something. You should think of getting contacts. You look lovely without your glasses. Go and see Grace, she'll sort you out. I guess you've had those glasses a long time?'

Tegan cringed. At least none of this would matter tomorrow. She peered at some photographs propped up on the shelf in front of her. Rhiannon smiled. 'That's one of Dad's pictures of Rhys' party.'

'It was lovely.'

'Thanks. Rhys had a great time and that's all that matters.'

Rhiannon went back to styling Tegan's hair. Finally, she applied sticky stuff to her hair and started to dry it. The heat was shocking. Her head was getting hotter and hotter. She thought of hell, flames. She closed her eyes and pulled her head away.

'You alright?'

Tegan opened her eyes. Everything looked so normal. 'Fine.' She dug her nails into the palms of her hands. Rhiannon started again. Tegan sat rigid, waiting for the agony to finish.

'Come on. Look at yourself.' She gently lifted Tegan's head.

Tegan peered, and then put on her glasses. She was shocked. That wasn't her. All that hair shouting for attention. It looked so different. She leant forward and picked up the black headscarf from the shelf.

'Stop!'

'But you said I could.'

'I know, but I never dreamt it would be so lovely. Please don't cover it up, not yet.'

'I'm sorry, but I will have to put this back on.' Tegan picked up her headscarf and started to tie it on.

'Thank you very much' she said to Rhiannon, who hated the way she looked so upset. 'How much do I owe you?'

Rhiannon smiled. 'Nothing.'

'Oh but -'

'No, really, at least you know now how beautiful your hair can look.'

Tegan felt awful and was glad to leave. It was strange walking down the street knowing that under the scarf her hair looked so different. She glanced in a shop window, and then stopped. How vain she was becoming. She blinked back tears and, casting her eyes to the ground, walked quickly home.

Tegan was glad to get back to the cottage and sat knitting. Later, Cerys came back wearing a long sleeveless dark blue cheesecloth dress.

'That's pretty.'

'Well thanks. Mum will groan. She hates it.'

'I can't think why.'

'She wants me to be more glamorous.'

Tegan ran upstairs. Now was the perfect time. She came straight back down.

'It's, lush, it's so beautiful.' Cerys' eyes were wet with tears.

Tegan blushed. Cerys' gratitude was overwhelming. The shawl Tegan had knitted was a fine spider's web of blues and greens.

Cerys gasped. She held it up. 'It's perfect.' She wrapped it carefully around her shoulders.

Tegan blinked fast.

'When on earth did you finish it?'

Tegan smiled shyly. 'Five o clock this morning. I wanted to give it to you, to say, um, thank you.'

Cerys turned and gave her a hug. 'Well thank you. It's wonderful. I shall wear it tonight. So, how did it go with Rhiannon?'

'I think she was disappointed that I covered my hair up again. She spent a lot of time doing it.'

'Can I have a look?'

Tegan glanced around guiltily, and then took off her headscarf.

'Wow, what gorgeous hair. Do you really have to cover it up?'

Tegan nodded.

'Shame. Well here's a dress. Hope you like it.'

Tegan took the carrier bag containing a rather crumpled dress upstairs. It was a red silk shift dress, very plain, with some decoration around the neck line and short sleeves. She tried it on. It was tighter than she would normally wear but at least it covered her body and it felt very soft and luxurious.

'Can I come and see?' shouted Cerys bursting into the room.

'Wow, that looks really good. It's posh, you know, designer, but I've never worn it, could never get it over my hips. Look at yourself over there.'

Tegan nervously walked over to the mirror. She wouldn't have recognised herself.

'You look lovely.'

Tegan blinked, embarrassed. 'It's OK?'

'Of course. I think even Mum will be impressed. I brought you some flat black shoes. I hope they fit.'

191

'Thanks. So is Robert coming tonight?'

'Oh, I forgot to tell you he's giving us a lift. Now, before we go I want to sort through some photos. I thought I'd make up a kind of montage.'

They went down together and Cerys spilled the photos on to the table. 'We need to find a selection, you know, starting with their wedding. Here, that's a good wedding photo.'

Tegan picked up the picture. Hannah was wearing a long white one-shoulder Greek-style dress.

'Apparently that was by some designer called Halston, popular in the seventies. Even then Mum wanted the best. Dad looks funny, though.'

Tegan looked at a confident young man, black hair curling over the collar of his white suit, grinning at the camera. 'They make quite a couple.'

'I think they were, you know, very fashionable. I suppose your parents must have got married about the same time. Did they look like this?'

'We don't have any photographs.'

'Oh, right.' Cerys sounded bemused. 'Look, here are the two bridesmaids. Of course the older one must be your Mum.'

Tegan looked at a self-conscious young woman with beautiful long blonde hair, wearing a long plain dark silk green dress, clutching a small bouquet of white roses. 'I don't think that can be her-'

'It must be. I mean, she wasn't the flower girl-'

Tegan looked closely. 'I suppose it could be her. Yes, I can see it now. I've never seen her in a dress, make up-'

'Surely to go out?'

'No. No, we don't dress up, go out, never.'

'Well, anyway, take a copy. There's loads here.'

Tegan peered at some more. 'Where's Philip then? ... Hang on, this is him.'

He was sitting next to Sarah, stiff, upright, in a dark grey suit, unsmiling, same round glasses. It was frightening how little he had changed.

'He looked an old man even then' said Tegan.

'You don't seem very fond of your Dad' said Cerys.

'We just don't have much in common.'

They found lots of pictures, some including Cerys.

'I was such a chubby child' laughed Cerys. 'Look at me covered in chocolate in my high chair, bet Dad took that one. Ah, here's one Mum would like.'

Tegan smiled at the immaculate child in flowered dress and matching bows in her hair. She stood beside an enormous cake with six candles. Tegan stared. It wasn't fair. Why hadn't she had parties, pretty clothes, and people making a fuss of her?

'When's your birthday?' asked Cerys.

Tegan blushed. 'I'm not sure-` she said quietly.

Cerys took a deep breath. 'You must know.'

'Not really.'

'Well, maybe, you know, when you go back you could ask. You have a right to know when you were born.'

'I suppose so. Anyway, what does it matter?'

They heard the sound of a horn outside

'Ah, Robert' said Cerys. She blushed with excitement.

Tegan looked out at a muddy Land Rover.

'Sorry, not exactly a limousine' laughed Cerys. Tegan had never seen her so happy. They picked up their things and went out into the darkness. Tegan clambered awkwardly into the back seat of the Land Rover. She smiled shyly at Robert. He was huge, not fat, but he seemed too big for the car. His hands dwarfed the wheel; his feet covered the pedals. Then Cerys jumped in. Tegan watched as he smiled at Cerys like she was a rare jewel. They didn't seem to need to speak. Tegan fumbled for her seat belt. They drove off into the darkness, and then, all too soon, they arrived at the manor.

Chapter Twenty Four

Tegan was aware that the old Land Rover stood out from the rows of smart cars at the manor but Cerys and Robert seemed oblivious. As they walked up the gravel path Cerys pointed out the plants and shrubs in the garden. When they entered the house, Tegan noticed people putting presents on a side table.

'I didn't bring a present. I'm sorry, I didn't think-' she said to Cerys.

'Don't worry. Right, let's put this thing up.' Cerys took the card with the photographs on and propped it behind the presents.

Ellis came over to them. 'Evening. Don't you two look lovely?'

'Thanks Dad' laughed Cerys.

'Tegan, I got a text. Your glasses are ready for collection.'

'Oh, sorry, but I won't be able to get them. I'm going back tomorrow.'

'Now, none of this nonsense. You can't go back there.'

'I am allowed to, and I want to.'

'Really?'

'Yes. Honestly. Thank you for letting me stay, but I have to go back.'

Ellis sighed. 'Well, shall I post the glasses to you?'

Tegan shook her head. 'Oh no. Please don't. I should never have gone.'

She was surprised at how upset Ellis was becoming. Was it because of the glasses?

'I'm so sorry to have wasted your money' she added quickly.

'The money doesn't matter,' he said, ' but it seems so sad that you are going, just when we were all getting to know you.'

Suddenly he put his hands on her shoulders and then kissed her on the cheek. 'Take care then, you know where we are now.' To her horror she saw that he was blinking back tears. He coughed and walked sadly away.

Tegan looked around the room. Most of the women were far more glamorous. She saw Rhiannon wearing a miniscule green dress, her fabulous hair studded with tiny stars. There were a number of extremely little black dresses, and some very long clingy evening gowns. Tegan was surprised at how immodestly so many of the women dressed.

Robert hung back. Cerys put her hand in his.

'Come on, let's find something to eat,' said Cerys.

A fair haired young man staggered over, large glass of beer in hand. 'Who's this gorgeous female Cerys?'

'Just piss off Bryn.'

He shrugged and walked away. Tegan noticed Rhiannon grabbing another glass of champagne. Then Hannah appeared. She was wearing a very understated but beautiful long green dress. She looked startled when she saw Tegan.

'Well I never, you're wearing that dress.' She inspected her more carefully. 'It's much too big of course but you almost get away with it. Good figure under there. If you got rid of that hideous headscarf, wore decent shoes, yes, you could look something. You've more class than most in this room.'

'Wow, high praise' said Cerys, laughing.

Hannah turned scowling to Cerys, and then her expression changed. 'Hey, where did you get that shawl?'

'Tegan made it for me' said Cerys.

'Really?' Hannah looked at Tegan in amazement. 'You made this?'

'We made things like it in the Community.'

'Well you have a real talent there,' said Hannah appreciatively.

195

'I've put up some photos up on the hall table Mum' said Cerys.

'Oh thanks. Not that I suppose your father will notice. Tegan, have you phoned your Dad yet?'

'Not yet-' said Tegan.

'I'll send him a text. Tell him you'll be there late afternoon?'

Cerys scowled at her mother. 'I don't see why Tegan has to go back at all.'

'Tegan knows it is for the best. Right, I must circulate. I don't suppose your father is looking after anyone. Oh, good evening Robert,' she added stiffly.

Robert grinned down and simply nodded. Hannah seemed at a loss as to how to handle him so she simply walked away.

'You must be the only person I know who is not in awe of Mum. It's great,' said Cerys proudly.

'She's alright. Not that happy, I guess' said Robert.

Amy came over in a long black lace dress with long black evening gloves and bright red lipstick, her tattoos slightly incongruous.

'Hiya' said Cerys.

'Robert, I'm impressed. Don't usually get you socialising,' said Amy.

Robert smiled. Amy grinned at Cerys. 'See you've resurrected 'the dress'.'

'I like to think of it as a timeless classic' Cerys joked.

'That's a lovely shawl, though. Looks like something my Mum would sell.'

'Tegan made it, didn't you?'

'Any news on the kitten?' Tegan asked anxiously.

'Not yet. Trouble is, there are a lot of kittens around at the moment. I hear you helped out at Rhys' party. You going for sainthood or something?' said Amy, laughing. Tegan didn't reply, not sure if Amy was laughing at her.

'How's work going?' Cerys asked.

'Actually, it s all very exciting. Fiona who owns the sanctuary has asked me to go and see her.'

'Why?'

'Some kind of plans for the centre. I'll find out at nine o clock tomorrow morning.'

'You're seeing her? Where?'

'Central London.'

'But how the hell will you get there in time?'

'Ah, straight after this I change into sensible clothes and drive through the night.'

'Good gracious, you'll be shattered.'

'No. I wanted to be at the centre all day. This is the best way.'

Cerys raised her eyebrows. 'You're twp, you are.'

Rachel, Amy's mother came over. She was dressed in layers of silk and velvet. 'Amy, are you definitely driving off tonight?'

'Yup.'

'I don't like you driving at that time. What if you break down or something?'

'Don't fuss Mum. I'll be fine.'

Amy put her arm around her mother and gave her a hug. 'Now, look at this shawl Mum. Tegan made it. Lovely, isn't it?'

Rachel peered at it intently. 'It looks good. You say you knitted this?' she asked Tegan.

Cerys took off the shawl. 'There you are Rachel. You can have a proper look.'

Rachel held the shawl up to the light. 'It's perfect, very good. Where did you learn to knit like this?'

'In the place I lived in London.'

'I am getting a huge demand for hand made clothes and accessories, particularly using local yarn. Would you be interested in making some things for me?'

'Oh, I'm not good enough for that' said Tegan, confused. 'In any case I'm going back to the Community tomorrow.'

197

'Oh that's disappointing' said Rachel. 'I pay good money for this sort of work.'

'Really?'

'Yes, of course. We're talking high end of the market. Now, Amy, have you seen your brother anywhere?'

'He'll be arriving with Angharad later. She'll want to make an entrance.'

Cerys turned to Tegan. 'I want to take Robert to see the garden. Will you be alright?'

'Fine' said Tegan. She turned, but Rachel and Amy had gone. Everyone seemed to be talking, drinking. Then, in the distance, she saw Angharad arriving, looking stunning in a strapless, pink lace evening dress. Behind her, Sam followed, looking scruffy but attractive in his evening suit. Tegan panicked: she couldn't speak to him, and at least tomorrow she would never have to cope with him again. Tegan spied a side door, and slipped out of the room. Opposite, she saw a door ajar and sneaked into a small room. There was a table covered in coats. It was cool and dark. She walked over to the window, tried to breathe slowly. Maybe she could hide in here all evening?

However, Tegan soon found that was not possible. Sam came in, dropped Angharad's wrap on the table, coughed, and asked 'Escaping?'

She turned as he spoke, but looked away, wishing he would just leave her alone.

'Have you got into the woods yet?' he asked.

'Mmm.'

'What did you think?'

'OK.'

'The kitten wasn't micro-chipped then? She's a nice little thing. Did you see the red kites, you know, in the woods?'

Tegan shook her head. Sam approached her, pleading. 'I'm sorry for what she said.'

She blinked and looked down. 'I wish you'd been honest, not pretended you thought I was normal.'

'Oh God, Tegan. What's normal anyway? Why do you worry so much about what people think of you? You need to have the courage to be yourself.'

'That's easy for you to say. I'm glad I'm going, getting away from here.'

'You're going?'

'Back to the Community, tomorrow.'

'But I thought-'

'Apparently if I repent I can.'

'And do you? Repent?'

'I'm sorry I ever left.'

Sam stood next to her. 'I thought you said you were pleased you'd come.'

'I was-'

'So did you get to the woods?'

'Cerys took me to see the Holy Well.'

'What did you make of it?'

'It was peaceful. Not sure about the statues, though.'

'Why?'

'Nothing. You wouldn't understand.'

'Come over here,' he said gently. He took her to the window, and pointed to a sky bursting with tiny stars. Tegan looked, and shuddered. She moved back. Sam saw her face.

'You don't need to be frightened of everything.'

'The blackness, the night-' she whispered.

'But it isn't all black. It's full of stars. "Seren" they call them in Wales. We have no street lights, not many buildings around here. I've seen meteor showers, once even the Milky Way. It's extraordinary.'

Tegan looked again. There really were thousands of stars. Suddenly, the door burst open.

'Sam, there you are.' Angharad came in smiling.

'Hiding away again. Evening, Tegan. Still got the headscarf, how sweet.'

Sam grabbed hold of Angharad's hand. 'Come on. Let's go and mix.'

Angharad looked surprised. 'Well, keen to socialise. You are improving. Right, see you later, Tegan.'

Tegan turned back, breathing hard. Her head hurt. Tears burned her eyes. She heard footsteps in the room, guessed it was someone bringing in a coat. But then she felt a hand gently on her shoulder. She turned, hoping it was Sam. However, she was surprised to see James. 'We didn't get a chance to talk much in the pub the other night.' He stood very close. 'Studying the stars?'

'Sam was telling me about them.'

'Sam? You don't want to be waiting for him. He's completely under Angharad's spell. He'll never come out of it. Whereas me-'

She felt his hand on her headscarf. He gently started to pull it back off her head. Tegan started to panic.

'I knew it. You have lovely hair. And, you know you, are very attractive. He stroked her face and then kissed her on the mouth. She pulled back but he pressed against her. She froze. 'Don't!' she cried.

'It's alright.' He kissed her again, hard and roughly on the mouth. She tried to push him away but his hands started to caress her and he pulled her tightly into his body. She tried to scream but her throat constricted. The scream could not escape. It was strangling her.

Chapter Twenty Five

Tegan became frantic. The harder she struggled against James the tighter his grip seemed to become. Her heart was racing. She was shaking.

Suddenly, the light came on. 'What the hell's going on?'

Hannah stood by the switch. 'James, I think you'd better get ready for the concert.'

James went to argue, but instead left the room. Hurriedly, with trembling hands, Tegan put her headscarf back on.

'Are you alright' asked Hannah quietly.

Tegan nodded, too upset to speak. What ever must Hannah think of her?

At this point Cerys also appeared. 'Mum have you seen...? Oh, there you are, Tegan. Are you alright?'

Tegan nodded miserably, but inside she felt terrible, soiled, and defiled.

'You look after her' said Hannah to Cerys. 'She just felt a bit unwell.'

'Fine. Come on, Dad's put on a concert. That will settle your nerves' said Cerys.

Tegan went with Cerys, who led her into a large panelled room. It had a grand piano and plush seating. The guests were slowly filtering into the room and sitting down.

Cerys said, 'I sent Robert down the front. Come on.'

Tegan sat, trying to calm herself down as the concert got under way, but it was so hard. She dug her nails into the palms of her hand. The pain started to distract her. This was the wicked world she had been warned about. Ellis stood at the front. He coughed. She looked up, aware of a subtle change of atmosphere. It was very quiet.

'And now, finally, for something very special. As many of you know, we have someone staying with us. I have discovered she has a very special voice and it is with great pleasure I am going to ask our guest Tegan to sing "Ar Hyd a Nos".'

Tegan's face was burning hot. Was this a joke? It must be.

However, Ellis looked at her eagerly. 'Come on, don't be shy. I have the words here.'

Everyone started to clap. Tegan couldn't move. Ellis went over, took both of her hands and pulled her off the seat whispering, 'It'll be fine. Come on, I'll sing with you if you like.'

'No. Please, no. I can't do it.'

He ignored her, went and sat at the piano, and started to play the introduction. She stood up and looked at the room full of people, watching her, judging her. It was all wrong. Her throat hurt. She felt dizzy. She could feel James's lips on her, smell the beer. It was all her fault, standing here dressed like a slut. She stood staring at the people and started to scratch the palm of her hand as hard as she could. She couldn't breathe. Her throat was hurting so badly. She turned to Ellis in panic. He smiled encouragingly. She shook her head violently. Suddenly, the room spun round very fast, and she fell. In an instant everything went black.

Tegan opened her eyes to find a strange woman leaning over her. 'I'm Nadia, a doctor. You fainted,' said the stranger. Tegan blinked and pushed herself up. Her head was still spinning.

'Take it easy,' Nadia said.

Tegan sat very still, aware of the sound of chairs scraping on the floor. She felt embarrassed and very sick.

Bethany came over. 'Is she alright?'

'Yes, just fainted' explained Nadia.

'I'll take her to a seat' said Bethany. Tegan walked slowly, holding on to Bethany's arm. She was breathing deeply.

All she could think was that she mustn't be sick. Cerys brought her a glass of water, and she sipped it slowly. Gradually, the nausea subsided.

Ellis came over to her. 'I'm sorry. I thought it would make her want to stay, you know, if it had gone well-'

Bethany interrupted. 'Ellis, I think Tegan needs to recover. Talk again with her tomorrow. I'll take her back to the cottage now.'

Tegan looked over at the people leaving. Her head was clearing. 'Actually, I don't want a lift thank you. I need to talk to Amy.'

'Tegan, you need to go home' said Cerys, concerned.

'I need to talk to Amy' repeated Tegan firmly.

'OK. Well, I'm just going to find Robert. You sure you're alright for a minute?' asked Cerys.

'Of course' replied Tegan. Cerys left her and Tegan walked over to Amy.

'What time are you leaving, going to London?' she asked Amy urgently.

'I'm planning to go now. My stuff is in the car.'

'Can you take me, give me a lift?'

Amy blinked. 'I suppose so. Are you well enough to travel?'

'I'm fine. Please, I was going to London tomorrow anyway, but I need to go right now.'

'Your decision, but you'll need to get your things, won't you?'

'Yes, but I can be really quick.'

Amy smiled. 'Fine, I've already said goodbye to Rhiannon, so we might as well just go. I think things have pretty much wrapped up here.'

They found Amy's car, a small tatty red Volkswagen Beetle, and drove straight to the cottage. Amy said she would wait in the car.

Tegan ran into the cottage and up the stairs. She pulled out her case, took off the red dress, hung it carefully on a hanger and put on her own skirt, blouse and cardigan. Carefully, she packed all her things. She left the boots, jeans and jumper that Cerys had given her. Then she thought about the coat. Maybe in the Community they would let her wear it for gardening. It was so warm, and she knew Cerys didn't want it any more. She packed it carefully, and then looked at the mobile phone. Should she leave it? She needed to phone Philip: better take it with her. She put the picture of her mother as a bridesmaid in her pocket and then ran down the stairs. She glanced at the bookshelves. She felt a momentary pang of loss. In this room she had had a freedom, a comfort she had never known. But the price had been high, too high. Her old coat felt cold and thin as she put it on. Then she left the cottage, pulled the door firmly behind her and walked towards the car.

As she got in, Amy smiled at her. 'OK, got everything? Does Cerys know you're going?'

'I'll send her a message.' As she sent the text she felt guilty. It was not the way she had wanted to say goodbye to Cerys. Then she phoned Philip.

'Philip speaking.' Her heart sank.

'It's Tegan. Please can I speak to Mum?'

'Why?'

'I'm coming back.'

'Tonight? You are ready to repent?'

Tegan took a deep breath. 'Of course. Can I speak to Mum now?'

'Alright. I must go and inform Daniel.'

Her mother came on at the other end.

'Are you truly repentant Tegan?' asked Sarah.

'I really am. I was very wrong to rebel. The world is a wicked place.'

'How will you get here?'

'I have a lift.'

'Who with?'

'Amy, a girl from the village.'

'It's very late to be travelling. You know there is always a price to pay for disobedience? You understand that?'

'Of course.'

'Good. We will see you in the morning.'

Sarah lay back in bed, exhausted. It had been a difficult few days. No food, the isolation, the looks of disdain. But she had not broken. She had paid her penance. She would not sin again. She heard Philip coming back to the room.

'I've told him' he said.

Sarah got out of bed and put on her threadbare dressing gown. 'What did he say?'

'Obviously, she can't just come back as if nothing has happened.'

'Of course not. She will have to go through what I've been through. It's only right.'

'Sarah, there is more to it than that. It will take a lot longer. We must be sure she is pure, unsullied by the world.'

'What do they plan to do?' She tied the belt of her dressing gown tightly.

'Daniel is being very merciful to allow her back. He will do what is necessary to make her fit for the community. You must realise, Sarah, just how grievously she has sinned.'

'Of course.'

His face showed no emotion. 'I am going down to join the vigil. The elders will pray for wisdom regarding Tegan.'

She nodded, and watched him leave.

Amy and Tegan drove through the night in silence. Amy seemed preoccupied. Tegan was relieved. She needed time to think. She was excited about seeing her mother, but also trying to prepare herself for repenting. Was she sorry? Yes, maybe she was now. She thought about James, the concert. She would be glad to get away.

At about three in the morning Amy suggested they call in at the services for coffee. They went inside. It was very quiet. There were a few people, all sitting alone. Tegan remembered the money Hannah had given her. 'Let me buy you coffee. Would you like something to eat?'

They went and sat down. Tegan felt like she was in a bubble, cut off from the world. The striving had stopped. She was going back to the Community, and she had nothing to prove.

'You must be shattered,' Tegan said to Amy, watching her hurriedly eating a large piece of chocolate cake.

'Adrenalin is keeping me going at the moment.'

'But will you have to drive back later after you've seen this woman?'

'I've friends up here. I'm going to park outside their house, tube it in and then crash with them tonight. I'll drive back first thing in the morning.'

Amy wiped her mouth on her serviette. 'So you're going back then?'

'Yes.'

'So, this Community, is it some kind of commune? All equal, sharing kind of thing?'

Tegan sighed. Soon, no more questions. 'Not quite. Daniel sets the rules. We're happy to do what he says.'

'Sounds a bit sexist.'

'No, his visions are from the High One.'

'Really?'

'I don't expect you to understand.'

Amy shuddered. 'So why were you thrown out?'

'It's quite complicated.'

'Daniel, what's he like then?'

'He's very passionate about his vision.'

'Is he a bit crazy? '

Tegan looked at Amy. She spoke firmly. 'No, and we choose to do what he says.'

Amy shrugged. 'It's your life.'

They walked back to the car. It was still dark. They drove the rest of the way towards London in silence. The traffic was getting heavier. London was waking up. They stopped on the outskirts in front of a large house. It was half past six, and light was breaking.

'My friends live here. I'll park and get the tube in.'

'Oh, right. Well, thank you for the lift.'

'Hang on, why don't we get a drink over there in the café, then I'll go on in to see my friends? No-one will be up yet.'

Tegan frowned. She didn't want another grilling.

'Please' said Amy. 'I don't know about you but I'm starving. Promise, no talk of religion.'

Tegan realised she was hungry and so together they went over to the old fashioned café. It was busier inside than Tegan expected, mainly men eating large cooked breakfasts. Amy ordered bacon and eggs. Tegan ordered egg on toast and they sat down to wait for their food. When their meals came Amy tucked in enthusiastically. After a few mouthfuls she slowed down and said 'I'm not going to nag, but let me give you my mobile, just in case.'

'I was going to ask you to take the phone back for me.'

'You hang on to it. Come on, let's swap numbers, just in case.'

Tegan did it to keep Amy happy. She ate some of her egg. It was hot, and tasted better than she expected.

'The thing is, Tegan, some people, they just have to control other people,' said Amy.

Tegan gritted her teeth, annoyed that Amy was badgering her again about the Community. She stared steadfastly down at her egg, but Amy continued.

'God knows why, but the point is, they will do what ever it takes, put people down, and frighten them, anything it takes.'

Tegan put down her knife and fork. 'What are you talking about?'

'This chap Daniel, he sounds a bit of a control freak.'

'He's not' said Tegan upset. 'He's a prophet, and I obey him willingly, just like everyone in the Community. I don't expect you to understand, Amy, but this is where I belong.'

Amy sighed. 'OK. Sorry. Finish your breakfast and then we'll go.'

They finished eating in silence, and then Amy said 'Why don't you come over and meet my friends?'

Tegan shook her head. 'No, thanks. I think I'd like to get on now.'

'Really? Where do you need to go?'

'Bethnal Green station.'

'Oh, right, you can get straight there on the tube. Go to the end of this road. You'll find the entrance there on the left. I remember going to Bethnal Green with the girls for an art thing, takes ages, but you don't have to change. Central line is the one you want.'

Tegan smiled, relieved that at least she was only on one train. 'Thank you very much for the lift and I hope your meeting goes well.'

To her surprise, Amy gave her a hug. 'You take care now. And, remember, phone me if you need me.'

Tegan started to walk to the underground station. She had forgotten the noise and smells of London. She looked at the endless buildings, concrete paths, and litter. People pushed past her. She stopped and closed her eyes, tried to transport herself back to the mountains. For a brief moment she was standing outside the cottage, breathing in the air, the freedom. Then someone pushed her from behind, an ambulance screeched past behind her, sounding its siren trying to get through the traffic. She walked down the street and went in the station entrance. It was confusing as the tube started over ground. Still, at least she would be in daylight a bit longer.

When she bought her ticket she checked her route. It was a long journey: Amy was right. The train was waiting as it was the beginning of the line. She got a seat easily. Soon the train jolted and started the journey. Tegan became mesmerised by the sound of the train, even found her head nodding forward. She realised how tired she was but forced herself to stay awake. She didn't want to miss her stop. Slowly the train filled up. She was surrounded by people, and, finally, the train reached Bethnal Green. She got off and walked with a crowd of people out of the underground, and started to walk towards the Community.

She glanced over at her park: she would still have that. Standing outside the iron gates, she noticed for the first time how imposing, forbidding they were. Suddenly, all her confidence drained away, her heart started to race, pound in her chest. She pushed open the gate, and walked across the forecourt. She felt very sick as she climbed the stone steps, and with shaking hand she rang the door bell.

Chapter Twenty Six

Tegan stood on the doorstep, waiting. Eventually the door was opened by one of the older women, Martha.

'Tegan, we were expecting you. Come in,' she said sternly.

Tegan took a deep breath and entered. The house seemed to envelope her, claim her. The white walls, the threatening but familiar Bible verses, the clock, the distant smell of cooking: all shouted that this is where she belonged. She glanced at the board, March 11th, only eleven days since she was last here. The verse was "This know also, that in the last days perilous times shall come. 2 Timothy 3:1"

'The men are at special vigil,' Margaret was saying. 'You are to come to the women's room. We are all busy working. We have so much to do, and of course extra knitting because of you leaving.'

'I'm sorry. Is Mum in there?'

'Of course.'

Tegan followed her into a dingy cold room with long wooden tables. At each sat a woman on a hard chair knitting or sewing. No-one looked up. Tegan blinked. She had never noticed before how frumpy and colourless they all appeared. In a corner, isolated, she spotted her mother, sitting very still, unsmiling. Tegan walked over to her. She was shocked at how tired and old her mother looked: her face was tight and grey. Tegan saw some of the children sitting quietly reading old tatty Bible story books with black and white pictures. She wanted to take them to the library, show them a whole world of beautiful books and stories they didn't know existed. She was wondering where Elizabeth was when she saw Esther. Her face was drawn, tired. A toddler sat at her feet; a baby slept in a cot. Tegan glanced at her swollen belly.

'Another one on the way, then?'

'The High One has seen fit to bless us with more offspring,' Esther said, but her voice was flat. The light and fun had gone from her.

'Of course,' said Tegan, mentally checking herself. She must be careful how she spoke.

Sarah stood up, touched her arm. 'Come and talk.'

They went into a small room that led from the women's room and sat down together on an old wooden pew. Tegan glanced down at her mother's bandaged hand. 'What have you done?'

'I was foolish.'

Tegan looked closely at her mother. 'Are you alright?'

'The reason I may look a bit pale is that I had a long fast this week. I have done penance. We have all paid the price of your rebellion. The Community is undergoing a particularly harsh time of trial. We feel your rebellion is part of that.'

'I'm so sorry Mum. How is Philip?'

Her mother's face tightened. 'It has been very hard for someone who holds such an important role in this Community to bear the burden of such a rebellious daughter. It has been a difficult time.'

'I am so sorry. I have been so sinful.'

'Did you stay pure out in the world?'

'I tried, I really did, but it's been so hard.'

Tegan burst into tears. Sarah sat very still next to her. Then she reached out, and placed her hand on Tegan's. Her hand was cold but comforting. Tegan realised how tired she was, tired of being strong. When the sobbing had subsided her mother spoke.

'Maybe now you know what I've been trying to keep you from all these years.'

'I think I do. I don't wear the right things. I don't understand what people mean half the time. People go to pubs and drink alcohol. They wear terrible clothes. They touch you, and it's horrible. They think I'm a freak Mum. They think I'm mad.'

'But did you stay pure?'

'I hope so Mum. It is good to see everyone again. By the way, where is Elizabeth?'

Her mother's mouth tightened. 'Unfortunately, she has been taken.'

Tegan went pale 'She died?'

'No, no. Deborah's sister, a heathen woman. She got some court order and Elizabeth has been taken to live with them in Ireland.'

'So does Daniel see her at all?'

'No. He won't visit her out in the world. From what I heard Elizabeth does not appear to miss the Community. With no-one to guide her she has completely lost her way.'

Tegan pictured Elizabeth with beautiful books, a pretty bedroom. She couldn't help but be glad Elizabeth was somewhere else.

'Were Ellis and Hannah kind? What was it like living in the manor?' asked Sarah.

'I spent most of the time with their daughter, Cerys. She was really kind. You see, I didn't stay in the manor. No, I was in a small cottage nearby.'

'A cottage?' Her mother sat forward.

'Yes.'

'Tell me about this cottage.'

'Well, it was weird. The cottage was like the one you used to make up stories about, you know among the mountains. I found it, well, it was peaceful.'

Tegan went on to describe the cottage, the hills, and the woods. Sarah closed her eyes, listened.

'And Mum, look what I found-'

Sarah opened her eyes. Tegan pulled out the wedding photograph and held it in front of her. Sarah glared at it. She refused to touch it. 'Put that away. Why did you bring such a wicked thing here?'

'But Mum, you look so pretty.'

'It was a long time ago.'

'Ellis told me you sang solos then.'

Sarah's face darkened. 'I was proud and vain.'

'Are you sure? I mean, isn't it good to have gifts, to use them?'

'Stop this, Tegan.' Her mother sounded angry, frightened.

Tegan shook her head. 'I'm sorry, I just thought-'

Sarah looked at the photograph, not daring to touch it. 'Get rid of that as soon as you can, burn it.'

Then Tegan saw that her mother was looking at the locket she was wearing.

'You need to stop wearing that as well,' Sarah said sharply.

'I was wondering who the people in it were?' asked Tegan.

Tegan saw her mother blush and then she realised. 'It's you! Of course. So, who was the man? The photo is all scratched.'

Her mother looked at her, alarmed. 'This is sinful nonsense. You must get rid of that as well. The pleasures of the world have no place here.'

'I understand for adults, but I did wonder, you know, for children, why we don't have things like birthday parties, let them have some nice books and things?'

'You know why. We never wanted you to crave worldly things.'

'But I don't even know when my birthday is-'

'We have the Community birthday. That is enough.'

'But I have a right to know when my birthday is.'

'You have had a privileged upbringing. You are being extremely ungrateful. Look at Elizabeth. Who is warning her about the perils of hell, the eternal suffering that awaits her if she does not stay pure, that any time the end may come and she will be left alone in a world of trial and tribulation?'

Tegan stared at the fanatical gleam in her mother's eyes. 'But she's so young. Do you really think she should be told things like that at her age, to live life paralysed by fear?'

'I have told you many times. It's good to be frightened.'

213

Tegan looked closely at her mother. She sat rigid, her hands tightly clasped. 'Are you frightened a lot of the time Mum?'

Sarah nodded, but slowly. 'Of course, but it's alright. I wouldn't want to relax. Fear gives purpose to my day. It is the reason I live.'

'Why don't you sing any more?'

'Life is about sacrificing yourself, your own needs and desires, for a greater good. It is obedience to Daniel's words. I learnt to sacrifice myself, my singing, my academic achievement. I know now to trust Daniel and vigil.'

Tegan bit her lip. 'Ellis took me to an optician-'

Sarah went very red. 'He had no right to do that. You should have refused.'

'But the tests the woman gave me, I could see so much better.'

Sarah stood up. 'It seems to me, Tegan, you have come back here with a very critical spirit. It is essential you show how repentant you are. You know the medicine of the world is evil. It stops people turning to the High One. Daniel has taught us this for years. You have strayed a long way from the truth.'

'But Mum-' Tegan grabbed her mother's arm. Her mother flinched and pulled her arm away.

'What's the matter Mum?'

'My arm is sore. That's all.'

Tegan pulled back her mother's shawl. The arm looked red and inflamed. 'That looks bad.'

'It's alright. Just a reaction from my hand.'

'But you should get something for it.'

'You know Daniel would not approve.'

'But that's not fair-'

Sarah didn't reply but seemed to be staring at the doorway. Tegan was momentarily held by the look of sheer terror on her mother's face, and then followed her gaze.

'What isn't fair?' asked Daniel, his voice cold and menacing. She felt her heart beating fast. She was finding it hard to breathe.

214

Chapter Twenty Seven

'Daniel,' said Sarah, her voice in awe. She got off the seat and went down on to her knees, but Daniel ignored her and turned to Tegan.

'What isn't fair?' he repeated. His voice was quiet but terrifying.

Tegan's mouth felt very dry. She couldn't swallow.

'What?' he repeated.

'That Mum should suffer,' she stammered.

Daniel came closer. 'You think we should be going to an evil world for help?'

'I don't know-'

She heard Sarah gasp.

'How dare you doubt me? You are worthless. You should be grovelling on the floor for forgiveness.'

Tegan looked at her mother, head bowed, trembling. It was what Daniel expected, but she stayed on the bench. She stared at Daniel and realised he looked smaller than before. She noticed the staining on his beard, the way the white shirt clung to his fat stomach. She watched as he took her mother's hand. Sarah, in a dream, stood up, her eyes fixed on Daniel.

'Daughter, you have fasted and prayed this week?' he asked.

'I have. I am truly sorry for my sins and I beg for forgiveness and mercy.'

'You are forgiven. I think now you had better leave us.' Sarah quietly, ghost-like, left the room.

Daniel turned to Tegan, his voice hard. 'You will go to the isolation room, immediately.'

Tegan's heart sank. Of course, she would have to go there. She hated that place. It was a cold windowless room with its own toilet and shower. She looked at Daniel, but he just

215

glared and turned away. She picked up her bags and followed him through the women's room. The women bent their heads in silence as they passed. Tegan had never noticed how much tension there was in the Community. Before they left the room, she watched as Daniel turned and scanned the room. No one dared breathe. Tegan didn't lower her eyes. She was looking at Daniel. She looked at his face, the arched eyebrows, and the thin snarl of a smile. She understood for the first time how much he relished control but despised those who submitted to him. Her gaze met his. He glared at her, waiting for her to bow her head. But she continued to stare. His breathing quickened. His eyes grew larger. The longer she held his gaze, the greater the fury she saw in his eyes. But she kept staring, and slowly she saw something else creeping in: panic. A hint of weakness she had never seen before. He scowled and roughly grabbed her arm, dragged her out of the room, along the corridor. He pushed her down a short flight of stairs and threw her into the pitch black room. He stood, filling the doorway.

'I thought you had come back repentant for your sins, but still in your soul I perceive rebellion.'

Tegan screwed her eyes up. In panic, she realised that Daniel could be about to cast her out again. She couldn't go out there again: she had to save herself. 'I am sorry, sorry for going to the library, having coffee with a heathen man. I want to come back. I belong here.'

'Are you prepared to completely submit your will to that of the leadership, to accept the chastisement and discipline of this Community?'

Tegan looked down. She suddenly felt sick, very frightened. She stammered 'Yes, yes, of course.'

Daniel nodded. 'So do you understand the world to be a wicked, evil place?'

Tegan suddenly pictured the hills, the skylark, Cerys. She pushed the images away.

'I do,' she said quietly.

Daniel came close to her. He held her face. 'There is something wrong here. I look into your soul. You have been contaminated.' He spoke in a hard whisper. His hand was squeezing her chin. 'I sense you are holding on to the world. Don't you realise that anyone outside this Community is vile, corrupt and deserving of eternal punishment?'

Tegan stepped back.

'I don't understand,' she said hoarsely.

She saw his eyes harden.

'It is not your place to understand, to think. You have to accept what I tell you.'

'But some people out there, they helped me, looked after me. How can they be completely evil?'

Daniel stepped forward. 'How dare you question my teaching? You will repent. You will be sorry.' He was shouting. She saw him approach, his face contorted in anger, and then suddenly a vicious blow sent her flying into the wall. Her head was spinning. She crouched in a ball, waiting for him to strike her again. He turned away, and slammed the door. Darkness, pitch blackness. She heard the lock turn. She was alone. She tried the light switch, but it didn't work. She groped her way to the bed and crawled onto it.

She lay, her face and head thumping, listening to the traffic outside. The thought crept into her head and the voices grew louder. Daniel was just a man, an ordinary man, who told lies to make people follow him. She trembled at the heresy, but the thought wouldn't go away. She had seen that look. He didn't love anyone here. He despised them all. When she asked questions, he shouted, hit, but never answered. But she wanted to stay here, didn't she? She knelt on the floor and tried to do her vigil. 'Come quickly Oh High One. Come quickly Oh High One.' She repeated the words, loud, frantic, like a drowning man, trying desperately to hold on to her faith. Her eyes started to close, so tired.

Tegan had no idea how long she had slept but she was startled awake by the door being flung open. She lifted her head, stiff from being bent over, blinked at the shaft of light coming from the hallway. It illuminated Philip in an eerie shape. He

217

looked stern, his eyes brighter than she had ever seen them before.

'I have spoken to Daniel. I have left him at vigil where we have been kneeling for many hours. You bring nothing but shame on this family.'

She stood up slowly, and approached him, in a dream. 'I am sorry. Please let me stay.'

He looked at her face and then his eyes went down to the locket she was wearing.

'What is that?'

'Mother gave it to me.'

'I have never seen it before.'

With a shaking hand Tegan opened the locket. 'It's her, it's my mother. Who is the man? Is it you?'

Philip screwed his eyes up, and tried to make out the picture in the dim light. He pulled her towards the light and looked again.

'Take it off,' he demanded.

Tegan put her hand over the locket and shook her head.

Philip went to grab it, but she clutched it. She saw his hands were shaking, and then realised it was fear, not anger that she was witnessing.

'Why does this scare you?' she asked.

'Nothing scares me. But Daniel must never see that.'

Tegan looked closely at the hunted expression on Philip's face, saw his eyes darting around. Shocked, she realised for the first time just how much fear her parents lived with. But her mother had said it was good, hadn't she?

'Philip, how do you really feel about Daniel?'

Philip stood very still. His eyes seemed to glaze over. 'Daniel is omniscient. He is the prophet of the High One. He is our leader and he is never wrong. It is our privilege to follow him.'

There was a quiet cough. It was Daniel. 'Philip, what are you doing here? I didn't say you could come in here.'

Philip turned in a panic, his face again creased with fear. He knelt down. 'Daniel. I'm sorry, really sorry.'

Tegan was horrified to see Philip shrink back. She should have been pleased to see this man who had bullied and shown her so little love all her life humiliated. But to see him as a little scared boy was disturbing. Now she realised why his threats had so often left her cold. He was a child desperately trying to copy a grown up, Daniel.

'Leave him alone!' she shouted at Daniel.

Philip stepped forward. 'Tegan, that's enough.'

Daniel walked over to Tegan, grabbed her hair, and pulled her head back. 'How dare you defy me? I am omniscient. I am never wrong.' He spat in her face as he spoke. It was disgusting, and suddenly anger welled up in Tegan. This man was a bully. He did make mistakes. She remembered the optician. The world had been kind, and then there was Deborah. He was pulling her head back, her neck felt like it would snap, but the pain fed her anger.

'You were wrong about Deborah-'

She felt his grip tighten. 'Don't you dare-'

She stared at his face. Why wasn't she frightened of him any more? For some reason the hate she felt for him was drowning the fear. That emotion was so much stronger. It gave her courage. He looked at her, the grip weakened and he pushed her away.

'That is it. We were willing to show you great mercy and forgiveness. Now the High One has revealed to me the blackness of your soul. We are to cleanse this place. You are evil. I cast you out and this time you will never, ever return.'

Tegan stood up defiantly, staring at him.

'From this time forth you are cursed' shouted Daniel. 'Your name has been blotted out of the lamb's book of life. Every night will be a foretaste of hell.'

'You are evil' Tegan said quietly. 'No one should have to live here. My parents will not stay here. I am taking them away.'

'But they want to stay. They will never leave.'

His smugness infuriated her.

'You are lying' she said.

219

A quiet, firm voice said 'No, it's true Tegan.' Sarah had arrived. She stood in the doorway.

'You must go and we must stay.'

'No' pleaded Tegan. 'Come with me. Don't stay with this man. I know you care, you helped me last time I left.'

'I repent of that' said Sarah. Sarah turned to Daniel, 'Tegan is no longer my daughter. She is dead to me.'

Daniel nodded slowly, smiled at Sarah and then she knelt in front of him. He laid his hands on her head in blessing.

Tegan shuddered in disbelief, and then a pain in her head grew, became unbearable, a thick strong band being pulled around her head tighter and tighter. Her mother stood up and without so much as glancing at her, left the room.

Daniel looked over at Philip and then at Tegan's bags. Without speaking, Philip picked them up. Daniel roughly held her arm and pushed her out of the room, and along the corridor. They passed the women's room. The door was ajar. Tegan glanced in and saw her mother sat with them, her head bowed. They all looked so old, dull, and bitter. She had grown up with many of the women. Some had bathed her knees when she had fallen over, read her stories from the old books, taught her to sew, plant seeds, cook. It hurt so much that all the love had been conditional on her conformity. They didn't even look at her now. No secret tears would be shed for her, and she had ceased to exist.

Daniel pulled her towards the front door. Philip opened it and then Daniel pushed her down the steps, took her bags off Philip and threw them on top of her as she fell. Her glasses fell off. She picked them up but the lenses were smashed. She put them in her pocket. Slowly, she got to her feet, shaking. She looked back just as the door was slammed shut. Tegan wiped her face roughly, picked up her bags, turned, staggered across the forecourt and pushed open the iron gate.

Chapter Twenty Eight

Tegan staggered over to a bench in the park. She looked around at the trees in the early evening light. The beauty, the hope, in the blossom now trying to escape from the buds made her feel more alone, desperate. Tears slowly, aimlessly, fell down her cheeks. Shocked, she sat motionless, barely breathing. She looked down at her knees and hands. They were badly grazed. Blood, like tears, tricked down her legs. Her arms and her head throbbed. The physical pain was strangely reassuring, wounds she could see. 'You are dead to me' her mother had said. Maybe her mother was right, she was dead. If all her past, her beliefs, were a lie, then what was left? Nothing. She was nothing. She had ceased to exist.

It started to rain harder. Cold spots hit her face. A drunk came over and sat next to her. She didn't move. She didn't know where to go. A group of teenagers arrived, drinking and shouting. She stared at them. She had no energy to be anxious. She sat getting soaked, the rain easily penetrating her thin coat and headscarf. Her tears mingled, became one, with the rain. Her nose was running. She saw blood dripping down onto her coat. She didn't have a handkerchief. She used her sleeve.

Eventually, she was aware that it was getting darker.

'We're shutting up now' called a man. He came over and looked down at her. 'Hey, are you alright?' She followed his gaze to a can of lager that was lying on its side next to her. She realised the liquid had been soaking into her coat. She got up. The park spun round. She tried to walk as steadily as she could. She couldn't bear for the man to think she was drunk. Her feet squelched in her shoes, her wet headscarf clinging to her head. She glanced over at the Community house. The lights were on. They would all be at vigil. Had they forgotten her already? Her mother would be in there chanting, 'Come Quickly Oh High

One'. Tegan knew the experience would be soothing. Her mother would soon start to be light headed, numb, all her anxieties forgotten. Maybe that is what it is like to be on drugs, drink alcohol?

Tegan started to walk aimlessly away, but it was hard; her head was spinning. The nausea overtook her and she was very sick. People who passed her looked at her in disgust. She didn't care. She had to walk, but it seemed pointless, so she started to count her footsteps. It was mindlessly comforting. She was aware of people pulling down the metal security blinds on some of the shops. The pubs were coming to life. There was a café, lights on, looking cosy. She saw couples, groups, slowly emerging for a night out. No-one looked at her. She went to walk down a dark alley. The night time, the demons waiting to show her hell. She must keep in the light. She walked on. She glanced in the smart cafés and restaurants. Weary, she found a seat, sat down and closed her eyes. But she felt too vulnerable. She got up, started to walk again. Red buses and police cars passed her. Eventually the London Eye came into view, far away, shining like a beacon. She must walk to the light. It gave her somewhere to aim towards. Her sodden feet hurt. She could feel the blisters forming, rubbing. Although she could always see the Eye, it was a long walk. She tried not to stop at all. It would be so hard to start again. She stumbled along for hours. She crossed the river over one of the bridges. When she finally arrived at the Eye, the area was still crowded, despite the time. She desperately needed to sit down, but out here she was so vulnerable. Then she looked over and saw Waterloo station. She walked towards it, climbed the huge stone steps and entered.

Inside was quieter. Tegan was aware of people looking smarter. They seemed to be avoiding her. The large clock said eleven. She went up to the next level where there were cafés and bought coffee. The woman serving her smiled sympathetically as she handed her the coffee. Tegan found a seat in the corner and turned away from everyone. She realised how little money she had left. What was she going to do? At last she could sit down. She sat back, and went to rest her head on the window but it was

222

too painful. She had to sit upright. Her neck hurt but she managed to close her eyes and rest.

She was woken by a hand on her shoulder.

'Wake up, station's closing now' said a man. She glanced at the large clock: it was one o'clock. She kept her face away from the man and started to walk out of the station. She was very stiff. Her arms and ribs ached. She was cold and she knew she must smell of alcohol and vomit. The streets seemed a lot quieter now. She walked back across the river over the bridge. She saw Charing Cross Station. She guessed it would be closed. In a doorway she saw a man huddled up in a sleeping bag. On him sat a scruffy dog. As she looked at the dog, content, loyal, she wished she had such a friend. She remembered Dylan. She had nobody. She started to cry, quietly, sadly, alone.

She saw the lights of a McDonalds. She was very embarrassed at the way she looked but she had to get out of the cold. It was surprisingly crowded. What were all these people doing here at this time? She went to order coffee but caught sight of herself in one of the mirrors. She was shocked and turned away, but everywhere she looked there were mirrors. Her headscarf was sodden, her legs were filthy. But it was her face: no wonder people had asked her if she was alright. The left side of her forehead was swollen, badly bruised. There was dried blood in her hair. Both her eye sockets were badly swollen and her cheek looked twice its normal size. Her lip was cut and there was vomit on her collar. What had people thought of her? Tegan went into the toilet. Using toilet paper she tried to wipe the blood away but it hurt too much to touch her forehead. A woman came into the toilets and their eyes met in the mirror. The woman looked at her as if she despised her. There was no pity. She went back into the restaurant and went to order coffee. She was too embarrassed to look at the person serving and sat as far away from people as she could. The food smelt appetising but she daren't buy any. A lot of people in there were on their own. She wondered how many nights some of them had spent like this.

She noticed a few others clinging on to one cup of cold coffee, their pass, like hers, to stay. Those people were all sitting

223

alone. She saw one girl was asleep. Another stared, her eyes deep with pain and loneliness. She looked out of the window, saw dawn creeping over London.

A girl came and sat down opposite her. She was wearing a track suit top and jeans. Her face was grubby, her nails black. 'Not seen you here before.'

'No.'

Tegan looked at the girl. She seemed very young. 'Why don't you go home?'

'Mum chucked me out.' Tegan looked at the girl as she explained. 'My Mum got a new boyfriend, Brian. He gave me drugs. Mum found them, accused me of using, and she said I had to leave. She wouldn't believe me when I told her Brian had given them to me.'

Tegan looked at the girl. She had spoken quietly but there were no tears. The girl stared at her. 'So you, what happened?'

'I was thrown out.'

'Like me' said the girl, who stood up and left.

Tegan felt in her pocket for a tissue, looked out of the window. It was getting lighter. She had a slight feeling of relief. She had made it through the night. Then she thought to herself, for how many years had she woken up and thought that? She was aware of the cold, damp clothes. Her head hurt. She shut her eyes. At that moment her phone rang. She went to get her phone out. Her arm ached as she lifted the phone to her ear.

'Tegan?'

She didn't recognise the voice.

'Tegan?' The voice spoke again. 'I just wondered if you're OK? I've phoned a few times.'

Tegan stared at the table. A group of very drunk boys came in shouting and swearing.

'Tegan, where are you?'

'McDonalds. Who's this?'

'It's Amy. What the hell are you doing in McDonalds? Have you been to the Community yet?'

'I've been thrown out again.'

'Oh God. What will you do?'

'I don't know.'

'You must come back with me. Listen, I'll come and pick you up. Which McDonalds are you in?'

'I don't know.'

'Ask someone.'

'Oh hang on, then.'

Tegan walked up to the counter and waited for someone to look her way. 'Excuse me, um, where am I? I mean, this McDonalds, where is it?'

'The Strand, love.'

'Thanks.'

'It's on the Strand' she told Amy.

'Fine. I know where that is. Wait outside, OK?'

She heard Amy moving about. 'Listen, you stay there. I'm on my way. Look for me out of the window. I'll be in the car. I don't want to park.'

Tegan finished the call. She glanced at her reflection in one of the many mirrors. She couldn't let Amy see her looking like this. She had to change. She got up and went back to the toilets.

It was difficult in such a confined space, and her left arm was getting increasingly stiff and painful. She opened her case and took out clean clothes. Then she took off the wet, dirty coat, skirt and blouse, and put on a clean skirt and blouse. The dirty skirt and blouse she rolled up and put in the case. The coat she left out and put on the coat that Cerys had given her. She looked in the mirror. Slowly she undid her headscarf. She tried to shake her hair free but it was in wet greasy clumps. She did up her case, pulled up the hood on her coat and left the toilet.

She went out of McDonalds and found a bin. Into it she pushed the coat and the headscarf: out with the rubbish where they belonged.

Chapter Twenty Nine

Tegan waited outside McDonalds, watching each car as it passed. At least she wasn't so cold now, although her head was spinning and the nausea was returning. Eventually she recognised Amy's car. She pulled up her hood, and when the car pulled up she quickly put her bags on the back seat and sat next to Amy. Amy peered at her and wrinkled up her nose.

'Are you OK?'

'I fell over. I'm sorry. I was a bit sick.'

'What ever happened?'

'Nothing.'

Amy turned her attention to coping with the heavy London traffic, trying to ignore the curses of other drivers as she tried to get back into lane. Once they were clear she was able to talk. 'So you're sure you're alright?'

'Yes.'

Amy was very chatty. 'Sam sent me a text. Wales lost to France in the rugby yesterday. It means France have won this year. Hard to believe Wales won the Grand Slam last year.'

Tegan sighed. She was so tired, but somehow it was comforting to have Amy chatting on. She wanted to keep her going.

'How did your meeting go?'

'Oh great. Fiona flew in from America two days ago. Anyway, she has been in consultations with the Welsh Assembly and wants to extend our centre to become a wildlife sanctuary kind of thing.'

Tegan closed her eyes. She felt very sick. Amy's voice sounded a long way off.

'I said are you alright?' Amy was asking.

'Just tired.'

'OK. Well, I'll put the radio on. I could do with concentrating on my driving.'

They drove with a white wall of music. Tegan tried to breathe slowly. She couldn't be sick. She drifted in and out of sleep.

After they had crossed the Severn Bridge, Amy said, 'The services are ahead. I need caffeine.'

Tegan looked out through the windscreen. It had started to rain. 'I'll stay and sleep.' She determinedly turned away from Amy and pulled her hood well over her face. Amy swore at the weather and ran out. When she returned Tegan continued her pretence of sleeping. Amy turned on the radio and they continued on their journey. Eventually they started on the steeper, narrower, valley roads. Tegan found the nausea returning. Her head was throbbing. She knew she was going to be sick.

'Can you stop?' she asked urgently.

Amy pulled over. Tegan grabbed the door handle and dived out of the car.

She pushed back her hood and was very sick.

Amy came over and spoke behind her. 'Are you alright?'

Tegan stood up, and then Amy saw her face. 'Oh my God, Tegan, why didn't you say?' Amy reached out to touch her arm. Tegan flinched.

'What the hell has happened?'

Tegan's eyes filled with tears. She couldn't speak.

'Come on, back in the car. We need to get you to a hospital.'

'No, no. I can't go there. Please don't take me to a doctor.'

'Hey, OK. Listen, get in the car and I'll take you to the cottage.'

'Do you promise?'

'Of course, come on.' Gently, Amy helped her with her seat belt. Tegan sat back and closed her eyes. At least she didn't have to hide her face. She tried to think about going back to the

227

cottage but nothing seemed to make sense any more. They pulled in somewhere. Tegan had the impression they weren't far from the village. Amy got out of the car and made a phone call.

Cerys was in the manor garden when the call came from Amy.

'Hi, you on your way back?'

'Yes. Listen, it's not just me. I have Tegan.'

'I thought she was going back to that community.'

'It all went wrong. And, listen, she's in a really bad way, Cerys. I don't know what's happened but she's injured. I don't like the look of her head. She's just been very sick. I think she's been wandering the streets most of the night.'

'Oh my God.'

'I'm bringing her straight to the cottage. She needs to see a doctor but goes hysterical if I suggest it.'

'I'll come round.'

Cerys went to the back door, removed her boots and went to find Ellis. She heard him playing the piano and went straight over to him.

'Alright love?' he asked, his hands hovering over the keys.

'It's Tegan, Dad. Amy's bringing her back but she's in a bad way. I don't know what's happened to her.'

Ellis shut the lid of the piano. 'Duw, what do we do?'

Cerys looked at her father, useless as usual in a crisis; then saw her mother coming in.

'What's up?' asked Hannah.

'It's Tegan. She's with Amy. She's coming back.'

'Coming back? What's happened?'

'I don't know, but she's not well. Amy thinks she should go to hospital. I'm going to the cottage to meet them.'

Hannah turned pale. 'Has she been attacked or something?'

'I don't know. I have to go and see her.'

'I'll come too' said Ellis, his back to Hannah.

Ellis and Cerys left and drove straight to the cottage. Cerys could see the lights were on, went to knock on the door, but found it was on the latch. She pushed it and went in. She was hit by the obnoxious stench of vomit. To her horror, Tegan was curled up on the settee, foetus-like. Amy was standing helplessly staring at her.

'She's worse than I imagined.' Cerys whispered to Ellis. She glanced at her father. He was staring at Tegan, horrified.

Amy came over to them. 'She's just been sick again. I've called an ambulance but Tegan doesn't know. I hope I did the right thing.'

'Of course' said Cerys. She went over to Tegan, knelt beside her, and spoke gently. 'What's happened? Tell me.'

'Cold, tired,' mumbled Tegan.

'Has someone attacked you?'

Tegan shook her head. 'No. It all hurts.' She started to sob.

Cerys tried to touch Tegan's arm to comfort her but Amy intervened. 'No, don't. That arm hurts.'

At that moment Amy saw the blue flashing light of the ambulance, and the paramedics came in. Tegan seemed to become more alert. She looked like a petrified animal.

'Who are you? What are you doing?' She looked accusingly at Amy.

A female paramedic stepped forward. 'It's alright. Tell me what's happened.'

Tegan tried to speak but burst into tears.

'OK. Can I just check a few things?'

'No. Leave me alone.'

Cerys came over. 'Please let them, Tegan. I'm so worried about you.'

Tegan closed her eyes in resignation. After a brief examination the paramedic said 'We need to get your arm checked properly, and those head injuries.'

'Not hospital.'

'It would be best. You know, if you have broken bones they need to be treated straight away.'

'I'll come with you. Don't be scared' said Cerys.

'I mustn't take drugs. I mustn't be hypnotised.'

Ellis, who had not moved from the end of the room, came forward. 'Tegan, you must, you have to go.' He spoke sternly. Tegan blinked, but nodded.

The paramedic asked Cerys if she could speak to her in the kitchen. 'She seems very confused. Has she been taking any kind of drugs, do you know?'

'I don't know. She wouldn't normally.'

'We definitely need to get her in. I'm worried about those head injuries. She also seems to be in shock. Tell me again what has happened to her.'

'She went to London yesterday to see her mother. There was some sort of bust up. She spent the night on the streets and then got a lift back here.'

'Right. Can you get some bits together for her? We must take her in.'

Cerys found Tegan's unopened case. As she went through Tegan's clothes she was struck by how few things she actually possessed and how old they all were. She had already seen Tegan's skirts and blouses, but the nighties were thin, cheap and shabby, the underwear grey and shapeless. A few basic wash things were in a plastic bag. It gave Cerys a new and upsetting insight into Tegan's life. She put the things in a carrier bag and then spoke to Ellis.

'I want to go in the ambulance with her, Dad.'

'Fine, I'll drive. I'll wait in the car. Think I'll be in the way if I come in.'

'I understand Dad.' Cerys turned to Amy. 'Thanks so much. You must go home now. You must be exhausted.'

Tegan found herself being helped into the ambulance. Cerys came with her and held her hand. Tegan lay in the ambulance with a gathering sense of panic. She had had so many warnings about the evils of the medical profession, been told so many stories of their heathen practices.

The paramedic kept checking her. She thought they were meant to make her feel better, but her head was thumping and her arms hurt. The ride was bumpy. Eventually they reached the hospital.

'Right. We're taking you into Accident and Emergency first, and then I expect you'll be admitted to a ward.'

Tegan was taken into a brightly lit, busy place. Some people quietly sat on chairs looking pale and ill. Some were drunk and shouting. She was pushed past them to a side room. A doctor came and examined her. She hated lying there in this alien environment. It was all so intrusive. Cerys stayed with her, held her hand.

'We need to X-ray your arm, and then I'd like to admit you. I'm concerned about that bump on your head.'

Once the admission procedures had been sorted out, which seemed to both Tegan and Cerys to take for ever, Cerys said 'I'll leave you now. I'll only be in the way but I'll be in tomorrow to see you.'

Tegan looked very scared.

'It's OK. They'll look after you. Dad's outside. Really, don't worry. You try to rest now.'

Tegan watched Cerys leave. She was alone with strangers. She was moved to another trolley and wheeled up to the ward by two porters. The hospital corridors seemed dark and quiet. She and the porters were the only ones in the lift. The voices of the porters were over-loud and bright, as if they were pretending this was all normal.

She was taken to the X-ray department. It was dark. It was very uncomfortable as the people there made her put her arm in different positions. They kept retreating while the X-rays were taken. Why? Was it dangerous? She felt abandoned and very vulnerable. Finally she was taken to the ward.

A nurse helped her put on her old nightie and then brought her water and a flannel to wash her face, hands and knees. 'There, now. Let's settle you into a bed. The doctor has written you up for these. They'll help with the pain.'

The nurse held out some pills in a little plastic cup.

'No. I won't take them.' Tegan couldn't bear any more.

'Come on now-'

231

'No. I want to go home. Please let me go.'

'That wouldn't be a good idea, would it? Not now. You just try to rest. Alright?'

The nurse left her and quickly found a doctor. He came over and touched Tegan's hand.

'Get off. Don't touch me. Leave me alone. I won't let you kill me.' Tegan was very scared. Her fears and panic came tumbling out.

The doctor sat next to the bed. 'No one is trying to hurt you.'

'Yes you are. I'll go to hell, burn for ever in the lake of fire. That's what they said. What if they're right? I don't want to die.'

'Calm down. It's OK. You're safe here. You just try to rest.'

The doctor left her and went to talk to the nurse. Tegan lay back and clung on to the sheet, curled on her side. She daren't close her eyes. Who knew what they would do if she went to sleep?

Chapter Thirty

The next morning Cerys rang the hospital to find out how Tegan was.

'Ah, I'm glad you called' said a nurse. 'Dr Richmond wondered if you could pop in this morning to see him.'

'Why, what's the matter?'

'He'll explain when you see him.'

'OK, what time?'

'About eleven?'

Cerys, very concerned, went to find Ellis. He had been very strange the night before. He had hardly spoken and then gone off walking when they had returned. She found him on his own in the music room

'Hi Dad. You alright? You look done in.'

'I walked a long time, went to that well of yours, and did some thinking.'

'Where's Mum?'

'I've not seen her since yesterday. I found a note, and it just said she's gone out.'

'Dad, the doctor wants to talk to us about Tegan. What do you think is the matter? Do you think they have found something serious?'

'Oh, Duw. I'll come with you love.'

'OK. Can we leave soon? I need to pop into a few shops.'

They drove to Aberystwyth in silence. Cerys shopped and then they went to the hospital. They went straight to the desk on the ward. Cerys approached a nurse 'We were asked to come and see Dr Richmond?'

The nurse sighed. 'Could you wait in here? I'll have to try and find him.'

The room they were taken to was small and airless, full of odd chairs and an old television. After a few minutes they started to wonder if they'd been forgotten, but neither had the nerve to ask what was happening. Eventually a harassed-looking doctor appeared. His white coat was hanging open and he looked in need of a hot meal and a good night's sleep. He pushed his fingers through his brown curly hair and addressed Ellis.

'Right, what relation are you to Tegan?'

'I'm her uncle. Cerys is her cousin.'

'Are there other close family, parents, or partner?'

'Her parents are in London, but she has been thrown out of her home, so we're the closest family she has at the moment.'

'OK. Well, we've run a number of tests.'

'And?'

'Nothing serious, but I do have a few concerns. I would like to have access to her medical history. Can you tell me who her GP is?'

'Why, what's the matter?' asked Cerys.

'Has she a history of substance misuse, psychiatric problems?'

'Not that we know of. Why?'

'It's something we think needs to be looked into. Do you have the contact details for her GP?' he asked Ellis again.

'No. Tegan doesn't know who she was registered with. I don't think she'd been to a doctor for years, since she was young.'

'So had I better speak to her mother?'

'You can try, but it'll be difficult. You know, the community where she lived is very secretive and reclusive.'

'Do you mean it's some kind of cult?'

'I don't know, maybe-' Ellis mumbled.

'Dad, it's a very odd group' interjected Cerys. She turned to the doctor. 'She has had a very strange life.'

'Can you tell us how to contact this community?'

'It's called "The Last Week Community". I can give you her father's mobile number. To be honest I can't see him being much help.' Ellis told the doctor the details.

'Thank you. When she leaves here will she be going back to London or staying with you?'

'I hope she will stay with us. I got the impression she really can't go back now.'

'I would like her to be registered with a doctor here then.'

'She could come to our doctor, Nadia, Dr Khan, I should think. She's lovely.'

'Can you give me her details as well please?'

Ellis wrote them down.

'I'll catch up with you later,' said the doctor, standing up.

'Can we go and see Tegan? I mean, I know it's not visiting time.'

'I think that would be a good idea. You may be able to reassure her.'

'Thanks.' Cerys turned to Ellis. 'There's no need for you to stay.'

'I'll wait. You go and see Tegan. Then I need a quiet word with her. Go on, you go in first. I'll be in the corridor.'

Cerys went to the nurse's station. Everyone seemed to be rushing and preoccupied. Eventually a nurse noticed her. 'Yes?'

'Doctor Richmond said I could visit Tegan.'

The nurse frowned. 'Really? I'll take you to her.'

As they walked the nurse said 'Dr Richmond is a law unto himself, but, still, I suppose he's very conscientious-'

Tegan was in a ward with three other patients. She was lying curled up, her back to the door, looking very vulnerable and child-like. Cerys walked around the bed and touched her hand.

Tegan's eyes shot open. 'Cerys, have you come to take me home?'

'How are you feeling?'

'What's going to happen to me?'

'When they say you can go, you can come back to the cottage. I'll stay there with you.'

Tegan's eyes filled with tears. 'She said I was dead to her. It really hurt, like she really wanted me to be dead-'

'Who, who said such a horrible thing?'

'My mother-' Tegan sobbed into her pillow silently, her body heaving.

'Tegan, that's terrible.' Cerys sat, close to tears herself. Slowly, the sobs subsided. Cerys handed Tegan a tissue. She wiped her face.

'I hope you don't mind' said Cerys shyly, 'I went and picked you up a few bits for while you're in here.' She handed Tegan a bag.

Tegan frowned but sat up and peeped inside the large carrier bag. She carefully took out a soft blue cotton nightie with tiny white sprigs of flowers and lace around the neck. There was a light negligee to match. She gasped.

'For me?'

Cerys smiled.

'They're brand new. They're lovely, so pretty,' Tegan said, touching them in awe.

'There's more.'

Tegan pulled out a pretty white rose-decorated towel, and a wash bag to match. Inside was a new toothbrush, scented shower wash, shampoo and a new hairbrush. Tegan picked the items out, felt them, smelt them. She held the towel to her face but then burst into tears.

'Are you OK?' asked Cerys.

'I've never been give such lovely things. Thank you. Thank you so much.'

'We're cousins. We're family.'

'Do you think you could bring me in some clothes from the cottage? You know, the jeans and things? I don't want to wear my Community clothes any more.'

'Of course.' Cerys touched Tegan's hand gently. 'You've had a terrible time, haven't you?'

'I'm so confused. I don't understand. Was it always like that or have I changed? You know I was thrown down the steps.

That's when most of this happened.' She cautiously touched her cheek.

'I'm glad you've come back.'

Tegan nodded, still crying.

'Dad wants to see you now, OK?'

'Alright.'

Tegan lay back in her bed, and then she saw Ellis approaching. He was walking slowly. He seemed smaller, older. He came and sat next to her bed. She turned her head on the pillow to talk to him.

'Oh God, you look terrible' he said. 'Sorry, I shouldn't have said that. How are you feeling?'

'Cerys brought me some lovely things. She's been so kind'

'You two, you get on well don't you?'

'Yes, I'm very fortunate to have a cousin like her.'

'Um, right. I think I'd better just come out and tell you. Cerys is not your cousin.'

'What?' Tegan frowned. She was so tired. She tried hard to concentrate.

'The thing is, Cerys is your half sister.'

'She can't be.' Tegan scowled. What was Ellis talking about? She was too tired for this.

Ellis sat nervously stroking his beard. 'I don't know an easy way to say this. The thing is, Tegan, I am your natural father.'

'What?' she asked quietly. She rolled her body over on her pillow, curled her body slightly and looked at him intently. Their faces were very close.

'It is true. I am your father' said Ellis.

'But Philip-' she said desperately.

Ellis touched her hand. 'No, it's me. I'm sorry.'

Tegan stared at him. He looked so sincere. 'But how is it possible? My mother?'

Ellis looked down. 'Yes, your mother is Sarah.'

'But that would mean-'

237

'I'm afraid the story does me no favours. It happened in the first year of my marriage to Hannah. She was nursing at a hospital in Cardiff. I was working for the Welsh National Opera there. Anyway, Hannah was in the hospital choir with Sarah and she asked me to go and help them out. Well, obviously I'd met Sarah before. She was our bridesmaid, but I hadn't heard her sing. You know, we'd never got on. She was so strict and she and Philip were together and very fanatical. Anyway, she sang a solo. It was a revelation. She sang like an angel.' He looked down and blushed. His voice became more uncertain, quieter. 'After rehearsal she stayed to practise on her own and, well, it was just the two of us. It just happened.'

Tegan stared. 'No. No way would my mother have done that.'

Ellis grimaced. 'I'm sorry, but it's true. It was wrong. We both knew. We didn't speak about it when we next met. A month later Sarah found out she was expecting you. Before she told me, she told Philip.'

'She told Philip?'

'Yes. She felt she had to break off the engagement. She intended to raise you on her own. Philip, however, surprised her by saying he still wanted to marry her, have you as his own. Nobody was to know, not even me.'

Ellis swallowed hard. 'Sarah got married the following month. It was a very small wedding, but Hannah and I were invited. After the service, Sarah told me she was pregnant. She felt guilty, thought I had a right to know. She made me promise to keep out of things. I was so shocked. I didn't want to disown you, but Sarah insisted I have nothing to do with you. She did agree to give you my mother's name, Tegan.'

Tegan remembered the 'T' on Cerys' necklace.

'The other thing that was agreed was that my name would go on the birth certificate. It seemed right to be honest about that' said Ellis.

Tegan frowned. 'Philip agreed to that?'

Ellis sighed. 'Yes, he would not have wanted to lie on an official document.'

'But what if I'd seen it?'

'It could have happened. If you ever wanted a passport, for example, but that would not be for a long time. Sarah and Philip had strict control of your life.'

Tegan rolled on to her back, stared at the ceiling. So many mixed emotions. Horror and anger at her mother, a faint glimmer of relief that Philip was not her father. But Ellis, what did she feel about him?

She turned her head. 'You had nothing to do with me?' It was an accusation.

'I wanted to help, but, as I said, Sarah wanted nothing to do with me. The only thing she took was £500, a kind of emergency fund, nothing else.'

That explained the money. Then she thought of Philip, remembered the tears last time she had seen him at the Community. All these years Philip had held on to the secret, lived a lie. It must have really hurt him.

Then she screwed her eyes up. 'What about Cerys and Hannah?'

'They don't know. I've often wondered if I should tell Hannah, but somehow there didn't seem any point in upsetting her. I think, however, it is time to tell them. I want you to feel like you are part of a family here. This is where you belong now. I want you to stay, stay permanently, here in the cottage.'

Tegan blinked. 'Really?'

'Do you know your full name?'

She shook her head.

'Tegan Mai Williams. Pretty, isn't it?'

Tegan found it hard to speak. She saw Ellis waiting for a reaction but she felt numb. How was she meant to feel? So many lies.

'You should tell Cerys. I don't know how she will feel. I mean, you've lied to her. She will be very hurt. She may want me to go.'

'I don't think she-'

'Go now. Go and tell her.'

Ellis seemed to hear the urgency in her voice. He nodded and left her. Tegan lay thinking. Her mother had lied to her, pretended to be so upright. How many more lies were there? Who could she trust or believe any more?

Ellis found Cerys sitting in the corridor.

'OK, shall we go back?' she asked.

'I think we'd better talk first' he said nervously.

'What's the matter? Is it Tegan?'

'Let's go and get a drink.'

Once they were sat opposite each other, Ellis saw Cerys looking at him expectantly.

'I have just told Tegan something. I think maybe I should have told you and Mum this a long time ago.'

'What is it Dad. Are you ill?'

'No, nothing like that. It's about Tegan. You think she's your cousin, don't you?'

'Of course,' said Cerys, screwing up her eyes.

Watching her was agony. He had to just blurt it out.

'She's not your cousin. The truth is Tegan is my daughter. You and her are half sisters.'

Cerys put down her coffee cup, blinked really fast.

'What?'

'Tegan is your half sister, my daughter.'

Cerys was breathing fast, her face very red.

'But that would mean you had slept with Aunt Sarah, Mum's sister?'

He nodded.

'Dad, you are serious, aren't you? This isn't some kind of game?'

He shook his head. He couldn't speak, and he wanted her to shrug it off.

'You slept with your wife's sister, and for twenty seven years have kept it a secret that you have a child. My God, Dad.'

'I'm sorry' he mumbled.

'Does Mum know?'

He cringed. 'Not yet.'

'Dad, you mean you've told Tegan and me, but not Mum?'

'I didn't know what to do.' Even to him it sounded pathetic.

'All those lies, Dad. You slept with her sister, had a secret child together, and then carried on living a lie.'

'I haven't seen Tegan for years. They didn't want it. When she came here was the first time I've seen her since she went into the Community at five years old.'

'But you knew when she was coming. Dad, you shouldn't have told me that she was my cousin. Lying to me, to Mum, God, even the doctor. You just told him you were her uncle. Dad, this is terrible.'

Ellis put his head in his hands. He had expected rows with Hannah, but not Cerys. Cerys always understood, always took his side.

'I thought maybe you'd like finding you had a sister' he said.

Cerys stood up. 'Dad, you haven't just given me a puppy for Christmas. You've turned my life upside down.'

She started to walk away.

'Where are you going?' called Ellis

'I'm going home. Someone needs to look after Mum.'

'Look, I'll drive us.'

He saw Cerys glance at the door and then she sighed. 'OK, bit stupid for me to get the bus. Anyway, I can make sure for once you don't take the easy way out. You're going to tell Mum everything.'

Tegan lay in bed, waiting anxiously for Cerys to come back, to tell her everything was alright. There was a large clock over the entrance to the ward. Tegan lay staring at it, watching the seconds, the minutes, and then an hour pass, but Cerys did not return.

Chapter Thirty One

Cerys sat next to her father driving, staring ahead. She felt so angry. How could her father have betrayed her and Mum like this? All though her childhood she had lived with this man who would be away for long periods of time, missed all her school concerts, sports days, times she was ill, and yet she forgave him every time he walked in through the door with smiles, hugs and presents. She had thought her mother difficult, resented her for not being the same. Now she felt he'd played her for a fool.

They drove up to the manor. The first thing Cerys noticed was that the workmen's lorries had all gone, then that the front door was open. Her mother had driven her car up to the steps and the boot was open. She saw the look of alarm on her father's face as they approached. He stopped the car and jumped out. Hannah was coming out of the house carrying a small case.

'How is Tegan?' Hannah asked stiffly.

'I think she'll be alright-' he stammered. 'Hannah, what is going on?'

'I'm going away to think.'

'What is going on?' he repeated.

'I have sent all the workmen home.'

'Why?'

'Ellis, I'm fed up with it all: the house, the money, and your lies.'

'Lies?'

She sighed wearily. 'Oh really, Ellis. We're too old for this nonsense.'

Cerys was standing next to her father. She knows, Cerys thought, somehow my mother knows about Tegan.

'What are you talking about?' Ellis asked.

'Tegan, I know about her. I knew as soon as I saw her,' Hannah said, pain and anger fighting to be heard in her voice, but her face expressionless. 'You're her father, aren't you?'

Ellis nodded dumbly. She continued her judgment.

'I guess it was when I was pregnant with Cerys that you slept with my sister?'

'I'm so sorry-'

Cerys watched as Hannah put down her case. The solid mask on her mother's face slowly melted, tears pricked her eyes, and her thin lips trembled. Cerys realised that her mother deep down had been hoping her suspicions were wrong, but now there was no denying the truth any longer.

'How could you, Ellis? All our married lives you've kept this secret from me but I have always wondered, I've been too frightened to ask. All the time it's been like fighting an invisible enemy.'

'All this time you've suspected?' asked Ellis incredulously.

Hannah nodded. 'I saw the way you looked at Sarah when she sang, did the maths when Sarah gave birth. I know Philip would never have slept with her before marriage. And then, of course, Tegan was given your mother's name. All these things made me wonder, but I really knew when I saw Tegan-'

'How did you know then?'

'Ellis, really,' said Hannah, exasperated. 'She's the spitting image of your mother. She is so obviously your child.'

Cerys watched as her father crumbled. 'I'm so sorry' he said. The words had never sounded so inadequate.

'Was it all an act when she came? I mean, have you been seeing Tegan secretly?' asked Hannah, her voice hard.

'No, Sarah didn't want me to have anything to do with Tegan.'

'You should have told me. You should have faced up to what you had done.'

Cerys saw her mother suddenly looking at her as if she had just noticed she was there.

'Has he told you?' Hannah demanded.

243

'Yes,' she said. 'Just now.'

'I'm sorry, you must be in shock,' said Hannah gently.

'Look Hannah,' interrupted Ellis. 'Come inside and sit down. Please, let's talk.'

Hannah shook her head. 'I have to get away. I'm not saying I'm leaving you. I don't know what I'm doing, but I need to get away from you. You know there is so much of you. You fill my head, and I want to be able to think.'

'But what do you want? I can't undo the past. Did you want me to send Tegan away?' pleaded Ellis.

'Ellis, this can't be just brushed away. In any case, does Tegan know yet?'

'I just told her.'

'So I was last on the list to be told,' said Hannah coldly. Then she turned to Cerys, 'I'm sorry to abandon you. Please ring me, come and see me. I'm only going to a hotel.'

Cerys walked towards her mother. 'I'll be fine. I have Robert. Are you alright?'

Hannah nodded. Cerys took her bag and put it in the car. She saw Ellis was standing apart from them, watching, but excluded.

'Bye Mum. Keep in touch' said Cerys.

Hannah kissed her briefly on the cheek and drove away.

Cerys turned to her father. He was in tears, but they didn't touch her. She had no spare emotions for him, not now. She walked away into the garden back to her home.

Tegan lay in bed all afternoon. Evening visiting time came. She looked over as visitors arrived. For the first time, she was aware of all these strangers coming into a room where she was lying in her nightie. It was very odd, them in their coats, carrying bags, cases, or holding the hands of self-conscious children. The patients were like the inmates: vulnerable, trying to sit up, look alert, like it was a perfectly normal situation. However strange she might feel, though, Tegan wished someone, particularly Cerys, would come to see her.

She saw people starting to say good bye, and then she saw Cerys. She was walking slowly towards her. Tegan sat up, searching Cerys' face.

'I'm so sorry' stammered Tegan. Cerys sat down and touched Tegan's hand. Tegan went to speak, but then, to her horror, Cerys bent forward and burst into silent, heart wrenching tears.

'Cerys, I'm so sorry. You don't deserve this' said Tegan.

Slowly the storm subsided. Cerys wiped her face. 'You are the only person who shouldn't be saying sorry. Dad and Mam are having their usual drama, and as always I have to sort myself out.'

'That's not fair,' said Tegan.

'It's the way it has always been. Both of them so absorbed in their own worlds. I told you I could trust my parents. Well, now I don't know, do I?'

'Your Dad should have told you, but maybe he didn't want to upset you.'

'I suppose so. You know, I can already feel myself feeling sorry for him, damn him.'

'Would you like me to go, leave here?' asked Tegan quietly. 'I mean, you can all go back to how it was before, like I'd never come.'

'No, please stay. Things can't ever be the same, can they? Anyway, you and me, well we get on alright, don't we?'

Tegan smiled. 'You've been wonderful to me. I don't know how I would have coped without you.'

'So, how do you feel about it all?' asked Cerys. 'I mean, Philip is not your father. My Dad is. It's a bit mind blowing.'

Tegan sighed. 'You know, I'm so tired. I don't think half of it is going in.'

Cerys smiled back. She looked around.

'Heck, everyone else has gone. I'd better go before I get told off. See you tomorrow, OK?'

Tegan watched as Cerys left the ward, relieved that they had made their peace.

$\otimes$

The next morning Dr Richmond came to see Tegan.

'How are you feeling today?' he asked.

'Much better,' she replied. 'Can I go home now?'

'You can go today,' he said, 'but I'd like to get a few things in place before you're discharged.'

'What do you mean?' asked Tegan, frowning.

'I think you should be registered with a doctor down here.'

'Why?' Tegan couldn't understand why the doctor was fussing like this. She just needed to get home and rest.

'Because you are going to need care when you leave here.'

'But you said nothing is broken.'

'I think, Tegan, you need to talk to someone professionally about your problems. This could be arranged through your GP.'

Tegan sat up, blushed. 'I'm not mad. I know I've been a bit difficult in here, but I'll be fine once I get out.'

'You're not mad, Tegan,' said Dr Richmond patiently, 'but can you honestly tell me you are happy, that you feel able to cope?'

Tegan shrugged. 'I can get by, stay in the cottage, do knitting.'

'But that's not really coping with life, is it?' he persisted gently.

'Well I don't know. Cerys will look after me.'

'Don't you want to be able to look after yourself, live a normal life?'

'But I don't even know what that is,' said Tegan. 'My life has been so different. I get so confused.'

'You know, I think you must hurt inside a lot of the time,' said the doctor.

Tegan tried to swallow. She blinked back tears. She couldn't speak.

'It could help you cope, you know. To talk to someone who would understand, who could help you. Now, would you be happy for me to talk to Dr Khan, the doctor in your village? See if she can take you on?'

'I suppose so.'

'Good. You rest now. The nurse will let you know when you can contact family to come and fetch you.'

Tegan watched the doctor walk away. This was crazy. There was nothing wrong with her. She waited anxiously until a nurse finally told her she could ring Cerys. This she did, and then showered, and washed her hair. She was sitting in a chair when Cerys arrived.

'Hiya, I brought clothes,' said Cerys, holding out a bag.

'Thanks. Hang on. I'll pull the curtain and change.'

She put on jeans and a T-shirt of Cerys'. It felt good to put on normal clothes.

She pulled back the curtain. 'Ready.'

Initially Tegan walked quickly, but she soon slowed down. Her legs felt very weak, shaky, and out there in the corridor it seemed so much nosier and busier than the ward, like she was emerging from some kind of cocoon. She felt fragile. She held on to Cerys' arm as if the slightest wind would blow her away.

Tegan sat back in the car and looked blankly through the window.

'Have you spoken to your Dad yet?

'I did last night. We'll be alright.'

It seemed strange to see people just walking and shopping after the traumas of the past few days.

They arrived at the cottage. Tegan stepped out of the car and took a deep breath of the fresh, intoxicating air. She was suddenly aware of the wind blowing her hair. Without the headscarf it had been set free. Then she looked around her. So much had changed in a short time. Then, among the grass, she saw some orange poppies.

'These are like the ones in your pictures aren't they?' said Tegan, kneeling down. She touched their delicate petals. They felt like tissue paper.

247

'Meconopsis cambrica, the Welsh poppy. Plaid Cymru have just taken them as their logo. Fantastic aren't they? They self-seed everywhere around here. They can be yellow or orange. These are a few early ones.'

Tegan gently held one to her nose. 'There's not much smell, is there? Maybe a bit sweet?'

She stood up and continued to gaze around her. It was staggering. She felt she'd been away for a long time. Those initial feelings of being overwhelmed by the wildness, the space, all came back. In the distance she saw Sam and Angharad with Bracken. Sam waved and they started to approach her.

'So you came back,' said Angharad. 'Heard you had some kind of breakdown.'

Tegan looked at Sam, who seemed oblivious to Angharad's words. Instead, she could see his eyes tracing the marks on her face. He flinched as if they hurt him, then said, 'The red kites are still down there. I keep checking to see if they have started to build a nest. If they do and you're up to it we'll go down and I'll show you one day.'

Tegan nodded.

'So you've got rid of the headscarf?' interrupted Angharad.

Tegan put her hands to her head, suddenly feeling naked, ashamed.

'We ought to go,' said Sam. 'You take care, now. Remember, this place is special. You'll get better now.'

Cerys and Tegan went into the cottage. This time it felt to Tegan like coming home. The room was clean, quiet. Tegan sat down tentatively on the sofa while Cerys boiled the kettle. Tegan wanted to cry. She didn't know why.

'Why don't you go and cwtch up in bed, have a rest?' suggested Cerys.

'Where's Dylan?'

'Up with - well up at the manor. It's easier if he's there for the time being.'

For the first time Tegan noticed how pale and tired Cerys appeared.

'What's happened about your Mum? Ellis has told her now?'

'Well, actually Mum has gone to a hotel.'

'She's left your father?'

'Don't worry. This has been building for a while. Mum just needs some space, I think.'

'Have you spoken to her?'

'Yes, she sounds alright actually. Dad looks completely lost but she's not just letting him off the hook this time. Anyway, come on. Let's get you tucked in.'

Tegan went up to her room and took out her pretty new nightdress. She hadn't wanted to wear it in the hospital. She didn't want it tarnished with those memories. She held the soft cotton against her face, and put it on. It felt luxurious. She had never worn anything that felt so comfortable. She saw that Cerys had unpacked her things. Cerys came up and knocked on the bedroom door. She brought in a vase with a few poppies in and a book for Tegan to read.

'Thank you,' said Tegan.

'I'll be just downstairs. You rest now.'

Tegan lay down. She was worried about Ellis and Hannah, concerned it was her fault. She picked up the book. Of course, she had no glasses. They were broken. She tried to peer at the print but no, she couldn't read it. She laid back. Her senses all seemed heightened. She heard the birds outside. The room seemed so light, bright and quiet after the hospital ward. She turned on to her side, and then reached up to the etching of the owl, glanced at the poppies. They fitted with the owl for some reason. It was as if they were the same pieces of a jigsaw, but there were so many other pieces missing she had no idea what picture they would make. However, she was more convinced than ever that she had not imagined that feeling when she first came here, that feeling of familiarity, of something that happened deep in her past that she needed to uncover.

Chapter Thirty Two

Tegan had slipped into a deep sleep when she was awakened by a knock at the bedroom door. She was opening her eyes, trying to reorientate herself, when someone walked in. 'Hello, I'm Dr Khan, Nadia. I heard what happened. I wanted to pop in and see how you are.'

Tegan recognised the doctor from her fainting fit at the party. 'I'm much better,' she said quickly.

'Good. I've had a chat with Dr Richmond. He has asked if you could be registered with me. I am happy with that. Are you?'

Tegan nodded, not knowing what else she was meant to say.

'Good. Well, can I have a look at your injuries, see how they are healing?'

Tegan lay down passively as Nadia checked her head, shone lights in her eyes, and finally felt her ribs. Tegan was surprised to see how extensive the bruising was now, and her arms as well as her side were black and deep red.

'You say all this was done by a fall?'

Tegan nodded. Nadia waited but she said nothing else.

'You've had a rough time of it, haven't you?'

Tegan couldn't speak.

Nadia sat back. 'OK. Now, you rest. I want you to come and see me tomorrow morning. I'll see you about half eight. Is that OK? We need to chat about a few things. If you need anything before that, though, do ring the surgery. I'll have a word with Cerys about bringing you.'

After she had gone Cerys came upstairs with a mug of coffee. 'OK?'

'I think so. I have to go and see her tomorrow.'

'Don't worry, she's really good. You'll be fine.'

Later that evening Tegan went downstairs. She was stiff and dizzy, but glad to get out of bed. Cerys was in the lounge.

'I was thinking of watching a DVD. What do you think?'

Tegan looked blank. 'Sorry?'

'You know, a film.'

Tegan panicked, and then realised that, of course, there was no reason not to. It had all been a lie. Cerys was looking at her, waiting for a reply.

'I was thinking of Pride and Prejudice, the one with Colin Firth. Fancy that?'

Tegan tried to work it through. She had read the book. That was fine. She took a deep breath.

'OK then. Let's try.'

She sat down nervously and watched fascinated as Cerys slid the DVD into a slot on the machine. The film came on. It was very loud, the colours bright. She curled up on the sofa. Cerys made them some soup and bread to eat while they watched. They saw three episodes. Tegan wasn't taking a lot in, but it was comforting.

'You alright?' asked Cerys.

'Mmm. You know what I miss?'

'What?'

'Knitting. I wish I had some knitting.'

'You could see if there is anything for Rachel. She seemed keen.'

'Maybe. I don't think I'm good enough for that, though.'

'Well, you could see if she wants to give you a trial or something. She really liked my shawl and she doesn't throw around compliments. We could go in tomorrow when we go to the doctor's.'

When she went up to bed Tegan thought about the vigil, but got straight into bed. Daniel had been right to panic when she doubted him. He knew that if she doubted one thing then slowly the whole thing unravelled. But her mother believed all those things. Her mother, a clever, intelligent, woman, had chosen to believe Daniel's teaching, like a fly that relished being stuck in a web. She seemed to choose to stay enmeshed in the fear of his teachings. She looked on her bedside cabinet at her book of Daniel's Revelations, picked it up, and flicked through it. What if it was all lies? The verse in the frame? She put them both in the drawer. She heard her yellow clock ticking. It was unnerving, but she couldn't think why. She picked it up and put it in the drawer.

When Tegan woke the next morning she lay in bed motionless. It was as if every scrap of energy, every emotion, had been drained out of her. She could hear light rain pattering on the window and lay watching the droplets aimlessly meander down the window pane. She could hear Cerys downstairs getting breakfast. She didn't want to get out of bed. She wanted to stay there for ever.

Cerys called up. 'Breakfast's ready.'

She didn't reply. Cerys came upstairs.

'You alright?' asked Cerys.

Tegan shrugged. She couldn't speak.

'It's the doctor's today.'

Tegan still didn't reply.

'Look, you get up. I'll get some coffee and toast.'

Tegan forced herself to get out of bed, every footstep an effort. She couldn't be bothered to wash; she just threw on some clothes and went downstairs. There she took a sip of coffee, a nibble of toast and they left the cottage.

They drove to the doctor's in silence. They were the only ones in the waiting room. Soon Nadia called her in. 'So, how are you feeling?'

Tegan shrugged.

'OK. Well, let's have a look at you.'

She gave Tegan a thorough examination.

'Physically, things are healing well. How are you in yourself?'

Tegan swallowed. She couldn't speak.

'You have been through a huge ordeal. Dr Richmond suggested talking to someone, didn't he?'

Tegan nodded.

'I have someone in mind. She's called Liz. She's a qualified psychotherapist, very well regarded in medical circles. She works with a small group in a building attached to a medical practice in Aberystwyth. I'm sure Cerys will know where it is. I spoke to her and she could see you a week Friday. We're lucky: she's had a cancellation.'

Tegan frowned. 'I don't see the point.'

'You look very unhappy.'

'I feel nothing.'

'I would like you to go and chat to Liz. Just see how it goes. It may help.'

Tegan sighed. She just wanted to get out. 'OK.'

'Good. The details of the appointment are at reception.'

Tegan stood up.

'One more thing-'

Reluctantly, Tegan sat down again.

'I know this is difficult for you, but I would like to talk to you about medication.'

Tegan sat back stiffly. Nadia knew what she was thinking.

'I know, but let me explain.'

Tegan listened. What the doctor was saying sounded reasonable. Of course, Daniel would not agree, but then he'd been wrong about so many things.

Nadia looked at her carefully. 'I can see you're worried. Tell me, what's the problem?'

'I suppose we were never allowed to take medication. Will this play with my mind?'

Nadia shook her head. 'Oh no. I have put you on a small dose to start. It will just help bring some of that anxiety down. You'll be able to talk to Liz, work through some of the things that have damaged you.'

Tegan nodded. 'Well, alright. I can come back, can't I, if I don't feel well on it?'

'Of course. I want to see you regularly for a while, and of course any time you are worried, just make an appointment. I will tell the receptionist to fit you in that day. You can have this made up in the pharmacy here, alright?'

Tegan nodded.

'Good. Now, take care, and just rest. You are very tired,' said Nadia.

Tegan left the room. She went to reception and was given details of the appointment, then she found Cerys. They went to the pharmacy, picked up her prescription, and walked across the square. Tegan glanced over at the gift shop.

'I don't suppose you want-' asked Cerys, following her gaze.

'I don't know' Tegan said, sighing.

'I'll come with you. You said you missed it.'

Tegan shrugged, and followed Cerys across the square. She hoped that Rachel wasn't going to need to chat. She took a deep breath and went into the shop. Rachel was sat on a stool behind the counter sewing.

'Morning, Cerys. Ah, Tegan, I heard you'd come back.'

'Tegan wondered if she could do a trial for you,' said Cerys.

Rachel puckered her brows. Tegan panicked. Of course she wasn't wanted. 'It doesn't matter,' she mumbled, and started to turn away.

'Stop, sorry,' said Rachel. 'My mind was miles away. You say you want to do some work for me?'

'Well, if you would like, I could do a trial,' said Tegan quietly.

'I would like a shawl like you made Cerys. Would that be alright?'

'Yes, I suppose I could manage that. I have a pattern and needles. I need to buy yarn.'

'I'll obviously supply that.'

Cerys was looking down at a large sculpted wooden rabbit. 'That's clever.' She touched the smooth wood.

'Alan did it,' explained Rachel. 'He doesn't get much time, but they sell well.'

Rachel put down the white shawl she was embroidering.

'That's beautiful' said Tegan, gazing at the intricate silver embroidery.

'It's for Angharad, for the wedding. She asked for it, but I don't know. I think she was humouring me. Bet she never puts it round her shoulders. Still, there we are. I'll do it for Sam. Now, come and see my Aladdin's cave.'

Tegan and Cerys followed her into a room with shelves full of beautiful yarns and silks. Rachel seemed to relax in there.

'It's my dream, all this. Come on. Let's sort out things for you.'

'So, when do you need the shawl by?' asked Tegan.

'ASAP I suppose, but don't rush and make mistakes. I have built up a reputation for the highest quality work and that's why people pay so much.'

'Right. Well, I'll take this back and make a start.'

'Good. Let me know when you've finished.'

Tegan and Cerys went over to the shop, bought some food and then went back to the car.

'Why don't you bring Dylan around later?' asked Tegan.

'Are you sure?'

'Yes. I miss him.'

'OK then. I'll take you back and then pick him up from the manor'

When she returned, Tegan found her things for knitting and went to her room. She spent a lot of time resting in bed for the next few days. Sometimes Dylan would come up and lie next to her bed. She was surprised how quickly the days went and how much she slept.

It was the following Tuesday when she finally woke feeling a bit better. At last the world looked a bit brighter. She could feel a trickle of energy flowing through her veins. She got out of bed, and opened the curtains. The sunshine outside reached her. She felt tearful, but like something inside was thawing. She went downstairs.

Cerys smiled. 'You're up early.'

'I felt like it. I really felt like getting up today,' said Tegan earnestly.

'That's wonderful.'

'I would like to go out. Are you busy today?'

'I don't have to be anywhere. Why?'

'Could we go for a walk? Maybe you could show me the well again?'

'Of course. Have some breakfast and we'll go down together. I've wanted to tell you about the well, properly. You know, it may help you.'

Tegan put her coat on, and stepped out of the front door. Dylan went bounding ahead of them. She found her legs felt quite weak and shaky but she could feel a hint of warmth from the sun. The smells of the fields had changed. They were rich with spring flowers. In the woods there was a rich heady smell.

'Wild garlic' said Cerys, anticipating Tegan's question.

As they approached Tegan could see the sun glinting on the surface of the pond. It sparkled in a magical way. She found a large stone nearby and sat on it, breathing in the peace of the place.

'This feels a million miles away from London. All my troubles seem like a dream.'

'It has been really rough for you, hasn't it?' said Cerys.

'It's been horrible' she admitted. 'I feel very lost, not sure what to do next.'

'You've taken quite a battering, haven't you?'

'I'm so shocked, you know, about my mother. I mean, she's not the person I thought she was. How could she have sinned like that?'

'Well I don't know. My Dad was as bad. In fact, it is awful to think that he slept with his wife's sister. Not sure I'd use the word sin, although I don't condone it. It was very wrong. But then, everyone makes bad choices, don't they, sometimes?'

'But my Mum always pretended to be so perfect. She would have been so critical of anyone acting like she had done. It's so hypocritical.'

'I don't know,' said Cerys. 'Your Mum sounds a very complicated sort of person. If you don't mind me saying, she seems pretty messed up and she has been pretty terrible to you.'

Tegan touched the water. Although still cold it was not freezing like before.

Cerys put her head on one side. 'Remember you asked me about those pieces of wool on the bushes?' She pointed to the scraggy bits of wool hanging on nearby hawthorn.

'Mmm.'

'I think it's time I told you about it.' Tegan was caught by the intensity of Cerys' voice. She was about to share something deeply personal, like a child opening a secret box to reveal her most treasured possession.

'You see, it's the healing idea,' said Cerys. 'The ritual that has been handed down for hundreds of years is that you take a piece of wool, dip it in the water and then wipe it on the part of you that is ill. Then you take the wool and hang it on the bush.'

Shyly, Cerys produced from her pocket a piece of white shaped wool. 'You don't have to, but I wondered if you wanted to do it?'

Tegan's eyebrows rose. She wasn't sure. Would it be very evil, wrong? Would it hurt her in some way?

'Look, I told you I didn't believe in all those things like the tarot and things. I haven't just replaced them with this. I've been very careful. There is nothing magical in the water, and any healing will be done with hard work and the help of professionals, but for all that there is something soothing about it. My Nanna, your Nanna, used to do it all the time. I remember when I fell down once, and grazed my knees on the gravel outside the cottage. She brought me here and bathed it with wool.'

'And did it get better, you know, instantly?'

257

Cerys laughed. 'Of course not. Nanna took me back and put Savlon on it. But all the same, having Nanna wash my knee was very comforting.'

Tegan took the piece of wool and dipped it in the cool water. Where to wipe? All of her hurt, every part. She wiped her face, her head, and then solemnly took the wool and hung it on the branch.

They sat quietly and then Cerys said, 'Dad is going to see Mum today.'

'Really?'

'She sent him a text, said she was ready to talk.'

'What do you think will happen?'

'No idea. Those two... Still, I hope they sort things out. They need each other. They both sound so lost. Anyway, come on. Let's get back to the cottage.'

Ellis had parked and went to the reception of the smart hotel where Hannah was staying. He told them who he wanted to see while trying to push away the mental calculations of how much it was costing for Hannah to stay in such a place. He found Hannah sitting reading in a large conservatory. It was light, warm, and in the centre a fountain gurgled. Like several other people, Hannah was sitting on a sun lounger wearing a white robe, reading.

'Looks relaxing' he said.

She agreed. 'It is, really calm. Well, until you walked in anyway.'

He sat down awkwardly on a sun lounger next to her.

'I've missed you' he said quietly. 'I've been thinking. I do realise I've been rather selfish. I want to make things better between us.'

'Really?' she asked sceptically.

'I've already done things,' he added quickly.

'Like what?' she asked.

'I've contacted the trust, agreed to sign. The manor will be largely owned by them.'

'Really? We weren't too late?' she said, suddenly interested.

'I caught them just in time actually,' he said, sheepishly. 'They had started looking at somewhere else, but when I said what Cerys had done to the garden and what you had already started they were very enthusiastic.'

'Excellent.'

'Something else as well.' Ellis reached into his pocket and took out a golden envelope.

Hannah took it from him, opened it, and sat reading. Then she looked up, speaking in a whisper, 'An organised holiday, a holiday taking us to some the great art galleries of Europe.'

'Well, I thought if it was arranged like this I couldn't back out, you know, sneak you off to concerts. This way we have to go to the galleries.'

Hannah grinned. 'You make it sound like some sort of penance.'

Ellis smiled. 'Maybe it is. Still, I'm not a complete philistine. It will be interesting.'

'Have you seen the dates? It takes most of October. What about the job in the university?'

'I've turned it down.' Ellis saw Hannah's face. She knew how much this had cost him. 'You're right. We need to do more together.'

'I'm impressed, Ellis. I really am. But, you know, it all hurts. I can't pretend nothing happened.'

'I know, but please let's at least try and start again.'

'How is Tegan?'

'I've kept away to be honest, but Cerys tells me she's a bit better now. She'd been through a hell of a lot. I don't understand how Sarah could be so cruel.' He stopped.

'I don't either, to be honest,' said Hannah. 'I think you know that Tegan should stay.'

'Really?' said Ellis.

259

'Yes, and, well, I will come back. This place, well, it's a bit lonely actually. But this is a new start, Ellis, no just papering over the cracks. You've really hurt me this time.'

'I know, I am so sorry.' Then Ellis took a deep breath. 'Actually there is one more thing, the one thing I haven't told you.'

'What is that Ellis? No more children I hope?'

'No, not that. It's about the cottage. It's the one thing I thought I could do to prove you are now my priority, you come first.'

Slowly Ellis explained.

Chapter Thirty Three

The next day Tegan was sat on the sofa when Bethany arrived.

'Tulips today,' Bethany said as Tegan let her in. She sat next to Tegan on the sofa. 'How are you doing?'

'Bit better thanks.'

'Good, well I'm glad you're back with us.'

Tegan put down her knitting.

'Bethany, before I went away you said something to me about being in a cult.'

'I'm sorry. I wasn't very tactful. I have read a lot since then, talked to people, tried to understand things better.'

Tegan sat forward. 'I need to know. Please tell me. I feel I'm going mad.'

'Do you really want to hear all this? I mean, now. You must be exhausted.'

'I am, but I need to understand. My mind, my head is full of stuff I can't make sense of.'

Bethany nodded. 'I'm no expert, OK, but I will tell you what I learnt. Actually, one of the first things I read is that if you think someone is in a cult, don't say that to them.' She grinned. 'Then I found out that the word cult is not used so much, that they are now called things like High Demand Groups. There are different sorts of groups, some more destructive and dangerous than others.'

'And did you find out anything about my group?'

'It was difficult. It is quite small and secretive.'

'But you did?'

'Just a bit. Actually, I contacted someone who is working in London. He works with people from different sorts of cults and sects.'

'And what did he say?'

Bethany seemed to lose her nerve. 'I don't know Tegan. I'm not sure I'm the right person to be talking about all this.'

Tegan leaned forward, and spoke earnestly. 'Please, I have to know the truth. I'm so lost. All I've been told is lies. My life has been a lie. Please tell me what you heard.'

'OK. This man said that he had heard things about your community. He actually went to a meeting where Daniel, your leader, was speaking.'

'And-'

'In his opinion he thought Daniel was a very disturbed individual, dangerous.'

'Dangerous?'

'Yes. He said he had many of the traits of the leaders of destructive cults. He was very concerned for anyone living in the Community.'

'Really?'

'Yes. I also read that an ex-member had raised concerns about the financial practices going on there.'

'I don't think that can be right. We lived very frugally. So how are you meant to know if a group is dangerous?'

Bethany sighed. 'From what I remember he said that a destructive cult is one that exploits its members, tries to control them. They demand you worship, follow unconditionally, a leader.'

'You mean like Daniel expected us to accept everything he said?'

'That's it. They have to make you feel that they are the only person who can save you, and if you disobey them you will go to hell.'

'I suppose he did say things a bit like that, but you know some of the people in the Community were very bright. Surely, if Daniel was fooling everyone they would have known?'

'You know, I used to think that it was only troubled, needy people who joined cults. But I was reading that actually cults want bright, dedicated, idealistic, energetic people to raise money, do the work of the group, and recruit new people.'

262

'Actually the Community existed before he came. I'd been there for about five years. So I suppose he had people very ready to accept his teaching. I mean, my parents had always told me about the end times, that I would be left, go to hell, that sort of thing. When Daniel arrived, slowly it became more about following him. He was the chosen one, you see, the one who had visions. Slowly, he became the supreme leader. I wonder how he managed to keep them believing in him?'

Bethany took a deep breath.

'What? Tell me.'

'Well, it's complicated. He said leaders can use methods called thought reform or mind control.'

'We weren't brainwashed.' Tegan was horrified. 'We weren't walking round like a load of robots.'

Bethany shook her head. 'No, that's not what he meant. It's like they use a number of things which break down a person's sense of self.'

'Like what?'

'Things like isolating members from the rest of society so that they can't think critically about what they are being taught. They are taught the world outside is wicked and evil.'

Tegan frowned. 'That's what Daniel said.'

'Also, members are kept very busy, no time for thinking. In fact, they are told all the time what to do, what to think, wear, eat, when to sleep.'

'I don't know. It all sounds so negative but, you know, that can be quite a nice way to live. Out here, all the time you have to make decisions. It's exhausting.'

Bethany smiled. 'I can see that, but the problem is that the members can end up living always in fear. All the creative side of a member is squashed. You have no autonomy, no sense of who you are. It can lead to all sorts of problems.'

Tegan lay back. It was so much to take in.

'Do you have any books or anything I can read?'

'Yes, of course. You can borrow them any time. I could leave them in the porch for you to pick up if I'm out.'

Bethany stood up. She looked worried. 'I hope I'm doing the right thing telling you all this. It's one thing to know things in your head, but to live with the consequences is very different.'

'Do you know about Ellis?'

Bethany nodded. 'About him being-'

'My father, yes.'

'I had heard.'

'You mean it's all round the village? So what's everybody saying?'

Bethany bit her lip. 'Well, let's say no one was too surprised. Ellis has always been very flirtatious, and, you know, the older folk, they remember your grandmother. Apparently you do look ever so like her. Anyway, don't you worry about all that. They'll have moved on to something else in a day or two.'

'But Hannah has come back. Ellis rang Cerys last night.'

'That's really good. Hopefully they can sort things out properly now.' Bethany stood up. 'I'd better leave you in peace. I hope what we talked about helped. I'm no expert, you know.'

'I'm meant to be going to a therapist on Friday.'

'Really. Good, I'm so glad.'

'We'll see,' said Tegan. 'Can't say I'm looking forward to it. You know, maybe I just need to rest.'

'Try to go. Really, it could help you.'

Tegan shrugged, but the more she thought about it the less inclined she was to go.

When Cerys returned later, she said to Tegan, 'Dad was asking if you are coming to choir tonight.'

'He feels like doing it then. You know, after all the upset.'

'Oh, you know Dad. Bounces back pretty quickly. So, what do you think?'

'I don't know,' said Tegan. 'I mean, I don't know how I'm meant to be with him now.'

'He did say that you may find it awkward, said he would try to act normal.'

264

'But what will the village think of me? I mean, my Mum wasn't married when I was conceived. And then they find out I'm the choir master's daughter.'

'You're living in the past. Look at Rhiannon. If she hadn't been the vicar's daughter nobody would have blinked an eyelid. Don't worry; probably make people accept you more not less. You know, you're officially part of the village, not some stranger from London.'

Tegan shook her head. She would never get the hang of things out here.

After an early evening meal Cerys said, 'Right, we need to go. Dad said that, if you were going, to get there a bit early.'

They drove down to the church hall. Tegan was surprised how small and unglamorous it was. She had expected them to be in a large building similar to where she had been for the concert.

Ellis came over to greet them. 'Well done Tegan. I'm so pleased you've come.' He looked very tired, but he smiled. 'It's OK. I don't expect to be called Dad or anything. Let's just carry on as we did before, eh? Now, I'll put the heating on, and then we can do some singing exercises to warm you up. Come on, Cerys, you can do this as well, make Tegan feel less self-conscious and, in any case, it'll do you good as well.'

Cerys groaned but went with Ellis and Tegan to the piano.

'First I'm going to do some breathing exercises with you.'

Eventually, Tegan heard the door of the church hall open.

'Well done. You know, Tegan, you have a very good voice, something special there. Don't you neglect it now.' She turned to see who was coming in, and was surprised to see that most of the village seemed to be in the choir. She saw Angharad arrive, firmly holding Sam's hand. Then Sam untangled himself and made for the piano.

Ruth came bustling over to Tegan and Cerys. 'Tegan, Ellis tells me you have joined the choir. I have your folder ready.

265

Apparently you are to be with the sopranos. The next concert is on May 1st. That will be held at the manor; outside if it's dry.'

Ellis came over to them. 'Thanks so much, Ruth. I don't know what I'd do without you.'

'I'm sure you'd manage.'

'No, you know me. Couldn't manage without you.'

'I don't think I know you at all, actually. I'll go and sort out the music with Sam.'

Cerys grinned at Ellis, who had gone red. 'Bit of a put down, Dad. I think she's found out her idol has feet of clay.'

'I don't know what you mean. Let's get on with this damn rehearsal.'

He shouted to everyone to go to the stage. Reluctantly, people picked up their folders and started arranging themselves. Tegan stood next to Cerys. Sam sat at the piano, sheets of paper arranged on the top. Ellis chose the first song. He found the music, and the rehearsal began. Tegan had to use all her concentration, but was completely wrapped up in the singing. She was between Cerys and Grace, both strong singers. Slowly, she relaxed. She loved the feeling of singing with other people. The harmonies worked well. Ellis seemed magically to blend the different voices into one lovely sound. Sam's accompaniment was excellent, not just technically, but he seemed to make the piano sing with the choir. Sometimes the music stirred up such strong emotion. Her throat would tighten, and it hurt too much to sing. Then she would listen, try to relax, and join in again. Time went quickly. She was surprised when they finished.

Ellis came over to her. 'How did you find it?'

'I enjoyed it a lot more than I expected. It's emotional, singing, though, isn't it?'

Ellis nodded. 'It is if it means anything to you. It will get easier. Now, remember, you need to pick up those glasses.'

'I may be going to Aberystwyth on Friday.' She looked down. 'You know, therapy. Maybe I could call in then?'

'Make sure you do. Are you alright for getting to Aberystwyth?'

'I think Cerys is taking me.'

He looked around and saw Ruth leaving. 'Oh, she's gone.'

Cerys laughed. 'You've really upset her, Dad. Come on, me and Tegan will help clear up.'

'Heard from Mum, love?' Ellis asked Cerys.

'Yes, she sounds alright. What are you going to do Dad?'

'I've been thinking. Don't worry. I've got it all in hand.'

Cerys grinned and shook her head. 'There's no putting you down, is there Dad?'

Ellis grinned back, and then turned to Tegan. 'I could do with a quick word, actually. Come over here.'

They sat on two of the plastic chairs.

'It's about money,' said Ellis. 'You really can't have much now at all. I know I will pay for your glasses, but there are other things, clothes and stuff.'

Tegan blinked hard. 'I have started working for Ruth actually. You know, shawls and things.'

'That's great, but it will take a while to make any money at that. I'm glad you're doing that, though, and I don't want you to feel you have to rush into anything else. I have put some money in an account for you, and I have a card for you.'

'Oh no. You can't give me money.'

He looked at her sternly. 'I want you to have this. Now, make sure you use this card. Sign it on the back. This is the pin number. Learn it and then destroy it. You can get money out of machines with it, or pay for things in shops. Cerys will help you if you get stuck.'

Tegan wanted to reject it but practically she knew he was right. She had very little money left. She took the card.

'I'll pay you back one day.'

'What ever. I know you're not used to spending money on yourself but you must use this.'

'Well, thank you. It's very kind.'

Tegan turned away.

'Good luck on Friday,' he called.

Tegan sighed. How she could get out of it?

267

Tegan had her excuses ready when she went down to breakfast on Friday morning.

'I can't be going to the therapist' were her first words to Cerys.

'You have to at least give it a go.'

'No. I've thought about it. I'm getting better. I don't need to go. I have plenty of people around to help me now, and I don't need it.'

'But, Tegan, you told Nadia you'd go. You know, you're still shouting out a lot in the night. Please at least give it a try.'

'But I have stomach ache. I don't think I can.'

'Look, let's at least get to the place. I'll wait for you. You know you can walk out any time you want to.'

'Can I?'

'Yes, and I'll be there waiting. I promise. Listen, if we go early we can go and get your glasses first, which would be good, wouldn't it?'

'Yes, I suppose so' Tegan agreed reluctantly. 'Do you think we could park up by the optician, not the sea front?'

Cerys looked surprised but said 'If you like, of course. Come on, then, let's go.'

They got in the car. First they drove in to the village and stopped at the vicarage, where Tegan found a carrier bag of books and papers hanging on the door handle.

When they arrived in Aberystwyth they parked down a side street. They walked up the steep street, seagulls screeching and gliding on the winds above them. Tegan shot a look at the birds. She felt her breathing quicken. She stopped, wanted to hide.

'You alright?' asked Cerys.

'Yes, it's OK.'

When they arrived at the optician Tegan felt another surge of panic and wanted to run, but she stopped herself. Take it slowly. She felt calmer, and they went in.

Jenny was there again typing on her computer. Her nails were black today.

'I-' Tegan was aware that Jenny was looking at her face. 'I wondered if my glasses were ready?'

'Oh yes.' Jenny seemed confused. Tegan wondered why.

'Wait a second. I'll see if Grace wants to fit them or if I can.'

She disappeared for a few seconds and then returned. 'She's on her way.'

Grace came out smiling, and then looked at Tegan. 'Are you alright?'

Tegan smiled. 'Yes, much better thank you. I was wondering about my glasses.'

'Well they're ready. I was just thinking that your eyes look rather sore.'

Tegan glanced over at the mirror. She had forgotten about her face, still bruised. No wonder Jenny had looked at her so strangely.

'Oh, this. It's OK. I fell. It's much better now.'

'OK then, let's see how these fit.'

She handed Tegan her new glasses. Tegan put them on. She blinked, startled by the clarity of things around her. She looked at a notice on the wall. She could read it easily.

'It's incredible. It's like seeing for the first time.'

She looked around in wonder.

Cerys approved. 'They suit you. You look really pretty.'

Tegan blushed. Grace checked the fitting, and Tegan was about to leave.

'Hey, don't go without making another appointment. I want to see you in three months. Come back sooner if there are any problems.'

Tegan made an appointment, and they left.

Tegan walked through the streets looking at everything they passed. It really was like she had never seen before: everything so clear. She could read the names of the shops, the prices in the windows. She looked at Cerys and could make out the details of her face.

269

Cerys caught her staring at her. 'What are you thinking?'

'Well, I can see you properly now.'

'Oh no.'

'No, it's nice. We look like sisters.'

'I suppose so, but you are a lot thinner. Oh, here we are.'

Tegan looked nervously up at a modern single-storey building. Inside, a rather harassed but efficient woman took her details and told her to take a seat. She sat on a hard plastic chair next to Cerys. There were different medical posters about immunisations and pregnancy on the walls. After a few minutes a woman of about forty, with blond curly hair, wearing a homely, chunky red jumper came into the room. The woman looked over at Tegan hopefully.

'Tegan?'

Tegan stayed in her chair, frozen.

'Hi, I'm Liz. Come on through' said the woman easily.

Tegan followed behind her, slowly, glancing at the front door that was ajar. She could run, get away; she didn't have to do this.

Chapter Thirty Four

Tegan fought the desire to escape, and followed Liz into the therapist's room. It was light and bright with plants scattered around. Liz indicated the chair for Tegan to sit on. On a small table strategically placed were a clock and a box of tissues. Tegan sat rigid; frightened she would say the wrong thing. She didn't want this woman to think she was mad.

'So what's brought you here?' asked Liz.

'I was told to come by the doctor.'

'And why do you think that was?'

'I suppose I came back from London in a state. She was worried.'

'Dr Khan has told me you were in a community called the Last Week Community.'

'That's right. I was brought up there by my parents, well my mother and step-father.'

'And you left?'

'I was made to leave, twice.'

Liz didn't speak. It was awkward. What did she expect her to say? The silence continued. Tegan had to think of something.

'The first time I was cast out because I rebelled. Then I tried to go back, but that didn't work out either, and then I ended up in hospital.'

'So your mother and step-father-'

Tegan looked down, dug her nails into her hands. 'They are still there. I shan't see them again.'

'Tell me about your Community.'

'I think it may, well, it may have been a cult.'

'Why do you think that?'

Tegan explained what Bethany had told her. She spoke as pragmatically as she could. She had to show this woman she

271

didn't believe it any more. She stopped. Liz didn't appear to be reacting.

'And how do you find it living away from the Community?'

Tegan shrugged again. She glanced out of the window. She saw people outside shopping, chatting, all so normal. 'It's OK,' she said.

Liz waited.

'Well, sometimes it's difficult,' Tegan admitted. 'In the community I didn't need to make any decisions, worry about money. That was all done for me.'

'But you say you rebelled?'

Tegan bit her lip. 'I went to the library, made friends with someone-' She stopped, silence.

Liz said quietly, 'So, how do you feel now you've left?'

'Bit awkward. Silly things frighten me. I am starting to understand that some of the things I was taught weren't true, but, you know, I can't help missing it sometimes. I feel, well, lonely.'

'Leaving a group such as yours can be extremely difficult. You have lost your family and the only way of life you knew. In many ways it is like going through bereavement.'

Tegan blinked, swallowed hard. Liz was right, but she didn't want to react here: she mustn't cry.

Liz leant forward. 'I know the words are hard, but I hope it helps you understand some of the reasons why you are hurting and in such pain.'

'I feel guilty. You know, I have somewhere to live, money. I should be fine.'

'No. Don't underestimate the level of hurt you have been through.'

'One thing that was difficult was that they told me that everyone in the world was evil. But some people are very kind. They have helped me a lot.'

'That must have been confusing.'

'It was. And I'd been told that the optician would try to blind me, could not help me. And yet when I went with Ellis I found I could see properly for the first time in my life. I can't understand what is so bad about that.'

'Tell me, is there anything in particular that upsets you at the moment?'

Tegan shrugged. She looked out of the window, looked at the sky.

'The red kites. I don't know why I put my hands on my head when I see them. I panic.'

'You are frightened?'

'Yes I was, but I don't know why-'

'When it's happening, the birds are above you, try to think how you feel. What are you thinking?'

Tegan closed her eyes. Slowly, she remembered, and then it became vivid. She could feel the panic growing. 'They are trying to get me.'

'Who?'

'The birds.'

'And how do you feel?'

'Hot, sick.'

She opened her eyes and started shaking. She clutched the arms of the chair. 'I don't want to talk about this. I should never have come. I was happy before I came in here.' She put her face in her hands and started to sob, hard sobs that hurt, that didn't make anything feel better.

Liz leant forward. 'It's alright, Tegan. Breathe slowly now.'

Tegan started to calm down, wiped her eyes, and looked at her lap.

'Sometimes,' said Liz gently, 'something called a trigger makes you vividly recall something from your past, gives you a flashback. That is much more than a visual memory: it's very real; you are back there; a smell, a taste, you see everything. Can you tell me, when you get these panics seeing birds what do you see?'

Tegan sat imagining the red kites swooping over her. 'The huge flying beasts on my wall: that's what I was thinking of.'

273

'Can you describe them?'

Tegan described her picture.

'And when would you see these beasts?'

'At the end, you know.'

'The end?'

'You know, it's the end of the world. Huge flying monsters will rise out of the sea. They will pull the skin off my face. I will scream, but nobody is left to help me.' Tegan stopped.

'When did Daniel and the community first talk to you about these things?'

'I don't know. I remember Philip telling me that if I was not a good girl him and Mum would disappear. I would be left in the world on my own, and all these nasty things would happen to me.'

'How old were you then?'

'Oh, five or six, I suppose. He told me about hell as well.'

'Hell?'

'Mmm. Well, anyway, Daniel, he came when I was about ten. He taught us a lot more. He showed us films, which was odd, because we'd never been allowed to see TV or films, but he said these were different.'

'What did he show you?'

Tegan dug her fingers deep in her hand. 'I can't remember. It's a long time ago.' She felt very sick.

They sat in silence.

'So what can I do, you know, when I see birds, to stop being frightened?' asked Tegan.

'You can try some kind of grounding techniques.'

'What are they then?'

'It's a way of putting yourself in the present. Try and stop yourself going back to the traumatic memories that have been triggered. So, for example, you can stamp the ground, grind your foot into the ground, feel the chair you are sitting on, notice the smells around you, the colours, and the sounds.'

'Oh, OK. Maybe I'll try that.'

'But be gentle with yourself. Rest, read a book after. It can be very tiring.'

They talked more about the nights, about vigil.

Then Liz said, 'So you say your community was isolated. There must be some things that are quite difficult now.'

'Going into pubs is hard. We were told it was evil, and now, although I don't think that, I still feel ill when we're going in. It's like when Cerys lights the fire, or when I go out in the dark; it's things that frighten me but I don't seem to be able to calm myself down.'

'Can you describe how you feel physically?'

'My heart thumps very hard. I feel like I'm very scared, wonder if I'm going to die. I feel hot, sweaty, and sick. I can't think straight. It's very frightening.'

'Does this feeling last a long time?'

'I don't know.'

'What you are describing sounds like a panic attack.'

'What?'

'When we feel frightened or anxious our body produces a hormone called adrenalin.'

'Hang on. Deborah did that in biology with me. Fight or flight?'

'That's right. The adrenalin makes your heart beat faster to take oxygen to those parts of the body that need it. You breathe faster, sweat. You become more alert.'

'Ready for attack?'

'That's right. These changes make your body able to take action and protect you in a dangerous situation, either by running away or fighting. Once the danger has passed, other hormones are released, which may cause you to shake as your muscles start to relax.'

'But you say that's normal?'

'Yes, but a panic attack is like an exaggerated version of this. It comes on quickly and you experience things like you described, the heart thumping, sweating. It's very frightening.'

'Is there something I can do to stop myself feeling like that?'

275

'There are a few things. One thing we could do is work on some simple breathing techniques.'

'What do you mean? I'm not doing yoga.'

'This is just breathing. I'll show you.'

Liz talked her through deep breathing.

'Ellis showed me that when he was trying to help me sing' said Tegan.

'Sing?'

'Yes, you see, it gets stuck. My throat hurts. Philip said it's judgment for being vain.'

'Philip?'

'He's my father. No, my stepfather.'

'OK, so did the breathing help?'

'Actually it did.'

'Good.'

'Maybe I could do it when I'm trying to go to sleep. I'm very tired a lot of the time.'

'Something else that might help you when you feel very anxious is imagining a safe place to go to.'

'Oh, I've already done that. My mother made up stories about a cottage. Even now I have found I could think about it as a place to go when I was very frightened or scared.'

'Tell me about it.'

'Actually, it's very like where I'm living now.'

Tegan closed her eyes and described the cottage. She felt warm, at ease. She could smell it, feel it.

She opened her eyes.

Liz smiled. 'It sounds wonderful. Think of somewhere in the cottage you particularly like to sit, where you feel safe. Use that when you need it.'

Tegan nodded.

'Now, we are allowed more sessions. Would you like to carry on?'

'You mean I have a choice?'

'Of course.'

'So you can help me more, can you?'

'Yes, one of the things we can use is something called cognitive behavioural therapy or CBT.'

Tegan flinched. What was going to happen to her?

'It's alright. It's just sitting here talking like we've been doing. We'll look at how the way you think affects your behaviour and how you deal with problems. The aim is for you to gain control of your fear and distress by changing the negative way you think about your experience.'

Tegan didn't understand this. It sounded very complicated.

'Do I need to talk any more about my past?'

'Well, CBT does tend to focus on the present rather that the past, but I do think in your case we are going to have to look at your past as well.'

'But I don't like thinking about the stuff I was taught.'

'I can understand that, but, you see, some of the things you were taught were so frightening that you have never processed them, thought them through. We need to do that together so that you can move on.'

Tegan again felt lost but she had to admit that the session today had been helpful. Maybe it was worth coming again? 'So I have five more sessions?'

'Actually, I want to request more. We have a lot to do. And I don't want to rush things.'

'OK. Yes, I will come again.'

'Good. I'm really glad. Your next appointment would be next Friday, March 31st. Same time. Would that be alright?'

Tegan nodded.

'Good. Now, I have something I'd like you to do for next time. I wonder if you could write about yourself as a child, either when Philip or Daniel was talking to you, what it was like sitting there, how you felt. It's part of this trying to understand the past. Do you think you could do that?'

Tegan nodded. 'OK.'

Tegan left the room and found Cerys, who was sitting reading a magazine.

'Alright?' asked Cerys.

'I suppose so. I'm very tired now though.'

On the way back to the cottage Tegan said 'Can we pick up Dylan, bring him home with us?'

Cerys smiled. 'Of course.'

They called into the manor. Everybody seemed to be out. Dylan came bounding towards them, and jumped into the car ready to go with them.

When they got back to the cottage, the first thing Tegan did was find a book to read. It was fantastic to pick up any book off the shelf and be able to read it easily. She sat on the sofa and Dylan leapt up next to her. She was so engrossed in her book that she didn't notice the time.

'I'll close the curtains,' offered Cerys. 'Look, I know you're engrossed in your book, but would you mind if I put the television on? I want to see a gardening programme.'

Tegan bit her lip. Her heart started to race. It was the unpredictability that frightened her. Any minute it could change, she had no control. She looked over at the remote control. Of course, she did have control, and she could switch it off any time she wanted. Surely it wasn't any different to watching a film? Nothing terrible was going to happen. Millions of people watched TV everyday, and they were fine. She had watched films and been fine. This was no different. Dylan came over to her, somehow sensing her unease. She stroked his ears, and then started to concentrate on her breathing. It was only a gardening programme. She could do this. She glanced over at the knitting bag. Maybe if she was knitting it would help.

'OK.'

Cerys sighed with relief and turned on the television. Tegan went and found the knitting. She sat down and picked up the pattern. 'Gosh, this is clear.'

Cerys laughed. 'You're really appreciating your new glasses, aren't you?'

'I'll say. Wow, I can see the knitting so much better. I should be able to knit faster now.'

The programme was a garden make-over. Cerys and Tegan sat commenting on the pros and cons of what was being planned.

'The trouble is,' said Cerys, 'it's more, like a building project, so much wood and concrete. I suppose it saves looking after lawns and things.'

After a while Cerys said to Tegan 'OK?'

Tegan nodded. 'Yes, thanks. I'm fine. It's hard to believe that something that seemed such an issue is actually fine. I'm sitting here watching TV and I haven't been struck down. The end of the world hasn't come, nothing. It's incredible.'

Chapter Thirty Five

Early the next morning Tegan decided to go for a walk over the fields. Dylan was delighted to go out so early and ran in front of her. The bird song was rich, the air cool and clean. She closed her eyes, let it envelope her. When she opened her eyes again she was surprised to see Sam and Bracken close to.

'How are you feeling? Hey, you've got new glasses?' said Sam.

'Yes. I'm just getting used to them.'

'I'm going to see how the red kites' nest is coming on. Fancy coming?'

Tegan agreed and they started to walk toward the woods. Suddenly, a kite swooped overhead. She couldn't speak. She could handle this, and it wouldn't hurt her now. She tried to quieten her breathing.

'Look, they're definitely building the nest. That nest will be lined with sheep's wool. They keep adding to it all the time. I must let the red kite association know. It's nice and quiet round here. Hopefully nothing will disturb them.'

They automatically started to walk into the woods. Tegan glanced around, but Dylan wasn't far behind them.

'Hey, now you're back you'll be able to do a proper study of the owls; try and get out at night. It's so exciting.'

'Mmm-'

Sam smiled. 'I know, you don't want to go out? Are you still scared, you know, of the dark and things?'

'A bit.'

'You mustn't be like that. You know, I come up here purposely a couple of times a month after dark, walk up in the hills. It's fantastic, another world.'

'Aren't you scared?'

'Oh no. I love the night. Hang on, shush. Look, up there.'

Above a nesting box a tawny owl sat roosting.

'See, it's holding itself against the trunk. Well camouflaged, isn't it? You see smaller birds, like tits, will gang up on it and attack it.'

'Oh?'

''Fraid so.'

Tegan was very excited. She had never seen an owl before, and to be so close! Quietly they walked away until they reached the well, where they sat down.

'Look, why don't I come back later when it's dark, take you out? It's a while since I've done it,' asked Sam.

'Oh no. I mean, I don't think I could.'

'Come on. Of course, you have to be more careful walking at night but I'll bring all the right gear.'

Tegan smiled at his enthusiasm, but said 'I don't think Angharad would like that.'

'Maybe not. Hang on, I'll phone her.'

Tegan stood listening to Sam explain the plan to Angharad. She could hear that Angharad wasn't too impressed. Finally the call was finished.

'Well, there you are. She has the option of coming.'

'Do you think she will? I mean, we shouldn't go if she doesn't want to, should we?'

'She can come if she wants to.'

Tegan tried to smile and said quickly 'I could ask Cerys.'

'Great.'

They reached the well and sat down, Dylan noisily lapping up water. Tegan leant forward, scooped some water and splashed it on her forehead. It was very peaceful. Bracken lay down, chin on the ground, one eye open watching the birds, but clearly with no intention of moving.

Sam's phone suddenly smashed the stillness. 'I'm still with Tegan. James, best man? No way. What now? OK.' Tegan glanced at him. His face creased anxiously, his spare hand scratching the back of his neck. He ended the call.

'Sorry, I need to go and see Angharad. Wedding plans,' he said abruptly.

'That's OK. I think I'd better be going.'

'Now, don't forget tonight,' he said, smiling.

They walked back through the woods; both quiet.

Tegan went back into the cottage and had started making breakfast when Cerys came down. 'You're up with the lark.'

'I took Dylan out. It's a lovely morning. We met Sam. He showed me the nest, very exciting.'

'You must show me later.'

'He knows so much about birds and nature doesn't he?'

'Yes.'

'You know, he said he'd take me out tonight, explain all the things you can hear at night. He said I wouldn't be scared then.'

'Did he now? Is Angharad going?'

'Oh, I think so. I was going to ask you if you fancied it as well.'

'I doubt it. I'll be tucked up watching telly by then. I can't see Angharad coming, unless she wants to keep an eye on you two.'

'Oh no, there's nothing like that.'

'Seems to me you two have quite a lot in common actually.'

'He's engaged. There's no point in even thinking like that.'

Cerys grinned. 'I'll believe you.'

That evening Cerys and Tegan had their tea and then sat watching TV. Cerys was closing the curtains when Tegan sat up.

'Sam's coming soon. Will you come as well?'

'I'm sorry, but not tonight. I'm done in. Go on, you'll be fine if you ignore Angharad. Take Dylan for company. He'll love it.'

'That's a good idea.' Tegan went to find the lead. She looked out of the window. Her stomach was starting to tighten. Her hands felt hot. She tried to remember her breathing, but it was hard. Then she saw car lights approaching. Tegan put her coat and boots on, and picked up the biggest torch she could find. Sam knocked on the door and she let him in.

'Ready then? Evening Cerys,' he shouted, 'coming for a night hike?'

'No thanks. I think I'll watch the telly. You must be mad. Is Angharad with you?'

Sam laughed. 'No, I knew she'd bottle out. It's just me and you Tegan. Ready?'

He looked down and saw Dylan's eager face. 'Ah, I see you're coming as well.'

Tegan stepped out into the darkness. Dylan rushed off. She caught glimpses of the white in his coat but he certainly wasn't going to stay close to her. It was all too exciting. Then the panic hit her. Her heart felt it would burst out of her chest. Her throat was tight. She couldn't breathe. She started to shake, sweat. She felt like she was going to die. She stood very still. Sam turned. 'Alright?' Then he saw her.

'Hey, what's up?'

Tegan couldn't speak.

'It's alright. Come on, let's get back inside,' he said quickly.

Gently he put his arm around her shoulders and knocked on the door. Cerys came and, taking one look at Tegan, led her gently to the sofa.

'Come on in' she called to Sam.

Dylan came running in, wondering where everyone was.

Tegan started to calm down, now feeling very embarrassed.

'I'm so sorry' she stammered.

'Hey, it's alright,' said Sam.

'How about a drink instead?' suggested Cerys.

Sam took his coat off and he and Cerys sat chatting. Tegan felt exhausted but didn't want to go upstairs. She didn't want to be alone.

Angharad was back at the pub. She was put out about Sam's night walk but not prepared to stumble around in the dark just to chaperone him. She saw James come in. He was scowling. He leant on the bar. 'Whisky, double.' He saw Angharad look at him. 'It's OK. I walked here. Aim to drink away my troubles.'

'What's up with you?'

'It's home. Mum and Dad just argue all the time lately. It's miserable, and now there's all this business over the flat.'

'Your Dad told me your Mum wants to sell. That still going ahead then?'

'Of course. I'm surprised you knew about it, though.'

'Your Dad was in here talking. He's fed up about it. Do you think your Mum will get her way?'

'I should think so. She usually does with money.'

Angharad put down his whisky.

'Why doesn't your Dad put his foot down? I don't mean to be rude, but your Mum, well, she was very lucky to get someone like your Dad in the first place.'

He took a long sip, and sighed. 'Dad likes money you know, and he married a rich woman. Without her he'd never have had his designer clothes, Ferrari. She spoils him, me as well for that matter, but at the end of the day what she says goes.'

'That's a bit pathetic isn't it? You men need to lay the law down in that house. I mean, look at you, still living with Mum and Dad. Time you flew the nest, isn't it?'

'Why? I want my own place one day. Living at home, Mum pays for all my clothes, even the car, and I stand a chance of saving up.'

'Surely your Dad could set you up with something? I mean, as an architect he must have all sorts of connections.'

'You'd think so, wouldn't you? No, he just goes on about making my own way, but on the wages Mum pays, how am I meant to? It's hopeless.'

James took another long sip, draining the glass, and looked at Angharad. She took the empty glass away.

He put his hand on hers. 'Anyway, you seem a bit serious as well. What's up?'

'Oh, nothing. Tell me, this girl Tegan. What's she like?'

'Tegan? She's weird, but an interesting girl. You know, there's something about her despite her terrible clothes. I tried to come on to her at the party but no luck. Doesn't exactly flatter a chap. Still, it's intriguing. Mum said she tried to go back to that place in London but for some reason she's come back here again.'

'Yes, shame. Ruth told me she'd had some kind of nervous breakdown, though she looks alright to me. Did you hear about Ellis?'

'What's that?'

'Turns out he's her father. Ruth's furious.'

'Oh, that. Yes, Mum was having a good old bitch about it, though for some reason she's blaming Hannah. She likes Ellis, thinks he adds a bit of class to the village. Tegan's done alright though. There's money in that family.'

'I suppose so. Anyway, I was going to ask you. How do you fancy being best man?'

James grinned. 'Isn't Sam meant to be asking me that?'

'Oh, you know him. I have to organise everything.'

James frowned. 'He does want to get married, doesn't he?'

'Of course.'

'OK. Just wondered.'

Angharad took her hand away from under James', and refilled the glass. 'There, a double and decent stuff this time. It's on the house.'

'Hang on, what's going on?'

'Let's say I have a proposition for you.'

'Go on. I'm intrigued.'

285

'This girl, Tegan.'

'What about her?'

'I think Sam has taken a fancy to her.'

'You're kidding. I can't believe you've got competition. This must be a first. And from Tegan-'

'I wouldn't call her competition. No way. It's just I reckon she's worked on Sam and now he fancies himself as some bloody knight in shining armour.'

'Mm. Actually, that's possible. There's something about her. She's so vulnerable.'

'She has something then? You men seem to be attracted to her for some reason.'

'I suppose so. I reckon she's a virgin. Always a novelty. Anyway, what's this proposition?'

Angharad wrapped a golden lock around her finger, and looked thoughtful. 'You know she has that cottage rent free. Could make a nice escape for you from the parents?'

'Eh?'

'Well, why you don't get together with her, just for a while. Move in, you know, for a few weeks.'

'Hang on. She's been ill, hasn't she?'

'Think it was just mental stuff. She'll be alright. Maybe a bit of male company is just what she needs.'

'And you don't want her spending time with Sam?'

'Exactly.'

'You want me to get Tegan out of the picture?'

Angharad smiled and leant forward. 'Come on, it could be fun.'

'She spurned me once, you know.'

'Come on, James. About time you took on a challenge. These local girls are too easy.'

James grinned smugly but then grimaced, 'But her clothes-'

'I can help out with that. She's already ditched the headscarf.'

'I suppose it would be a change, bit of a challenge.'

'Go on then. Give it a shot. Get your phone out. I got her mobile number from Sam's phone.'

James put in Tegan's number. 'Long time since I've dated a virgin.'

Angharad took his empty glass and filled it again. 'This one's on me too' she said, handing it back, and then she added more seriously, 'Dad's got a fifty year old single malt in the cellar. It's yours if you keep her out of the way for a bit.'

James grinned and lifted up his glass. 'Then you're definitely on.'

Back at the cottage Cerys Tegan and Sam sat talking till late. Tegan had started to relax. She enjoyed Sam's company. They found some of the books she'd been reading about the Cambrian Mountains and looked at them together. Eventually Sam looked at his watch. 'Gosh, it's midnight,' he said, and then his phone rang.

'Hi. Yes, I'm just leaving. What now? I've got work in the morning. OK. I'll drive there now.' He stood up. 'I have to go. Angharad needs me. She's been in the pub but wants to do some work now. I have to go.'

Tegan hid her disappointment. Angharad, it would always be her. He would always go back to her.

Chapter Thirty Six

The next morning, Tegan, aware she was tired and fractious, turned down Cerys' offer to go to the manor and stayed in reading and knitting. The day dragged on. She wondered if she would hear from Sam, but there was nothing. However, in the afternoon she was surprised to receive a text from James.

'Hiya, Sam gave me your number, wondered if you fancy a drink this evening?'

Tegan was shocked. Why on earth was he asking her out, and why had Sam given him her number? When Cerys came back she showed her the text.

'Avoid him,' said Cerys. 'What ever you do, don't go out with him.'

'But why would Sam give him my number? He must think it would be a good idea-'

'Oh, I don't know. Whatever, keep away from him.'

Tegan remembered James at the party and blushed. Cerys was right: it wouldn't be a good idea. She replied that she was busy and then sat down to have tea with Cerys.

When Tegan went to bed that evening she thought more about the text. Had she been too quick to turn James down? After all he was very good looking. She remembered him singing; it had been wonderful. Of course, it had been embarrassing at the party, but she had been different then. Maybe she should have been flattered that he made a pass at her. After all, Sam wouldn't have given him her number if he was awful. It may be that Cerys was just being over-protective, had forgotten she was twenty seven. All her life people had hidden things from her. Maybe it was time she started to enjoy life.

Tegan got into bed and remembered the writing Liz had asked her to do for Friday's therapy session. She was reluctant. Why rake up all that stuff? Still, she had better do what the therapist said. She found paper and pen, sat up in bed, and closed her eyes. Where to start? Slowly, a memory came creeping back. Early on a Sunday evening, Daniel was speaking. She must have been about ten. She sat, hard plastic digging into her thighs. She hurt her neck as she strained to look up at Daniel. She knew there was a tight knot in her stomach. What was he saying? Tegan picked up her pen and started to write. Tears trickled silently down her cheeks. It was all so real.

When she had finished she put the paper down and lay back in her bed. Exhausted, she fell asleep, but she was not transported to a quiet peaceful place. She was plunged into a terrifying world. She woke herself up screaming, and tried to read, but every time she went back to sleep the dreams became more real, more violent. She crawled out of bed at five in the morning, sweating and exhausted. She went downstairs and made herself coffee, trying not to disturb Cerys. She had never been this bad before therapy. This was crazy, and she knew what to do now with panic attacks. That was enough.

'My God, Tegan, you look terrible,' said Cerys when she came down.

'I feel it.'

'Are you ill?'

'It's this therapy. I had to think about stuff and write it down. I had an awful night. That's it, Cerys. I'm not going again.'

'But you said it helped-'

'I learnt some useful things, but that's enough.'

'But-'

'You and Nadia said if I wasn't getting on with this I could stop. Well that's it. I'm stopping.'

'You can't, Tegan. You've been ill. You have to go,' pleaded Cerys.

Tegan felt irritated. 'No, I don't have to go. Liz said that. You don't know what it's like.'

'But it's for your own good. You want to be more independent, don't you? Well, you need to get better.'

'Cerys, I am twenty seven. I need to make my own mind up about this.'

'But you ought to go.'

Tegan bit her lip. She didn't want to argue with Cerys.

'Look, I'm off to the manor now. I've put cheese and ham ready for a sandwich.'

'Oh thank you,' mumbled Tegan. 'I might go out, up the hills.'

'Don't go too far. You still get very tired,' said Cerys.

Again, Tegan did not reply, but for the first time she couldn't wait for Cerys to go out. She was tired of being bossed about all the time.

The next few days were awkward. Tegan found everything Cerys did irritated her. She knew how much she owed her but somehow that made it worse. They went together on the Wednesday to choir and she saw Sam. He came over to speak to her in the break.

'How are you doing? I really enjoyed our walk.'

'I'm fine thanks.'

Angharad pushed past Sam. 'What's this I hear about you turning down the handsome James? That must be a first for him.'

Tegan shrugged.

'Tegan doesn't want to be going out with him,' said Sam firmly.

'For God's sake,' said Angharad. 'Don't you take any notice of him, Tegan. James is a decent bloke. Look at him.'

Tegan glanced over at James, talking to a pretty girl. He really was very good looking, wearing jeans and a blue T shirt.

Angharad grinned. 'Yes, good looking, isn't he? I tell you, if I wasn't engaged-'

Tegan looked at Angharad. Did she mean that?

'I don't think I'm his sort,' she said quietly. 'I mean, he goes out with very pretty women doesn't he?'

'Don't underestimate yourself. He asked you, didn't he?'

'I suppose so' said Tegan.

Ellis called them back to the practice. Angharad grabbed her arm. 'If he asks again, what ever you do, don't turn him down. Let me know. I'll make sure you look fantastic. I reckon it's time you lived a little, don't you?'

When they were walking back to the cottage afterwards Cerys asked her stiffly, 'So what was Angharad talking to you about?'

'Actually, she was telling me to go out with James.'

'Don't listen to anything she says.'

Tegan didn't reply. They walked back in silence.

The following evening Cerys said she was going to the pub with Robert and asked Tegan if she would like to go with them.

'Might as well,' Tegan said moodily.

Robert came and picked them up. Tegan watched Cerys chatting to Robert in the front. They were very close now. She felt left out. At the pub she started to calm herself, and then realised Cerys had walked off with Robert and abandoned her. She squashed the panic and went in. She found them at the bar.

'What are you drinking?' asked Robert.

Tegan looked around the bar, so many people drinking alcoholic drinks: why shouldn't she? She could do what ever she liked.

'Large glass of wine please.'

Cerys frowned. 'Are you sure?'

Tegan glared at her. 'Yes, of course.'

They sat with a group which included James and Rhiannon. James grinned. Then Tegan remembered the party. She took a deep gulp of her wine, and looked down. The effect was fast. She felt light headed.

'You drinking now then?' asked James.

She looked up defiantly. 'I've joined the sinners.' She finished her drink quickly.

'So why did you reject my offer of a drink?' he asked.

She blushed, looked down. 'I don't know' she mumbled.

291

'I'm not used to it, you know. I was very hurt.'

'I'm sorry' she replied.

'Well, I don't give up that easily,' he said. 'Want another one of those?'

'OK.'

James fetched the drinks.

Rhiannon was in high sprits. 'Good to see your hair, Tegan. It looks gorgeous, doesn't it, James?'

'It certainly does.'

The evening went quickly. Tegan stood up, feeling very giddy. James grabbed her arm, and whispered in her ear. 'Look, how about Saturday? You know, that drink?'

The wine was making her very confused, but it seemed a good idea. 'Why ever not? Yes, great.'

'Pick you up about half seven.'

She staggered over to Robert's Land Rover. Cerys helped her get in. Her head was swimming. On the way she heard them talking.

'You and me should stay at your place tonight, celebrate you having a roof.' She saw Robert squeeze Cerys' knee.

'Oh no, not tonight, you know, I can't- Tegan.' Cerys was trying to whisper, but Tegan heard.

Cerys turned around. 'What was James talking to you about?'

She peered blearily at her. 'Actually, he was asking me on a date again.'

'I hope you turned him down again. I don't know what he's playing at.'

'Actually, I thought I might go.'

'Just don't, Tegan.'

Tegan took a deep breath. 'You know, Cerys, why don't you and Robert go back to your place tonight? You don't need to babysit me any more.'

She saw Robert grin. 'We could take Dylan.'

'Oh no,' said Cerys.

'Really, I'd prefer it. I need to be on my own a bit now.'

They had arrived at the cottage.

'OK, then,' said Cerys tightly. 'Tegan obviously would like some space. I'll go and pick up a few things and Dylan.'

Cerys ran inside, gathered her things with Dylan and left the cottage quickly. She didn't really speak to Tegan.

It seemed very quiet when Cerys had gone. Tegan felt her head spinning. She slumped on the sofa, put the TV on and watched mindless programmes for an hour. She received a text from James. 'Saturday at 7.30. Dress up, it'll be a night to remember.' She smiled, staggered upstairs and fell into bed.

Tegan got up early the next morning and phoned the therapist. She left a message on the answer phone postponing her appointment until the following week, although she had no intention of ever going again. She sat back, drinking coffee with a sense of relief. She didn't need that; she had a date tomorrow, and she could handle this. She was going to make more coffee just as the phone rang. Her heart raced. Maybe it was James?

'Hello' she said nervously.

'It's Amy. Listen, I'm a bit stuck. Pam, my receptionist, wants to cut her hours. Fancy a few mornings a week, basic pay but not too arduous?'

Tegan was trying to think straight. Amy was very much awake and talking fast. 'Oh, I don't think so.'

'Come and see. Really, I think you'd like it.'

'But I don't know anything about clerical work, and have no experience of the computer.'

'Oh, you'll pick it up in no time.'

Tegan floundered. Amy carried on.

'Come on. Come down now and have a look. Tell you what, I'll come and pick you up, say, about nine?'

Tegan agreed without thinking about it. She showered, put on her jeans and waited for Amy. She ran out to the car.

'I expected you to make more of an effort for an interview,' joked Amy.

'Oh sorry-'

'Only joking. How are things?'

'Alright thanks.'

'I hear you have a date with James tomorrow.'

293

'How on earth do you know?'

'Oh it's everywhere.'

'So do you disapprove? Everyone seems to.'

'Worried about James, I suppose. He has a reputation you know, slept with lots of women in this part of Wales. Just don't feel you have to be one of them if you don't want to. Right, here we are.'

Tegan had imagined a dark depressing place but she was pleasantly surprised.

'It looks very modern,' she said to Amy as she showed her around.

'It is. Fiona has put a lot of money into it. We work hard getting the animals ready for new homes.'

Despite the cleanliness, though, Tegan found it hard. Some of the stories were heartbreaking. They saw dogs and then the cats.

Tegan's heart leapt. 'That's the kitten I found, isn't it?'

'Yes. I'm surprised no one has adopted her.' Tegan put her hand through the cage bars. The kitten rubbed up against her. They went back to reception and Pam on the desk explained what the work entailed.

'We'll obviously be a lot busier once we're the wildlife sanctuary,' said Amy. 'So, how about it?'

Tegan screwed up her eyes. 'I could do, but the thing is I have one condition.'

Amy grinned. 'Really? What is it?'

Tegan's face was deadly serious. 'You may not like it, but this is something I really want to do.'

Chapter Thirty Seven

Amy looked at Tegan, more puzzled now. 'What do you mean? What condition? I can't pay you any more.'

'It's not money,' said Tegan, sounding less sure of herself. 'It's the kitten, the one I found. Please can I adopt it?'

'Really?'

'Yes, I'd really like to,' she said more firmly.

'Have you owned a cat before?'

'No.'

'OK. Let's go through what's involved first.' Amy went through it all in minute detail. Tegan still wanted to adopt.

'OK. Let's try a week, and then a few weeks, initially and see how it goes. Equipment-wise we sell all you need here, so let's get you sorted out.'

It was fun choosing the things. Even more, putting the kitten into a box to take home. Amy gave Tegan a lift and once at the cottage helped her to settle the kitten in.

'She's been spayed and micro-chipped. All her injections are up to date, but don't let her out for a while. She needs to get to know you. Do you have a name you want to use?'

'Seren, star. That's what I want.'

'Good choice. Well, use it lots and get her used to being called to it before you let her outside. In a few weeks let her out just before a meal for a short time and then call her back.'

Tegan was very excited, watching Seren investigate the living room. Amy left. Tegan sat entranced, playing with Seren and stroking her. She sat on the sofa and Seren jumped up on to her lap. She could feel the heat from the white fluffy body on her knees, the vibration of the deep purr. Tegan felt her relax, and carefully sat back. The two of them sat in peace, resting.

That night she took Seren and her basket up to her room. Seren soon jumped out of it and on to the end of her bed. Tegan smiled down at her and the two slept well.

The next morning she checked her phone. She was missing Cerys, and wondered if she would hear from her, but there was nothing. She didn't really want to text her. She wanted to go ahead with the date first. It would take very little persuasion to back out.

Seren settled down after her breakfast and Tegan slipped out of the cottage. She started to walk across the fields. She was surprised to see Angharad with Sam out walking.

She was even more surprised to see Angharad start rushing towards her.

'I was hoping to see you,' said Angharad excitedly.

Bracken ran up to greet her, followed by Sam.

'He's pleased to see you,' said Sam. 'I heard about the kitten.'

'Yes, it's exciting. She's so sweet, slept on my bed last night.'

'Amy told me she'd landed on her feet. What's her name?' asked Sam.

Tegan smiled shyly. 'Seren. You know, star.'

Sam smiled. 'That's perfect. I will have to come and check on her soon.'

'Yes, thanks. I'm keeping her in for now. Amy said to let her get to know her name first. I would be very nervous about letting her out yet. She's eating well. I thought her eyes looked a bit sore, but they look better now.'

'Good. Well, let me know if they get worse. I'll come and see her.'

Angharad pushed forward. 'Enough of this animal talk. I hear you have much more exciting news than that.'

Tegan looked at her blankly.

'James,' shouted Angharad. 'Your date with James.'

'Oh yes, I'd forgotten. How did you know?'

'James was very excited. Sent me a text last night.'

'Really?'

'I told you. You don't want to go out with him,' said Sam sternly. 'He's not good enough for you. Don't go.'

'Oh God, listen to him,' laughed Angharad. 'Honestly, he'd have you in a convent. You go. James knows how to give a girl a really good night out.'

Tegan shrugged. 'I'm a bit nervous now actually.'

'Why? Most of the girls around here would do anything to be in your place.'

'But I don't even know what to wear. I mean, do I wear jeans or one of my skirts?'

Angharad unsuccessfully tried to hide a look of horror. 'Do you have any money to spend on clothes?'

'Well, Ellis gave me a card. He said to get new things, but-'

'Right, you and me, right now. Aberystwyth, shopping,' said Angharad.

Tegan stared. 'Shopping? Now?'

'Yup.'

'You said you wanted to see the nest,' protested Sam, looking at Angharad.

'No time for that, clothes to buy. Right, see you in about fifteen minutes Tegan?'

'But Seren. I can't just leave her,' protested Tegan.

'She'll be fine. Come on. I'll drive us. We won't be long.'

Tegan thought for a moment. If anyone knew how to dress, act on a night out, it must be Angharad.

'OK. See you then.'

Tegan ran to the cottage, and sat playing with Seren. She quickly tired and Tegan had settled her down just as she heard Angharad arrive. She grabbed her coat and the bank card Ellis had given her and ran out. Angharad drove quickly into town.

Once there, Tegan regretted her impetuousness. She had no idea how to clothes shop, no idea what things cost, what size she was. She was going to look such a fool. Angharad steered her into the first shop. Tegan picked up a long cotton skirt and a blouse.

'You're not serious,' said Angharad. 'You can't dress like a granny to go out with James. How many men have you been out with?'

Tegan was embarrassed. 'Well, once for coffee.'

'Oh my God. No wonder you don't have a clue. Right, the first thing you must learn is how to dress the way a man likes. That means short skirts, low tight tops, and high heels.'

'But I've never dressed like that in my life!'

'Exactly. And how many dates did you say you've had?'

Tegan blushed.

'Right, come on. I will choose exactly the right things for you.'

Tegan looked at Angharad seriously. She had never heard anyone talk like this. Men were to be obeyed, of course, but to flirt, dress for them, this was new. Angharad chose a tight top, and a short denim skirt.

'No. No way,' said Tegan.

'Try them. Come on, give it a go.'

Tegan went into a changing room, turned away from the mirror and tried the clothes on. The skirt was tiny. Her legs were exposed and cold. The top was very tight.

'Come on, out you come' called Angharad.

Shyly, she pulled back the curtain.

'My God, you look amazing. James will be so impressed.'

'It's all too small. No way am I going out like this. No, I can't wear these. I'm not going.'

Angharad stepped forward. 'Right, hand it over.'

'What?'

'Your phone.'

Tegan handed it to Angharad, who quickly starting typing.

'What are you doing?'

'There you are. I've told James how much you're looking forward to coming, and I've told him to pick you up at the pub.'

'Why?'

298

'Because I don't trust you not to bottle it and wear your jeans.'

Tegan screamed. '

'No, no. What have you done?'

'I am your fairy godmother. You shall go to the ball.'

Tegan grabbed her phone back.

Angharad touched her hand. 'Seriously, Tegan. Why ever not?'

Tegan looked back at her reflection. Why not? 'But how can I go out with someone like him?'

'Tegan, really, you look amazing. Trust me.'

'Really?'

'Yes, really. Come on. Now we need to elongate those legs.'

Angharad picked out a pair of needle-like stiletto heels. Tegan put them on and clung on to the wall.

Angharad laughed. 'You'll need to practise in the cottage.'

'I don't think Cerys will approve.'

'Cerys hasn't the first idea how to dress. Don't take any notice of her.'

'But she has been very kind-'

'I'm sure. But she's not going to help you mix, fit in. I'm not surprised her mother despairs of her. Honestly, she's hardly normal, is she?'

Tegan cringed: that word 'normal'.

She went back to trying to walk, but it was impossible. The skirt was tight, the top clung to her figure, and the shoes were killing her. 'I can't do this.'

'Yes, you can. You know what they say: "no pain no gain".'

'Really, I wanted some jeans that fitted,' said Tegan quietly.

'Well, I'll keep these things and we'll look at jeans.'

Angharad found her a pair of skinny jeans. 'Size six, I reckon.'

Tegan tried on the jeans. They were very tight but she settled for them, teamed with a T shirt chosen by Angharad. She went to pay. She was horrified at the cost but Angharad assured her that it was very little to pay for clothes.

'Now, have you thought about having your ears pierced?'

Tegan shook her head. 'Never.'

'Well you should come and get them done.'

Angharad linked arms with her. 'This is lovely, isn't it?'

Tegan smiled. It was nice to be with someone like this. All those times she'd seen girls shopping together, and now it was her turn. She smiled at Angharad. 'Yes, it is. Thank you.'

Angharad took Tegan down a side street and led her into a tattoo parlour. Tegan stared around. The walls were covered in pictures of tattoos. A young girl lay having a complex picture drawn onto her leg. It looked very painful, but the girl was talking to the man. Angharad guided her to the desk and they sat on a brown settee waiting their turn. She was very uneasy but she daren't back out.

Eventually it was her turn. She sat while a girl wiped her ear. The piercing was quick, but her ears throbbed. She chose the plainest studs she could see.

When the girl showed her what they looked like she stared in astonishment at her reflection. How had she come to have this done? Her mother... She'd be horrified, but then who was she to tell her how to live? Tegan felt anger burning inside: she was glad she'd had this done. Angharad just smiled.

'Good. Right, and now make up.'

'Make up? No, I never wear it. And in any case I can't spend any more money.'

'It's OK. Make-over is free.'

Tegan found herself taken into a smart beautician's.

A young woman heavily made up with talons as nails smiled at her. 'What do you normally wear?'

'Oh, nothing. I've never worn make up at all.'

The girl laughed. Angharad intervened. 'She's serious, you know.'

'Oh God. Right then. This will be fun.'

Tegan was embarrassed but the girl seemed to think it was exciting. Tegan sat in a chair. Her feet didn't touch the ground. The young woman started smearing foundation over her face. It felt suffocating. Her face felt tight. Then more layers. She didn't enjoy having her eyes painted and her lips felt like they would stick together.

Finally, the girl said, 'There you are, a new you.' She held up a mirror. Tegan blinked. Her first reaction was to want to wipe it all off. It was hideous. But Angharad came over and smiled broadly.

'Why, Tegan, you look fantastic.'

'But I don't look anything like me.'

'It's a new improved you. Look at your eyes. They are much darker blue than mine. With your black hair you look amazing. You should buy some of this, you know.'

Tegan looked again at herself. She wanted to be normal, fit in, and this was what it must take.

'OK.' The price shocked her. This would have to last a long time.

'I'll give you a lift back,' said Angharad.

As Angharad dropped her off she said 'Now come round and meet me at the Red Dragon about half six, OK?'

Tegan rushed upstairs, put her new clothes in the bedroom, and went back down to Seren. It was so calming to sit with her. The rest of the day seemed like some weird dream. Her ears throbbed. When Seren was sleeping she went up and put on the skinny jeans and T-shirt. She looked at herself in the mirror. It was incredible. Her hair and her face with make-up. And the earrings. Then she cringed. She was dressed like a whore. She looked again. Thousands of girls dressed like this. She must not think like that. She went down into the kitchen, and saw a half finished bottle of wine. She poured herself a glass, and sat down. She heard a knock on the front door, wondered who it was. Suddenly she felt very self-conscious. She went and opened the door. Cerys was there, looking uncharacteristically nervous.

'Oh, hello. You should have let yourself in,' said Tegan, trying to sound casual.

'I didn't like to-' said Cerys. Then she stopped, and stood staring at Tegan.

'Like the new look?' asked Tegan.

Cerys stood open-mouthed and then whispered, 'The make-up, the jeans-'

'It's a new me' said Tegan defiantly. 'Come on in. Fancy a glass of wine?'

Cerys shook her head.

'Hey, meet my new house mate' said Tegan.

Cerys looked down and saw Seren. She seemed to relax. 'Oh my God, she's' beautiful. She's not-'

'Yes. She's the kitten I found. I've called her Seren.'

'Star? Oh, how sweet.'

Tegan looked carefully at Cerys, realising that she too looked different, but it wasn't to do with clothes. No. It was her eyes: they were shining.

'You look really happy, radiant. Has something happened?'

'It's Robert.'

'Yes-'

'He's asked me to-'

'Marry him?'

'One step at a time. No, he wants us to live together.'

'Oh, right. So you'll live with him before you get married?'

'That's right. Actually, he'll be living with me. We're going to move into my house, have more privacy, like. It's so exciting, isn't it?'

'Of course, congratulations.'

'Robert's just gone to get some things. He'll be back for me in a minute.'

'Oh.' Tegan felt rather shocked. 'So you'll be there permanently now. Will Dylan go as well?'

'Gosh, yes. Can't leave him with Mum and Dad. Hope he's alright, mind you. Robert wants to bring his collies with him, of course. They're his working dogs, but so far they haven't got on with Dylan. Anyway, hopefully in a neutral place they'll be better.'

Tegan didn't say anything but was hurt that Cerys didn't seem to be thinking about her. She seemed happy now just to dump her.

'You'll be OK, won't you? I think you're ready for your own space now, aren't you?' asked Cerys.

'Of course. Look, I'm fine. I don't need you looking after me any more. Anyway, I'm out with James tonight.'

'Oh my God. Honestly, he's not your sort. He's been out with a lot of women, and he has, well, expectations, if you know what I mean.'

Tegan was annoyed. 'I think he could be good for me. Angharad said he likes me a lot.'

'When did she say this?'

'Today. She took me shopping. She showed me how to dress. She thinks I can look really good, normal.'

'Oh, I see. Hence the jeans and the make up.'

'I decided on those. Look, I had my ears pierced as well.'

'Oh, right.'

'And I have a mini skirt, heels, things James will like.'

'But do you like them?'

'That's not the point.'

'Look, be careful with Angharad.'

'Doesn't seem to me that you trust many people, including me. One minute you're telling me to do new things, but then you try to put me off.'

Cerys looked upset. 'I don't want you to get hurt.'

'I think I can take care of myself. I'm not a child, you know.'

'Of course not.'

They both stood, neither knowing what to say next. Then there was the sound of a horn tooting.

'That's Robert, I'd better go. Take care.' Cerys quickly left.

303

As she watched Cerys go, Tegan heard her phone. She picked it up, and gasped. It was a text from James.

'I love you. Will you marry me?'

Chapter Thirty Eight

Tegan's hands were shaking. James was asking her to marry him. She couldn't believe it. Cerys, Sam, they had been wrong. He loved her. But should she marry a heathen man? She pushed the thought away: that was old thinking. To think such a handsome man wanted to marry her! She played with Seren, her mind whirling, and that settled her down. She went upstairs, packed her high heels, top and denim skirt and walked down to the pub in a dream.

Tegan found it very strange to be going into the pub on her own. She pushed open the door nervously.

Angharad was waiting. 'Come on then, upstairs.'

She followed her meekly up the wooden stairs to Angharad's bedroom. The room was dominated by an enormous dressing table covered in make up products. The mirror had special lighting.

'Right, let's get you sorted out. You did bring the skirt and things?'

Tegan nodded.

'Good. Well, get changed.'

Tegan waited to see if Angharad would leave the room, but she stayed. She put on the skirt before removing her jeans, and reluctantly took off her sweatshirt.

'Good, now your hair.'

Angharad chose from a range of hairbrushes, used hair tongs and various sprays and mousse. By the time she had finished Tegan felt like she was wearing a wig. When she shook her head her hair didn't move. However, Tegan sat smiling at the mirror. None of this would really matter to James. He loved her, wanted to marry her. She felt sick with excitement. Maybe he would bring a ring this evening. It would be so romantic, like in Pride and Prejudice when Mr Darcy finally proposes to

Elizabeth, just when she thinks he couldn't love her because of all that had happened.

Tegan became aware of her face being pulled to one side. Angharad applied extra eye shadow, tons of mascara and lipstick. Then she stood back and smiled.

'Now you look ready to go out. Now, this date-'

'Yes?' asked Tegan, smiling.

'Now, it's not enough to dress for James. Remember, even if he's talking nonsense, make him feel like the most interesting, clever person you know. If he makes jokes, however dreadful, laugh.'

'He'd like that?'

'Yup. James is used to girls hanging on his every word.'

'Oh, right.'

Angharad coughed. 'I guess you don't have much experience, well, physically, with men do you?'

Tegan blushed. 'No. No, of course not. I shall wait until I'm married.'

'Um, right. Well, don't be too uptight with James. He's not, well, used to that sort of thing.' Tegan couldn't contain herself any longer.

'But you see, it's alright, look at this.' Proudly, she held the text up for Angharad to read.

To her surprise, Angharad burst out laughing, saying 'Typical James.'

'What do you mean?' she asked, confused.

Angharad looked at her. 'You didn't take this seriously, did you? You do know what day it is, don't you?'

'Sorry?'

'It's April 1st. April Fool's Day.'

Tegan could feel her voice shaking. She was frantically blinking back tears. 'What does that mean?'

'Oh, it's nonsense' said Angharad. 'Look, come on down to the bar. I'll get you a drink.'

Tegan glanced at her reflection. Suddenly she felt ridiculous, dressed up like some street girl. Fancy her thinking for a minute that any man would want to marry her.

'Cheer up. You look great,' laughed Angharad.

Tegan followed her unsteadily, tottering on the high heels.

Once they were down in the bar Angharad gave her a short glass containing a yellowy-orange liquid. 'Knock that back.'

Tegan did as she was told but was shocked. The liquid burned the back of her throat. She felt sick.

'There you are, your first whisky. Now I'll just text James and tell him you're ready.'

At that moment Sam came into the bar. He stopped and stared at Tegan. He looked upset. 'You're going on this date then?'

'Of course.'

Tegan was suddenly very aware of her cold, bare legs. She tried to pull loose the tight top.

Sam came forward, and touched her arm. 'Please don't go. You don't know what he's like.'

For a second she was tempted to go back upstairs, change and go home. But then she saw his eyes wander over to Angharad behind the bar. He had his girlfriend, but he didn't want her to have any fun.

'This is nothing to do with you,' she said, crossly pulling her arm away.

'It is. You deserve to be with someone who really loves you, who'll care for you.'

Suddenly, she felt rage burning. 'You have no right to lecture me. You have your girl. You have your happy ending.'

'It's not like that.'

'Well it should be. You're engaged to that beautiful woman and yet you go round looking miserable. It's not fair.'

Sam stood staring at her, his face deep red. He looked like he might cry, but she felt no sympathy.

Then James appeared. He strutted over to her, put his arm around her. 'Hello gorgeous.'

He grinned at Sam. 'Don't look like that. You're greedy, that's your trouble.'

307

Angharad came over. 'You two make quite a pair. I did a good job, didn't I, James?'

'Brilliant. Right, goodbye you two. Enjoy your wedding plans. We're off to have fun.'

Tegan found herself being led to a red sports car. She got into it with difficulty. It was very low down and she felt squashed. It was hard to sit decently in such a tiny skirt. James turned the key, lowered the hood, revved the engine and roared away. The wind tugged at her hair, a huge rush of adrenalin. The music thumped out, then Tegan became aware of the words "Need you to dance, I need you to strip, I need you to shake your little ass'n hips".

'We'd better turn it off,' she shouted.

James laughed, shouted back, 'No way, you must know this. It's called "Nasty Girl".' He turned the music up. Tegan cringed as people walking past glanced at them accusingly.

They arrived at a pub called the Ty Mawr and screeched into the car park. Tegan struggled out of the car, took a deep breath and followed James in. It was smaller than The Red Dragon, with low beams, and, although obviously popular, you could easily hear the young girl who was sat playing guitar, gently singing Welsh folk songs. It was beautiful, and for a moment Tegan stopped and listened, transfixed by the beauty of the music. James touched her arm and she followed him through the crowded tables. She noticed a few women glanced at James but he ignored them. Then she realised that there were men looking at her, not the usual confused looks but sly smiles. She felt herself blushing. She wasn't used to this attention. She was glad when they found a seat by the window. Here she could look out at the mountains, the late evening sunset coating the hillside in a pallet of reds and yellow.

James smiled. 'Glass of wine?'

Tegan looked around the pub. She caught sight of her reflection in a mirror and was shocked. What was she doing, dressed like this, out with a heathen man in a pub? Who was she? She realised James was waiting.

'Sorry?'

'I asked if you would like some wine.'

Tegan remembered what Angharad had said. 'Yes please. Large glass of white wine, thanks.'

He looked surprised but didn't comment. She sat feeling very self-conscious on her own and was relieved when he came back with a glass of wine for her and a coke for him. She gulped back her wine quickly.

He put his head on one side. 'What's going on? The clothes, the wine?'

'Do you think I look stupid?'

'Not at all. You look great. It's just you're being so different.'

'Let's say it's a new start.'

'Well I'm glad you started with me.' He put his hand on hers. Tegan looked over at the girl singing and then said,

'Don't you ever want to do more with music? You have such a lovely singing voice.'

'I'm happy as it is. It's no better than lots of others. I'm not Ellis. His life has always been music. He was single-minded, ambitious to get on. Not me. What about you? I hear you sing well.'

'I couldn't sing in front of people on my own. It would be too embarrassing.'

'You should have more confidence in yourself. You know, you're very pretty.'

He went and bought another glass of wine for her. She sat back, breathed slowly and gazed out of the window. When he returned she said,

'I feel so relaxed: beautiful hills, lovely music and, well, everything.'

'You must have lots of good times, boyfriends, in London.'

'No. I went for coffee with this chap Steve in London, but that was it.'

'You mean you never had a steady boyfriend?'

She leant forward and whispered loudly. 'Never. Never had a date.'

309

'I wondered. That's incredible.'

'Does that put you off, the fact I haven't been with lots of men?'

'Certainly not. I find it enormously seductive.'

Eventually they left the Ty Mawr. Tegan noticed the effect of the wine when she went to stand up, but James put his arm protectively around her and steered her to the door. As they drove back, Tegan began to feel very sleepy, but James chatted on. When they got back to the cottage he helped her to the front door. He went to kiss her.

She panicked. 'Would you like a coffee?'

He grinned. 'Cerys won't mind?'

'Oh, no. Cerys has left me. Robert has moved into her place. They're living together there now.'

'So you're all alone?'

'I suppose I am.' She opened the front door. Seren looked up from her bed and mewed. She went over, pleased to see her. As she leant forward her head spun. She felt very sick. Slowly, she stood up, staggered into the kitchen and started to make coffee. James came into the kitchen and took down two glasses. He pulled out a bottle of brandy from his pocket.

'Where did that come from?' she asked.

'Always have a bottle with me when I know I'm not driving home.'

She smiled, missing what he had said. He put his arm around her. He kissed her once and then more intensely. Tegan pulled away.

'What's up?'

'I'm sorry.'

'Hey, relax. Have another drink.'

She looked at the walls, and suddenly felt very sick again. 'I'm sorry. I can't.'

He put his arm around her again. 'Look, just relax. You'll be fine, and you're in the hands of a master.' He leant forward and kissed her again.

Tegan pushed him away again. 'Don't do that. Please. Look, I'm very tired.'

'OK. Please yourself.' His eyes narrowed. The easy charm seemed to melt away. He looked colder, more severe. 'I'm not going to beg. I'll leave the brandy. Ready for another night, eh?'

'OK, sorry' she stammered.

James gave her a final glance and started to leave the kitchen. Then he turned and spoke in a lighter, flirtatious voice, 'Fancy going to the cinema on Monday?'

'Cinema?'

'You know, that big place they show films' he said, mocking her.

'Oh, well. Yes, OK.' She was very anxious at the thought of going to the cinema, but then at least he wanted to see her again.

'Good. See you then.' She watched as he walked through the living room. At the door he stopped and called, 'Your cat looks hungry.'

She was puzzled at this and looked down at a sleeping Seren, wondering what he meant.

'I'll be off then' he called again, and left.

She went straight upstairs, listening as the car roared away. Her head was muffled from the wine. She cringed at the memory of the evening but then she thought that actually it hadn't been so terrible. She had been out with a good-looking man and he had actually wanted to sleep with her! She should be flattered. That finally meant she was normal, didn't it?

Chapter Thirty Nine

When Tegan opened her curtains the next morning the sun was shining. It seemed to light up the woods. She blinked at the brightness. She had a terrible headache. She staggered downstairs to make coffee.

She fed Seren, drank a glass of water, and looked out. It was a quiet, still morning. Then she realised it was Sunday. To think, all her life she would have had a day of fasting and vigil. Now she was here, nursing a hangover after a date with a heathen man.

She showered, and was dressing when she heard the front door open. She guessed it was Cerys. She would be partly pleased to see her, but dreading what she would say. Tegan threw on a top and ran downstairs.

'Morning,' said James.

Tegan froze. It was such a shock, an invasion of her privacy. 'How did you get in?'

He laughed. 'Took a key last night. You know, we could have a nice day together.'

Tegan was very confused. 'What do you mean?'

'Well, silly us both being on our own. I brought my own TV, something watchable, not that archaic thing. There's a good day of sport. You can make us a decent lunch. OK?'

Before she could answer he returned to his van and came back carrying an enormous television set.

'Just got this: biggest plasma screen I could buy,' he said proudly. 'I've also got a load of Top Gear DVDs. I just love Jeremy Clarkson, don't you?'

Tegan watched as he set up his TV. When he turned it on the colours and brightness filled the room. The sound was deafening and seemed to bounce off the walls at her. Eventually he had tuned it in. He looked back at her.

'Coffee?' he asked.

Tegan went into the kitchen, closely followed by Seren. She looked in the cupboards. It would have to be pasta for lunch.

James stayed all day, watching TV, grumbling at the lack of roast dinner, until in the evening he went to the car and brought in cans of beer and more DVDs. He spread his things everywhere. Tegan and Seren huddled together on a chair.

'I thought we'd watch Basic Instinct,' said James. 'The sequel is due out any day. 1 wanted to remind myself of the plot. How about some supper then?'

'I don't think I have much more food in,' said Tegan apologetically.

'Well I'll nip and get us a Chinese, won't be long.'

When he left Tegan picked up the remote control. She pushed a few buttons until the TV miraculously switched off. The silence was stunning. Seren came over to her.

'I'm sorry little one,' she said. 'He's taken over, hasn't he? Still, I suppose it's nice that he wants to spend time with us.'

James returned with a carrier bag full of tinfoil trays. 'Let's get this food sorted out and open this wine.' He turned the TV back on.

Tegan was pleased James looked so happy. He pulled around the coffee table and spread the tin foil cartons around. They seemed very greasy and hot. Tegan was worried about the table. But he was in such a rush. Finally he opened the wine and found some glasses.

'Right, come on. We're all set.'

Tegan sat next to him on the sofa. Seren curled up next to her. James had piled food on to his plate. Tegan wasn't hungry. Then the film started. She found the graphic language and sexual scenes deeply shocking. She glanced at James but he seemed absorbed. It must be her being prudish. This must be the sort of film most people watched. She tried to cope, but in the end she closed her eyes and tried desperately to be somewhere else. The film seemed to go on for ages.

James turned and grinned. 'Good fun, eh? Can't wait for the sequel.'

Tegan tried to smile but was just relieved when it finished. She felt she had woken from some horrible nightmare but couldn't shake it off. The images had been too brazen, too strong.

'Do you fancy a walk?' she asked.

'God, no. Let's watch another one. We could open the vodka now.'

'But surely if you're going to drive-'

'Who's driving anywhere? I hope you're not thinking of chucking me out again?'

She looked down.

'I want to take Seren up with me. It's late. I'll take her and her things.'

'My God. Alright, see you later.'

Tegan gathered up all the things and took Seren upstairs. All the time she was wondering what he meant by 'see you later'. She couldn't sleep with him, not tonight. But how was she meant to say no? She opened her window and stared out. The night sky was full of stars, little moonlight but beautiful. A moth swept past her face. She heard an owl. 'Tawny owl, territorial call' she thought to herself. It was very calm and peaceful. She heard the TV go off downstairs and started to panic. He was coming up. James entered the bedroom holding a bottle of vodka and walked over to her.

'Tired of TV.' He swigged the vodka. He pulled her towards him and kissed her. The bottle dug into her back. She froze, but she didn't push him away. I have to get used to this, she thought. I can't keep saying no. He'll think I'm a freak, not normal.

She felt his hand slide up her leg. She cringed, but said nothing.

'You OK?'

She tried to smile. 'Fine.'

'Come on, then.' He held her hand tight and started to undress her. She caught a glimpse of herself in the mirror. It was like watching a scene from that film: this wasn't her. He pulled

314

her roughly towards the bed. She immediately panicked. 'Get off. Leave me alone!' she screamed.

'Eh, what's going on? Look, just relax. Have a drink.' He lifted the bottle to her lips, and poured the liquid into her mouth. She started to choke.

'Come on,' he said. 'Take it slowly.'

The liquid filled her mouth. She gulped it down, gasped for air, and then he poured more into her mouth. She kept gulping. She felt she was suffocating, drowning. He pulled the bottle away. Tegan ran to the bathroom and was violently sick.

'Oh my God! You're a freak. That's what you are. A frigid, cock-teasing freak. I should never have let Angharad talk me into this.'

'Angharad?'

'God, yes. You don't think I'd choose a girl like you, do you? I'm doing this for a decent bottle of whisky. Don't you dare tell her what happened. I'm going down to get another drink,' he said moodily. 'I'll leave you up here with your damn cat.'

He left the room, slamming the door. Tegan sat on the floor next to Seren, who was curled up in her bed. She curled up tight next to her, sobbing quietly, trying to make herself as small as she could, and trying to disappear.

Tegan couldn't sleep; frightened he would come back up. When she saw dawn break she crept down to get a glass of water. She felt terrible. The room stank of stale beer and cold takeaway. She glanced nervously at the sofa.

James sat up, bleary eyed. 'Oh God, what a night. I have to be at the stables early.' He got up off the sofa, still wearing last night's clothes. 'I'll be off then.'

'Will we go to the cinema tonight?' Tegan asked.

James laughed, hard and cold. 'You are joking, aren't you? You just remember now, not a word to anyone about last night. I'm not having a girl like you ruin my reputation.'

He unplugged his TV, struggled to take it out to his van, and then came back for all his DVDs. Then he took the key out of his pocket. 'There you are. Don't reckon I want to keep a memento of this experience.'

Tegan stood with tears of humiliation streaming down her face. Then, to her horror, she saw Sam and Bracken in the distance. She watched, wishing for him to turn away, but instead James shouted over to him. 'Morning, Sam. I'm going home for some sleep. It's the quiet ones you have to watch, eh? Tell your fiancée she owes me a decent bottle of whisky.'

He laughed coarsely, got into his van and drove away.

Tegan, cringing, walked away from the window, deeply embarrassed. What ever would Sam think of her? To think she had been telling him to sort his life out. She heard a mewing and found Seren rubbing against her ankles.

'You want your breakfast, anyway,' she said.

She looked around the cottage. It was such a mess. In the kitchen she found the empty bottle of wine and the half-empty vodka. I could sit and drink all day, she thought. Just drift away, numb away all the pain and embarrassment. She heard Seren mewing again. She had responsibility now. She had to care for the kitten.

She picked up the bottles and determinedly emptied the vodka down the sink. She fed Seren, found a bin bag and a cloth, and started to tidy the room. When she had finished, she showered and dressed, went back down and made coffee. She realised that she was due down at the centre, so she settled Seren and started to walk down to the village, hoping she didn't meet anyone.

Tegan arrived at the centre to find Amy at the desk just finishing a call. She looked up at Tegan. 'Morning, that was a woman, a Mrs Abbot. She's found a cat and will be bringing it in later.'

Tegan tried to smile and look efficient.

'Hey, you alright?' asked Amy. 'You look done in.'

'It was a bit difficult' said Tegan.

'Has this anything to do with James?' asked Amy. 'Sam came back from his walk rambling on about him.'

316

Tegan cringed. 'Oh no, everyone will know soon. I've been so stupid. It's entirely my fault.' She burst into tears.

'Tell me what happened,' said Amy gently.

Once Tegan started, she found it a relief to tell someone about the weekend.

'God, I knew James was a prat but I didn't realise he could be so nasty,' said Amy angrily.

'Oh, it was my fault. You mustn't tell people that, you know, nothing happened. He would be so embarrassed.'

'I shan't say anything, but you should be jolly proud of yourself. He's a spoilt, selfish kid. You're well rid of him.'

'You think so?'

'Of course. Now, I'll make you a coffee before I go. You sit there and look after the phones. Hopefully it'll be a quiet morning for you.'

At that moment, Sam was approaching the pub. He was very angry. He had to speak to Angharad. He had a day off but he wanted to go to the centre. However, he was determined to see Angharad, and find out what was going on. He knew she had stayed at The Red Dragon the night before, and found John busily sorting out the bar.

'Good morning, son.' He grinned knowingly. 'Can't keep away, can you? Well, she's upstairs getting some extra beauty sleep, not that she needs it. Anyway, go on up.'

Sam nodded and went straight up to Angharad's bedroom. He knocked on the door and went straight in. He stood and looked at his sleeping beauty, as she slowly awoke, and sat up, looking even more beautiful dishevelled and without make-up.

'Ah, Sam. Hello, come and join me.'

He shook his head. 'What's happening with Tegan? You must tell me,' he said, his voice shaking.

'What is there to tell? She seems to be with James now. You should be pleased. She's done well there.'

'I wouldn't say that. I saw him coming out of Tegan's this morning. He shouted to me something about a bottle of whisky.'

Angharad laughed. 'Oh, that was a bit of fun, that's all. Sounds like he earned it then.'

'What? Was there some sort of bet between you or something? Did you tell him to do something with Tegan?'

'It was just a bit of fun. I said he could have one of those single malts if he got her in the sack. I did my part as well, took her out, got her some decent clothes.'

'Hang on, you came with me that morning, said you wanted to see the nest, but you were looking for her?'

Angharad grinned. 'That's right. I was going to find some way of getting her to go into town. I promised James. You couldn't expect him to take her out looking like she did.'

'That's so manipulative. That's horrible. Tegan trusted you.'

'For God's sake, Sam. Stop being so uptight. She looked really good and I'm sure he gave her a good time.'

'You two. What a cruel thing to do. She's so, so, vulnerable. She needs people to look after her, not to go tarting her up, and making bets about getting her into bed. You disgust me.'

'I disgust you? I'm your fiancée. What's she? She's just some weirdo, dowdy old spinster. I was doing her a favour. You just don't know how to have a laugh.'

Sam shook his head. 'It's no good, Angharad. I've known it in my head but this confirms it. There's no way I can marry you.'

'What are you talking about?'

'Me and you, we're so different. I've tried, I really have, but we've nothing in common. I don't love you. I don't even like you very much any more.'

'Now, Sam,' she said, getting out of bed, putting warm arms around his neck. 'No more of that.'

He took her arms away. 'I'm sorry. This really is it. You and me, it's the end.'

'But I can't manage without you.'

'You can. You know you can. You're beautiful, bright. My God. You can have your choice of men.'

'But I want you. I need someone stable, strong.'

'And you will meet someone else like that, but not me-'

'But your father-'

He stopped. 'What about my father?'

'The thing is, Sam, you do things for family that you won't do for outsiders. If we were to break up I would have to tell Dad about your father's background. He would definitely not recommend him for that contract and I am sure there are a number of people in the village he will feel obliged to tell.'

'My God, that's blackmail. You wouldn't-'

'Oh yes, I will. Just try me.'

'I feel like I have never known you. I've been blind. I never dreamed you could be so malicious.'

He stood staring. It was like he was seeing her for the first time. It was like opening a beautiful gold box and finding a poisonous snake hidden inside. He started to walk towards the door, stopped, turned, took off the signet ring which Angharad had given him, and threw it on the bed.

'I can't believe I fell for any of this. I was such a fool.'

Angharad got out of bed, ran at him, and grabbed his arm, her long claw-like nails digging into him. 'How dare someone like you think he can dump me?'

'What did you say?' He stopped, stared at her. Had he heard her right?

'You know what I said, you miserable little nerd. You'd never normally get someone in my league.'

He uncurled her hand from his arm and stood away from her. 'So, tell me then. Why did you pick me? I mean, you obviously don't love me.'

'No, Sam, of course I don't. But I have to get married. I'm not getting any younger. I want a home and kids. Is that so strange?'

'So why me? Why some miserable little nerd?'

'Because actually you're moderately good looking, got a steady job and I think you'd stay loyal. I wouldn't end up like my mother: divorced, chasing a string of younger men.'

'But haven't you ever met someone you really loved? It doesn't make sense, someone like you settling for second best.'

'Everyone thinks I can have what ever I want? Well it's not true, I can't have him.'

'Who? Who are you talking about?'

'That's a secret. Nobody knows about that. In any case, there's nothing to know now. The point is, I had to find someone else, and I chose you.'

'You mean, you thought you'd settle for me?'

She looked at him, held her head high. 'Lots of people make compromises in life. You were to be mine.'

'You are unbelievably selfish and arrogant. Thank God I'm out of this.' He stormed to the door.

'Come back this instant. I haven't finished with you.'

Sam didn't turn back. He opened the door and went downstairs.

John was waiting. 'What's going on? What have you done to my girl? Why is she shouting, crying?'

'It's off, John. The wedding is off. I'm sorry. I'll make up the money you've lost,' said Sam quickly, just wanting to get away.

Angharad appeared, running down the stairs. 'Daddy, he's leaving me. Stop him. Please, you must.'

John strode towards Sam. Although shorter, he was much broader and stronger than Sam.

'Come on, Sam. We all get cold feet.' He spoke in a menacingly calm voice.

'No, this has never been right. I'm sorry.'

John grabbed his jumper, pulled him close, their faces nearly touching. 'You make up with my girl right now. Nobody, I mean nobody, hurts her.'

Sam shook his head. John pushed him back and then punched him hard in the face. He fell back, banging his eye on the bar. Blood poured out of his nose. John stood breathing hard, a bull ready to charge again. 'No way will your father get that contract now,' he shouted. Sam stood up slowly, rummaged in his pocked and pulled out an old handkerchief. He held it to his nose.

Angharad come closer to the two men. She looked at her father. 'But Daddy, there is more, so much more, to be told about his family. Isn't there Sam?' She turned and looked tauntingly at Sam.

'Angharad, please' pleaded Sam, his words muffled by the handkerchief.

'I told you. If you break up with me I'm telling Dad.'

'Tell me what?' demanded John.

There was an icy silence. Then Sam shook his head. His eye was throbbing. It was no good and his nose hurt like hell. He had had enough. 'You must do your worst, Angharad,' he said. 'We're through.'

He turned his back on her and started to stumble away.

Behind him he heard John saying 'Angharad, tell me what's going on.'

Angharad replied in a loud voice 'Well Dad, just you listen to this. It's going to make your day.'

Chapter Forty

Tegan was sitting at reception at the rescue centre, hugging her mug of coffee, waiting for Mrs Abbot with her cat. She looked up when she heard the door open, thinking this must be them, attempted to look alert and friendly. However, the person arriving was Sam, holding a grubby handkerchief to a bleeding nose. Forgetting the embarrassment of the morning she sprang from her seat.

'Sam, what ever has happened?' she asked.

Blood was dripping through the hanky and his right eye was very red and swollen.

'John. He was very angry with me.'

'John hit you?'

'It really hurts.'

He was looking very upset, very sorry for himself.

'I'll phone Amy. She's somewhere around,' Tegan said, picking up the phone. When she had done that she guided him to a chair, where he slumped down.

'I've called off the wedding,' he mumbled.

'Oh no. I'm so sorry,' she said, adding quietly, 'What James shouted earlier, it was lies you know.'

'I guessed.'

She looked at Sam, but he wasn't really listening to her.

'So did John hit you because you called off the wedding?'

He went to nod but grimaced with pain.

'Is she alright?'

'She's fine' he said bitterly. 'I was just her backup plan.' Sam looked down.

'Oh no,' said Tegan. 'But, still, you didn't want to marry her, and so at least you know you haven't broken her heart'

'I suppose so,' he conceded. 'But Mum and Dad. It's a disaster.'

'What do you mean?'

Before he could answer Amy came rushing in.

'My God brawd, what on earth?' she exclaimed.

'John did it' Sam said. 'I broke off the engagement.'

'Well, that's the most sensible thing you've done for a while,' said Amy. 'My God, what a mess. You need to get to A and E.'

Amy looked at Tegan. 'Could you hold the fort here if I take him? If Mrs Abbot   comes, take the details. The cat can go into that empty basket until I get back.'

'Don't fuss Amy. There's no need for hospital' said Sam.

'Oh yes. I'm not worried about your nose. That couldn't be any worse, but that eye: it needs checking.'

Sam seemed too exhausted to argue, and soon they had left.

Not long after they had gone, Mrs Abbot arrived. Tegan thought quickly, remembered what she had seen Amy do, and soon the cat was booked in and settled into a comfy cage.

It seemed a long morning, but Tegan was surprised at how well she had coped. Eventually Amy returned alone.

'Everything alright here?' Amy asked as she walked in.

Tegan explained about the cat.

'Well done. Told you, you're a natural.'

'So how is Sam?' asked Tegan.

'He needed some kind of stitches on his eye but it's the family he's really worried about.' Amy sat down in a chair next to the desk.

'God, what a mess,' she sighed.

'What's the matter?' Tegan asked tentatively.

'I might as well tell you. I don't know what's going to happen,' said Amy. She took a deep breath. 'Before we came here, Dad was a vet on the Isle of Wight. He reported someone for animal cruelty, went to court and everything. The chap was given a fine, never went to prison. Anyway, he mounted this

323

huge vendetta against Dad. Posted all sorts of stuff about him on the internet, even wrote letters to the local paper.'

'That's awful' said Tegan. She remembered the gentle man she had seen in the pub.

'It was. The Isle of Wight is a small place. Word gets around. This man got hold of a picture of Dad when he was in his teens smoking cannabis. Heaven knows how. Dad had lived there all his life. Maybe some old friend sent it to this chap. Anyway, from this he built up a whole story that Dad was a drug addict. It was terrible. Some people actually stopped bringing their animals to him. Dad got horrible letters.'

'But surely your Dad could have challenged him? The police; can't they stop that sort of thing?'

'Dad's not one to fight. He kept saying this bloke would get bored and stop. But he didn't, and Dad slowly became very depressed. Mum was very worried, so in the end she contacted Glen who runs the practice here. He and Dad were great friends and he was expanding the practice. So he offered Dad and then Sam jobs here. We were all settling well, but now, well, I don't know what will happen.'

Tegan was puzzled. 'Why should anything change?'

'When we came here we made this stupid pact not to mention the past to anyone, but apparently one night Sam told Angharad all about it.'

'But your Dad had done nothing wrong. Why is it still a problem?'

Amy stood up, paced around. 'Sam is worried that John and Angharad are going to stir all that stuff up again. It's probably all there on the internet somewhere.'

'But your Dad can just say it's lies, can't he?'

'Well he should. Sam's worried, though, that he won't cope.'

'Oh dear. It's very serious, isn't it?'

Amy went to the leaflet stand and started mindlessly to rearrange the leaflets.

'It's stupid. I never wanted to keep it all a secret, but Sam said we should do what Mum and Dad wanted. And now

324

he's the one that's blown it, and he's in a right state. As it is he thinks he's let everyone down. Trouble is, Mum and Dad have made him out to be some sort of saint, which is crazy. I mean, no one's perfect, certainly not me.' Amy could not disguise the bitterness in her voice. She sighed. 'Well, he's going to have to own up to being human like the rest of us now.'

Amy glanced up at the clock. 'Anyway, enough of my family woes. It's time you were off. You've done more than enough for one day.'

'Are you sure?'

'Of course. To be honest I'm glad to be back here. I can cope with animals a lot better than people.'

Tegan left Amy and made her way back to the cottage. As she opened the door, the mess, the stale smells struck her. Seren came running up to her, and she stroked her. She looked around the room. It seemed tainted, spoilt by the weekend. She wanted it to feel clean and safe again.

She started to clean more thoroughly this time and then she went upstairs. It was time to clear out some of her past. At least getting rid of the physical things should be easy. She found some rubbish bags. In the black bin liner she put her Community skirts, blouses, underwear, and headscarves, then the denim skirt, tight top and shoes. Daniel's book and the framed verse she put in a carrier bag. Then she picked up her silver box. She didn't want to lose that. It was happy, good memories. She smiled, stroked it, felt the indentations of the words "Pen blwydd hapus", and wondered again what they meant. Then, carefully, she opened it. Inside, nestled in tissue, was a crystal owl. Tentatively, she took it out, and held it to the light, as she remembered doing all those years ago. She stood entranced as the light bounced off the surfaces, the colours rainbowing out. She put it on the bedside table. The rest of the stuff, the things in the bags could go. She didn't want them in her life anymore. She picked up the bin bag and carrier bag, took them downstairs and put them out for the next rubbish collection.

Chapter Forty One

The next morning, Tegan got up early, dressed, and sat down knitting on the sofa. Seren sat next to her. Tegan felt uneasy. Upstairs she knew was that letter she had written for therapy, that description of a little girl sat listening to frightening things. She knew she had been running away from that child, but deep inside her it was still there, frightened and alone. She wanted to be able to sit like this, quiet, to feel calm, not like she was trying to push away and hide from the past. Maybe Liz was right. Maybe she needed to confront this stuff, deal with it. Maybe then she would stop looking for someone else to tell her how to live, how to dress, what to do. She looked out of the window. She hadn't walked up the hills since she had come back. Seren was settled asleep. Tegan put on her boots and left the cottage.

It was windy but slightly warmer. As she got higher she relished the wind blowing through her free hair. She heard the sky larks, smelt the wild flowers, some so tiny she had to kneel to see them.

Suddenly she heard the screeching of a red kite above her. Instinctively, she put her hands on her head, and ducked. Fear gripped her, but then she remembered what Liz had said. 'I can handle this; breathe slowly; there is nothing to be scared of.' Slowly, she calmed down. She could feel her breathing slowing down and smiled. She realised that she had taken control of the fear. It felt exhilarating. She could control this. She would get stronger.

Each day for the rest of the week when she wasn't working or knitting she would walk up in the hills, and in the evening she sat with Seren quietly. She thought about texting Cerys, but wanted to go to therapy first.

So on the Friday she walked to the village and caught the bus to Aberystwyth. She was feeling strong, determined to show Liz how well she had done.

At ten o'clock she was sitting in Liz's room.

'You came back,' said Liz, smiling gently. 'How have things been?'

'OK.'

'Good.'

Liz waited, and then Tegan bit her lip and said, 'No. No, they haven't. To be honest, I've made a complete mess of everything.'

'What's happened?'

Tegan poured out the events of the past few days. 'So you see, I'm a complete failure.'

Tegan started to cry. It hurt. Her throat felt on fire, but still she sobbed.

When she had calmed down a little, Liz spoke. 'Listen, you haven't messed up. You are trying to learn to live. We all make mistakes. It's difficult for you. You weren't allowed to go through all the stuff people go through in their teens.'

'But to be doing it at twenty seven. Why did I just do what Angharad told me? What's wrong with me?'

'There's nothing wrong with you. This is not your fault. You were taught to blindly obey people. It's natural that you just followed her. But you are learning all the time. What you're doing takes huge courage. I know it seems more embarrassing, but just think: at the end of the date with James you took control. You told him to leave. You were very brave.'

'I suppose I did.'

'You have made huge strides; incredible. Don't do yourself down. I know you wanted to try to do things on your own, but was there any other reason you didn't come last time?'

'It was the writing you asked me to do. It made me feel terrible, gave me awful nightmares. I thought therapy was making me worse.'

'Tegan, you could have come and told me that you didn't want to do the writing. We take things at your pace here. You choose what you tell me.'

'Really?'

'Of course. Having said that, therapy can still be very hard. People have no idea, but, you know, you will get better if you stick with it. It takes courage, but I am sure you have plenty of that. So, did you bring your writing?'

Reluctantly, Tegan took the paper out of her pocket and handed it to Liz, who started to read it out.

'I am ten, sat on a big hard plastic chair. I am sat next to Esther. I am looking at my shoes. I am excited. They are red, and they used to be Naomi's. My arms are cold. There is a tiny window up high. I can see the sun. It is a sunny evening. I am tired and I want to go to bed but Daniel is saying he wanted to talk to just us children. Mum and Philip are next door in the big meeting. Daniel says he has an important message from God to tell us. We are all listening. Then he says, 'The end of time is going to be very soon. It could be tonight. If you are not ready, part of the elect, you will be left behind. Your Mum and Dad will just suddenly disappear and you will never see them again.' I know that is true. Philip has been telling me about it since I was little. Then Daniel says he has two films to show us. I am very excited. We have never watched TV or seen a film before. This is on a big screen. Daniel draws the curtains. It is very dark.

'The first film starts. The music is creepy. It makes me feel sick. There is a big yellow clock ticking. The radio is talking. There is a little girl in the kitchen, but she is all on her own. No-one is looking after the things cooking. She screams for her Mummy but she doesn't answer. Her Mummy has gone for ever. I close my eyes then. I am very frightened. I don't want to see any more. It seems to take ages, though. There is lots of screaming. At last the film finishes. I open my eyes, but then Daniel says there is another one. This time it is not real people acting, but the pictures move. There are friends walking. One just disappears, then a mummy holding her little girl's hand disappears. Terrible things happen, lots of screaming. I close my eyes tight. Then it finishes. Daniel says, 'That girl is you, Tegan, or you, Esther. You will look everywhere for your parents but they will be gone. You will be crying, shouting, but they will not hear you. The sky will then turn to blood. The beasts will come out of the sea. They will attack you and hurt you. Women who are having babies will scream in pain. The mountains will be on fire. You will be alone. And then God will judge you. Every single wrong thought or deed you have done, he will remember. You will be sent to hell for ever and ever. It is very hot fire. You will be thirsty and hungry but no one will look after you. You will stay there for ever and ever. You will be there on your own. Your parents cannot get you out.' I try not to listen, to think about my red shoes, but I can't. I want to get up and go but it's not allowed.'

Liz looked up. 'This happened to you when you were ten?'

'About then, although I'd heard a lot of it before. For years my parents had told me this stuff. It's just Daniel did it more forcefully.'

'It must have been terrifying.'

'Yes. I still find it upsetting to think about.'

'Do you think they should have been saying these things to a child?'

'He was trying to save me-'

'Would you say things like that to a child?'

'No, definitely not. No, never.' Tegan spoke firmly, angrily. How dare Liz think she was so cruel?

'Why wouldn't you?'

'It's horrible, so scary. To be honest, I'm not sure I'd want to say it to adults.'

'He told you your mother might disappear at any time?'

'I remember once I was in the garden and I went into the house and it was really quiet. I was sure that it had happened. I ran upstairs. I couldn't find anyone. I was crying, shouting.'

'What happened?'

'Daniel had called a meeting. I didn't know. They were all there in the meeting room. I was screaming. Daniel came out

329

of the room, and told me it had taught me an important lesson: to always be ready.'

Tegan sat back and looked at Liz. She wondered what she was thinking. Liz looked very concerned. Then Liz said, 'But you must have been petrified.'

'Well, yes, but I got used to it, you know, being frightened.'

'Why do you think they said such frightening things to you?'

'Mum said it was good to be frightened. It stopped me sinning.'

'Your mother thought it was good for you to be frightened?'

'When I was little she would sing to me at night, tell me stories, but she changed as I got older.'

'What caused her to change?'

'I've been trying to think about that. It must have been when Daniel came.'

'He changed things?'

'A lot. He brought in vigil, fasting, and life was a lot stricter.'

'And your mother followed all this?'

'Yes. If anything, she was more extreme than most. She fasts for days, does hours of vigil, you know, chanting the same words over and over for hours.'

'That's interesting. Why do you think she does it more than other people?'

Tegan shrugged. It was hard thinking like this. So much of her life she had taken the things people said and did for granted.

'I don't know. She never seems happy. The more she does the more she seems obsessed with it all.'

'Obsessed with what?'

'Doing vigil. She does it for hours.'

'What about your step-father?'

'I don't quite understand him. I always thought he was the tough one but now I'm not so sure. He, well, he seems unhappy but he will never leave. It was only recently that I found out he was not my real father.'

'Tell me what happened.'

Tegan told Liz the whole story.

'Do you think your mother feels guilty for what happened?'

'She gets very anxious talking about the past. She won't look at pictures and things.'

'And yet she gave you Ellis' address?'

'I know. It's odd.'

'You say Daniel introduced vigil?'

'That's right.'

'He seems to hold a lot of control over people.'

'Well, he is next to the holy one. We obviously had to do what he said.'

'You know, there are some leaders of groups who like to control others. They sometimes use something called mind control.'

'Bethany told me about that. Thought control, I think she called it.'

'That's right,'

'So that's what happened to me, you think?'

'Maybe.'

'So, my Mum, she may be influenced like that? You know, maybe she did love me once but she can't think straight any more.'

Tegan knew she was desperate. She looked pleadingly at Liz.

'It may be, yes.'

'I should go and get her, save her.'

'That wouldn't be a good idea at present. Your upbringing damaged you a great deal. You have a lot of healing to do. You must not underestimate how unwell you have been.'

Tegan blinked fast. 'But I don't want to think about all that in the past. It makes me worse. Surely it would be better to forget all about it. I mean, I had those dreams because of thinking about it.'

331

'I know that's tempting, but sometimes trying to avoid the memories is not the right way forward. Until you do that you will always carry that frightened little girl.'

They sat quietly. Tegan reached over for a tissue and wiped her eyes.

Liz continued, 'The trouble is, words can be very destructive, terrifying. When you are a child you believe everything adults tell you. Even at ten you still trust them implicitly.'

'Daniel said we should believe anything he told us. If he told us black was white then we must agree.'

'And would you agree with him now?'

'No, but inside I still get this really deep sense of fear, like I said with the birds. It can be other things as well.'

'Like what?'

'The fire. I hate it when Cerys lights the fire, but I feel so stupid, like I can't say anything.'

'Do you think the fire could be some kind of trigger for a flashback?'

'Yes, I suppose it reminds me of, well, you know.'

'What do you think?'

'Well maybe hell, but why should I still be scared when I don't believe in it in my head?'

'But remember when you were little. Daniel gave you those graphic images of hell, the heat, burning.'

Tegan pulled back in her seat.

'I can see just the words upset you. The problem is that you were very young when you were taught these things. I think they caused a kind of psychological trauma. Often, when someone goes through a traumatic experience the mind and the body can go into shock. Slowly, you may make sense of what has happened to you, process the emotions and come out of shock. However, sometimes a person can remain in that psychological shock. They feel stuck with a constant sense of danger and painful memories that don't fade.'

'Hang on. Are you saying this is happening to me?'

'Yes, I think so.'

'But nothing terrible happened. I was never in a crash or anything.'

'No, but you see, what they said to you, when you were little, these things were very real. Hell was very real. The end times in that film, it sounds horrific. There were even times when you thought these things were actually happening then and there, like when you came in from the garden and couldn't find people.'

'The dreams, you know, they feel so real.'

'That's because part of you still thinks of those things as true and real. It's why it's important to talk about these things. You have to try to process these scary things by talking about them in detail. Then you can learn to put them in the past, tell your body you don't need to be frightened of them any more.'

'But I didn't always listen. I would count the time and things.'

'It may have helped a little but the words still went in.'

Tegan sat listening. It was so much to take in. She wanted to dismiss all Liz was saying as nonsense, but how could she? The dreams, the terror: they were real enough and she had no idea how to get away from it.

'I'd like you to write to that little girl, to yourself, now as an adult, bearing in mind the things you know now.'

Tegan nodded, but she was not at all sure what she would say to that child. She was thinking it through when she realised Liz was talking about the next appointment.

'Next Friday is Good Friday, April 14th. Could you come a few days before, say this time on Tuesday?'

Tegan frowned.

'What's the matter?' asked Liz.

'Oh, it's the Good Friday. I'm sorry I don't know what it is?'

Liz quietly explained the Easter traditions to Tegan. She listened intently. 'I've seen Easter eggs. I remember asking Mum about them, but she just said it was a sinful tradition.'

'Do you still feel that?'

333

Tegan sat and thought about it. 'Well, no. I don't see why it should be. It's just what some people believe, but there aren't any powers or anything in the eggs, are there?'

'What do you think?' asked Liz seriously.

Again Tegan needed time to think. 'Well, they are eggs made of chocolate. Lots of people eat them that are alright. So I don't think they can be harmful.'

Liz nodded. 'Sounds reasonable to me. You see, you have a good mind, Tegan. You are a bright, intelligent woman. It is time you started to believe that and trust yourself.'

Chapter Forty Two

When Tegan returned to the cottage she saw Cerys walking over the field towards her with Dylan. Whatever she was going to say? Cerys saw her, waved and walked over. Dylan jumped up at her. Tegan stroked him, marvelling at how uncomplicated the life of a dog was.

'He's missed you.'

Tegan kept her eyes on Dylan. 'I'm very sorry.' Then she looked up. 'I was so ungrateful-'

'It's OK. Look, let's go inside.'

They smiled nervously at each other and went into the cottage.

Seren came running up to Tegan and at the same time Dylan came running in. He took one look at Seren and ran up to her before Cerys could stop him. Seren spat and hissed at him. Dylan immediately jumped back, and hid behind Cerys.

'You leave her alone' said Cerys sharply.

Tegan put the kettle on. Cerys took Dylan to the sofa. He sat down looking rather miserable, while Seren went and curled up on her bed.

'I came round earlier but you were out,' said Cerys.

'I went back to therapy. I've made a mess of things this week, Cerys. I'm very sorry for what I said to you. Of all the people here you have looked after me-'

'Hey, it's alright. I was probably being over-protective, but it's difficult to judge. Sometimes you seem fine, and then other times so vulnerable.'

'I know. I'm starting to deal with it now, though. You were right about James-'

'I'm so sorry about what happened.'

Tegan told her about the disastrous weekend. Cerys went red with indignation.

'Well, of all the nerve. How dare he just move in like that? Well, I never liked the bloke and I was right. Still, I'm sorry you had to find out the hard way.'

'So, tell me how are things with you?' asked Tegan.

'Really good, thanks. Robert and I are much better off in our own place.' Cerys glowed.

Tegan called Dylan to her. 'Come on, it's alright.'

He left Cerys, looking warily at Seren, and then flopped down on Tegan's feet.

'So how's Dylan doing?'

'Not brilliant, if I'm honest. The collies are just bullying him.'

'Well, you can always bring him here if he needs a break.'

'But what about Seren?'

'I think they'll be alright. She seems to have put him in his place.'

As they were chatting there was a knock at the door.

'You're popular today,' said Cerys.

Tegan opened the door to find Bethany. No flowers today. In fact, she looked very upset.

'Come in. Whatever's the matter?'

'Tegan, I don't know how to tell you. I'm so sorry.'

Tegan looked at Bethany, wondering what ever could have happened.

'Please tell me-' said Tegan.

'You remember the person I spoke to about your Community, the man who works in London?'

'Yes.'

'Well he's just phoned me. Something has happened at the Community.'

'What?'

'I'm so sorry, Tegan. I'm afraid Daniel, well, he's been arrested.'

'What? Why?'

'He's accused of fraud.'

'What do you mean?'

'I don't know the details, but he's accused of setting up some sort of illegal account or something. There was a lot of money involved.'

'But we had no money. We lived very frugally. I don't understand.'

Tegan sat down, shocked. 'It's devastating. If it's true, what will happen to the Community? Mum and Philip, what ever will they do? They gave everything to the Community, well, apart from that £500. They have nothing. But worse, what happens to their beliefs? They put all their trust in Daniel. He was their life. I mean, all of them in the Community. Daniel was everything to them. How on earth do they come to terms with the fact that everything they have believed in is based on lies? I can't imagine how any of them will cope.'

Cerys walked over and put her arm around Tegan. 'Maybe we need to ask Mum, see if she will phone them, find out what's happening.'

Tegan nodded. Cerys phoned Hannah. Hannah said she would talk to Ellis and decide what to do.

About an hour later Hannah rang back. 'Sorry, love. Philip is not answering his phone. Ellis will keep trying.'

Tegan sat anxiously, not wanting to eat.

Cerys looked at her puzzled. 'I know it's family, the place you grew up and all, but they've treated you so badly. Even your Mum. She never even came to visit you in hospital.'

'I suppose you're right, but it wasn't long ago that I was there, believing all the same things as them. I can't imagine how they are coping.'

Tegan and Cerys spent the rest of the day waiting for the phone to ring, but there was no news. Cerys said she would stay the night and Tegan was grateful. When Tegan went up to bed that night she wondered if she should be praying or doing vigil for the Community. She decided that there was no way she could go back to vigil, but she did kneel and say a prayer. 'High One, God, who ever you are and if you exist, please take care of Mum and Philip.'

She got into bed and lay back listening to the night sounds. She closed her eyes, but was aware for the first time of the loud ticking of her clock. She sat up and looked at the large yellow clock face. Of course, that's why it unnerved her. It was just like the one in the film Daniel showed them. She got out of bed and picked it up. Quietly, so as not to disturb Cerys, she went downstairs and found a torch. Then she opened the door, found the rubbish bag and put the clock in it. She looked up at the endless night sky. Tonight it was full of stars. She listened, starting to distinguish the fox, the bats, and the owl. The air smelt cool and clean. As she looked around her she realised the old fear, the crippling sickening fear, was not there, but she wouldn't want to go any further. She crept back into the cottage and up the stairs. Seren mewed a welcome and Tegan smiled as she saw her spread out on the end of her bed. Carefully, she climbed in and lay in the narrow space the kitten had left her. Her hand drifted up to the etching of the owl. She felt the roughly drawn outline. The moon was shining in through a gap in the curtains. Suddenly, she saw the hand, drawing the owl. She turned her head, and then she saw the face. She held her breath. It was so clear, but it couldn't be. No, it was impossible.

Chapter Forty Three

The next morning Cerys and Tegan were just about to phone the manor when Ellis and Hannah arrived together. Tegan ran to the door. 'What's happened? Are they alright?'

Ellis looked nervous. 'I'm afraid it's your Mum. She's in hospital.'

'Oh no. What happened?'

'She collapsed in the street. She's very unwell.'

Tegan took a deep breath, and then said, 'I want to go to her.'

'Are you sure? You've been through so much.'

'Yes, I want to see her. She is my mother. I should be there if she is, well, if anything was to happen.'

'I thought you'd say that. We'll take you.'

Tegan glanced at Hannah. There were tears in her eyes. 'I'm coming. I should see my sister.'

'I think we should go straight away,' said Ellis.

Tegan looked at Cerys in panic.

'It's alright. I'll look after things here, look after Seren. You just go,' said Cerys.

In a dream, Tegan found her coat, packed a few things and went out to the car. Together they set off on the long journey to London. She sat in the back, remembering the long journey with Amy. It felt a lifetime ago. They stopped for drinks but mostly kept driving.

They arrived in London late afternoon. Ellis dropped Tegan and Hannah off at the hospital while he went to park.

Inside was more like a shopping mall than a hospital. Eventually, Tegan and Hannah found a reception desk and took a lift up to the ward where Tegan was told her mother had been admitted. Hannah stayed close to her but they didn't speak.

Tegan stood at the entrance of the ward. She looked into a side room and saw Philip sat next to a bed. A nurse came to her.

'Can I see my mother, Sarah Williams?'

'Ah, there are three of you come from Wales?'

'That's right.'

'Well, it's outside visiting, but come through.'

Philip turned and saw her. He came out of the room.

'How is she?' asked Tegan

'Come and sit down out here,' said Philip guiding her to a chair in the corridor.

'What's happened? I heard about Daniel being arrested.'

Philip nodded slowly. He looked so old, frail. 'The police came. They've been asking questions for a while now.'

Tegan remembered the special vigil when she had arrived, the tension, and the look of panic.

'We believed it to be a time of testing. We undertook many nights of vigil, but Daniel was taken from us by the police.'

He stopped. She understood how much these words cost him to say.

'And Mum?'

'When the police came, it was awful. I've never seen her like that. She was hysterical, shouting that they couldn't take him. I took her to our room, settled her down and went to join the elders at vigil. I didn't realise that she left the house. She went to the park. That's where someone found her, collapsed, and called an ambulance.'

'What had happened?'

'The doctors think it's her heart, but, you see, she also had septicaemia from her hand.'

'The one she cut in the garden?'

'Yes. She was delirious when they brought her in, apparently. I'm afraid they gave her a lot of medicine. I hope she will not be too angry but I didn't know what to do. You know, Daniel was not there to consult-'

He looked completely lost.

'I think you did the right thing,' said Tegan gently.

340

Philip shook his head. 'She kept saying your name.'

'Did she?'

'Yes. I think you ought to see her.'

As Tegan walked to Sarah's room with Philip, she noticed Ellis sitting with Hannah. Philip ignored them. The room was small, white, with one chair beside the bed. Her mother appeared to be in a deep sleep. She had drips and monitors set up round her and looked very fragile. Philip gestured for her to sit down. He said he would be back soon.

Tegan sat watching her mother. She remembered lying frightened in hospital herself recently. Her mother had not come to her. For the first time she realised how wrong that had been. She had not thought twice about coming to her mother. Why hadn't her mother come to her? As Tegan watched her mother she suddenly realised her mother's eyes were open and she was looking back at her.

'Mum,' she said quietly.

'Tegan.' Her voice was warm, her eyes soft. Tegan swallowed hard. This was the mother who had sat next to her bed when she was so little and frightened and who sang to her.

Her mother's eyes drifted to the locket. 'Ellis.'

Tegan touched the locket.

'The cottage. The hills. I was happy there.' Her mother seemed delirious, her voice far away. Tegan frowned.

'Me and you, we picked orange poppies. Ellis played the piano, and we sang.'

Tegan stared. 'You came to the cottage?'

Her mother's smile deepened. 'Oh yes, I took you with me. So happy, but you cried. The dark, you were always frightened of the dark.'

Tegan sat forward. 'Did you draw the owl on my bed?'

'I said the owl would keep you safe.' Sarah suddenly closed her eyes and lay breathing slowly. Tegan sat with tears on her cheeks. Could any of this really be true?

Philip came back. 'Has she said anything?'

Tegan hesitated. 'Just a few words. Nothing much.'

341

'Ellis and Hannah are out there,' he said stiffly. 'I think you'd better get them.'

Tegan nodded. As she went to fetch Ellis and Hannah she saw Philip walking away. Ellis went into the room. He looked around uncomfortably, then at Tegan. She nodded at the chair. He sat down on the edge nervously. Hannah stood just behind. Ellis put his hand on Sarah's. She opened her eyes instantly. 'Ellis.' Tegan saw Sarah's eyes light up. She was the woman in the photograph again.

'Hello Sarah.' Ellis didn't smile back. He looked far more serious and sad. 'It's been a long time.'

'I was thinking about the cottage' said Sarah dreamily.

'You were happy there, weren't you?'

Sarah's smile grew. Ellis touched her hand and Sarah closed her eyes. After a little while a nurse came and asked them if they could leave as she had things she needed to do.

'Maybe we should get something to eat. We only had a drink and a snack at lunch time,' said Hannah.

On the way out Tegan saw a doctor talking earnestly to Philip.

'You go on. I'll just speak to Philip.'

'We'll wait just over there. This place is vast.'

'OK.'

Tegan went and joined in the conversation. The doctor turned to her. 'I'm Sarah's daughter.'

'OK. Well, I was just saying that we are very pleased. We've stabilised the septicaemia quicker than we hoped. Of course, we've a way to go, but she's out of danger.'

'So she's going to be alright?'

'It's certainly looking positive. Now, if you'll excuse me-'

The doctor rushed away before they could ask anything else. Tegan felt at a bit of a loss. What should she do now?

'It's good news then,' she said.

'I can't take her home yet though.'

'Of course not. She still looks very poorly.'

'I know, but she'll be very upset when she realises where she is.'

'I would like to see her again before we go.'

'The doctor advised leaving her now for the night. I shall go back to the Community. Where will you stay?'

'Don't worry. I'll talk to Ellis.'

She saw Philip's face harden. 'I may not see you again, so goodbye.' He turned and walked away.

It seemed to Tegan that the momentary softness had been papered over. There was to be no hug, no tender goodbye. She blinked back tears, and the pain of another rejection.

She went to find Hannah and Ellis. They broke off their conversation. Hannah looked at her seriously. 'I think you and your father had better talk.'

Tegan sat down nervously in Hannah's place next to Ellis.

'I need to tell you, tell you about the cottage.'

'What happened?'

'You and your mother came with me once to the cottage. You were very little-'

'So Mum wasn't just delirious. It's true?'

He nodded, and then he reached forward and touched the locket. 'That's when I gave Sarah the locket.'

'But how old was I? Surely Mum was married?'

Ellis cringed. 'She was. After you were born we only saw each other at the odd family occasion. I hadn't seen you for about a year. It was May Day. I was in Cardiff centre and bumped into your Mum. She was pushing you in the pushchair. I was so excited to see you, your mop of black hair and sparkling blue eyes.' Tegan saw tears glisten in his eyes. 'We chatted quite naturally. It was a lovely sunny day. Then she told me that she and Philip were moving to live in a community in London. I realised I may never see you again.' Ellis put his hand on hers. 'It seemed so final. Then she mentioned that Philip was away on a course that week, and co-incidentally Hannah had gone to her parents with Cerys. Suddenly I was desperate for you to see your roots, just once. The cottage was empty. My parents were away.

343

It seemed too good an opportunity to miss. I pleaded with your Mum to come with me, that day.'

'And she said yes?' asked Tegan, flabbergasted.

'Not at first, but there was something about that day: the sun, the music. We felt young and free. I couldn't believe it, but suddenly she agreed, said she'd come. We just went for one night. It was magical. The weather was perfect, and you toddled around the cottage so happily. We went to the well. I told your mother the stories my Mum had told me. She didn't really approve of some of them but she hooked on to the one about the owl.'

'But didn't Philip and Hannah wonder where you were?'

'Philip was on retreat. There was no phone. Hannah, well, I told her I had to go and check the cottage. I told her I was there on my own.'

'So I did remember it, the stone floor. I really could remember the feel of it under my feet.'

'Yes. I can't believe it, but, yes, you did, and the only time you cried was that night. Your Mum was sitting downstairs, just talking, but you were frightened. Your Mum drew the owl because I'd been telling her about the owl at the well. It was to make you feel safe. Your Mum bought you gifts that weekend. Do you know what they were?'

Tegan screwed up her eyes. She shook her head. 'No, I can't think-'

'You have them now, by your bedside.'

'The box, the crystal owl!'

'That's right. She had some money to buy herself some shoes. She used it to buy those for you, said she'd give them to you when you were older.'

'I think I was about seven. Funny, I was only telling Cerys about it the other day.'

'She bought them in a little shop in a village we stopped in on the way back. The box she got engraved at a jeweller's. She was very happy. It was like she gave herself a holiday just for those few days. Anyway, I took you both back to Cardiff. I gave your mother my mum's locket and the film of pictures we'd taken while we were away.'

Tegan sat in the hospital corridor, her mind far away. 'I can't believe I went to the cottage. It's incredible.'

'It's the main reason I have never wanted to sell it. You see, I never told your mother, but I kept hold of it so that if anything was to go wrong she could always come back there. I would make sure there was always a home for you. I was worried, you know, about the community thing. She told me Philip was going to give them all their money.'

Tegan said, 'So could Mum and Philip come there to live now if they wanted to?'

'That's what Hannah and I have been talking about. I've only recently told Hannah about the cottage. I had to prove to her I was not hankering for Sarah, for the past. I told her the cottage was now hers to do with what she wanted.'

'Oh, I see.' Tegan tried to hide her devastation, the thought of the cottage being lived in by strangers.

'You're not to worry' Ellis added quickly. 'We both agree you will always have a home with us. I promise you will never be homeless.'

She tried to smile. 'Thank you. Yes, that's very kind, but Mum and Philip?'

'Hannah will talk to them tomorrow. I think she will offer it to them.'

'Really?'

'Yes, she has a good heart, you know. I don't think I have always appreciated that. Anyway, we ought to go and find her. We need to find a bed for the night.'

Hannah had not gone far. No one spoke. They were all too busy with their own thoughts. They found a small hotel with vacancies. Tegan of course found it difficult to sleep. To think her mother had been to the cottage, and to see that wonderful gentle warm smile when she'd talked about it. And now her mother could go back, live in that wonderful place, and start again. Of course Philip would come as well. It was only right. Tegan tried to rid herself of a niggling resentment. The cottage

345

had been her refuge. It was hard to imagine them going to her shop, climbing her hill. It would be odd. That is supposing they want her to live with them. What if they said no, where would she go then? Her mind churned over the many ramifications until she finally fell asleep.

At breakfast Tegan guessed, from the exhaustion on their faces, that Ellis and Hannah had spent a lot of time talking.

'I rang the hospital,' said Ellis. 'Sarah has been moved on to the main ward. We are to go at normal visiting hours now, two o'clock. I was thinking-' Ellis looked at Hannah. 'How about we go and look at some of the museums, the National Gallery, the Tate? I've been promising we'd go together for years.'

'OK. Yes, that would be really nice. And Tegan, you must come. We have so much to show you.'

They went first to The National Gallery. They travelled by taxi, which was a novelty for Tegan. She was able to see famous places which, despite being brought up in London, she had never seen. They arrived at Trafalgar Square with the fountains and lions, and then climbed the stone steps into the National Gallery.

The whole experience was bewildering. First, to have her bags checked, and then into enormous rooms full of paintings. Hannah guided her. Tegan found herself catching her enthusiasm.

In the Impressionist rooms Hannah showed her Van Gogh's Sunflowers. The pain and beauty was compelling. Hannah told her that Van Gogh had described his sunflowers as a symphony in yellow and blue, how he would start painting at sunrise as the flowers faded so quickly. Tegan was quite relaxed until she noticed one painting by Rembrandt. Hannah came over to her. 'Ah, Belshazzar's Feast' she said.

Tegan just stared. Her hands were sweating; her breathing increased. The picture showed the biblical king, terrified, reading Hebrew words written by a ghostly hand.

'I've no idea what the words mean,' Hannah was saying. Tegan knew she had been shown this picture. The words had

346

been used to curse her when she was first thrown out of the Community. She looked at Hannah, white faced. 'They mean "You have been weighed in the balance and found wanting". It's what they said to me. I had failed. I was to be judged by God.' Tears filled her eyes, and a feeling of despair. Would she never be free from her past?

Hannah looked at her seriously. 'That was a terrible thing to say to you. You do know that? You know it isn't true, don't you?'

Tegan stopped, tried to think like Liz had told her. She took a deep breath. 'Yes, I suppose so. It's hard though.'

Hannah nodded. 'I shall take you to my favourite picture in the gallery' she said decisively.

Tegan was aware of Ellis hanging about, looking rather bored, but Hannah carried on regardless. They retraced their steps and Hannah took Tegan back to an Impressionist painting she had missed.

'This is The Water-Lily Pond by Monet. He bought a pond in Giverny in France which he transformed into a water garden, putting in Japanese-style bridges, and then he painted it at different times of day.'

'It's lovely. Cerys should see this. It would inspire her.'

'You know, I never thought of that. One day we'll all come here. Even better, we'll go together and see this garden. It's meant to be wonderful. It would be lovely to see it with Cerys.'

Ellis was really restless now, so they headed for Covent Garden. They ate pasta in the square. Tegan and Hannah left Ellis listening to buskers and went to look around the shops. Tegan spotted a small shop with long cotton skirts and floaty tops. Hannah cringed, but Tegan insisted they went in and she tried some things on to see if she really liked them.

'You know, they are not my taste but you do look lovely. Do you like them?'

Tegan looked at herself in the mirror. She had no make up on, but her hair fell loosely. She felt comfortable and pretty.

'I shall buy this top. It will go with my skirt at home.'

347

'Next time we'll bring Cerys. I think this could be just her sort of place. You know, I have always promised to take her to Chelsea, the flower show. We must work something out.'

Tegan smiled. She remembered Cerys talking about the things she had done with her mother when she had been a child. She hoped that the visits to France and the flower show materialised.

It was time to return to the hospital. Tegan was excited. There was so much she wanted to talk to her mother about.

They walked to the ward. Tegan saw her mother sitting upright. Philip was not there. However, as soon as she saw her mother's face she knew things had changed.

Chapter Forty Four

Tegan walked towards her mother's hospital bed. There was no smile this time, no greeting. Her heart sank. Her mother was like a different person from the warm woman she had spoken to the day before.

'Hello Mum. You're looking better,' she said, determinedly brightly.

'I am not happy about being in here. Philip came in earlier. I told him I want to discharge myself. There is a lot to do.'

Tegan noticed that Sarah only spoke to her. She had not even looked at Ellis and Hannah who were standing silently behind her.

'You've been very unwell. You know about Daniel?' asked Tegan.

'I understand he has been seriously misled. But the work goes on.'

'But how can it? Daniel was the leader. It was his vision.'

'No, he was but a messenger. The elders have had a new vision for the community.'

Tegan listened, baffled.

Her mother continued. 'The land the community building is on is very valuable. We bought it outright, you see, all those years ago. Fortunately Daniel had not re-mortgaged it. We can sell it for a substantial profit. We are going to set up a new community in Scotland, far away from the world. We will live a contemplative life, praying for the world, waiting for the end of time.'

'But who will be leader?' asked Tegan, faintly.

'The elders will work as a body. We believe it to be the right way for us now. Tegan, I have talked to Philip. We are sure it is right for you to come with us. I know there have been problems but this will be a new start. We will be far away from the wickedness of the world. You will be cut off from temptation.'

Silently, Hannah stepped forward. 'Sarah, I came here to offer you and Philip the cottage, a home. You don't need to go off to Scotland. I know I go on about it, but actually the cottage can be very snug, and you were happy there, weren't you?'

Sarah frowned. 'I don't know why you think I would want to live there. You are like the devil tempting me away from the truth. No, I shall never go there again.'

'Mum,' said Tegan, horrified, 'it's beautiful there, and very generous of Hannah to offer it to you.'

Hannah stepped away from the bed. 'Leave it, Tegan. That's it.'

'So, Tegan, are you going to repent of this worldly life and come and live with us?' asked Sarah.

'No Mum, no. I never want to go back to living the way we did. I don't understand you. You said you were happy there. You can be happy again. It's wonderful there. You don't have to be frightened any more.'

'Tegan,' her mother snapped. 'There is more to life than being happy. You should know that. And how many times have I told you, it is good to feel fear all the time, hold it close, never ever let it go.'

'But Mum-'

'Enough of this foolish talk. I offered for you to come back, a final chance.'

'No Mum, no. I never want to come back.'

'But what will you do?'

'Ellis has told me I have a home with them. I have work now. I can get my own flat one day.'

'Tegan, I fear for your soul. You know what the future without the elect holds. And Hannah and Ellis, you two remain hard set on the road to destruction.'

Ellis stepped forward, his face red with fury. 'How dare you speak to us like this? You and Philip are cruel and cold.

350

Maybe it's years of living in that community, but you know there was song, beauty in you, but you've killed it. And I shall never forgive you for what you did to Tegan. You failed to give Tegan the home every child has a right to, one where they feel loved and safe. You terrified her with cruel, evil, sadistic threats and lies. My sin is that I did nothing about it. I chose to ignore it and let this happen to her.' Ellis sat down, put his head in his hands and wept. Hannah put her arm around him.

The air was heavy with unspoken angry words. Then Sarah said, 'I think Ellis and Hannah you should go. I would like a few words with Tegan.'

'No. You won't hurt her any more,' said Ellis.

Hannah put her hand on Ellis' arm. 'I think Tegan should decide if she wants to stay.'

'Thank you. I will stay,' said Tegan, 'but please wait for me. I won't be long.'

When Hannah and Ellis had left the ward Sarah looked at her daughter. 'Do you agree with those wicked words of Ellis? You know I wanted to bring you up in the fear of the High One. I didn't want you to make the mistakes I had made. I wouldn't want you to hate me.'

'Mum, I could never hate you, but it doesn't mean I'm not badly damaged and hurt by the way you brought me up. I refuse to trivialise the harm and trauma you and the Community put me through. You know, yesterday, I saw the mother I occasionally glimpsed when I was very young. I believe that is the real you, and I hope one day you find her.'

Sarah reached out her bandaged, injured hand. Tegan held out her scarred hand, and they touched briefly. Tegan leant forward and kissed her mother on the forehead.

'I'm going now, Mum.'

'I will pray for you' said Sarah quietly.

'I will be living among those hills, Mum, the place I know you were happy' said Tegan.

For a moment she saw her mother's face soften. 'We will both be among hills, won't we?'

'Yes Mum, we will. You take care now. Goodbye.'

351

Tegan turned and quietly left the room. Outside, Ellis and Hannah were waiting.

'Alright? Come on, time to go to your home.'

'About the cottage-' said Hannah.

'Yes?' said Tegan, holding her breath.

Hannah smiled. 'It's yours. If you want it, that is?'

Tegan sighed with relief. 'I can stay there?'

'You can stay there for ever if you want. The cottage is to be put into your name. It will belong to you.'

Tegan gasped. She couldn't take it in. 'But I can't-'

Hannah smiled. 'Yes you can. It is what we want. Please take it.'

Tegan smiled. 'Well, thank you. Thank you very very much.'

Ellis beamed, and they left the hospital.

Tegan phoned Cerys as soon as she could. She had been anxious about telling her about the cottage, but Cerys could not have sounded more thrilled. 'What more could I want but a sister living in the cottage? Honestly, Tegan it's fantastic. By the way, your cat has done nothing but eat. Now travel safely, and see you soon'. When Tegan returned in the early hours, Seren was fast asleep on the sofa. 'Too full to move, I think,' said Tegan.

Tegan walked through the living room and into the kitchen. She touched surfaces, walls. This was her home. She took off her shoes and socks, stood on the stone floor, closed her eyes. Strangely, she noticed the distinctive smell of the cottage for the first time. It had been closed up and somehow the smell was concentrated: a mixture of wood, stone, and nameless but distinctive aromas seeped into her pores, calming and caressing her. She went upstairs to her room and sat on the bed, looking out of the window at a night sky full of stars. Then she reached out and touched the carving of the owl. Her Mum had drawn that, the warm, kind person who worried about her little girl being scared. Tegan lay down, resting her head on her pillow but still touching the owl. Tears welled up, but the tears jammed painfully in her throat. From deep inside she groaned. She curled up tight, and then she sobbed, grieved for the loss of the gentleness and softness, that life the cult had destroyed in her mother and that she had been denied.

She lay in the darkness. She could not sleep. In the corner she could make out the outline of the bag of books from Bethany about cults. She turned on her light and picked it up. One book contained accounts of people who had left cults, and been disowned by family and friends. They were very moving. She sat crying, reading of people who come out of cults to no support, about those who had become drug and alcohol dependent, seriously depressed; those who, many years after leaving, lived lonely isolated lives. She read of a man who had gone back to the gates of his community building years after being cast out and took his own life; of people who tied ribbons to the gates of loved ones who had refused to speak to them since childhood.

Although it was distressing, it helped her to feel less isolated in what she was going through. It helped her to see that her pain and hurt was valid. After a time, though, she put the books down. She got out of bed and walked around the cottage: her cottage, her home.

She looked over and realised that there was redness on the horizon. Tegan dressed, put on shoes and a coat, and went out into the garden. Early birdsong was starting, and as she watched the bright blaze of the first sight of the sun appeared. The brilliant yellow fire ball slowly, imperceptibly, crept higher, the dark blue sky around it streaked with reds, yellows. She remembered Hannah telling her about Van Gogh, painting the sunflowers at sunrise, and decided she would plant sunflowers in her garden just to look at them against this wonderful sky. She stood and watched the whole sunrise. The warmth reached out to her. Suddenly, she heard someone shouting her name. She looked round, to see Sam and Bracken coming towards her.

'You're up early' she called.

'Couldn't sleep, but marvellous isn't it? And I've some fantastic news. Look, come and see.'

Tegan followed Sam down through the field to the edge of the woods.

'We must be really quiet,' Sam whispered. 'Look, they've built a nest and the female is sitting there incubating the egg. They easily desert a nest at this stage.'

Tegan saw another bird arriving.

'That's the male feeding her,' he whispered.

'So how long will it be before the eggs hatch?'

'About thirty to forty days, and then fledging takes about seven weeks.'

'It takes a long time.'

They crept away, and started to walk into the woods. The bird song was rich and loud. Tegan noticed a robin singing on a branch.

'They're one of the first birds to sing in the morning and one of the last at night' said Sam.

They reached the well and sat together by the still water.

'How's your mother?' asked Sam.

'She's going to be OK, but it was a difficult visit. Still, I'm glad I went.' Tegan swallowed hard and then asked, 'So how are you? Your face still looks very sore.'

Actually, she had been thinking that, if anything, his face looked worse. The bruising was spreading back and dark red over his face, and his nose was still swollen and angry looking.

'Look a right state, don't I?'

'It'll get better. So what's happened about Angharad? Is she alright?'

'Oh, of course, you've been away. You haven't heard the latest.'

'What's happened now?' she asked, intrigued.

'I rang Angharad yesterday morning. We hadn't spoken since the split. I was worried how she was.'

'And-'

'She asked me to go round to her flat, said she needed to see me. I started to panic, thought that she might be about to do something to herself. I raced round in the car, rang the bell. It seemed to take for ever for her to answer. In fact, I had my phone out to call the police. Then she came to the door.'

He blinked, and scratched the back of his neck.

'She was in her nightie, but she looked fine. I was so relieved and then she asked me in. That's when I saw him.'

'Who?'

'The man she said she had always loved.'

'And who is it?' asked Tegan eagerly.

Sam ran his fingers through his hair.

'It's Wynn. You know, Wynn who is married to Megan.'

'You don't mean James' father?'

'That's right. He's left Megan.'

Tegan was dumbstruck.

'Angharad is in love with Wynn? But he's so-'

'Yes. He's much older than her.'

'Poor Megan.'

'Apparently, they'd been seeing each other for ages. She got tired of waiting for him to leave Megan. Then, when he heard we'd broken up he went rushing round to her. He's told Megan it's over, and now, after Angharad's exams, they're planning to go to New York, live in the flat. Apparently that was always their dream.'

'Good gracious.'

'Yes. It's awful really, but I must admit I'm so glad to be clear of her.'

'And your Dad?'

'That hasn't been as bad as I thought. He's lost the contract at the stables. He expected that. However, apparently John refused to have anything to do with all the other gossip, told Angharad it was a waste of time and he didn't go round muck racking. I think he thinks thumping me is a more honest response.'

'So you don't feel so bad then?'

'Not really. Maybe it's even done us all a favour, got things out in the open.'

'How is your Mum?'

'She's alright. Pleased I'm not marrying Angharad actually.'

A red kite flew overhead. Tegan's hands flinched, but that was all.

'Great news about the cottage then' Sam said.

Tegan laughed. 'How on earth?'

'Ah, Cerys went down the pub last night. She told Amy, who told me.'

'I should've known. Anyway, it's wonderful. I'm very lucky.'

'You deserve a bit of luck. Gosh, so much has changed for you, hasn't it? Mind you, I might be making some big changes as well.'

'What do you mean?' she asked anxiously.

'Can't tell you yet,' he said smiling smugly. 'Things to sort out, people to see and all that.'

Mystified and slightly anxious, Tegan stood up with Sam and watched him call Bracken. Together, they walked together back out through the woods. Sam left her and she walked back to the cottage alone.

Chapter Forty Five

When Tegan returned to the cottage she remembered that she had the letter to write for her therapy appointment the next day. She found paper and pen. She closed her eyes and tried to imagine that little girl sitting on the chair. She opened her eyes. She knew exactly what she wanted to say to her.

When she had finished, Tegan spent the day finishing the shawl for Rachel. Next day she packed the shawl carefully, and walked down to the village. She went straight to catch the bus to Aberystwyth. While she was travelling she received a text from Cerys.

'Have you got therapy? I could meet you after down the beach, want to give Dylan a good run. Are you free?'

Tegan cringed: the beach. She hadn't been down there since that first visit with Ellis. Maybe she should try. She replied with a time to meet and tried to push it from her mind.

When she was in her meeting with Liz she found that she was able to talk more easily.

'A lot has happened,' she said.

'Really?'

'I saw my mother.' Tegan explained all about Daniel, her mother in hospital.

'How do you feel?'

'OK I think. It was difficult seeing Mum. It was like seeing two different people and I don't really know which one is the real her. There were glimpses, you know, of a softer warmer person the first time I went in, when she was delirious, I suppose. Anyway, when she was better she told me she's determined to carry on in the Community. She can't let go of it all.'

They talked more about her mother and then Tegan took the letter out of her bag.

'This is the letter you asked me to write last session. I didn't know what to write, but after seeing Mum, somehow I was able to.'

Tegan handed Liz the letter. This time she didn't read it aloud but quietly to herself.

'Dear Tegan,

I can see you listening to Daniel. I know you are listening even though you are scratching your hand very hard and watching the clock. You are very frightened. You need to know that the things that Daniel is saying are not true. He is making those things up to frighten you. He's a dangerous man who needs to control people, even children. You will not go to hell and you will not burn for ever. You will not be left alone in a world full of blood and scary beasts. Stop worrying about your Mum and Dad suddenly being taken by The High One. It won't happen. It's alright: don't be scared. Not everyone in the world is evil. There are kind people in the world who will, one day, help you forget these horrible things. When you are older you will go to a beautiful place, full of hills and trees. You are a good person who can do good things. It is alright to feel happy and not to worry all the time.

Love,

Tegan.'

Liz put the letter down. She took a deep breath. 'That's very moving.'

'It's a bit frustrating though. You see, I know that what I've written is right, but then, it's like the past come out of nowhere.'

'What kind of thing reminds you of that past?'

Tegan told Liz about the painting in the gallery that had upset her so much. 'You know, it was so depressing. One minute I was fine and then I was so frightened and upset.'

'You know, it not only takes courage to get better, to face your past, but also perseverance. There is no quick fix. You spent all your formative years in the Community. The damage they did to you will not be healed in a few sessions of therapy. I'm so sorry, I wish it could be. Try not to get discouraged. You will get better, I'm sure. Just think, in the gallery, you didn't have a full panic attack, did you? And you are sitting now thinking about it in a way that you couldn't have done a few weeks ago.'

'That's true' said Tegan. 'There is something else.'

'Yes?'

'It sort of rumbles away inside. It's this frustration about all the things I missed. But it's too late now, isn't it? I mean, my childhood has gone. It's too late.' Tegan felt anger and resentment bubbling over as she spoke.

'Do you remember, I said that leaving the cult is like going through bereavement?' asked Liz gently.

Tegan nodded.

'One of the things you grieve for is that loss of childhood. It is very painful. Healing is a process. It takes time. And it is hard work.'

'It's not what my Mum would call hard work. I think she sees my life now as a waste of time. Sometimes I even wonder if she's right. I mean, when she was talking about the new place they were setting up, I could see the passion and vision for what she's doing. You know, she's waiting for the end of time, doing vigil to save herself from hell. Well, it makes my life knitting, walking and things look at the least a bit mundane.'

'Living a life that is not dominated by those kinds of extreme scenarios is something people coming out of high dependency groups often find difficult. But, you know, there is another way to live. A lot of that passion you saw in your mother is based on fear, and would you really want to live like that again?'

Tegan thought about the nightmares, the horrific flashbacks. 'No. No, I wouldn't want to go back to that.'

'I know at the moment sometimes it must feel like you are learning to survive, but, you know, life is multicoloured, not black and white. I am sure that slowly you will learn to find an excitement and joy in living.'

'You mean, like how I feel up the hills, or when I finish a shawl, sing a lovely song-'

359

'See, you've started already,' Liz said. 'You've done so well. There are lots of opportunities out there.'

'But I have no qualifications. There are so many things I can't do.'

'But you are bright. You could get some GCSEs at night school, some A levels, and meanwhile you could do some voluntary work in different things. Do you know what kind of things you'd like to do?'

Tegan frowned. 'I don't know. It's hard to think.'

'Well, you like walking in the hills. Is there anything else?'

'Reading, books. At a party, I sat with this little girl. I loved reading stories to her.'

'So maybe work in a library; write stories; teach.'

Tegan bit her lip. 'Gosh, you make it sound so easy, but what if I can't do it? What if I fail?' She felt herself close to tears.

Liz smiled gently. 'Tegan, you don't have to do anything. It's all up to you. You will find you will do things as you are ready. We are at the beginning of recovery from some very difficult things. You have to learn to dream. You've never been allowed to before. Take it slowly.'

Tegan sighed, suddenly very tired.

'Now, you know, I run a group for people who've come out of various high demand groups. It may help you to come to that some time, but we need to keep seeing each other one to one for a while. I have been told I can have the extra sessions. Would you like that?'

'Yes. Yes, I would.' Tegan glanced at the clock. Her hour was nearly up. 'There is one more thing' she said.

'Mm'

'It's the sea. I've to go there in a minute and meet someone. The thing is, I went there for the first time recently. It was terrifying. I couldn't look at it. I haven't been back since.'

'And why do you think you were so scared?'

'I don't know' said Tegan desperately. 'All I know is, I was petrified. I felt so stupid.'

360

Liz put her head to one side. 'Do you remember when you first came, you told me you were scared of the monsters. You had a picture.'

Tegan screwed up her eyes. 'The monsters in the red sky, coming out of the-' She stopped.

Liz waited.

Tegan breathed heavily. 'They came out of the sea.'

Liz nodded. 'Exactly, and when you were young and were told that you believed it was something that was real that would actually happen. All the fear and panic you felt when they were telling you those things come back when you see the sea.'

'But what do I do?'

'Well, how do you handle the birds now?'

'I think about my breathing, do that grounding thing, touch something, distract myself, tell myself I don't need to be scared: this feeling will pass.'

'Exactly. You see, you are developing techniques to cope. These triggers will surprise you sometimes, but you will get better and better at dealing with them.'

'I suppose so. I get frustrated, annoyed with myself.'

'Think of what you wrote to that little girl. She was so scared. You have to be kind, gentle, understanding of her.'

Tegan nodded. 'I think I see that. So now, when I go down to the sea, I have to be patient with myself, try all those other things, but not beat myself up.'

Liz smiled. 'You see, you have great courage. I'll see you next Friday and we can talk about it, but remember, I'm not going to judge you what ever you do.'

Tegan left Liz and walked down the street. Soon she caught glimpses of the sea. She could feel her heart starting to race. In with Liz it had seemed straightforward. Conquering this fear out here alone was very different.

Tegan stood on the pavement, stopped and tried to calm herself. Then she realised that she was in front of a florist, and decided to buy some flowers for Cerys.

Inside was a bewildering array of flowers in buckets and vases, all over the shop. A young girl engrossed in putting together a large bouquet came over to help her. Shyly, she went around, choosing a large bunch of yellow tulips and some white daisies, tied with a yellow bow. It made her smile, and the scent was delicate.

Walking down the street she held the flowers close and was soon at the sea front. She saw Dylan first, head down, smelling a large pile of seaweed. She heard Cerys running towards him, shouting.

'Don't roll in it.' She was too late and Tegan saw Dylan rolling, in ecstasies. Cerys looked up in despair and then saw Tegan and waved.

Tegan nervously looked past her at the sea. She smelt the flowers, and then, calming her thoughts, she walked towards Cerys. Suddenly, she found Dylan jumping up. She shielded the flowers and the bag with her shawl in from him, but stroked him, pleased to see him despite the smell.

'Hiya' said Cerys, gabbing Dylan. 'Hang on, I'll put him on the lead. We can go for coffee over there.'

While Cerys was sorting out Dylan, Tegan knelt down and touched the small stones on the beach. She listened to the waves sucking in the sand, and then raised her eyes to the sea. The sea was actually quite blue today, the sky a lighter shade of blue with streaks of white clouds. Her eyes were drawn to the horizon. She remembered her feelings when she arrived at the cottage: the vast wilderness of fields and hills. Here the wilderness was water. Tegan could see now that there was beauty there, but it gave her a restless feeling that she didn't find in the hills.

They left the beach and went to a café on the promenade. They sat down on metal chairs in their coats. A couple with a toddler and pushing a pram walked past, looking tired but determined to enjoy their holiday.

'These are for you.' Tegan held out the flowers. 'I wanted sunflowers, but it had to be yellow tulips this time.'

'Perfect, thank you,' said Cerys. 'So, how do you feel about the cottage?'

'I don't think it's sunk in yet, but it's wonderful. I hope you don't mind.'

'Of course not. I have my home. The cottage would never have meant that much to me. No, I'm pleased for you. Mum is full of plans to go and see some garden in France. She was inspired by her visit to the gallery with you.'

'It sounds a lovely place. By the way, I met Sam yesterday. He told me about Angharad and Wynn.'

'Shocking, isn't it?' said Cerys, her eyes wide with excitement from the gossip.

'I don't get why a girl who looks like her wants to be with someone so much older.'

'Nor me. It's embarrassing for James though. If anything, I always expected him and Angharad to get together. Mind you, they both need someone to massage their egos. I'm sorry for Megan though. She's very bossy, but she's OK.'

'I've finished my shawl. I'm taking it into Rachel' said Tegan.

'I'm sure it's perfect, but good luck. Listen, I'm on my way back. I can give you a lift if you like. I'm parked just along the front.'

As they walked together back to the car Tegan glanced over at the sea. No beasts in the sky; children playing; people walking dogs; all normal. She smiled and sighed with relief.

When Tegan arrived back at the village she walked over to Rachel's shop. She went in and saw Rachel's beautiful cream shawl on display.

'Hello Tegan.'

'I've finished the shawl,' Tegan said nervously.

'Great, let's have a look.'

Tegan had never seen Rachel so full of enthusiasm. Rachel inspected the shawl carefully.

'That's lovely. Well done.'

Tegan felt herself go pink with pleasure. 'I'm glad it's OK.'

'It's better than OK. It's lovely. You've done very well. I'm so glad you're going to be staying. I heard about the cottage.'

'Amy told you?'

'That's right. Now, can you face making more?'

'Yes please. I'd like to.'

'That's great. We must sort out employing you properly. I'll get Alan to do the paper work.'

'Sam told me all that had happened,' Tegan said, keeping it vague, not sure how much she was meant to know. To her surprise Rachel laughed.

'I can't believe how much stress we put ourselves though over all that. Still, you live and learn, as my mother said.'

'Gosh, that's good. Sam has been ever so worried.'

'Poor Sam. I've relied on him too much. He's so bright, you know, and yet so caring. I know I'm a typical mother who worships her boy, but he really has been such a support. I was worried to death about him marrying that girl.'

Tegan looked over at the shawl on display.

'Yes, I shall sell it. You know, Angharad would probably never have worn it, just stuffed it in a drawer somewhere. Anyway, let's find you some more yarn. I hear you are working for Amy now as well.'

'That's right.'

'Well, don't let her give you too many hours. I need you here. Actually, I was going to ask you if you could work in the shop sometimes while I go round some sellers.'

'Yes, I could do that.'

'Good. Well, let's find you some more materials.' Rachel then added hesitatingly,

'Sam talks to you quite a bit, doesn't he?'

'A bit-'

'It's just, well, has he said anything to you about making plans?'

'Yes. Yes, he has, but not any details.'

364

She saw Rachel's face fall in disappointment. 'Oh bother. I was hoping you knew what was going on. That's how he has been with me and Amy, very secretive. Not like him at all. He's going to London next week. He'll be away for a night.'

'Really? Well I'm so sorry. I've no idea.'

Tegan left the shop. It dawned on her that Sam may be planning to leave. He had talked about making changes. Her heart sank. She realised then that she would rather he didn't go away. In fact, she very much wanted him to stay.

Chapter Forty Six

The next evening Tegan decided to go to choir. She was very nervous about seeing James, but when she arrived he ignored her and stayed with his own group of friends. Ellis was practising in earnest now for the May Day concert. Megan came bustling up to Tegan with her music. 'Here you are. Now, Ellis wants to start on time.'

Tegan turned around to find Cerys grinning. 'What's going on? Where's Ruth?' she whispered.

'She's told Dad she doesn't want to be involved with choir any more. I wonder now if she had been hoping something more might come of their friendship. Anyhow, now that Mum and Dad are in relative harmony, I guess she's given up.'

'I'm surprised to see Megan out after what has happened,' said Tegan.

'It's her way of coping, I think. You know, keep busy, and it suits Dad. Mind you, she'll be bossing him around soon. She's not Ruth.'

'I suppose your Dad will miss Ruth.'

'Miss being hero-worshipped, I'm sure. John's pleased. He was always jealous of Dad. I used to feel sorry for him, but after what he did to Sam I'm not so sure. Some people say Sam should go to the police.' Cerys looked over at Sam sorting out his music on the piano.

'Really, do you think he should?' asked Tegan.

'Sam wouldn't want to. In any case, there are more rumours that John and Ruth may be selling up. You know, people didn't like what he did to Sam or Alan, and then with Angharad going off with Wynn, maybe he's had enough of the place.'

Ellis called them all to order. Tegan smiled over at Sam, who was sat at the piano. Apart from the bruising he looked a lot better.

At the end of the practice Ellis spoke to them all. 'Now I want extra rehearsals. Just because we will hopefully be in the open air doesn't mean we don't make this as good a performance as possible. You know that this is an important concert for me, so I think Megan has a list of the extra rehearsals.'

Megan officiously handed round the neatly typed timetable.

'Good,' said Ellis. 'See you all soon.'

Tegan and Cerys left together and went with a group to the pub. They met Sam on the way in and he offered to buy them drinks. Then they went to find seats. Tegan noticed James.

'I feel so embarrassed when I see him now,' Tegan said quietly to Cerys.

'Don't worry. Be grateful he's moved on. I hear he's pretty angry with his Dad though.'

Sam arrived with their drinks. 'Well, that was better than I expected,' he said, grinning.

'How was John?' asked Cerys.

'Actually, he apologised. He's really upset about Angharad and Wynn. He can sort of see why I might have had doubts. Mind you, he's well on his way to putting the whole blame on Wynn.'

'Well, Wynn had better be careful if he comes in here for a drink,' said Cerys.

'I'll say. He'd be a lot more upset by a broken nose than me,' Sam replied, laughing.

'Your Mum was asking me about your plans,' Tegan shyly hinted to Sam.

'Ah, I'm still not telling' he teased. 'Now, are you coming on the Llun y Pasg?'

'Sorry?'

'It's a Welsh Easter tradition, Llun y Pasg,' explained Cerys. 'We all get up before dawn and climb the hill behind your cottage. It's wonderful. Well, as long as it's not raining. We go

367

up and greet the dawn. People take a packed breakfast. You must come.'

'So is it dark when you set out?' Tegan asked nervously.

'Well, yes.' Sam looked at her thoughtfully. 'We never did do our night walk, did we?'

She shook her head.

'You don't have to come,' he said gently. 'Sorry, I forgot.'

'That's alright' she said, then added, 'I'd like to try it in some ways, but I'm worried. You know, it would be embarrassing to panic in front of lots of people.'

'Look, how about I come early,' said Sam, 'and we make our way up together? If it's too much we can go back. Otherwise, we can meet everyone up there.'

Cerys grinned. 'Go on, Tegan. You've come a long way since last time you tried it.'

'OK' said Tegan nervously. 'What time will you come, Sam?'

'About three in the morning, I suppose.'

'Three?'

'Yes, it will have to be that early.'

'Good grief,' Tegan said. 'It's hardly worth going to bed.'

'You know, I hardly notice time any more' said Sam. 'I work so many odd shifts. Somehow time doesn't mean that much now.'

'Well for most of us that's a very odd time to be out and about' said Cerys, and they laughed.

The next few days Tegan was busy with knitting and at the centre. The morning before the walk she went downstairs and, to her surprise, Seren went to the front door. Tegan still hadn't let her out. Tegan knew that she responded to her name now and at that she would want to come back for her breakfast. Logically it seemed OK, but she was very nervous. Slowly, she opened the door and together she and Seren went out into the garden. Seren sniffed the ground and made her way around the garden. Then, to Tegan's horror, she jumped over the fence into the field. Seren was very excited, scratched her claws on the bark of a tree, and instinctively started to stalk a bird. Tegan watched her, and then called her in. Seren came in reluctantly. Tegan realised that she was going to want to go out regularly now.

Tegan went to bed early that night. Cerys had shown her how to set the alarm on her phone. She set it for half past two.

No sooner had she fallen asleep than it seemed it was time to get up. She felt very tired and sick and was regretting the whole escapade. Still, Sam would be here soon. She washed, dressed, and left Seren asleep on her bed. It seemed very dark and quiet downstairs.

She gave herself time to prepare, to think, remembering things Liz had told her. The night was not something she needed to be scared of, not now. And that sickness and fear were from her past: they were not real. She would be with Sam, who knew the way. He would look after her. She ate some toast, had coffee, and soon Sam arrived. He looked very fresh, as if it was the middle of the day.

'OK. You ready then?'

She smiled but couldn't speak. After she had closed the front door and turned on her torch Sam held her hand, gently guiding her down the path and out into the field. She was breathing faster, but it was manageable. Then they started to climb the mountain. It was a full moon, which meant less stars, but the hill was well lit.

'If you turn off your torch your eyes will adjust much better.' Tegan did what Sam said. He reached out and held her hand again. 'It's OK. Come on, just watch your feet.'

As they walked she felt something fly into her face.

'What was that?'

'That's just moths. You'll stop noticing them soon.'

Half way up Sam suggested they stop and rest. Tegan looked down. The lights of the village shone brightly in the darkness.

Sam pulled out a thermos of coffee and some chocolate. 'I brought supplies.'

As they sat, the sounds and smells seemed accentuated in the darkness. It was very still. The heather and bracken remained motionless. It was very calm.

'Listen, you can almost hear the sheep breathing,' whispered Sam. They sat quietly.

Sam sighed. 'You know, this place, even at night is such a comfort. It wraps you up. It doesn't betray or hurt you.'

For the first time Tegan heard the pain he was feeling from the past few weeks. She put her hand gently on his, but then a loud squeaking startled her.

'That's the pipestralle bats,' he said.

Then there was a 'hoodoo' sound.

'Gosh, and listen. That's a long-eared owl.'

Slowly, Tegan found she was relaxing as Sam explained the sounds, the noises of the wildlife.

'Are you alright?' he asked.

She nodded in the darkness. 'You know I am. I'm OK.'

'This fear you have of the night, have you talked to your therapist about it?'

'A bit. Do you think I'm mad, you know, if I'm going for therapy?'

'No. I think lots of us could benefit from it actually. You know, if it helps you to feel more confident, more able to be happy with who you are, I think it's a good idea.'

She felt his fingers touch the scars on her hands. She had been using the cream Hannah gave her. Her hands were a lot better, but the palms were still rough and sore. She tried to pull her hand away.

'It's OK,' he said. 'You have been through so much, but look at you: you've more than survived. You've started a whole new life.'

She said quietly 'I do know I'm incredibly lucky, having the cottage and Ellis and things-'

'Yes, but you've also had lots of thing happen to you. It's hard for people like me to understand. You know, most of

370

your scars are inside. I can't see them. I wish I could, and I wish I could make all the hurt go away.'

Tegan looked at him. The sky was getting lighter and she could see his face. 'It's lovely that you care. Thank you.'

Suddenly, they heard voices and saw a small group of people coming towards them.

'Tegan' shouted Cerys.

Tegan stood up, waved, and the group came to meet them. She saw Amy, Rhiannon and Rhys. Bethany, Mark and Ellis had come.

'What's that?' she asked Cerys, looking at a large bowl in her hand.

'Ah, come and see. They all climbed the last part of the hill and looked towards a glorious sunrise. Then Mark took a large container of water out of his rucksack and poured it into the basin. Cerys tilted the bowl and then she said,

'We have it. Come and see, Tegan, 'her voice in awe. We have caught the sun dancing.'

With only just over two weeks to go until the May Day concert, practices gathered pace. Tegan went to choir, the rescue centre, did her knitting, and cared for Seren. Slowly, she started to sleep better. The constant nagging anxiety started to abate.

She saw Sam sometimes. He said no more about his plans, but seemed quietly excited.

One afternoon she was out weeding when she heard someone call her name. She looked up and was very surprised to see it was Rhiannon.

'Hiya' Tegan called. 'Don't see you up here very often.'

'God no. I'm no walker,' Rhiannon responded.

Tegan was puzzled as to why she had come but asked her in for a drink.

'It's lovely in here, isn't it' said Rhiannon, looking around.

'Thanks.'

'I'd like a place, you know, for me and Rhys one day; maybe Amy as well.'

Tegan felt she was looking at a very different person to the Rhiannon in tight clothes laughing in the pub. 'I suppose it can't always be easy living at home.'

Rhiannon laughed. 'No. No, it's not. But I don't have a lot of options. I completely messed up at school, and I earn a pittance at work. You see, Sian took me on and trained me up. I'm really grateful. I had Rhys, and I didn't want to take on anything else.'

Tegan thought of the things Liz had said. 'But you could do some things at night school, couldn't you?'

Rhiannon clasped her hands. She looked very nervous. Tegan wondered what was on her mind. 'The thing is, with some GCSEs I could go to college. You know, I always wanted to have my own place, complementary therapies, and things.'

'That would be exciting.'

'The thing is-' said Rhiannon.

Tegan sat forward, waiting.

'I was talking to Mum,' continued Rhiannon. 'She said her and Dad would pay for me to go to college and do English and Maths GCSE. I don't want to go on my own. There's a course starting in September. The thing is-' She stopped.

Tegan frowned. She didn't understand Rhiannon's embarrassment.

'Well, Mum said that you weren't allowed to do exams, and well-' said Rhiannon awkwardly.

'Oh' said Tegan, suddenly understanding. 'Were you thinking of me going with you?'

Rhiannon nodded. 'Please don't be offended and, of course, if you don't want to-'

Tegan grinned. 'But, yes, I'd really like to and it would be lovely to go with someone. That is, if I get on the course.'

Rhiannon smiled excitedly. 'I have the stuff here for you to look at. We need to apply soon. Have a look. It's not cheap, though. See what you think-'

Tegan glanced through the literature. 'I think I could do this if I work hard. I'm lucky I have no mortgage or rent. I could do some extra hours at the centre maybe. Knit a bit harder!'

When Rhiannon had gone, Tegan sat stroking Seren. She was nervous, excited but not overwhelmed, at the idea of the courses with Rhiannon. Yes, it was a first small step, and she could manage that.

There was a final rehearsal the night before the concert. The weather forecast was good. People were excited. Ellis worked them hard at the rehearsal. At the break Tegan talked to Cerys.

'Your Dad is very serious about this, isn't he?'

'He's always like this. Can't do anything half-heartedly when it's music involved. It's good, though, stops us getting sloppy. This May concert is always a bit special. I think Mum is going to be involved a bit more this year, part of the working together initiative.'

'What can I do? Shall I come up early? There must be loads to do.'

'Ah, Dad has said you are not to worry. Actually, Megan is organising everything. If you haven't been given a job, I'd keep your head down.'

'How is Dylan? It seems ages since I've seen him.'

'Things are a bit better, I suppose.'

'Well, bring him up to me for a day whenever. You know I'm around a lot. I'd enjoy having him, and Seren will just ignore him.'

'Actually, I'll do that. Thanks. He's happier up there than anywhere. Hey, have you heard the latest about Wynn and Angharad?'

'No, what?'

'Ruth was telling me. Apparently Angharad is furious. The day after Wynn left her, Megan signed a contract selling the flat in New York. It was in her name or something. So they are living in some flat in Aberystwyth now. Not quite the glamorous life she expected. Ruth reckons Angharad would like to go to France but I'm not sure what Wynn thinks about living with his mother in law.'

Ellis called them back for the rehearsal. At the end of the practice, Sam came over to Tegan.

'Can I give you a lift back? I need to talk to you.'

'Of course.'

They arrived back at the cottage.

'You go on in,' said Sam.

Tegan was puzzled, but went in to put the kettle on. She turned to see Sam coming in through the door awkwardly, holding out a bunch of wild flowers. 'For you.'

Tegan smiled as she took them.

'I think I'm muddling up all sorts of customs here,' said Sam, 'but apparently May Eve or Nos Galan Mai is important. You see, tomorrow, May Day, is seen as the first day of summer. I think they were meant to decorate the outside of the houses with flowers, but anyway I brought you a bunch instead.'

Tegan laughed. 'Well, thank you anyway.' She took the flowers into the kitchen.

Sam went and sat on the sofa. 'Can you come and sit here?'

She turned and walked towards him. He looked very serious. Nervously, she sat next to him on the sofa. 'The thing is, Tegan, I've come to talk to you about my plans.'

Chapter Forty Seven

Tegan turned to face Sam, her heart beating fast. What were his plans? Would his plans have anything to do with her?

'Tell me,' she said quietly.

'I have a new job.'

She remembered he had been to London and swallowed hard. It hurt to speak. 'What will you be doing?'

'I've been offered the position of vet in the new wildlife sanctuary they're going to be building. It's like my dream job.'

'New wildlife sanctuary?' she asked faintly.

'The one they're building at Amy's place.'

'You'll be working here, in the village?' she said, her voice shaking.

'Of course. I couldn't live without the mountains, and, well, the people.' Sam scratched the back of his neck. 'You do know I care a lot about you. You're the real reason I could never leave here.'

Tegan blushed and looked down.

'Don't you know how much you mean to me?' asked Sam.

'But I'm so odd, different-' she said, frowning.

'You're really not that different, you know. In fact, you're one of the sanest people I know.'

Sam smiled and then leant forward. Tegan lifted her head and leant towards him. He kissed her gently on the lips. Tegan could feel tears on her cheeks. Sam wiped them gently away.

'I'm sorry,' she said. 'I am happy, honestly. I can't believe any of this. It's like a dream.'

'It's true. I love you, Tegan.'

She listened, felt dizzy with emotion, overwhelmed.

'What is it?' Sam asked. 'What's the matter?'

Tegan bit her lip nervously. 'The thing is, Sam, I care a lot about you, but I have only just started to work things out for myself. I want to get some qualifications, sort out what I want to do, find out who I am. I'm sorry. Does that sound stupid?'

'Of course not. I understand. We'll take it slowly, I promise.'

Tegan breathed a sigh of relief, and Sam put his arms around her. They sat very still. After a while Sam sat back slightly. He spoke in a firmer voice. 'I met Ellis earlier. He asked me to take you out for the day tomorrow.'

'Really? That's odd. Anyway, there'll be all the preparations for the concert. Cerys said I didn't have to go but-'

'She meant it. They all want you to have a day out.'

'I don't think-'

'Listen, Ellis, Cerys, Hannah. They asked me especially to take you out. They want you to have a break. Please come.'

She shrugged, then grinned at him. 'Well, if you insist. Of course. I'd love to.'

The next day, Sam arrived at the cottage with Bracken. Tegan made a picnic and they went off high into the hills. It was blissful. The sun shone; skylarks sang. Bracken went off sniffing and investigating holes. Tegan had never felt so happy and free. The day passed quickly and she was surprised when Sam said it was nearly five o'clock and they ought to go back. They walked down the mountain holding hands, both tired and exhilarated from a day in the wind and sun.

When they reached the bottom of the hill they went into the cottage. Tegan fed Seren and went to make coffee. She was aware Sam seemed to be on edge.

'Come on then,' Sam said. 'Let's go round to the manor.'

'It's a while until the concert.' she said.

'I know, but we ought to go now.'

'But-'

'No, really. We have to go now.'

376

'OK. Well, I'd better change.'

Tegan ran upstairs. She put on her long skirt and blouse, brushed her hair, grinned excitedly at herself in the mirror and went back down.

'OK then, let's go' Sam said.

Tegan couldn't understand why he was so on edge and struggled to keep up with him as they walked quickly along the path to the manor. As they approached, Tegan caught Sam's arm. 'Stop. I can hear music.'

'Come and see' he said.

There were a lot of cars parked in front of the manor, which seemed strange. Why had everyone come so early? Sam took hold of her hand, led her through the manor, and out through the patio doors. Tegan stood, staring. She couldn't believe what she was seeing. It seemed that the whole village was there. There was a maypole, a barbeque, and a small group were playing Welsh folk songs.

Ellis approached her grinning, his arms open wide. 'This is for you.'

'For me?'

'Yes, look over there.'

Tegan looked up at the windows and read the banner.

"Tegan Pen-blwydd Hapus: Happy Birthday Tegan."

'But-' she stammered.

'It's your birthday,' said Ellis, gently.

Tegan gasped. 'Today, May the first. This is the day I was born?'

'That's right. Remember your middle name?'

'Of course, Mai.'

'Welsh for May. You know, every year I have held a concert somewhere for you. But now, here you are. It's truly wonderful.'

Tegan blinked away tears. 'All this time, unknown to me, someone, somewhere was celebrating my birthday!'

Tegan read the banner again. She said to Ellis, 'Those words, they're the ones on that silver box from Mum. You know the one she bought when she was with you, with the owl.'

377

Then she looked again at the children dancing round the maypole, her mind piecing together the final pieces of the jigsaw. 'The day my mother gave me the box and the owl, it was after we'd been watching maypole dancing in the park. So she had taken me there on my birthday. She actually gave me birthday presents.'

Ellis too now had tears in his eyes. 'I'm glad. I'm so glad. I've just realised. I didn't tell you, but the day I met you with your Mum when you were very little, the day we went to the cottage; that was your fourth birthday. Remember, I found you watching dancing in Cardiff with your Mum. So she bought the things on your birthday and then waited all those years to give them to you.'

Tegan stared. 'I came here on my birthday?'

Ellis gave her a big hug. 'Yes. I remember then thinking it was a shame we couldn't do you a proper party with friends and things.'

Tegan took a deep breath, so many emotions rushing around. Then she saw Sam coming towards her and immediately felt calmer.

'You alright?' he asked anxiously.

'Yes. Yes, I think so. It's so much to take in. I guess you knew all about this?'

'Of course. You're pleased, though, aren't you?'

Tegan nodded. 'Yes, of course. It's really lovely.'

Rhys ran at her, breathless with excitement. 'Mum said you'd never had a party before. Look, we've got balloons and jelly and everything.'

'Really? Wow, that's fantastic,' she responded.

'Are you going to open your presents?' asked Rhys.

On a table was a small pile of gifts. Tegan realised that the music had stopped. Everyone was watching her. She wiped away tears and walked over to the table. Rhys was very excited. He started handing her presents to open: a collection of Welsh folk music from Ellis; the skirt she'd tried on in Covent Garden from Hannah; from Cerys and Robert, plants; from Amy and Rhiannon earrings with tiny silver cocker spaniels; and from

Rachel and Alan a beautiful embroidered silk shawl. Finally, Sam took her to one side and she opened a small, leather box. Inside was a delicate gold Celtic bracelet.

'Welsh gold,' he said. She slipped it on her wrist. She leant up and kissed him.

'Come on now, Tegan' a voice said briskly.

Tegan turned to see Megan holding an enormous cake covered in white icing, pink flowers, candles and the words "Happy Birthday Tegan," immaculately iced.

'Thank you so much.'

Rhys, very excited, started to blow the candles out for her and she saw Megan scowl. Quickly, Tegan joined in. Megan relaxed and the whole village sang "Happy Birthday" to her.

Then they had a barbecue and played games, until dusk.

Finally Ellis called out 'Now, it's time for the choir.'

People sat in groups on the grass while the choir arranged themselves in front of them. Sam sat behind an electric piano set up for the occasion. The singing began. It had a magical sound in the open air; the voices seemed to blend into the garden. When they were singing the penultimate song, Calon Lan, Tegan started to brace herself for the final song. She and Ellis had discussed something. How she handled it was up to her. It was getting dark. Already the stars were shining. They finished Calon Lan. She looked over at Ellis, smiled and nodded. She was very nervous. He mouthed 'Sure?' Tegan nodded.

Tegan stepped forward. Slowly, the nerves crumbled, and she steadied her breathing. She stood upright, shoulders relaxed. In her mind she pictured a red kite, soaring high above the Cambrian Mountains. Sam gave her a note. Alone in the gathering darkness, she began to sing. As she relaxed her voice became fuller, more confident, until it filled the air. It had a mystical feel. People sat spellbound listening as she sang unaccompanied "Ar hyd a nos", "All through the night". Firstly she sang in Welsh.

Holl amrantau'r sêr ddywedant
Ar hyd y nos.
Dyma'r ffordd i fro gogoniant

379

Ar hyd y nos.
Golau arall yw tywyllwch,
I arddangos gwir brydferthwch,
Teulu'r nefoedd mewn tawelwch
Ar hyd y nos.

And then she sang the English version her mother had sung all those years ago.

Sleep, my child, and peace attend thee
All through the night.
Guardian angels God will lend thee,
All through the night.
Soft the drowsy hours are creeping,
Hill and vale in slumber steeping,
I my loving vigil keeping,
All through the night.

The words hung in the air. People applauded till their hands were sore. Ellis stepped forward. 'And now, dancing.'

The folk band began to play and the manor lit up with fairy lights.

People, shyly at first, started to stand in pairs, groups and then dance.

Sam came over to Tegan. 'Dancing?'

'Oh no, I don't know how.'

'Look around, Tegan.'

Tegan watched the people dancing. There were no set dances or steps. An older couple danced gracefully. Hannah was laughing as Ellis swung her round. Cerys seemed to be engulfed in a kind of bear hug by Robert. Amy and Rhiannon were leaping around with complete abandon.

'See, they're all just making it up as they go along.'

Tegan took his hand and stepped into the group and, laughing, danced into the night.

Acknowledgements

Thank you to my wonderful children Thomas and Emily for all their enthusiasm, encouragement and support. Thank you to Adèle Gerald Janet and Lucy who read earlier drafts and provided helpful guidance. Also many thanks to Felicity for inspiring me to write and to Kate for giving me the courage to do so.

About the Author

I was born in Cardiff and have retained a deep love for my Welsh roots. I worked as a nursery teacher in London and later taught Deaf children in Croydon and Hastings.

I now live on the beautiful Isle of Wight with my husband, where I walk my cocker spaniel Pepper and write. I have two grown up children.

'Free to Be Tegan' is my debut novel. It is to be the first of a series of novels set in Wales. The second will be set on the spectacular Gower Peninsula.

Contact me at marygrand90@yahoo.co.uk if you would like to be notified when my next book is released.

Mary Grand

28184041R00212

Printed in Great Britain
by Amazon